This Hidden Thing

This Hidden Thing

a novel by

Dora Dueck

CMU PRESS

Winnipeg, Manitoba

2010

CMU Press
500 Shaftesbury Blvd
Winnipeg, Manitoba
R3P 2N2

All rights reserved. No part of this publication may be reproduced in any form or by any means, electronic or mechanical, including photocopying, recording, or any information storage and retrieval system, without permission in writing from the publisher.

Cover: detail from *Seasoned Offerings*, mixed media, acrylic on canvas, by Agatha Doerksen.

Cover design: Karen Allen
Layout: Jonathan Dyck

Printed in Canada by
Friesens Corporation, Altona, Manitoba

The pages of this book are printed on chlorine free paper made with 100% post-consumer waste.

Library and Archives Canada Cataloguing in Publication

Dueck, Dora, 1950-
This hidden thing / Dora Dueck.

ISBN 978-0-920718-86-5

I. Title.
PS8557.U2813T55 2010   C813'.54   C2010-901897-4

for my children

This is a work of fiction. Correspondence to real people and their particular circumstances, apart from the obviously historical figures and events, is coincidental.

. . . there are . . . some secrets especially burdensome,
and there are many more in the world
than you would believe.

PAUL TOURNIER

. . . where I am folded, I am a lie . . .

RAINER MARIA RILKE

In worlds made of words,
where does silence build a house?

PART I

Five Years

1927 - 1932

1

"YOU'RE NOT WANTED," he told her that January morning in 1927 in a sideways voice, low and dull as if he'd expected it. "She says you're too fresh off the train."

"Not wanted?" Maria's head jerked in Peter's direction.

They were standing at the back steps of the large brick house, bending a little, like winter-ragged stalks of grass in a ditch, before the intense blue gaze of Edith Lowry, the woman of the house. They were waiting to get inside, to warm up, to have Maria start her employment.

"She has no idea what she'll do," he continued in the German dialect, "but she won't hire a girl without some grasp of the language."

Maria shuddered from astonishment, and the cold. She'd never been unwanted. And she'd never known such terrible chill, heavy and creeping, weighting her feet and hands like bricks. Such a deceptive, confusing cold, for the atmosphere was radiant, the sky bright and cloudless. Sunshine sparkled on the snow. It danced even in the shadow of the house where she and Peter waited. Danced in violet hues. But there was no warmth in it whatsoever.

Maria had no grasp of the English language. That was plain enough. She hadn't understood a single word – besides her name – of the English back-and-forth between Peter and the woman looming above them. She was completely dependent on him to talk for her. She'd seen the welcome pale as the other two conversed; she'd heard the woman's exclamations and the tinge of resentment in Peter's replies. She'd sensed that something was wrong. But she hadn't predicted this.

Not wanted.

The red brick house seemed to swell and reel while Peter elaborated the woman's dilemmas: her other girl already gone, the housework urgent. And now the help she'd hung on for couldn't speak for herself. Such a large and beautiful house, Maria was thinking, nearly bursting with its needs and significance, and its mistress filling the doorway of the porch that formed the back entrance, very fashionably dressed in a navy skirt and a light grey blouse with silver-streaked buttons, her auburn hair waved and piled and ornamented with silvery combs. Three steps up, and rigid, so dreadfully disappointed, she'd said, and Peter and Maria beneath her, both of them in brown – Peter's pants and jacket frayed and stained, Maria's coat misshapen from sleeping in it on their journey. They were immigrants.

Mennonite immigrants.

Maria had arrived in Winnipeg from Russia's Crimea just three days ago, together with her parents Johann and Susanna Klassen and the rest of the family. Peter Konrad, her uncle, had come two years earlier. He was the only living sibling of Maria's mother, and considerably younger – twenty-three – than she was, for a whole series of infants had died of various childhood diseases between them.

"I won't call you uncle," Maria, who was nineteen, had said that morning, setting out with him on the streetcar for this destination. "You're not nearly old enough." She'd felt brave and bold towards him, towards her new Canadian life, and he'd pretended to be hurt and teased her that her mother wouldn't like it at all. But she could tell he didn't mind.

He was rotating his cap in his hands. He'd removed it eagerly, deferentially, just moments before and seemed unsure what to do with it next, as if too little time had elapsed for its return to his head. The woman's words came at him quickly, he continued to Maria in an undertone, but the point of them was this: she had no use for a girl who was ignorant of the language. As if, he added parenthetically, a servant will be called on to deliver speeches.

The woman implied that he'd intended to mislead her, Peter continued, but this wasn't true; he was sure he'd been clear enough when he spoke with her by the telephone. He'd said, "To answer your notice, my niece, Maria Klassen by name, will soon be here." He'd written what he planned to say before he called, and he stuck to it.

"Will soon be here" was clear enough, wasn't it, that his niece hadn't yet arrived? And surely the woman would know, listening to his accent, that she wouldn't be arriving from England or the United States of America. There was plenty of call for immigrant girls from all the European countries; how did the rest of them manage? The porters weren't offering English lessons under the station rotunda, were they? He'd arranged this date to bring her by, he said, and Mrs Lowry went on to inform him, friendly-like as if the matter was settled, that the pay would be ten dollars a month. Starting.

Maria feared Peter was saying too much. With the translation so much longer than the original, he would surely cause further offense. "Peter," she said, "I understand."

Peter seized the narrow front lip of his cap with one hand and the worn round back with the other and lifted it over his head. He pulled it down quickly, as if to shield himself from a blow.

"She won't have you," he repeated, stretching the flat cap tightly over his thick coppery hair. "Not straight off the train."

Peter lowered his arms and slid his hands into his pockets. He hauled up the scrap of paper he'd consulted at every corner since he and Maria stepped off the streetcar just past the bridge on Academy. He stared at it as if demanding advice. But of course there was nothing new on it, just the address in his large pencilled writing and a roughly sketched map of their way to the Lowrys. He stuffed it away again and bent to pick up Maria's cloth bag of belongings.

In the emotion of their reunion in the CPR station three days ago, Peter had been as large and impressive in Maria's eyes as the grand terminal itself with its massive columns, marble floors, and shafts of amber light pouring from its high windows upon the travellers milling about the central hall. He was someone to lean on, in spite of his being young, barely older than the oldest of the Klassen children, in spite of leaving on his own to Canada, unmarried. Unbaptized. Mother's voice had always seemed to be rubbing at a scar when she spoke of it, how he'd abandoned their elderly parents, only she and Peter still living among all the children her mother had birthed, and what could *she* do for the aging pair, so much distance between the Crimea and Molotschna?

Then Peter turned out to be their Joseph in the distant land of safety and provision, for Maria's father changed his mind about staying to endure the trials foisted on the Mennonites in Russia. The ailing parents died, one soon after the other, so Mother's mind was relieved on that particular problem. When they wrote Peter they were coming, he replied he would do everything he could to help and Mother felt her prayers had been answered, for it sounded as if her brother had reformed his ways.

They'd been leaning on him from afar, and once they arrived, they leaned on him some more. Father clasped his young brother-in-law with a heartiness that got lost in his throat and rendered him speechless. Mother hugged Peter and bawled, and their sobs and laughter mingled so long the rest of the family grew embarrassed watching them and turned away. Brother and sister finally released their hold on each other and then everyone followed Peter to Immigration Hall.

They followed him meekly, willing to be contented with

this new homeland of theirs, and with him, their brother, uncle, and guide. He knew the customs, the habits of the land. He knew English. He would tell them what everything meant, he would teach them what they needed to know. He popped hard lemon candies out of his pockets for the younger children like a Father Nikolaus and teased the older girls with compliments, and he clapped Gerhard on the shoulder as best friends do, and then he charmed his "dear dear sister," Maria's mother, by presenting her with a gift of perfume in a tiny oval bottle. He amazed them all.

Now Maria realized Peter wasn't that far past stepping off the station platform himself. She heard the gap between his English and the woman's, his speech like a long day of planting potatoes, a trudge from one hole to the next, and hers brisk and expressive as if its back had never ached.

Then somewhere in the neighbourhood, church bells tolled. The sudden sound startled her, its tones so round and crisp and beautiful, but resolute too, almost stern in the cold bright air. *Not wanted?* Maria was aware of her immigrant brownness, the drab deportment of flight, of poverty, and she hated it. But hadn't they also been prosperous once, not so long ago, before everything in Russia was turned on its head by the Great War and the Revolution? And wasn't it true – and not to be dismissed – that God brought them out of it all? And wasn't she the second of seven, and the oldest daughter, with all the competence and affection that went along with that, with all the careful pride her parents had bestowed on her? She was loved. She'd been praised for her looks, her skills, her intelligence.

She couldn't just return, trudge back through the maze of streets they'd walked to this house, ride east along the route just taken west, watch the knot of her family that tightened as the streetcar tore her away from them loosen and fall open again, worry sliding over Mother's face like a veil, Father solemn but puzzled, the younger children mobbing her with their questions about why she'd been refused. Maria didn't want to work out but what choice did she have? Both she and her older brother Gerhard needed to find employment, and possibly Susanna – the sister next to her – as well. It was a momentous thing to start over, establish a family as large as theirs, pay off the travel debt. They all felt the responsibility.

Maria's feet tormented her with their hope of warmth in the house, behind the scowling and resistant Mrs Lowry. They were desperate to thaw and grow placid with heat, and then to get to work. Maria despised her thin, brown boots.

She grabbed Peter's sleeve. She pulled until he straightened. "Tell her I learn quickly," she commanded in a rush of air. "Tell her it won't take me long with the language. Say we're very, very sorry about the misunderstanding. Tell her I'm the oldest girl. Of us seven children. That I know how to work. That I've also been to school. I can't go back. Father and Mother are expecting me to work."

"You've been plenty rich," he muttered.

There was no time for anything but "Peter!" in dismay, and "Start then!"

He cleared his throat, removed his cap, addressed Mrs Lowry again.

When he stopped, Maria said, "Did you tell her everything? That I learn quickly?"

"You don't know the language."

"Tell her I'm good at learning language!" There'd been a shift in Mrs Lowry's demeanour, Maria was sure of it. "Say the same things over and over until she agrees. I'm not going back!"

Peter plodded through some more English sentences.

"Keep insisting," Maria said. "Repeat yourself."

Then she saw Mrs Lowry's body ripple in the cold, saw her give in. The English woman motioned for Peter and Maria to follow her and Maria leapt to obey, up the wooden steps, through the unheated back porch with its low roof and its windows arched with frost, through a second door and into a spacious, modern kitchen, Peter hurrying after her with her bag, his speech trailing to a halt. She didn't know whether he got around to mentioning she was good at languages or not. She had no proof of it, of course, but she would make it true, and therefore not a lie.

Maria found the kitchen warm and tidy, not chaotic as she'd been led to believe. Her feet thawed and tingled while Peter and Mrs Lowry reviewed the arrangements. The woman's manner hadn't softened, but she agreed to hire Maria. On a trial basis, Peter informed her in German. If she did well, she could stay.

□

That evening, Edith Lowry told her husband James what she'd done. She told him in the chattering, run-on way she reserved for matters he considered impulsive, or sentimental. She knew that James disapproved of sentimentality.

She'd hired a German girl, one of those Mennonites, she said, who didn't know a word of English. "An awful inconvenience, I know, but I decided by my sense of things. I think I'm a pretty good judge of character, don't you think so, darling? And I have to say, the girl was absolutely dogged. She gave me that impression, at any rate. It seemed a quality one might want in a servant. Our last girls have been far too relaxed about things."

Edith told her husband that she'd re-arranged her commitments for a month in order to teach Maria the rudiments of English and the rules of their household. Since she'd agreed to take her – her first inclination against it notwithstanding – she might as well throw herself into it. Make a decent job of it. She'd backed out of the Women's Auxiliary planning committee, she said, just for the time being, of course, and she'd let Iona know she'd have to forego their weekly game. It wouldn't be that difficult to find another partner, she'd joked to Iona, as long as her replacement wasn't that good, as long as they took her back, etc., etc.

She didn't tell James that in making these calls she felt herself elated by the freedom, by the opportunity – now that she'd been pushed into it by the girl's stubborn avowals, asserted through her relative Peter in his pathetic English – to drop for a month the tiresome and boring rounds of discussion every social or missions event at the church required before all the arrangements were finalized, to spring away from Iona for a change, since Iona short-noticed her often enough, and always rather casually too. Edith Lowry preferred more solitude than their particular class and striving allowed her, and the challenges that interested her were individual and domestic ones: decorating, encouraging advancements in the children's characters, creating what she liked to call the proper atmosphere of a home – linen-shelves properly layered and neat, meals served with promptness and regularity, the fruit cellar and spice cupboard stocked, jars of preserves aesthetically arranged, the jars not sticky. She liked projects that had obvious beginnings and obvious outcomes, ones she could manage without consulting other women.

Edith removed her stockings as she spoke, rolling each one slowly and carefully down her leg. James washed at the sink in the bathroom, the door open between them. She reiterated to him the risk she'd taken, the intuition required in a decision like the one she'd made, the commitment. She wanted him to know the size of what lay before her. Besides the problem of language, the new girl might be completely unschooled in the requirements of a civilized household – wasn't it mostly the peasant class coming from those parts of Europe? Although Maria seemed to have a kind of flair, Edith said, that suggested potential.

"And you've said, haven't you James darling, that the servants ought to please the eye as much as the tea cakes do?"

"I spotted her," James said, looking up, a towel in his hands. "And I agree. She's pretty."

"Now James," Edith said. She began to unbutton her blouse.

James Lowry had little interest in the subject of domestic help, as long as they had it. Nor was he fooled by Edith's concerns about the upheaval of her life. He heard her excitement. She was good at women's activities and organizations, good at keeping up friendships with the wives of his business partners or competitors and displaying her considerable natural charm, her instinctively understated snobbery. Woman's place was the subsidiary role, to be sure, linked securely to the home, but he preferred her delegating and directing its affairs in a way that reflected their upper middle class status, not in there with her teacher's attitude and love of the kitchen, sleeves pushed over her elbows. Edith had a personality that tugged her in opposite directions, James had always felt, and the prospect of her giving a month to a foreigner irritated him; he wished they had a larger house, more servants, enough servants to train one another. But, emerging from the bathroom, he glimpsed his wife's white neck and the curve of her white shoulder as she undressed and its loveliness stirred him to respond, "You're a born teacher, Edith, and I'm sure you've made the right decision, as you always do. You'll have her fit for us in no time.

"Just dress up while you're bound to her," he added, as if to console her, "as you yourself always advise."

Edith was grateful and lifted her head to him. "Yes," she said, "my philosophy of clothing." Edith believed in grooming one's hair and dressing well every day, not saving clothes for better occasions always around the proverbial corner. This general approach raised one's spirits, she'd say ("Goodness knows, there are days a woman would just as soon stay in her bed"), and impressed callers. Even delivery men.

And decent clothes made decent children. A prominent social worker said so in a magazine. Mothers ought to wake up to this, the article said, and Edith Lowry agreed. A little energy, a little foresight, intelligent shopping, costumes that emphasized not their separate parts but a stylish adherence to the whole was all it took to make a difference. "You immigrants," she was thinking – and must remember to advise her new girl later, once she learned the language – recalling Maria's flimsy, ill-fitting coat, "should keep this in mind. A little observation of how we're doing things in Canada, and you'll blend right in."

"Yes indeed," James teased, sitting down on the bed beside her, "your philosophy of clothing." He put his arm around her. "And mine, of unclothing."

"Now James," Edith warned again, but this time she was laughing.

□

The next morning, Edith Lowry brought sheets of paper, a bottle of ink, and a long-nibbed pen to the kitchen worktable and the lessons commenced. She set down key words, in capitals as if Maria were deaf. FLOUR SUGAR PLATE SPOON EGGS. During the first weeks, Maria was allowed to add the German word – *Mehl Zucker Teller Loeffel Eier* – beside its English counterpart. She wrote these words in script, small and subordinate.

The lessons consisted of reading, listening, repeating. Of doing, then doing again. Mrs Lowry's bible of the domestic arts was the thick *Canadian Cook Book*, where she'd also pasted recipes cut from magazines or written on pieces of paper, pasted them into any white space available, at the beginning and end and between chapters, even covering other recipes, ones she didn't like perhaps. The book crackled with brittle glue and its abundance of ideas, household hints, formulations for dishes and desserts of all kinds, as well as schedules for what should be done every day of the week. "If you know how to read, and can follow instructions," Mrs Lowry would say that day and many times after, "you can do anything." Maria thought the truth of this profound, after she'd grasped it. She liked its sequence and optimism. Her father too had done his best to buy his children books, in the days when he could afford them, and Maria loved to read. Her success seemed sure.

Family Vegetable Soup was the first recipe Maria learned. "Wipe meat," her mistress began, Maria stumbling after, "put in soup kettle, and cook slowly for 4 hours, skimming."

Mrs Lowry thrust the marbled slab of meat into Maria's hands, showed her the corresponding line, "2 pounds lean beef." Maria repeated the words while the brick of flesh, eerie and damp with blood, bore down on her palms and wrists. She'd handled meat in Russia, eviscerating chickens, butchering pigs, stuffing sausages. But now, in this context, in English, she feared she would gag. She hauled up a deep breath, and then another, telling herself she needed to stay, not daring to look down at the meat until Mrs Lowry took it from her and put it in a pot.

"Cook slowly for 4 hours," Mrs Lowry read, "skimming." The Lowry kitchen had a modern electric range. Turned to its lowest meant "slowly." Running the ladle over the churning water to catch the rising brown foam, "skimming."

Mrs Lowry pointed at Maria's head. "Learn the English word for everything," she said. She stopped and wrote, THINK IN ENGLISH. Maria knew the word English, and the word think, it had something to do with her head; it must be *denken*. She nodded.

Then Mrs Lowry led Maria into the dining room, held four fingers to the clock, swam them lightly in four circles. "Four hours," she said. She'd carried along the recipe book and pointed at the relevant line. Maria nodded. Her new mistress made one connection after the other – objects, names, sounds, meanings – and Maria nodded and nodded, shaking down the information.

There were many things to do while the broth simmered on the range. Mrs Lowry produced a dry mop and a carpet sweeper from a closet in the kitchen. SWEEP, DUST, she wrote. She wagged the broom in Maria's hands. "Sweep, sweep," she said. She marched out of the kitchen with the carpet sweeper, pushed it vigorously over a rug at the door. "Sweep."

Maria echoed "Sweep" and she nodded.

Mrs Lowry pulled a cloth out of the same closet. "Dust," she said. "Dust, dust, dust." She flourished the cloth over a table, a wood edging, the hat stand. Her navy shoes clicked on the floor. She was wearing a dark green dress, of wool, with a high collar from which a tiny star-shaped brooch hung on a pin. The brooch swayed gently whenever Mrs Lowry moved. Like a lullaby, Maria thought. The day wasn't half over and she was tired.

"Sweep and dust," Mrs Lowry said. Her long arm drew in the library, the dining room, the foyer. It circled the face of the clock. These jobs should take an hour.

An hour. For Maria, an interlude, an hour's reprieve from ignorance and the strain of listening. An hour to prove she was an excellent duster and sweeper. She dusted the sitting room, dining room, library, everything swiftly, thoroughly too: in each room all the edges of wainscoting, in each room the shelves and tables and picture frames. There was no dust on any of these surfaces, but Maria understood the rituals of domesticity. The necessity of prevention.

Swiftly and thoroughly she swept the rugs with the carpet sweeper, the hardwood floors with the soft mop, the kitchen and porches with the broom. In between, Maria stole glances at the paper with the capitalized words she had to learn, trying to fix them in her mind's eye and her mouth as if they were dogma, fix them so well there wouldn't be doubts when she needed to use them or know what they meant. She was conscious of Mrs Lowry enlarging and fading at a distance while she worked, sometimes glancing through doorways, never quite watching her but, like a faint reflection, changing angles as Maria moved.

Maria couldn't linger over any one thing; her hands

flew. Still, they were loaded with concentration and skill; they were like instruments responsive to her mind. Instruments that perceived, in their turn, the hard handles of the broom and sweeper, the soft yielding of the dust cloth, each surface they touched.

Good thing she'd been taught to work. In Russia, they'd usually had household help, besides the farm hands, but Mother believed in her daughters doing their share. "My own dear daughters have to know," she'd tell them as if addressing a third party. "How will they ever run a household?"

Mother had grown up poor in a cottage at the end of her village, and fairly vaulted from one Mennonite class into another when she married Father. She liked to remind her children – and she told the story with a tone of awe – that God had blessed her very much. But she also told it like a fable, with a moral at the end of it. She'd close off with strange, bleak sentences like "Who can imagine the future, for good or for evil?" or "Beyond the fine hill of today, lies the valley of tomorrow."

Good that she did, thought Maria now. Poverty had come true for Mother again. True for all of them. Maria working out – who would have believed it a decade ago?

But at least she knew what to do.

The hour ended and Mrs Lowry seemed pleased with Maria's dusting and sweeping. Except for the porch. She didn't need to sweep the porch, and not the lion pillars either. Maria nodded. She couldn't explain why she'd done so. She'd seen them through the window, those witless half-blind cubs, completely lacking in fierceness, their grey stone heads and forepaws tufted with snow, and she was drawn to them although she'd found them oddly incongruent when she and Peter came up the walk to the house the day before. Now she'd forgotten herself, opened the door, swept them bare. She probably let cold air into the house.

Mrs Lowry shook her head to it all, though her mood today was encouraging. But she didn't care about the lions, whether they were snow-covered or cleared. Mrs Lowry hugged herself, shivered, growled "Brrr" and then she mimed putting on a coat and boots, shovelling and sweeping the steps, the walk. When she was satisfied that Maria got her meaning – *not now, not in this sequence of tasks* – she took her upstairs where the beds had been stripped to air. MAKE BEDS, she ordered on Maria's page of words.

On the second floor too there were surfaces to dust and sweep, and there were bathrooms to wash, fresh towels to hang, banisters to polish. There were stockings and gloves to wash by hand. Then Maria and her mistress returned to the main floor where there was a kitchen to tidy, a pudding to make for supper, and a lesson on preparing the chops.

❑

The house mattered. She'd liked it as soon as she saw it. These were the streets, Peter remarked, where the better-off of Winnipeg lived. Not the really rich, but the rich enough. She'd realized as much, tramping in from the streetcar stop, the hum of the traffic diminishing the further they went, the crunch of their boots on the hard snow more obvious, the houses widely built, widely spaced. She'd found herself alert, reverential in the silence created by the larger portions, and proportions, of everything here, houses and streets and yards and air.

While they walked, or paused for Peter to look at his small drawn map, Maria stared around her. She wondered which house she would get. As if she'd come to claim a prize. That one, with its two-peaked roof? The one with the large bow window? With the turret? The second-storey porch? The columned porticos? The pretty trim around the door?

Then, there it was: square, red-brown brick, white-framed windows in symmetrical pairs on the first and second floors, a small pair in dormers under a high black roof. The house was plain, but elegant in spite of it, its simplicity clearly intentional and not for want of an imagination. Only the stone lions flanking the door seemed out of place, requiring a house even larger, with more elaboration.

But they were cubs. And she liked that house. She liked it immediately and she wanted it. And she got it.

□

She intended her letters to be a pleasure, something her parents and siblings, who had travelled on from the city to settle in southern Manitoba, would pass from hand to hand or hear aloud at the table, then keep. Something to comfort as much as inform them. Amuse a little too, if possible. She imagined the letters gradually forming a pile, tied with a ribbon (she pictured a ribbon in a creamy pale pink hue, the colour of dried apples) and kept in a wooden box, or in a leather case with an ornamental clasp.

My dear family, Maria wrote, in German of course, in her first correspondence home, *I was so happy that you let me know that you arrived in Winkler, and that you are all in good health. The Lowrys are treating me well, and I cannot complain. I am getting enough to eat and am beginning to understand what must be done. Each day has certain tasks. Mrs Lowry goes by some pages at the front of her recipe book that list the duties of a maid. There are some foods in this house I am not used to. I wish I could let you taste them. I think you would find them interesting, or else you would laugh. Mr Lowry works in an office somewhere. He seems to be an important person in his business. I make his porridge and set out his breakfast the night before. I come down early to make his tea and egg. He eats alone and always reads while he eats. He rarely says Good morning, but he is not unfriendly otherwise. I think he is just preoccupied. There are two girls, Eleanor and Frances. They are about the ages of Susanna and Katherine, and are almost like twins. They look alike, but for the difference in height. They laugh a lot and seem to be merry girls. And there is a boy who has two names: Robert Russell. But they usually call him Bobby. He is a noisy, energetic boy who also goes off to school every morning. He is just starting to eat his supper with the others, and it seems that he is having some trouble learning his manners. More than once he has been sent upstairs from the table and then I am told to bring him food on a tray. He looks so ferocious when he is angry that it is hard not to laugh. If I do that he scowls all the more. But he does not stay long in these moods. So far Mrs Lowry sends the laundry out, except for the handwashing which I do in a tub in the cellar. She seems satisfied with me and I think I will last. Your loving daughter and sister, Maria.*

She didn't want to worry them. She didn't even hint at the disorientation of the first days, weeks, months, how she'd feel normal all day, able to concentrate, mind and body coordinated, but then at the end of it, while leaving the kitchen, find herself overwhelmed with a sensation of lightness, as if her skull would unhinge and float away. As if one or more limbs would soon disappear. She knew this couldn't happen, yet the sense that it was possible, even imminent, was so strong she would lean against the table or doorway, and clutch her head or body, panting, until she was able to move.

Then she ascended the narrow steep stairway to the maid's room over the kitchen. She put her hands and her knees on the worn wood and pulled herself up. Once she fell asleep for a while. She crawled because of her exhaustion, and because she feared she would fall. Just moments before, her head had been light and unreliable, little more than an empty bucket on her neck, yet on the stairway it threatened to tilt as if her brain was a rock shifting from side to side. She would be unable to maintain her equilibrium if her head flew backwards or forwards. So she clung to the ground. Sometimes her heart pounded in panic.

Reaching her room was every evening's victory.

Maria's quarters were dreary. The maid's stairs and bedroom were constructed of lesser materials than the rest of the house, the floor of painted fir, the walls a dull tan colour without ornamentation of any kind, the room and passageway lit by single uncovered bulbs. Her room had a narrow closet, a cot, an old table and chair, and a shabby chest of drawers.

But she liked it. Its utter lack of beauty spared her the effort of noticing or caring for it in any way. She thought of the room and the things it contained by their German names. Although she felt vaguely guilty violating Mrs Lowry's instructions, she couldn't help herself. German adhered stubbornly to these surroundings and to the pleasant muscular rest that gradually overcame her body once she accomplished the journey from kitchen to garret. English words might be running through her head, but she was so completely finished by evening, she didn't have the power to rein them in or mentally fasten them onto the objects around her.

Maria's unvarying routine in the early weeks settled her somewhat. She untied the apron and removed the maid's cap. She put the starched, frilled cap and apron in the closet, the pins on the dresser. (For day work, Maria wore housedresses of pale blue or white, supplied by Mrs Lowry but required to be meticulously clean and pressed. For late afternoon teas or serving dinner, especially if the family had guests, her serving uniform was a black dress with a dainty white apron and a tiny white cap.) She combed her hair and washed, scooping the water towards herself in slack cupped hands, losing much of it but eventually getting clean by slow dabs over her face and body. She rinsed her undergarments and hung them over a short line in the corner. Her bathroom had a sink, an untrimmed mirror, a single shelf, and an unpainted chair. Her toilet was in the basement; in the evenings and during the night she used a chamber pot.

The day-long strain of learning made Maria mute to anything original or to further discipline. Back home, her family would be gathering for the evening devotional reading, so she read her Bible too, but she let the book fall open where it would, accepting whatever appeared before her eyes. Usually she ended up somewhere in the middle books: Psalms, Job, Proverbs. She read a verse or two. She rarely remembered what she'd read.

She might write a letter then, but usually she wanted only to sleep. She closed the Bible, pulled the string to turn out the light, dropped to her knees. Half kneeling, half lying over the bed, she mumbled the prayer of her earliest childhood.

Lieber Heiland,
mach mich fromm,
Das ich in den
Himmel komm.

Loving Saviour,
make me good,
So that I may
enter heaven.

Once in bed, blissfully horizontal, she might stare for a while at the sky through her opened curtains, might attempt, in a last effort to learn something new, to get a sense of how the moon's phases exhibited here, how lighted the sky might be, or how dark. But soon her eyes fell shut and then she lay in her own inky darkness, trying to recollect who she was. Maria Klassen. How she'd been in Russia and on the ship and on the train. Who her family was and the way they'd arrived and how they'd be listed in the *Mennonitische Rundschau*, the German periodical. ***Klassen:*** *Johann, 44. Susanna, 43. Gerhard, 20. Maria, 19. Susanna, 16. Katherine, 15. Hans, 11. Wilhelm, 5. Margarethe, 3.*

Her family always appeared to her lined up like that. Father, Mother, Gerhard, Susanna, Katherine, Hans, Wilhelm, Margarethe. And Mother pregnant. (She'd told Maria this on the train, close to Winnipeg. "We'll have another mouth to feed after yours is gone to work," she'd said, her voice as flat as the snow-covered plain outside the window.) In order by birth, and posed in front of columns and ferns – not real ferns but a painted prop, as if they'd decided to have a photograph made by one of Russia's Mennonite photographers with his elaborate backdrops.

Then her stomach hurt. They seemed to be speaking to each other, but they wouldn't speak to her. They didn't even realize she was there. They couldn't visualize her world. She set them in place, they were all together, but they couldn't set her in hers. None of them had been to this house where she lived and worked; they knew their lives with each other, but they didn't know hers. She, not Uncle Peter, was like Joseph now, Maria thought bitterly, at least in this respect: *for Joseph knew his brethren, but they knew him not.*

Peter was the only one, in fact, to whom Maria could imagine confessing her struggles and fears, confessing the truth. Not that things were bad, just that they were difficult. He'd seen the house, he'd been inside, he'd met Mrs Lowry.

But she couldn't tell Peter either. It hadn't ended well the day she was hired. Everything was arranged, and he wouldn't leave. He stood there, muttering "*Na ja . . . Na ja . . .*"

"Go and greet the parents," Maria had urged him in the dialect, positioning herself beside Mrs Lowry. "Tell them the house is a good one."

Peter didn't move. "Do things the way they tell you," he said. "Just the way they want."

Did he think she wouldn't know as much? Mrs Lowry left the room for a moment and Maria stepped close, forced Peter backwards, hissed at him as though he were a dog. "Go!"

So he went, injury flickering in his eyes, and then she glimpsed him through the kitchen window, bobbing past in the mauve shade of the house, his cap in his hands, his reddish hair unruly. When he stepped into the full sunshine of the driveway his head caught the light and flamed up orange. It shone with a kind of purity, it seemed to her, as if it were the wisdom he could have offered her still and she had missed. She'd been stunned with remorse and knew she'd have to make up for it.

But on the terrible nights of her first months, when Maria finally reached her dreams, neither Peter nor her family was anywhere to be seen. She had only the house. Polished hardwood against her knees, dishwater searing her hands, dust in her eyes from shaking the rugs. The brass oval on the dining room side of the swinging door, cool against her arm, and English voices throbbing in her ears. Words on paper fluttering around her. She tried to snatch them with her mouth but her throat clamped shut and refused to help. Schedules and recipes teetering in front of her as high as she could reach but she hadn't gathered the ingredients yet and people waited at the table!

In her dreams, she was snarled in masses of colour, unfamiliar sound, and the beauty of wood, and her tasks weren't finished. Light fell through leaded glass into rainbows on unexpected places – on her hands and the chintz of the sofa and chairs, the rose walls, the built-in flour bin, the copper kettle. She was carrying vegetables from the cellar but there were scones to make, and oatmeal, and what good were potatoes and carrots for that? Someone at the table kept calling for her, but when she rushed in to answer, the diners refused to say what they wanted. She wasn't subservient enough, she was going to be dismissed. Then they would exit the room, turn out the lights, force her to grope through the house in the dark. Porcelain bowls and the stove top gleamed, white as the moon. At the fireplace, the brass poker shone as if alive, wearing a thin, malevolent smile.

□

The next time the Lowrys ate Family Vegetable Soup, Maria made it alone. She followed the English words and it turned out as she remembered it should. She ladled the steaming soup into the magnificent cream-coloured oval tureen. Intertwined wreaths of painted green ivy wound around the top of the bowl and the lid. Maria carried the dish through the swinging door. "The soup," she announced, as she'd been taught.

She said it badly. The article "the" gave her trouble. She heard Mrs Lowry's "Try again." She felt the children's eyes on her: Bobby's, round and curious, Eleanor's and Frances's, disdainful. She sensed Mr Lowry glowering; he hated delays of this kind. Maria saw Mrs Lowry's lips part with anticipation as she attempted the announcement again, parting the way a mother's mouth opens and closes with each bite a toddler takes while she feeds him with a spoon.

"Better!" Mrs Lowry exclaimed. "Much better!" Her smile seemed warmly confiding. Maria lowered the soup like a red bouquet to the centre of the table, then hurried back to the kitchen while they ate. A buzzer on the floor near Mrs Lowry's chair would send her the signal to remove the soup course.

When Maria gathered the soup plates, she noticed the tureen was nearly empty. She surged with pride as she took it to the kitchen. Hearty eating, she believed, compliments the cook. She wanted to share her sense of achievement with her teacher – Mrs Lowry – who'd followed to assist with the second course. She crooked an arm around the tureen and, with her other hand, traced the curving vine high on its rounded belly. She held the vessel in that caressing way and turned to put herself in Mrs Lowry's way. "The soup!" she declared.

There was an answering silence in the room like the crack of a whip. Mrs Lowry plunged her finger into the cooling leftover soup in the pot on the stove and held it there between the carrot slices, potato chunks, and beads of fat, the dainty white stone in her dinner ring hovering reproachfully just above the liquid. "This is the soup!" she said. Her voice was tight.

Then she stabbed at the tureen with her soup-wet finger. "And *this*, the tureen!"

Maria felt her body filling with shame. It was seeping into her as if she were a labyrinth of holes. Had she known the difference? Had she been thinking tureen, or the contents? It was all one piece to her, altogether soup. She knew its similarity to the German word *Suppe*, had become enamoured with her quickness in learning, had lost her senses over the beautiful bowl. They'd had beautiful things too, in Russia.

Her foolishness blurred the room. Maria leaned into the counter and was only dimly aware of Mrs Lowry carrying the meat and potatoes to the dining room, of the door closing between them. She dropped into a chair and the Lowrys shrank to a murmur and clatter behind her, like a thunderstorm moving away, rumbling without threat at an ever greater distance. She knew what had happened. It was more than forgetting the words. She'd forgotten she was a servant. She'd crossed a line of enthusiasm. Intimacy. How could she have been so careless? Her duty wasn't to initiate: it was to receive the moods Mrs Lowry projected, moods that varied from day to day, even within a day. Maria felt she couldn't breathe. She grasped the obligation of the servant for what it was – a restriction of her very being to the will of another woman, not her mother. (A mother's will had its compensations of affection at least.) The thought of it, the endless prospect of it, seemed like a pressure upon her throat, constricting her supply of air.

Someone was standing at her elbow. Mrs Lowry had taken the serving bowls out of the dining room without calling for her help. Maria heard her mistress ordering her to eat, heard her leaving, the dessert tray with the fruit compote and sweet biscuits in her hands.

Maria warmed herself a bowl of soup. It tasted bland. When I'm finally in charge of this kitchen, she said to herself, when I'm not only cooking but deciding the menus – and I will be soon, soon I will be for sure! – then they'll get *Suppe* to exclaim about, never mind the words for it. Soup seasoned strongly, with a toss of this and a toss of that, tasting as I go, not following numbers on a page like a slave, a real soup – soup with strength, as Mother would say, a soup like the Klassens eat, not insipid like this English-recipe-book soup of the Lowrys. I'll put in dumplings – *pelmenje* – not this tasteless noodle they call macaroni. They'll cry out with their praises but I'll turn my face away!

That evening Maria washed every plate, every cup, every utensil with stubborn and deliberate kindness. She took her time with each piece and she saved the tureen for last. She drew fresh, hot water for it. When she picked it up, the reproach of her error repeated itself, just as she had to repeat words over and over, learning the language. And once again she'd forgotten the word for the large special bowl.

But it seemed a forgiving thing in her hands. It seemed not to mind her mistake, or her friendly admiration either. Call me *Schuessel* – bowl – it seemed to console her out of its cavernous white interior. Or *Gefaess* – container. Or whatever you want for now. There's a knowing beyond names, it seemed to say, and you can only learn so much in one day, or a week, or a month. You're doing well, it seemed to be telling her; Mrs Lowry isn't here and she'll never know.

Besides, Maria reminded herself, she could avoid the word if she had to. Find a substitute, or figure out a way around it. She was aware of the need to hone the immigrant sensibility, the cunning carefulness for every unfamiliar situation, the ability to wear ignorance if required, the slyness of the one deemed inferior, but growing – perhaps – in subtle ways even more clever than those she served and on whom she depended.

But she had forgotten the carefulness. Next time she would keep herself in check.

Maria washed and dried the tureen as gently as if the china were skin, as if it were her youngest sister Margarethe just after a bath. Her motions, slow and tired, were the affectionate rub of prophecy. The day is nearly over, she told herself, and tomorrow will take care of itself.

☐

Edith Lowry sat at her desk, facing east, the morning sun dropping its gentle sheen like rain onto the shrinking snow, a detail she could be noticing, really noticing – "paying attention," as she thought of it – for her letters, this particular day neither spring nor winter but part of the transition between the seasons. Her mother and sister-in-law enjoyed the results of her paying attention; "how interestingly you describe things, Edith," they said, though not her sister Gladys of course, she being even farther west than Edith – in Saskatchewan – and knowing plenty herself about the prairie climate and landscape and how things progressed, filling up her springtime notes with recitations of everything she'd planted and as the summer wore on, how everything grew, and the flowers – three buds, four buds, five on the rose bush . . . and then the harvest; good or bad, they heard about it. How monotonous it got after a while!

Or, she could be reading. Again she was reading several

books at once: Cather, Hemingway, and someone new, de la Roche. And annoyed over it too, but the new books were always recommended more quickly than they could be read, page by page, she and James discussing the books they read, though never very deeply, Edith thought, it was rather as if James meant to grill her, as if he needed to discover whether she was still intelligent or was yesterday's evidence merely circumstantial? She could forgive him for that, it was simply the way he was, and sometimes she told him, as casually and indirectly as she could, what happened by the end of a book, not even hinting he might not have time to finish it himself, or even begin the book for that matter, and she didn't mind either, hearing him drop something she'd given him into a sentence in front of their friends.

"He's made two of you lucky, Edith – and happy," her brother Charles told her once. "First Adela, then you."

"My fortune on the back of her misfortune," she'd retorted, thinking perhaps it was they who'd made *him* happy. "I'm merely complimenting you, Edith," he'd said, "you're fortunate, is all I'm saying, and don't you think it says something too, coming back for a sister? My sisters attract prosperous men, that's what it says about our family, our upbringing, considering the poverty not so very far back."

"Is prosperity all you can think of, Charles?" she'd asked, to which he laughed, and said, "Precisely and only that. Prosperity."

She was staring outwards, out of the rose and green room with the heavy green curtains now opened. She loved the delicate lace of the snow and sun in its shadows and variations, whether describing it in a letter or not, and she wasn't going to start calling Maria every morning to pull the curtains and run her bath; she could emerge to do it herself, far too impatient to wait. "You have no idea how delicious it is, Edith," Iona had said in her particular voice for this subject, "to have the sun sweep over you in that position, to have it hit you all disheveled, all sleepy and remembering the pleasures of that night . . ."

"If, if, if," Iona had giggled then, meaning Edgar must have dispensed with his customary hermit's routine on the sleeping porch. This the same Iona who pronounced Edgar an excellent husband, really the best, not bothering her much. "It gives you the right start for the day," she'd gone on, "having someone to let in the light, prepare a bath, bring coffee; even if we can afford only one maid for ourselves now there are niceties we should allow ourselves, don't you agree, Edith my dear? Why else is there a bell-pull beside your bed?"

I consider myself plenty smart enough, Iona my trifle, she was thinking now, and well enough adapted to our position and class, but this much I'll decide for myself. Why should I deny that I wish to open my own curtains, Iona my piddling?

Edith, Edith, she scolded herself, how positively hateful you are this morning! Isn't Iona your dearest friend? You were stupid enough to warrant her fullest scorn over the dress you gave Maria – should she ever know of it, that is. Which it's not likely she will, as you'd rather swallow a snake than mention your little *faux pas*.

Edith sat there, not writing a word, not reading a word, not concentrating, her thoughts in tangles. She couldn't even say what they were about, just so much running of the mind and worries together, and the retorts she imagined to things already said. Did others also live their lives this way, she wondered, this constant conversation in their heads, or was it her deficiency alone? In ten days, Mother would be here, the annual visit west, no use writing her now, there was nothing new anyway, and as for her sister and sister-in-law, she simply couldn't begin, as much as she loved them, to strew the gaiety of her life over the page as if it consisted of petals. She had no heart to rouse their admiration or their envy today. She really didn't. She wasn't as shallow as that.

She wished she could write their oldest, James Edward, her yearning for him a repetitive thing, full of worry, but in his last letter he'd said, "The letters should go in order, you know, as in a tennis match; to receive so many volleys from you in a row before I can return them is exhausting, so Mother be easy and let me breathe in between; surely you've forgotten the demands of life at the university; you should be glad I'm studying hard and can't be writing as often as you'd like, plus I know you'll be delighted that I've gotten into quite a circle here with obligations of the tastiest kind (and how!) but don't worry, it's exactly what Daddy would approve of, etc., etc." Written in that rushed style he affected, as slick and confident as his combed-back hair, the rebuke intended to be light-hearted no doubt, as jaunty as his handwriting though actually he'd always been a rather sloppy boy in that respect and Edith hadn't minded either, secretly hoping it showed him too brilliant to submit to ostentation on a superficial level, although even then he got the punctuation and the syntax generally correct. She recollected it now as a single gush, not adding the pauses or stops that changed the meaning, she knew, the dashes that could take the irritation she felt at his youthful paternalism out of it, if she could just let it, but she wanted to feel it, the sting of it, to feel sorry for herself, especially since James had remarked that his son sometimes wrote him care of the firm. Well, why shouldn't he? They had so much to share that she wouldn't understand. But it hurt; she felt left out by the two of them again. What was wrong with her writing the boy twice or three times as often as he wrote in return? She wrote her own mother whenever she felt like it, never thought of correspondence strictly "in receipt of." But now she felt she had to wait.

She'd loved James Edward already as a baby, the first time Adela brought him to Ontario where she was school-teachering then – "to show him off to Auntie!" She'd done her best for him when he became her own responsibility. She ought to be grateful for the camaraderie between James and his son, which hadn't been there earlier. Smoking together after supper, and the elder James clearly pleased with the younger and his reports of the university (though less his marks than his social connections, it seemed), as if he could see through them into the future and knew the successes written there. A wise move for the boy to study in the East, see other parts of the great Dominion, especially the province of their origins, to let him sow some wild oats if he absolutely had to, James would say, though Edith thought it rather unchristian of her husband to approve of these inconsistencies.

Her husband was a good man, though: good enough. She *had* been lucky, as her brother Charles said. She had plenty to be thankful for, she told herself. Happiness had to be taken out of what was given her, love leading on as heat, not forced and twisted as if a piece of metal could be altered stone cold. Courage – no snivelling now – no tears, she told herself.

Once James Edward was finished, set up in the firm, back in the city, she could dispense with letters. It was too hard to find the proper voice for letters to a grown son anyway; all would be different once he was home. It was not that she expected to have him entirely at home ever again, perhaps weeks here and there during the holidays, some months in the summer, days at the cottage, but in Winnipeg at least, and some day perhaps with the Ruth he had talked about last time home. He called her Ruthie so what else could she have done but imagined her a slender frail thing with her childish name retained, and then in the photograph, there she was, a big girl, as if she'd spent her life in a sailboat, so strong and outdoorsy she looked. And in her hand, a cigarette. "She's fast?" came Edith's mother-reaction, blurting out, because it surprised her. The laugh to answer her was perfect, low, the son charming and confusing, putting her off with his acquired ambiguity. "Not too fast, Mother. Just fast enough."

Oh, the boredom of tumbled thoughts, nothing in focus, nothing needing to be narrowed and pinched off. She was done with the strain of getting Maria fit to serve them – my, oh my, but she'd taken that on without any idea what it could involve! It had worked, yes it had, in spite of James not wanting her wasting her time with it. For weeks she'd put off tea, bridge, the readings, the mission circle; she'd missed plenty, everyone keen on mah jongg now, and when she tried to explain they just wondered why she hadn't found herself an English girl, why bother with an immigrant of that kind? Iona sighed; they all sighed. They reminded her to test Maria's honesty, a cheap glittering jewel or money hidden where it would be found as she was cleaning, hidden deep enough that it might have lain there a long time, offering the choice of being taken or returned. Then one would know whether the girl could be trusted with the things. Edith hid a loose brooch stone and she had it back the same morning. Maria seemed disappointed, as if she'd guessed what Edith was up to.

And Edith was chagrined and said so to her friends. "They're honest," she said.

"Yes, I've heard good things about those Mennonites," Iona said, in a chirpy voice, "they're not as bad as the others."

But she shouldn't have given her the dress. The new dress. That was her weakness, too much of the do-gooder in her. She knew what James would have said had she told him. "Don't give your breeding away where it falls short," and "Please, Edith, don't waste your generosity." She was so often right about things, but sometimes so completely wrong it shamed her. Compassion ought to be channelled properly, not spent rushing off to Eaton's when the girl looked wan, from loneliness Edith supposed. She'd seemed altered, nothing specific to point to in terms of her work, but an expression of pain behind her smiles, as if she'd begun collapsing somewhere unseen, behind a façade.

So she'd bought the dress, brand new, bought it in blue, patterned with leaves in sprays, because the girl was dark and it would suit her best of all the colours. It was current, and relatively cheap. It wasn't as if she'd purchased something terribly expensive. It did look pretty though, it did, the slipover style, the kimono sleeves, the panel effect from the neck, the tuckings, quite something she would have chosen for herself had she been younger, in Maria's position.

But then Maria couldn't grasp it was for her! "I bought it for you," Edith kept saying, until she thoroughly regretted the attempt and Maria finally seemed to understand and muttered "thank you," that awful "tank you" though, coarse sounding. By then nothing would have been enough, though actually, it was far too much. Maria stroked the dress and fingered the pleats, tried to make something of it in her own way. Poor dear, she'd probably never seen or felt anything like it, out of the hovels of war and revolution. And the worst luck of all, Eleanor walking in and asking why Edith was giving Maria, the maid, a new dress, making the question a hook.

Edith kept herself contained and told her daughter to save her questions for later and Eleanor had flung tempestuously on her way again, not caring a bit, her posture said, what her wicked stepmother did. Oh, it was such a struggle with the girls sometimes.

She liked this German girl from Russia, that was the point. She was extremely efficient. If they could hang on to her . . . But she should have been more visibly grateful, instead of acting as if she was used to admiration. Receiving the gesture, once she'd figured out that it was meant for her, as if she deserved it.

So Edith went shopping again, bought something for herself. Gorgeous fabric made of silk and cotton crepe to commemorate Queen Maria of Roumania's visit to the continent, but bought to commemorate only herself. Gold-flushed, red and dark green, very expensive. She rushed to the seamstress to have it made into an evening dress, something suiting her age but also beguiling! And then she used the rest of the afternoon reading the women's pages and magazines that had piled up. "Evelyn was twenty-one – rather too thoughtful to be a flapper, and much too pretty to be a frump," one story began, and she fell upon the sentence as if it were a description of her. She murmured the latest colours aloud so they would flow smoothly in her speech. In the blues: navy blue, baby blue, Queen blue, French blue, poudre blue. And after that the beiges: rose, cream, tawny, and monkey skin. Gooseberry green and bird grey. Athenia rose. Silks in pheasant, Peter Pan, or orchid. Wood grey and creole.

Tomorrow she would fit the dress. She was sure it would suit her; James would say so and so would James Edward, once he was home for his summer vacation. She should have taken an egg cup of Mrs Pinkham's Compound this morning, she thought to herself, it would give her a lift better than the heavy sound of "Hold thou thy cross before my closing eyes" playing like a gloomy organ in the cavern behind her eyes. She had memorized dozens of hymns as a girl and never noticed until recently what they were all about. Her men were indisputably gallant, she had to admit, they would notice and mention the dress, they might compliment her while Maria served them silently in her neat black and white uniform. From now on she would give the girl her hand-downs, the worn and out-of-style things. "It keeps them in good humour," Iona would say. Years from now, perhaps, the dress of Roumanian crepe. But she'd be wearing it first, chatting with her husband and her eldest son, these dear ones she'd sworn loyalty to for her own dear sister's sake; the three of them would be chatting and Maria would serve them something sweet with their tea, triangles of cinnamon toast perhaps, of which James Edward was inordinately fond.

□

Maria had no idea there was another son in the family until spring, when James Edward came home from his studies in Toronto. Mrs Lowry instructed her for tasks, not about the family or its history. The only family details Maria needed to learn were their tastes, their habits, as they affected her work: how each liked their egg, what she ought to do for the girls when cleaning their room and what the girls were supposed to do for themselves, what Bobby ate for a snack after school. That kind of thing.

She had one day's warning. The third-storey room needed "refreshing," Mrs Lowry said; James Edward had sent a telegram, and was on his way. Cleaning the room, Maria saw it for the first time, and then he was home. "James Edward, our oldest," Mrs Lowry stated, pointing to him at the dinner table.

Maria described him in a letter home as tall (taller than his parents), very blond (blonder than his parents), talkative, and busy. For herself she gathered further observations, as she did for everyone in the family: how easily he smiled, how quickly his smile disappeared when the need for it passed, how his bony shoulders moved in a kind of stubborn shrug when he walked, as if to deflect opposition or some qualms of his own.

He brought more noise to the house, the heavy run of feet up the stairs two at a time, his habit of starting conversations with people before he was close to them, his first sentences like a call. He was an additional person to cook for, a hearty appetite. He was another set of names for Maria to learn. Difficult for her to say, separately and together. She had to pause to start, keep it slow, lengthen the sounds. The English "J" was hard for her in any case. She practiced "James Edward" as she practiced other names, until she could say them correctly.

Maria liked him. Why wouldn't she? "Hello, hello, hello, Maria," he'd said, laughing, to his mother's half-introduction, as if there was something funny about sets of threes. She let James Edward remind her of her older brother Gerhard, whom she was missing, just as she had linked Bobby to Wilhelm, and Frances and Eleanor to her sisters. Perhaps in some way the Lowry children could stand in for her faraway siblings and her interrupted Mennonite life.

□

When Maria entered the dining room after dinner to clear away the last of the dishes, the parents and oldest son were still at the table, though they'd pushed their chairs back and seemed to be rising. Mrs Lowry's face was pink. She was in the middle of laughing. Her husband's arm had caught her round the waist as she was getting up and for a moment they were suspended there in their obvious delight, as if posing. The dessert tray had iced cakes left on it, plump and tempting, and the white napkins discarded on the dark blue tablecloth looked cheerful, like sailboats on the sea. Someone had opened the window and a warm spring breeze blew in. Altogether, the room seemed possessed of benevolence. Maria could almost imagine, in fact, that she'd chanced upon something unusual, a certain effect occasioned by all these elements in this particular combination for this particular moment. James Edward had dropped back in his chair instead of standing and was grinning widely at the picture his parents made, as if their happy entanglement was all his fault.

Edith Lowry's hand plucked at her husband's neck while his arm crept further. His wedding ring glinted like the tinkling of a tiny bell as it appeared around her skirt. Her face descended towards his and she kissed him, on the highest hairless point of his forehead.

Maria was startled by a pang of envy – not of the couple alone but of James Edward too. His pleasure in the scene. His presence as witness, his by right, while hers was accidental. And awkward.

But they'd all turned to look at her because Mr Lowry said, "Maria! What in the world did you put in the sauce?"

She was nervous, conscious of her still-rudimentary English. "You like? You like?" she sputtered. "I make again."

After she said this, the three Lowrys broke into fresh laughter and the combined force of their laughter in their individual timbres threatened to knock her off balance. They were laughing because of her answer. Her arms shook. She reached for some plates, for ballast. Just as quickly the elder Lowrys turned their attention away from her; they seemed about to nuzzle again. Maria turned too, trembling, grateful to give them their privacy. But she felt James Edward's eyes on her.

She saw amusement persisting on his mouth while his gaze grew serious. Curiosity, assessment, and approval seemed to follow in rapid succession. The uncertain meaning of his watching confused Maria even more than the laughter. She fled into the kitchen holding only two plates.

◻

But James Edward was nothing to her then. She had Aron Ediger to contemplate: *that* hope and possibility. She and Aron grew up in the same Crimean village and they'd been passing on the walkway in the village late one afternoon; for some reason they'd halted; they'd talked there, uncertainly at first, then easily, beside the white stone wall. The fragrance of the acacia trees hung in the air and his smile reached her exactly, mouth to mouth it seemed, a direct hit.

She'd noticed that smile as if for the first time, after living four farmsteads down the village street from him all her life, after seeing him so often. He was simply Gerhard's friend. She had thought him imprecise and unambitious, but after their conversation she noticed that when he opened his mouth to laugh or smile or sing with his low musical voice, Aron was transformed, and he seemed someone else, his goodness unmistakable. Maria watched the young men of the village race horses down the central street and then she realized, Aron usually came second, but sometimes he was first.

"Aron Ediger has his eye on you," her cousin Lena teased Maria in a jingly tone. Maria denied it but she knew it was true. She didn't want to speak of it. Not to Lena, who envied her.

The night before the Klassen family left the Crimea,

Aron delivered a songbook to Maria. He said it was a gift from his father, who conducted the local choir which Maria had recently joined, and from the other singers too. Now Aron seemed unusually timid and their exchange on the stoop had more empty spaces than words in it, but Maria was genuinely happy over the book. She paged through it and it must have given him the impetus and the time he needed, for he declared he wanted to emigrate too. Could they write one another, then, until it was possible for him?

Maria answered, "Yes, of course." She'd been surprised how calm she felt, how sure. She wasn't nearly as nervous as he was. She told him she would gladly reply to any letters he wrote. She told him they would be sending cousin Lena's family their address as soon as they had it.

And Aron had written as he'd promised.

The letter arrived in April. It was a single, folded sheet inside a pale, thin envelope, as if emaciated from the journey. *Dear sister in the Lord, Maria,* Aron had written. It sounded as stiff as Sunday clothes but Maria loved that opening, the formal affection she felt in it, its theological emphasis.

Greetings from the Crimea, the letter continued. *I thank you for the address forwarded me by your cousin Lena. It is very truly a great joy for me to write to you, Maria. There is not much news from the village, but I can say this, the uncertainty has no end to it yet. We have noticed no improvement in our affairs. I am keeping well. My father is ill and cannot do the work alone. My mother worries and prays for some change in our situation. I think you will be able to guess what that might entail. But Father is quite unable to consider it now. He thinks it a futile wish. I do hope you will think about me and my dilemma. And may I be very bold and ask whether you will consider waiting for me there? I do not wish to persuade you beyond what you may be ready to do, but I miss you very much. I wish I had not hesitated so long to indicate my interest. I fear I squandered the opportunity and now you are gone. In these last days the words of Psalm 37:4, 5 have been meaningful to me, and I leave them as a friendly greeting. Aron Ediger.*

Maria felt the letter was remarkable. She felt Aron was remarkable. Not one sentiment turned the wrong way, not a single word misspelled, perfect love and piety combined. She practically memorized it from repeated readings, all the while composing her answer in a series of drafts over a week's time. She might have remained in Russia, she realized with a small shock; he implied as much. Only his shyness in approaching her had set the plan in this new direction, and how providential it was, how much better that he should follow her! She was sure her parents wouldn't have left Russia without her. And given the choice, would she have stayed? She was glad to be spared that decision.

Of course she would wait. Waiting wasn't in doubt as she wrote and re-wrote her reply. It was the expression of willingness she wanted to get just right – so Aron might marvel at her letter as she'd marvelled at his. She had to convey the right amount of eagerness, the right amount of reserve, ample room for him and God's will too. She leaned to a little more reticence than he'd shown, not that she felt it (in fact, she longed to be enthusiastic) but because she was sure this a feminine characteristic he would expect and appreciate. When she was satisfied with her words, she posted the letter and began to wait, as she'd told him she would.

❑

Maria believed her life as a domestic would be short-term, that Aron would soon reach Canada from the Crimean Peninsula, that they would marry, settle somewhere near her parents, raise a family of their own.

While she waited, she got through the worst of it at the

Lowrys – the first months. By spring, she could follow Mrs Lowry's instructions for an entire day. She knew the routine, the deviations from routine. Time within its larger structure of past, present, future had returned to her, the kind of time that belonged to adults. She'd hated the childlike experience of time that ignorance of the language imposed on her, time without proportion, living moment by moment, task by task, someone else announcing what would happen next. But she came through it, and she could speak and understand. It was astonishing, thrilling really, how the learning of language grew, how she was building a solid parallel line of English words beside her long, rich German vocabulary. She liked to consider the words side by side, to see them in tandem, to say them.

She'd grasped that *Fruehling* is spring, and then the season itself showed up. She'd been carrying the smaller rugs out to shake one morning and felt something altered in the air and then it struck her as surely as if she'd tripped and landed with her nose in the exposed black earth of the flowerbed that the seasons rotated and spring followed winter here in Winnipeg too. Happiness poured in as if some unknown anxiety had been relieved, as if in some unconscious but significant part of herself she hadn't been completely sure the laws of nature existed in the New World as in the Old. Had she actually feared she was finished with certain fundamental things forever? These were immigrant fears, certainly, and now she knew they weren't true.

Spring in her Crimean homeland was field larks soaring into the sky from their nests in the grasses, and mulberries, and acacia flowers hanging in clusters. The steppe a painting of lilies and violets, and red and yellow tulips. She remembered how as children they'd startled grouse and field chickens and cranes when they played, and how, in turn, the birds' beating wings had startled them. Here the landscape and climate were different, but the sense of hope and exhilaration was exactly the same. Here there were robins and lilacs, tulips too, and that shy green of the very earliest leaves, pale and glossy, reminding Maria of newborn calves.

Her father came to see her.

"Papa!" Maria cried, opening the front door to the bell. "Papa?" Just that week Mrs Lowry had given Maria a compliment, saying she'd learned quickly, and here her father was, like an angel to reward her. He looked as he did when they parted outside the streetcar the morning she was hired, wearing the clothes he'd worn upon arriving in Canada, the grey suit, the dark flat cap. His short greying beard was neatly trimmed to the same length, and the longer ends of his thick moustache curved upward and outward at the very same angle. Then it was winter, now it was spring and therefore summer soon, but he was the same.

A robin watched the meeting at the door, head cocked and still, and new grass was pushing through the residue of winter on the lawn. Clusters of red tulips stretched out of their beds. Mrs Lowry called, "Who's there, Maria?" from the middle landing and rushed down to see, but that awkwardness over – for she'd been officious and in Maria's opinion, shrill, and her father sober, evaluating – father and daughter sat in the kitchen while he asked questions, though he seemed distracted by her uniform and the things in the room. He smelled of damp wool, strong soap, perspiration. He muttered regrets about her being a servant, about his need of his children's support.

"Mother insisted I come," he said. "She doesn't trust the words of letters."

"She can trust mine!"

"The reality of Canada isn't exactly what the letters we got in Russia led her to believe." He smiled for the first time in the visit.

Maria couldn't think of what to say to that so she brought out the waffle iron and set it before him on the table. It was still quite new and the round lid and fat legs gleamed. The tray had ebony handles. He said, "Well, this is a servant that won't talk back."

"Papa!" she laughed. Maria's father loved machines of all kinds, equipment for the field or modern gadgets like this, anything he could touch and operate, or imagine his womenfolk using. (Everything but the telephone, which he resisted all his life.)

But the visit was short. He hadn't come just to check on her, he said, he had business in the city too. And he would take this opportunity to tell her in person that the child Mother carried had come into the world. It was a girl who died within the hour of her birth. Mother was still recuperating in bed, he said. It wasn't clear what went wrong; the delivery itself was uneventful.

Father's large hands were opening and closing over his knees as he spoke. The hands seemed as white as they were at the end of their travels from Russia, the nails perfectly clean; he hadn't found work during the winter and a move to a place of their own still lay ahead of them. It was Gerhard, Susanna, and Maria who were working. Maria slid her hands, nicked and reddened, under her apron.

"So we have a grave here now," he said, as if some necessary obstacle had been overcome.

He asked again if Maria was well, if she was getting enough to eat. He asked if the Lowrys were church-going people and Maria said, yes, they usually attended. She felt calm and pleasantly meek in his unexpected presence, and then her father left by the back door, before she'd given him anything of her loneliness, sympathy, or joy.

Maria restored the waffle iron to its place in the pantry. She set the water to boil and lowered the tray for tea. When Mrs Lowry entered the kitchen, intending, she said, to put out tea for her friend Iona and herself this once so Maria and her father could have "a good hard visit," she was surprised to find him gone. She asked Maria if she'd given her father a bite to eat. She might have offered, Mrs Lowry said.

Permission granted now, after he was gone!

Mrs Lowry took her favourite teacups out of the butler's pantry, the green and gold ones. "He didn't stay very long," she said. "I thought he'd stay longer."

"He came with others."

Father was dependent and the visit seemed miniscule, useless now. Mrs Lowry was having Iona in and they would linger over their tea and sandwiches. Talk for an hour or more. "Thank you, that will be all, Maria," Mrs Lowry would say once they'd been served. "Iona and I will just linger over our tea."

Linger. It was a word for those who'd been here a long time. For those who had everything.

Then Mrs Lowry said it was too bad she didn't get into the kitchen sooner, for Maria's father might have taken something along.

"Something? Something along?" Maria heard the sloppiness of her mouth, her thin, weak "th" sounds. Mrs Lowry had taught her that her tongue had to touch her top teeth, inside, to say them properly. But it wasn't a habit yet. She felt like Moses: *not eloquent, and slow of speech, and of a slow tongue.*

"A little something for your family. What we're not needing."

It was all so confounding. What kind of little something?

Maria remembered the accumulating crusts from sandwiches. "Bread? What we cut off? My family – they like pudding out of bread."

And she thought of the bacon fat, not used here, and the cake in the cupboard, the one that flopped. "Looks grim, that's for sure," Mrs Lowry had said. She told Maria to throw it away, to make another. Maria couldn't bring herself to toss the cake; she was eating it, slowly, herself.

"What you do with the crusts is up to you."

"I'll run after – "

"Was he on foot? Do you know where he went?"

She didn't.

"Well then," Mrs Lowry said, "it would be foolish to go dashing after him."

Maria felt herself blushing. She busied herself with the tray, shifted the plates, the creamer, though they needed no re-arranging.

Then, from the unpredictable Mrs Lowry, "Why don't you make us a bread pudding this week? I haven't had that since I was a girl. Do you need a recipe?"

"I have it in my head."

Maria longed to say that her mother had borne a baby, that the baby died, that Mother wasn't well but recovering. From the birth and the death. She wanted to quote her father's "So we have a grave here now." Something of their own, dug into the earth. Roots. Mother's greatest difficulty in leaving Russia was over the graves. The grave of her first child, also named Maria, and the graves of her parents in the Molotschna.

But Mrs Lowry might wonder why Maria had neglected to ask the child's name. She might pose other questions Maria couldn't answer. She would think her ignorance and her father's brief stop represented the extent of their bonds. She wouldn't know how deeply the Klassens cared for one another.

"Your father is a fine-looking gentleman, I can say that much," Mrs Lowry said. "He looks younger than I would have expected. And I trust everyone in your family is well?"

"They are well," Maria said. "Thank you."

But she remembered her mother's lack of emotion on the train while revealing she was pregnant, and she wondered again what that signified and whether now, perhaps, the child's death was a relief. It seemed impossible; she was sorry she'd thought it. Where did ideas like this one originate? Forgive me, forgive me, her mind sighed heavenward as she peeled potatoes later. But every peel that dropped seemed only to remind her how ignorant she was, in fact, about herself, but especially about what went on in the heads of her father and mother.

☐

Years later Maria looked back at herself as if paging through an album and saw how clumsy and swollen with trying she'd been, how driven by fear that she would stumble or meet the end of Mrs Lowry's patience just around the corner. That she would begin weeping in front of her and be dismissed. But on those same pages of her memory, there she was, descending the stairs with a smile, over and over, growing fond of the house and its objects, contented to be where she was, Aron's letter playing in the background of her concentration like a quiet, lilting song. No strain or mortification too great, if only she could stay and do what had to be done. Drawing from some reservoir of hope. Resilient.

At some point she'd begun to read more methodically in the Scriptures again, using them the way she'd grown up hearing them used, everything open to layers of meaning, lessons extracted from every line or fragment of a text. Figures, types, and applications. "This was the law of the leper in the day of his cleansing," she read in the Pentateuch, *Two birds alive and clean, and cedar wood, and scarlet, and hyssop . . .* If birds feel, there's drama here, she thought. Two birds, alive and clean, watching and nodding sweetly from their basket cage while preparations unwound around them. Cedar, scarlet, hyssop. And water, which had to be running. The birds alert to the human hands. What did their imprisonment signify? Why the earthen vessel standing outside the bars?

One of the birds was killed. *That* neck wrung under water; *that* bird used for blood. How was it chosen, and the other bird chosen to live? *(The living bird loosed into the open field.)* Were the birds compared, by sex or size, colour or character? Or was it simply chance, the bird that happened under the fingers reaching down when the lid was opened, that bird taken? The other, not taken but released? Every morning, she thought, her courage escaped defeat like the one freed bird. Father and Mother had decided, the circumstances demanded it, and she obeyed. Every morning, she thought, she was let loose into the Lord's mercies for another day.

2

LIKE GEESE, WHOSE journeys to and from their nesting places mark the Canadian seasons of spring and fall, Mrs Lowry and the children migrated north to their Victoria Beach cottage on Lake Winnipeg when the school year ended. Their cottage was green and white, and tucked among birch and evergreen trees. They called it "cozy but comfortable." They'd added the screened verandah the summer before, which made a difference, they said. It gave them more room, and peace from mosquitoes.

Maria was "the Help," so she was taken too, like the trunks and boxes loaded with things the Lowrys couldn't live without. Things they transported back and forth at the beginning and end of the holidays.

Life at Victoria Beach had a primitive quality about it, which Maria found astonishing at first, especially when things were so fine and modern in the city. Beach residents seemed pleased to have their amenities reduced for months at a time, however, for the sake of sand and sun and water. They seemed relieved to return, as if they'd returned to their original selves, as if urban progress and conveniences were a burden they'd been forced to enjoy through the winter out of duty – to country and King.

They went to some effort, in fact, to maintain the contrast to the city. If they planted flowers they did so randomly to effect that the blooms had sprung up wild. They praised the quiet, natural atmosphere of the place in conversation and in the newsletter they published. They all spoke of Victoria Beach as the most attractive beach in Manitoba. They especially liked the story of the visiting minister from England who'd said in the Sunday service at the clubhouse that the landscape reminded him so forcibly of the flower-bordered lanes of the old country, he'd felt entirely at home.

Maria's work was harder at the Beach. She carried bags from the station, unpacked the trunks, cooked on a woodburning stove that she had to light and tend. The cottage was badly arranged and there was no cross-breeze in the kitchen. She washed clothes on a scrub board.

But she liked Victoria Beach. (How could she resist?) She ate with the family, even when the men came for the weekend on the "Daddy train." The meals were simpler, just one course, and sometimes she heard someone say "Delicious!" or "This tastes wonderful, Maria!" Everyone's appetite grew because of daily exposure to sun and water; everyone devoured whatever she put on the table.

My dear parents and siblings, Maria wrote in July, *Greetings from Victoria Beach. I wish you could join me here for a day. It is very pretty. We all find the water refreshing to our spirits. This is the most attractive beach in Manitoba and has an excellent advantage over all the other Lake Winnipeg beaches. A visiting preacher said it reminded him very much of England, his homeland. The houses are hidden away among the trees and everything is kept as natural as possible. The people like to get out of the hot city and rest in the wild. No automobile traffic is permitted here, so it is very quiet indeed. Mrs Lowry and the children will spend most of the summer in this place and Mr Lowry joins us on the weekends.*

I told you, didn't I, that their oldest is home from his college for the summer? He works as a clerk in his father's firm. Most of his other time he spends with friends. Every day, I have several hours free, so I'm having a bit of a holiday too. Mr Lowry saw me writing and offered to take my letters along to the city. He said I could send as many as I liked, he would buy the stamps and mail them. He said this offer would last as long as I work for them. I am to put my letters beside his breakfast plate. I think it is very considerate of him and as you can imagine, it has touched me and made me thankful. I wonder if the lovely surroundings made him think of it. He is a kind man, but simply too busy in the city to notice much of what goes on around him. I am often invited to join the family in their activities here, but today I declined to go along to the water. I am on the verandah instead, writing you, dear parents, dear siblings. I hear the sounds of happy children at a distance, and it makes me think of my own – my own – dear family. Bobby tells me this is a very large lake, as far from one end to the other, north to south, as you could travel in three days. I cannot say if it is true, but the water stretches as far as the eye can see. Sometimes it is rough, at other times quiet. It is a lake with a mind of its own and all we can do is adapt to its moods.

Did you celebrate the Diamond Jubilee? I attended with the family. Mrs Lowry said we were celebrating Canada, no matter who we were, so on this day we would all go together. I think she was proud to have me along, because of what I represented. There I was, standing just behind them, watching the wonderful parade. The floats showed the history of Canada and all the nations who are part of it now. Bobby loved it. (Did the Mennonite papers say anything about it?) There was a ship with sails set, and a turning windmill, and even a waterfall dropping ten feet. (I got the number from the English paper, with Bobby helping me find it.) We went to Assiniboine Park for a program and picnic. The paper said 50,000 were there. I found my friend Helene Janzen among all those people, isn't that something? – I was so happy, Mother,

*to read you are on your feet again. Your lines to me were
a treasure. Never lose courage. Mrs Lowry told me I can
take a week off later this summer to come home for a visit.
Your loving daughter and sister, Maria.*

☐

At Victoria Beach, the Lowrys slept late. By the time
they rose, the sun had been up for hours. The entire resort, in
fact, hardly wakened until noon and rarely reached its peak
until evening. Then people stayed up late, into the long light
of the summer season, long after Maria had gone to bed in
her tiny alcove off the kitchen where she had a narrow cot
and a small square window facing east that she kept open
through the night. She woke early then, into a dark that was
no longer darkness but humming with pre-dawn expectancy,
the sense of imminent light, the first notes of birds. She often
stole out of the cottage to watch the sun rise. She had hours
at her disposal. As long as she was back to wake the household with the crackle of fire and the sweet hazy smell of
wood smoke, as long as she made the Lowrys' mid-morning
breakfast.

Sometimes she perched on the verandah while the
light transformed the thicket in which the cottage stood, but
usually she descended the cliffs fronting the lake to walk on
the sand, cool from the night, to bask in the play of colour on
the lake as the sun rose behind her. She loved the morning's
modest pink flush, the quiet lapping of the waves, the peace
and mystery she felt in the meeting of water and sky. The
horizon was momentous to her – because it was so straight,
because the lake was so large, because of its pearl-grey
tones. It seemed possible then that Victoria Beach belonged
also to her, not only to its cottagers.

The sand was fine and white, and – at the water's edge
– sculpted anew from the work of the waves through the

night. It seemed to wait for her, for her feet to mark it first. She liked to imagine, striding barefoot along the beach, arms swinging carelessly the way rich folks could walk, that she was one of the Lowry girls. Not one of the two sisters, Frances and Eleanor, who existed already, but an older one in addition. She walked with the airs she'd had on her family's Black Sea holiday years before, years before when they'd been prosperous. She turned her toes downward into moist sand. She pretended her dress was white, the fabric light and flowing, a pale blue sash around her waist. She pretended her hair was bobbed, bouncing in the breeze.

The only person Maria met early mornings, walking his dog, was Mr McCormick, who lived on the avenue be-hind the Lowrys. He bent his head slightly and always said Hello in the courteous way she associated with elderly men of distinction. But when the old man McCormick and his wife came visiting – "wandering over," they called it – at the Lowry cottage in the evening, he never acknowledged her. Perhaps he didn't recognize Maria as the girl he passed in the morning. Perhaps she looked different down there on the beach, pretending.

□

How that boy could beg! Seven-year-old Bobby circled his mother's chair like a ball of wool unwinding, pleading in every way he could think of to go down to the water. And just as steadily, his mother said no.

No, she said, because it was late, because they'd baked in the sun all day, because she'd just settled down in a chair to have a drink and read a book (couldn't he see?), because there was a dance at the clubhouse and no one else would be at the water. Because a wind had come up. Because she didn't know where in the world he got his harebrained ideas. ("Never mind what harebrained means," she said.) Because the sun was heading to bed and she was tired and the girls were never around when she needed them and there was no one else here. Overlooking her, Maria thought to herself. She too had just settled herself in a chair, to embroider.

Bobby pestered until his mother looked up and said, "Oh Maria, he's so desperate for a swim. Could you go down with him? I'll follow later, I promise."

"I don't need anyone!" the boy said. "I know how to swim."

"Oh stop it, Bobby! You can't go alone!"

Maria recognized the mounting impatience. In a moment, the peaceful atmosphere of Victoria Beach would be shattered in the Lowry cottage. "I'll go," she said. She set her handwork aside and got up.

"It's that or nothing, Bobby!" Mrs Lowry warned. "And sticking close to shore."

She sang out to Maria as they left, "Oh thanks, thanks so much! I'm afraid I've come to the most exciting part of my book."

Bobby was fretful and dashed ahead. He could wheedle, tease, and enjoy Maria, but tonight he had no use for her. By the time she had planted herself at the water's edge to supervise, he had stripped off his shirt and waded in. As Mrs Lowry predicted, the beach was deserted; there must be something truly special going on at the dance.

Maria called to Bobby in a friendly, coaxing voice but he ignored her and made a noisy show of splashing and springing about in the water. She shivered and crossed her arms over her breasts. The warmth of the day was slipping away with the wind. It seemed a melancholy wind, stirring about in the trees and grasses that clambered up the cliffs behind her as if lost. Clouds hid the sun but it trailed its regrets in spite of them, in wisps of red and orange across the sky.

She listened to the wind and the slap of the waves against the sand. She waited for Bobby to tire.

"Water cold?" she called.

"No! It's warm!" he said. "Now I'm going to swim."

"Play here!" Maria cried. "Play here!"

But if the water was warm, she thought, perhaps he had the right idea, swimming now. It was a good place to be, perhaps, while the air cooled. She wished she had a bathing costume. She also knew how to swim. She swam three times, on the Black Sea holiday. It had come quite naturally to her.

She wasn't a good swimmer, of course, not after three attempts, not a swimmer like James Lowry or his son James Edward who left the land behind as if they had no need of it, and returned as unconcerned, as unwearied, as they had left. But she could swim, she was sure of it; she'd paddled and pulled, water-borne. It was exhilarating, those three times.

But it seemed a long time ago, and she had nothing to wear for swimming. She would never spend what she earned on an item like that; her money went home to the family. For their survival. To pay the travel debt. She would never swim with the Lowrys or other Victoria Beach cottagers, either, prancing half-naked into the water as they did, giggling and shrieking over a splash or two. As if the transition from one element to another was a major expedition. She wasn't one of the privileged now, strolling at the Black Sea, speaking of it with awe and a feigned indifference so casually combined, *at the sea!*

But perhaps when alone, on an evening like this?

The wind moaned, the waves quickened against the shore. Maria yawned. She felt herself swaying a little with weariness and snapped back to attention. Didn't Mrs Lowry realize these wishes of Bobby were simply his postponements for going to bed? She'd be stricter with that boy if he were hers. But in other ways, easier on him too.

Bobby pushed into the water up to his chest and turned to wave. So, they were still friends. Maria waved back. He was walking backwards and then a bank of oncoming water spilled over him and knocked him off balance. He righted himself. He seemed to be laughing.

Maria watched Bobby advance against the waves, still

walking instead of swimming, it seemed: up to his shoulders, his neck. The sun slipped lower behind its cloudy veil, sank into its shining casket of water for the night. But a remnant of light remained, a golden incandescence behind those clouds like a lamp behind a curtain. A pair of pelicans passed overhead.

And then she was watching with longing the odd-shaped but elegant birds, just two of them in the sky, and each there for the other, as if they were the only pelican pair that existed, like Adam and Eve in the Garden of Eden, needing no one else. Not like her, alone on the beach, and far away from everyone who mattered to her. She wondered whether Aron was thinking of her.

The birds grew smaller and smaller in the distance but the gradual departure of their togetherness only deepened Maria's loneliness. Then she remembered where she was, and why she was there. She searched the water for Bobby. He was still on his feet, it seemed, but she couldn't tell for sure.

"Come back, Bobby!" she shouted. "Your mother said to stay close to the shore!"

Bobby paid no attention. Maybe he couldn't hear her. Maria lost sight of him, then found him again, or his head at least, bobbing like a ball on the surface. She couldn't judge which direction he intended to swim. He usually swam with his father or brother beside him, but he didn't go far. She glimpsed his arm in the air. She waved back. She was shivering, but if the water was warmer than the air it would be hard to persuade him to return. Knowing Bobby, he'd come back when he was ready.

Maria tried to keep the boy's head in view, but it jumped away from her and then the water filled with leaping, disappearing heads trying to trick her. "Get back here," she muttered.

She was suddenly uneasy. He was going too far. Maria flipped off her shoes and ran into the lake. Just up to her knees. Just to see him better.

Bobby was right; the water was warm. She felt stones under her feet, and walking further in, hard sand in ridges. She couldn't see Bobby; couldn't see him anywhere. What would the Lowrys say? She'd been inattentive; she'd been staring enviously at the bird pair sailing home to its nest.

Maria moved still further. She'd changed into a skirt and blouse for the evening and the skirt was full, the hem wet now and dragging. She yanked it up and pushed forward. The water hit her legs. She felt the water's cold boldness as it pushed through the garment and touched her thighs, as it reached her underclothes, her hips, then turned warm, like a wrap.

She was hurrying into the vast dark lake and remembered Bobby saying, three days to cross, and here she was in it, the first time. Perhaps a minute in. It was hard to run against, the water like hands blocking her abdomen. The sound of it around her was thick and resistant too. She couldn't be sure that Bobby was in danger, but she'd lost sight of him. She might be blamed. She had to get closer and find him.

A broad plank of water struck Maria's chest. She gasped for air, twisted, and then she saw a woman descending the wooden stairs down the cliffs and realized it was Mrs Lowry, descending as if she'd fallen. She heard a scream. Had she, Maria, screamed, or was it her mistress? When she turned back into the lake she caught sight of Bobby, floundering and going under. She started to paddle, awkwardly and urgently, the way she recollected doing it years earlier in Russia. Her skirt and petticoat billowed around her in some slow pattern opposite the movement of her body. She saw Bobby, rising. Flailing.

Maria shouted to him that she was coming. The skirt was like a tangle of seaweed around her legs. She needed to be rid of it. An awful decision, though, for she wouldn't find it again, and what if this was simply Bobby's joke, or her imagination? She had so few clothes.

She fumbled at the buttons, ripped and pushed the skirt

and the petticoat away. She shouted to Bobby again. The words seemed stones that sank before they reached him. She was paddling badly, but her legs were free. She couldn't stop now; she was sure there was no bottom under her feet. And Mrs Lowry was waiting. Mrs Lowry never entered the water. She claimed to be terrified of the lake. Maria would have to do it alone.

Bobby surfaced and Maria gained on him. She reached him, lunged for his neck, his arm. She had some solid body parts – had him, like gold in her hands.

But she'd stopped – just the briefest of stops – and stopping, she lost her rhythm, her knowledge of how to swim. She knew she had only a moment to recollect it before they both went down, only this moment to resist the onslaught of panic just beyond it and the fear she would die. *God help me! Help me please!*

Bobby was a smart boy. And perhaps he was sorry for his disobedience. He put his arms around Maria and didn't fight her at all. He trusted her and then it came back: how to paddle him home to his mother. Legs scissoring, arms reaching and pulling. Not as she swam in the Black Sea, giddy with water's remarkable propensities. Not as anyone swims. She must be a sight, she was thinking even in the midst of it, the way she kicked and rowed and plunged, heading for the frantic Edith Lowry who had actually stepped into the water, waving her arms at them like a beacon.

Bobby hung on and Maria worked shoreward. He grew heavier. Water threatened her throat. Maria coughed to dislodge the collar of liquid around her neck. The motion must have frightened Bobby for he tightened his arms around her, raised them higher. She felt herself choking.

She remembered her father's "You're not afraid," proud of the Black Sea holiday and his children. And Mother's surprise, or maybe disappointment – "You're really not afraid?"

She couldn't be afraid! Bobby was fighting her now and the pain shot into her stomach. A small boy, but so heavy!

A thin, wiry boy, and what was the matter with him that he didn't help, didn't swim? His legs bound her like a rope and where should she struggle first? For her arms, legs, mouth?

A command pierced the air above the waves. "Stand, Maria! Stand!"

Maria put down her legs. There was sand under her feet. Her head cleared the water. She could breathe.

The sand was firm and their ascent was brisk. Maria's blouse plastered coldly against her skin and her legs grew longer as the water receded. She sensed their length, their whiteness, the taunt of the wind upon their nakedness. She was ashamed of the entire episode and missed her skirt, wherever it was.

Mrs Lowry met her with a jolt. She grabbed Bobby's arms and they pulled him together, so much lighter as he seemed now, over the narrow bar of stones and onto land. Maria toppled then. She felt her hand scraping her lips, sand on her teeth.

When she lifted her head, she discovered a towel stretched over her buttocks and Mrs Lowry kneeling and wailing admonitions, forcing Bobby up. The boy retched with a marbly, gushing groan. His mother crouched against him.

"Bobby?" Maria's voice seemed to depart her mouth at a distance.

Mrs Lowry cried, "He's alright! You saved him, Maria!" Her head dropped into her hands. She was sobbing. Against the wind and water it sounded as heartwrenching as anything Maria had ever heard.

Then Mrs Lowry flung her head up and her face looked ferocious in the darkness. "If I'd been here, I couldn't have done it!" she said.

She clapped Maria's shoulder. "You saved him, Maria. You saved him!"

"I was drowning," Bobby wailed. "I was going under."

Mrs Lowry wrapped the boy in her arms. "Shh-hh-hhush,

Bobby," she soothed. "Everything's fine. Maria saved you and everything's fine."

After a while, her voice vehement, she said, "I think it was a miracle." Maria wasn't sure whether Mrs Lowry was speaking to her, or to herself.

□

If a miracle, there were elements of foolishness in it too, Maria sometimes thought in the weeks that followed, after Mrs Lowry's gratitude had subsided. It came back to her sometimes, the whole scene like a tremor, and it all seemed vaguely shameful, even ridiculous. But she'd saved Bobby's life. What was shameful in that? And she'd gained some advantage. Mrs Lowry declared she was beholden to Maria forever. She said she'd buy her a new summer skirt to replace the one shed in the water, and she'd buy her a winter skirt as well, once they were back in the city. Something of fine black wool. As a reward, she said. "That would be useful, wouldn't it?" she asked. "A black skirt?" Maria agreed that it would.

□

Another evening at Victoria Beach, the girls off with friends again, and James spending the weekend in the city, Edith Lowry thought, because of meetings or something, he'd said. No break, then, from being in charge of the family. And James Edward, who *had* come for the weekend, no help either. He turned into such a child at times.

A hot, sticky evening, mosquitoes and flies whining against the screens, sensing a change in weather or just wanting in, as insects always did, never content where they were, and the sky growing darker. Edith heard the first thunder, at a far distance, then another, and knew the storm was coming their way. She remembered the mess in the yard where Bobby and the girls had played. Where Bobby was playing still, she saw as she stepped outside, on his haunches and peering at something in his hand.

He looked up and she saw his mouth opening to explain what he'd found, but there was no time to wait for that. "It's going to storm. It's going to thunder and flash!" Edith cried. "Help me clean up the things."

She was picking up blankets, hats, books, and toys, and Bobby wasn't helping. At the edge of her hurry and fluster she saw that he had shot up and to the door. She saw that he had nearly collided with Maria, who was coming out to assist. She heard his high, scared voice. "There's going to be a terrible storm, Maria!"

It was only ten days since the episode in the water, and he was still afraid of everything. Edith saw him lock his arms around Maria's legs, saw her bending and rubbing his back, heard her soothing. "Only wind, Bobby, only wind. You're not afraid of wind."

"I'm so afraid of wind!"

"Only wind, Bobby, only wind."

The wind was ripping at her patience, that's what the wind was up to, Edith thought, annoyed at the boy's protestations of fear, and Maria's repetitious consolation.

And now she'd dragged the boy inside.

Edith had told Maria it would take time for Bobby to settle down. She'd informed her that he would likely need a lot of reassurance.

But she hadn't instructed her to provide it.

Edith chased a piece of newspaper, caught it – a shrub caught it for her, that is, and then she had it, and then she had everything, and the cottage yard was ready for rain, and she burst into the cottage, dishevelled and hot, her arms full. Annoyed but pleased that she'd battled the scattered things into one load so quickly. She let the door slam.

Maria was sitting in the rocking chair and looked up. A blink of dazzling white, and then a crash of thunder.

Bobby had curled into Maria's lap. And Maria was sitting in her chair. The chair they all knew as Edith's, all called "Mother's chair."

James Edward occupied the entire cottage sofa and more, his feet sprawled over one end, his head propped up on a pillow on the arm of the other. He was absorbed in a book.

But there were other chairs.

"The sky is giving a story," Maria was whispering, rocking the boy ever so slightly. "Light. Noise. Just a story."

Then she was reciting some German ditty to him, in a sing-song voice.

"You should have been helping," Edith barked, and she meant the three of them, James Edward – so capable of shutting away his little brother's fears and all the signs of weather changing around them – and the cringing Bobby, and Maria. Most of all Maria, to whom Bobby dashed now every time he had a spot of trouble.

Maria was trying to push the boy from her lap, but he only clung harder, and Edith could see she was nervous. "He's afraid," she was saying. "Because of the storm." Her hand hovered over Bobby's pinched-shut eyes.

Edith felt a surge of energy – and she knew it was envy and anger – that propelled her to the pair in her chair. She fumbled for Bobby, rougher than she wanted to be, and Maria worked along with her, she knew, prying the boy's hands loose and pushing him away.

"Maria's the maid, Bobby," Edith scolded. "You come to me when you're afraid."

She pulled until he yielded, whimpering as she tugged him into the bedroom. "Maids come and go, but your mother's always here," she said. She said it loudly, over the wind moaning around the corner of the cottage.

Edith sank onto the bed, drew Bobby onto her lap, finding coos instead of words now, a softness and sympathy that felt rote to her, until he relaxed against her, until she relaxed as well, her sounds now weary and authentic. The two of them sat a long time, she thought, until she noticed that the quietness had come to the outside too, as if the storm had vanished without even beginning. So there hadn't been any rain?

Bobby had fallen asleep. She would slide him gently out of her arms and onto her bed. He could sleep in her bed tonight, she decided. Then she heard James Edward speaking in the other room, heard him say, "Would you like to hold me on your lap?"

He must be speaking to Maria. So the girl had stayed in the chair, empty-lapped and looking doleful?

A pause, and again, James Edward. "Really. I'll come sit on your lap."

Edith heard the girl stand, heard her quick steps away into her own room, indignation in them, or maybe confusion.

And James Edward, snickering. "Shucks, Maria, all I meant was, I wish I was small again."

Edith wanted to shout at her eldest to stop being an idiot, but she was in no mood yet to defend Maria, and Bobby was now so calm, his damp hair like a tonic against her neck, and she didn't want to waken the child or frighten him with anything else.

□

When Maria saw her brother Gerhard coming towards her at the Winkler station with his large rapid stride, his patched but neatly-pressed clothes, in that lean, determined manner of his, the homesickness accumulated inside her since January was exhaled in one happy breath. It had gathered there for many months, a constriction on her lungs, taking up space. By the time her brother reached her she felt cleansed of her pining. Just the sight of him was enough. The abiding sense of Mrs Lowry and the children in their cottage, surrounded by balsam and pine, disappeared. The strenuous week, just past, of washing, waxing, and buffing the floors of their house in Winnipeg, vanished. Her aching back, the sore knees, the polishing machine, whose heavy vibrations complained through her body for hours afterwards, were forgotten. Gone too was the large empty house, where for five days only a cup or a glass in the sink spoke of anyone living there besides herself. "I'll eat at the Club this week," Mr Lowry informed her and Maria had no idea what James Edward had done for his meals.

Gerhard had come to fetch her in a borrowed car. It belonged to a neighbour, he said, for whom he'd done some field work.

Maria said the horse and wagon would have been fine; that's what she expected.

"Father insisted," he replied.

Maria was pleased. Her father's generosity had always revealed what was possible, financially; the car must reflect a positive turn in their situation.

"But," said Gerhard, once they were seated, "it's because the man has no money to pay me for my work. He wants us to use the car a few times to cover what he owes."

So the vehicle was no indication of things going well: poorly, rather. Gerhard chuckled. It wasn't such a wonderful automobile either, he said. It was prone to break down. Although he knew how to fix it, he said. It was a hot August day and the car reeked of oil and dust as it clattered through the powdery streets of the small Manitoba town.

Gerhard toured Maria homeward through the village where the Klassens had lived their first months in Canada, with a family of conservative Mennonites. Descriptions in her father's letters took physical form: there the immense barn and house, all under the same roof, where they crowded together – two families – and then, a half-mile or so distant, the granary where they camped a month in late spring, waiting to take possession of the farm they were presently renting. Maria looked at everything he showed her, but not for long. These places were past; they were bits of text in Father's neat hand, historical references upon which she had no need to dwell. She listened languidly as Gerhard explained the area's composition, who was here and why, who was leaving. He said the earlier group, the Mennonites of the 1870s, were granted land in chunks and could settle in islands of their own; they'd formed village communities like those in Russia; some of them, the most inflexible to change, were moving on again, to Mexico or Paraguay. Large-tract settlement wasn't possible now, he said; the immigrants of their migration were squeezing in where they could, attaching themselves to their own people here and there, though the ones who had left unexpectedly helped the newcomers by freeing up good farms for sale. But the Klassens' farm was rented – and could be purchased perhaps – from an *Englischer*, and not in a village: Mother was finding its stand-alone isolation nearly unbearable, sociable creature that she was.

Father had sketched all this in his letters and Maria was unable to absorb the information again. She let it float on the joy that filled her at the station; she was buoyant with antici-pation, half-realized already with her brother beside her, of landing at her own small colony of safety – her family. They were nearly there, Gerhard had said, and for one week neither she nor her mother would be alone.

"Here it is," he said as the car rattled off the main road. Their farm: the future they were building by her help, in her absence. She saw unpainted sheds scattered like boxes at the end of a long and narrow lane. The middle one must be the house, the one on the left, the barn. Size-wise, neither seemed to gain much as they approached. Then Maria saw the door of the house opening and closing and her mother and siblings emerging one after the other onto the drab, bare yard. Waiting for her, in a row.

Gerhard stopped the car with a final and decisive clank. Mother, Katherine with Margarethe in her arms, Hans, Wilhelm, streaming towards her. Her mother lifting a corner of her apron to dab at her eyes and then the whole apron slipping up and over her head in a single fluid motion and her hand immediately smoothing the hair the apron might have disturbed. Now Maria saw clearly, each of them squinting at her against the strong summer sun, and her memories of them and their reality snapped together; they were real and solid before her. She hugged them all, felt them against her, flesh and bone. She was home.

A bank of poplar bush shimmered in the heat behind the house, perhaps a hundred yards away, but there were no trees on the yard. Several chickens lolled against a sagging mesh enclosure in the narrow shade of a decrepit-looking henhouse and a dog lay under the porch, panting. He'd lifted his head to the commotion but didn't move. To the right Maria saw a field of wheat, its rows like shining silver ribbons. Heat seemed to rise from the hard grey ground, penetrating even her shoes.

"Come in, come in," Mother urged. "It's very hot." They moved as one into the bar of shade against the house, Maria in the middle of the pack, while Gerhard returned to the car. He would take it back to the neighbour, Mother explained, and then walk home.

Again Mother was urging them inside but Maria's sisters and brothers were acting shy of her and waited for her to enter first. Maria laughed and sprang up the two wide wooden steps. The house drew her inside. It was pleasantly dim and cool. All the curtains were drawn.

Maria's eyes adjusted; she saw that the house was very small. Only two rooms. The family's clothes hung over ropes strung between the corners of the smaller room and divided that space further in two, providing some privacy, a double bed on one side, a double mattress on the floor of the other. A crude, freshly-made ladder leaned against the wall of the main room. "In summer," Wilhelm, who had edged close to her, whispered proudly, "the boys sleep in the attic."

There was very little room, very little furniture, but everything was clean and in order. The dishes were washed and stacked on a shelf over the worktable. The stove top glistened, the lamp glass had been rubbed clear. The clothes draped over the rope were laid in a way that suggested a pattern to their placement.

Maria's mother pulled a chair away from the table and seated Maria like an honoured guest. How strange and awkward it felt for her, but what a relief! Then Mother pulled out another chair and sank into it beside her eldest daughter. She put her apron and her hands into her lap. She'd been rounded with her pregnancy when Maria saw her last, and now she was flattened somewhat as if deflated, except that her lower stomach still bulged under her, like a reminder of the past. Her bare tanned legs seemed to grow out of her shoes, thin as a girl's legs but covered with coarse brown hair.

The ugliness of her mother's legs shocked Maria. She wished now she hadn't worn stockings – fine silk stockings passed along to her by Mrs Lowry because each of them had a tiny tear. They'd torn at the top, out of sight; they were easily mended. Maria wished she'd removed them at least, on the train before arrival. But her mother's eyes shone, moist with emotion, and the children's were doe-eyes, wide and tentative.

Katherine perched on the floor beside Maria. She fingered the hem of her sister's dress. She touched a stocking. Maria was wearing the blue dress Mrs Lowry had given her several weeks into her employment. She patted the ribs of Katherine's high, tight braids to reassure her. Wilhelm saw this and he knelt and touched Maria's ankle too. He let Maria tousle his hair and press his cheeks between her hands. "Oh Wilhelm," she said, thinking of Bobby, "I've missed you."

And here was Margarethe, still a pudgy toddler, tugging at Maria's arms, suddenly insistent, as if she'd finally remembered this stranger. Maria lifted her up and wrapped her arms like a blanket around her. The child acquiesced immediately to her enclosure.

Maria felt her mother watching everything. She'd

grown up under that azure gaze, full of love but expectation too. Admiring, or reminding. There was no rebuke in it now. No envy.

And the way they clustered around her! Something could be made, perhaps, of wearing stockings and a pretty dress to a poor hot farm. Instruction, or inspiration. Maria heard herself speaking and felt herself astonished, for it was more than half a year since she'd told these children stories, a long time since she'd spoken unbrokenly and with authority. She cradled Margarethe and bent towards Katherine to recount to the sister who was clearly becoming a lovely young woman the particular circumstances of receiving this particular dress. The goodness of her mistress and her own amazement. Because it didn't fit her well enough, she said, Mrs Lowry passed it on to her, and it fit her of course, and she'd been thrilled with the style; it was very fashionable, wouldn't they agree? She wore it to the celebration of the Diamond Jubilee. She'd written about that, remember? The big day had been chilly, and threatening rain and Maria had no hat so Mrs Lowry rummaged through her things and she found her a scarf. A red scarf. "The colours of the day!" she'd exclaimed.

"As if it was the flag," Maria said. Katherine smiled and rested her head against Maria's leg.

Maria spoke of other dresses too, not hers of course, but the clothes Mrs Lowry – and they all practiced saying her name – and her daughters pulled out of their closets, even for the everyday. Maria knew her father wouldn't approve of this emphasis so early in the visit but he wasn't here and Mother's eyes were as thirsty upon her as Katherine's, just as eager for the tales Maria was spinning out of colours, fabrics, pleats, and stylings. Every garment had a story's potential: a beginning, a plot of numerous and various occasions, an ending full of memories. This blue dress of hers, for example, patterned with leaves, had already made an impression on the other Mennonite domestics at their meetings at the Mary-Martha Home. One of them sketched it, to copy its pattern to sew. And now she'd worn it on her first visit home.

Hans and Wilhelm stared at Maria as if mesmerized. But they started to fidget as the womanly tales of clothing wore on, and then turned into the details of the Lowrys' house and habits, extended even longer because of their mother's relentless curiosity how this or that was done. Hans poked his brother, Wilhelm poked back.

"Go catch gophers then!" their mother exclaimed. "Off with you! Sitting around like lazy sheep heads, as if there's no work to be done!"

"They earn three pennies a tail," she told Maria as the boys shuffled out.

Mother twisted in her chair and extended her apron, preparing to put it on again. She sighed. "I've worried more than I should," she said. "I think of what can happen in a city. The traffic, the dangers . . . You haven't been in danger, have you?"

"You can see that I'm fine."

"Are you ready to stand before God?"

Maria's eyes filled unexpectedly with tears. "*Mutti*, you know!" She'd missed her mother's questions, even their constant need for reassurance, for consolation, but not a question like this one, something basic, something Mother knew – and the doubt in it! As if Maria might have become another person. As if she were that weak and susceptible.

"It doesn't hurt to ask ourselves," her mother said stiffly, in spite of Maria's tears. "To be sure." She sighed as if it had been a hardship for her as well. Then she touched Maria's arm – a brief and mild touch – as if to heal the awkward but necessary exchange.

Maria swallowed, then asked, "But how is it going with all of you?"

So Mother began to talk, and she talked and talked some more, until Katherine got up and served them something to eat, and she was talking still when Susanna arrived from town, from her day job as a domestic, her face red, her hair and neck streaked with perspiration from bicycling. She dropped two coins in a tin cup. Maria leapt surprised from her chair to embrace her sister.

"Where did the afternoon go? We've been visiting all afternoon! Eating Mother's pickles and *platz* —"

Susanna said, "Oh Maria, I'm sure you weren't just sitting, that wouldn't be like —"

"I've been sitting."

"She and Mama sat here all afternoon," Katherine said. "Talking."

"It's true," Mother confessed. "As idle as a Sunday."

Hurt crossed Susanna's face like the shadow of a hawk over a field, and the rims of her eyes grew pink. Except for the bits about the dresses, Maria thought defensively, the bits about Lowry housekeeping customs, Susanna hadn't missed anything. She hadn't talked that much and what she'd said, she could tell her sister later. It was Mother who talked — talked out her life in the Manitoba village and then in the paper thin house on the farm, talked out her concerns and discouragements, laced with her familiar expressions of gratitude and reminders of blessings, things Susanna knew plenty well enough. Maria had merely started her off, and then she'd listened.

"They have me leave just before supper because they don't want me eating with them," Susanna complained. "I cook and have to smell it till I'm hurting with hunger and then I have to leave."

"So near to starving you're not," Mother said. "One day in the year Maria's home and we don't have supper ready."

Maria insisted Susanna rest while she and Mother fried potatoes and set the table with bread, pickled watermelon, and buttermilk. Father came in from the field work, Gerhard returned from the neighbour's, the boys bounded home with three gophers as their bounty. The entire Klassen family was together around the table. "No one is missing," Mother said triumphantly as she took her seat.

The meal was delicious. Only one course but it was enough, and then Maria's father opened the Bible for the customary reading. A New Testament chapter in the morning, an Old Testament chapter at night. In this way they read through it all. History, genealogies, poetry, or prophecy, no matter what came up, it was their text for that day or night. (This is how Father believed it had to be done. The daily reflections of the *Kalendarblatt* – the tear-off devotional calendar – weren't sufficient for him, though he and Mother read these too.) In Maria's absence, they'd reached the first Chronicles of the Kings, chapter twelve:

> *Some Gadites defected to David at his stronghold in the desert . . . brave warriors, ready for battle and able to handle the shield and spear, their faces . . . the faces of lions . . . swift as gazelles in the mountains. Ezer the chief, Obadiah the second, Eliab the third, Mishmannah the fourth, Jeremiah the fifth, Attai the sixth, Eliel the seventh . . .*

Father read the Hebrew names smoothly, as if they were the names of his friends. Maria bowed her head, her eyes resting unseeing on her empty plate with its spatter of crumbs and bits of fat and pickle juice. She listened with a sharp awareness of the daily event, less to the text than her father's voice, sounding in the crowded over-heated room as cool as water gurgling over pebbles, his voice beautiful over the ancient sacred words, and all of them in a posture of obedience to the habit of these words, twice a day. She'd missed them, that many times.

> *The commander of the men called to David,*
> *We are yours, O David!*

We are with you, O son of Jesse!
Success, success to you,
and success to those who help you,
for your God will help . . .

After the reading and Father's prayer, Maria produced from her bag the box of Corn Flakes bought with Mrs Lowry's grocery order and charged against her wages – her gift to the family. All of them marvelled at the crunchy orange petals, tasting a few each before setting the box aside for tomorrow's breakfast. The girls washed the dishes. Then Maria invited Susanna for a walk along the lane.

It had grown late but the air was still very warm. Clouds of pink and mauve lined the western sky. The field of grain beside the lane lay dark and solid as if asleep. Meadowlarks and whippoorwills called out of the dusk of the fields and clusters of gnats whined around them as they walked, but the impression upon Maria was one of complete quiet and calm. She put her arm into Susanna's. "And what is it like, at *your* work?"

What it was like poured out. "They're a family as big as ours. The mother is sick. She lies in bed, that's why I'm there. They don't seem to care about it much. As if they wish her dead. Her husband shouts at her. He shouts at the children. He shouts at me. It's nothing special, that place. If he didn't pay me at the end of every day I wouldn't think they had any money at all. He practically throws it. Thirty-five cents a day. He thinks his wife ought to be better by now. Every evening I'm glad to leave. In the morning, my stomach aches for dread."

"Your job is harder than mine," Maria murmured.

"But it aches more if he greets me by saying I'm not required for the day. Then there's nothing gained from the going and coming, and Mother will be disappointed. The money we earn hasn't gone for the travel debt. Not yet."

"Did Father say that?"

"It's no secret."

"We'll have to work a long time!"

Susanna withdrew from Maria's arm and stopped. "Maria," she accused, "what else?"

"I thought . . . it would go sooner. How long?"

"It will take time to get the farm going properly," Susanna said, a forced brightness suddenly sounding in her voice as if she'd recollected and taken on her mother's words.

It fell as quickly. "But this farm is no good. That's what my boss always says."

"Have you told Father?"

"He'll discover it himself, if it's true. Good we're only renting . . . But maybe he says it to be mean. I don't know."

The sisters turned around at the main road and wandered back along the lane to the house. They walked slowly, not speaking now, as if their thoughts and the lane must be tested under their feet. A faint band of light and colour still soft-ened the western horizon. Maria heard their steps, hers and Susanna's, stepping as one.

"Do you like your home in the city?" came her sister's voice. "What's it like there – in Winnipeg?"

In Winnipeg? Pronounced so wistfully, the name sounded strange.

Did she like her home in the city? The question wasn't that simple. The crops of the bad farm, in the field at her right, seemed smaller now, insubstantial in the night. Perhaps she was getting used to the city. But, for her sister's sake, she said, "I'd be glad if I didn't have to go back."

"I feel that every morning."

"Isn't there another place you could work? Tell Father how it is."

"Tell Father! You and I, Maria, are keeping the family alive."

Katherine ran to meet them then and they couldn't discuss it further.

□

It was the night before Maria would return to the city. They'd been busy every day. The garden Mother planted on the flat behind the knoll of trees needed attention. There were peas and beans to preserve and Mother took advantage of the extra help to cook rhubarb jam and gooseberry jelly. They also went visiting. None of Father's close relatives had come to Canada, but there were second cousins in the area and there were friends from the Crimea. Everyone was glad to see Maria. In one week, she became thoroughly acquainted with the new life of her family.

But Maria didn't tell anyone that she saved Bobby from drowning. She'd fully intended to, hadn't she? She'd wanted to share it personally instead of by letter but it hadn't seemed quite right for that first day at home nor quite suitable for the second. She couldn't find a good way to begin; she couldn't find an opening wide and obvious enough. Such an important story should have come up within the first hour or two, but postponed once, she postponed it further and each postponement increased the problem of introducing it. And now it was too late. She rolled from side to side on the narrow cot they'd obtained for her, borrowed as the car had been, puzzling over why she hadn't given that episode away.

Had she feared that telling would diminish it? That she wouldn't know how to shape the narrative, then find it skewed, distorted, one part over-emphasized, the other not enough? That she'd be misunderstood, or questioned? That either panic or success might fail to be revealed; that the outcome might seem coincidence instead of divine intervention as well? Or too much intervention, not enough coincidence? Too much her effort, or not enough?

Mrs Lowry said Bobby owed his life to Maria. Did Maria find this too hard to believe? Or did she fear to worry her family retrospectively, make them think her existence apart from them was full of unexpected peril?

She ought to have shared it with Susanna at least. Susanna, barely seventeen, in the midst of her trials. She recalled her sister's disappointment when she and Mother visited on her first afternoon at home, intimately, Susanna supposed, without her. But would she receive the story as a gift, or would she be envious? She might not grasp the meaning Maria needed for her sojourn in Winnipeg, that she had a purpose – already manifest in this incident – beyond the wages she earned for the rest of them. In her chafing, discontented way, Susanna might raise doubts over how close to drowning she or Bobby had been. Might probe at Maria's memories, and alter them.

All week Maria had been poised, and not that comfortably either, beside her sisters' mindless patter. Susanna and Katherine already knew a great deal about the Mennonites in the farms and towns around them, about everyone in church. They gossiped about it all. Moustache-Hiebert, so pious in public, and then, it was said, beating his wife. The Friesens' neglect of their animals. And the latest – the Dycks' daughter Elizabeth, not married but expecting a baby. It was an enormous scandal, fresh this very week. Susanna knew what Mrs Fehr had said, and what the Dycks had said – the father one thing, the mother another – and the shamed grandparents, he being a preacher and she so smug. They weren't just any family, those Dycks. Susanna and Katherine exchanged speculation about the baby's father, who it could be and why Elizabeth refused to say. It might have been a salesman; or one of the village youth. Several names had been mentioned. Some people, they said, confessed to disbelief; others said it was no surprise, not about Elizabeth. Mother disapproved of the girls' talk. The church would deal with it, she said. But even she seemed too eager for the dealing to begin.

Maria didn't know Elizabeth, but she pitied her, so exposed. So *known*.

Was that it? Was Maria marked with this flaw, an unwillingness to let her life be known by others? A preference for privacy? It seemed a kind of selfishness. She was able to talk about clothes easily enough. And she helped herself to as much of others' lives as she could, to strengthen herself for returning. But her own self? That, she hoarded. One peril of the city, the preachers said, was anonymity. Had she succumbed already, so soon, to its temptation?

Perhaps it was simply the distance. Or a way of getting older. She thought she'd missed the sense of oneness inside the family, telling everything; yes, she'd grieved its loss and yet – once back – she hadn't told the others much beyond the superficial things. She hadn't let them know much at all, neither the horrors, to spare them, nor that she'd been, according to what James Edward said before he'd suggested he sit on her lap, a "heroine," a word new to her then but one she'd found in Mr Lowry's library dictionary afterwards. She'd left her family against her will, but now it seemed necessary. Chosen.

Maria slept fitfully. The mattress was lumpy. She dozed, then twitched awake, supposing herself in her quarters at the Lowrys, then realizing it wasn't so. She listened to the creak of boards and beds, the breezes puffing against the walls and into the open windows, the curtains lifting at wind's breath. She listened to Father's snoring through the thin wall of the other room, Gerhard's snoring in the attic, Susanna's clicking of her teeth and lips as she slept. This is my centre, Maria thought, where I belong. Think of what it's been, think of that.

But she was thinking of the Diamond Jubilee parade, and Mrs Lowry – who so loved "occasions," she always said, especially involving progress or patriotism – animated and almost girlish-looking, wearing a new navy hat with silk trim that shimmered every time she turned from Bobby to her daughters or leaned forward to speak to Mamie MacPherson just down from them or to her husband James. Maria had watched the floats, and she'd watched that hat.

She too had been gripped by the fervour of the day. The

telephone company's float rolled past, with its huge map of the country showing that east to west was connected by telephone, and in that moment, Maria transferred her loyalty. The Mennonites had been part of something tremendous in Russia but now they lived here. Then and there she decided she wouldn't waste her future on a gold-to-ashes past. Later, at the picnic, everyone, no matter who they were, rich or poor, wore tiny pins or buttons or Jubilee flags and the granddaughter of Canada's first prime minister posed in a final tableau, draped in white fur and crowned with maple leaves while figures of various races stood below her to represent the stream of people who'd turned their backs on the countries of Europe. Maria was in that crowd, and one of them. People who'd poured into Canada. Clamoured for it. *Her* country.

But Maria's parents were not as enamoured. Mother said, "I can leave the wash on the line at night, and nothing is stolen," her voice thankful, but at the same time so many indignities had been suffered here already, small resentments, annoyances that their former status went unknown, unrecognized. Mutterings of the common herd about them, all that Low German babble. *Ich denke der alten Zeit, der vorigen Jahre*, they might say, quoting the Psalms, I'm thinking of the old times, of the years before. They were submissive, chastened in their poverty, grateful of course, but sometimes bitter too.

Maria drifted to sleep at last and dreamed wildly. She was running down Portage Avenue, practically flying into Eaton's, her reflection in the show windows giving her a navy coat and matching hat, shoes with pretty heels, but when she turned she saw Susanna behind her, and her mother too, and some of their friends. She darted into the store; they rushed by on the street. They were running to find a house, they said, and when she finished shopping, she should join them.

But the store closed around her like a room without an exit and everywhere she went, it was empty. All the racks and counters were bare. There was only one table in a far-off corner, piled with potatoes. Mrs Lowry was peeling the potatoes. She didn't look up. A pan of gooseberries waited on a shelf nearby and bread dough surged out of a bowl. A banner waved in her face.

The banner contained a single German sentence, written in long black letters: *Die Stadt kennt kein Mitleid, sie schaetzt keine Traenen.* Maria read the words loudly, once, then twice, but Mrs Lowry wouldn't raise her head. She had a hat on now that covered her face. Maria remembered: Mrs Lowry doesn't know German. "The city has no sympathy," she shouted, "it doesn't shed a tear." She remembered that Father had thrown her the banner when she ducked into Eaton's and the family ran past. It fit into her palm when she got it. She herself had unfolded it, watched it grow. She herself had strung it up along the wall over Mrs Lowry's bowed and diligent head.

□

The domestics of Winnipeg got Thursdays off. Thursdays from noon. On Thursday mornings Edith Lowry expected Maria to clean up the kitchen, tidy the common rooms, prepare lunch, bake something in advance for tea. This was no problem. It was possible on Thursdays to rush through chores. Everything Maria did Thursdays was a cheery farewell and a promise. Tomorrow I'll be here to look after you again, she told the house in her hurry; today is my day away!

Maria's new friend Helene Janzen called for Maria at the back door promptly after lunch. Helene worked in a house six blocks away. As soon as they greeted one another in German, their lives seemed whole. Their Mennonite conference of churches had organized a centre for the servant girls in the city called the Mary-Martha Home and this was where they headed.

Helene was large, not plump so much as big-boned, her face friendly and open, her personality generous and easy to know. She was much freer in every way than Maria was. When her skirt bunched up between her legs as they walked and she stopped to untangle herself, she reached up directly under her coat, laughing, and yanked it down, almost indiscreetly though not in a loose kind of way. Helene was popular with the girls at the Home. Everyone called out "Hello Helene!" when she and Maria arrived, as if relieved she'd made it. Soon, because of Helene, everyone knew Maria too. (What Maria would do for Helene in turn would be to introduce her to Gerhard, who married her.)

On Thursdays, Mrs Lowry gave Maria a small sack with her supper in it. She insisted on coming into the kitchen and assembling this herself. Maria didn't know if this was a component of employment stipulations for domestics or if Mrs Lowry wanted to prevent her leaving the house with more food than she should. When it came to food, Mrs Lowry vacillated between splurging and scrimping. But the bag supper was the same from week to week: two roast beef or pork sandwiches and an apple. The girls got coffee at the Mary-Martha home.

Getting to the Home was part of Thursday's pleasure. The Home was in the North End and, if weather permitted, Maria and Helene walked to save the fare. But whether by foot or by streetcar, they felt they were themselves again. She and Helene would say this – "Oh, I feel I am myself again" – and it always made them giggle.

There might be some business to attend to on the way, perhaps at the shoemaker's, the dentist's, Eaton's. Sometimes they strolled for a while through the aisles of the department store, or went into the basement where they felt at greater liberty to examine the merchandise. They touched blouses, shoes, scarves, and dresses. There was so much of everything at Eaton's to admire and often after they left, Maria felt contented, as if she'd purchased a whole basket of things, not minding that she hadn't spent a penny. She was careful with her money, the little she kept for necessities.

She expected that someday the Klassen family would be well off again, she and Aron Ediger under the great family umbrella too; there would be time enough, someday, to spend and buy things from Eaton's. Maria decided that when it came, she would go over and shop at the Hudson's Bay store as well.

The North End wasn't like Crescentwood where Maria worked. The houses in the North End were tall and close together. They stood on narrow lots and appeared to have risen quickly, in clusters instead of individually. Just down from the Girls' Home, for instance, there were five houses in a row with identical peaks that Maria found amusing, as if they were too plain to be noticed on their own, too modest and unassuming, but noses in the air when they stepped out in a group, side by side.

It wasn't just the houses. The difference was the details: a headless doll in the snow, a verandah door open to the wind, "To Let" signs, a tin teapot on an inside window sill. The yards were tiny, the front porches nearly meeting low fences at the street. The back yards were tiny too, taken up with a shed or piled with wood. And always the sense of people about – children playing on the walks, or men and women leaving their houses or coming home to them.

The railway was the border between Winnipeg's North and South, the line of demarcation. The North End was crowded with Jews and immigrants – not every kind of immigrant, of course, but those from the eastern European countries, those called "foreigners." The South End was the other Winnipeg, dignified and genuinely local, rooted here and not foreign at all. At least that's how it thought of itself, and so did Maria.

If the contrast jarred, it was never for long. Maria understood how matters had to be. She crossed the border gladly enough, because her own people too – those few who had chosen to live in the city instead of on farms – resided in the North End. When they could afford it they would move on, but here they were for now. And here too, the Mary-Martha Home, its windows glowing with homey, welcoming light.

On Thursdays, the Girls' Home buzzed. All those voices, repressed in their workplaces for a week, now released at high pitch. Everyone had stories, and something to say about "my lady." When the girls were alone in their English or Jewish houses, the stupid things they did and the scolding of their mistresses hurt them inside, as if their hearts beat on broken glass. But in the Home, on Thursdays, they told one another these mistakes and what they were up against, how awful their employers could be, and when the others nodded and understood, or had a story to match, it didn't hurt nearly as much as it had when they were alone. Sometimes they laughed so hard they cried.

They ate their supper lunches together with the coffee supplied for them. They read the German newspapers: *Der Bote, Der Zionsbote, Die Post, Die Mennonitische Rundschau*. The world felt closer because they knew what was happening in other places.

And they sang, and then, in two or three or four-part harmony, they knew for sure they weren't alone. They even had a special song about their Mary-Martha Home. Their voices swelled on the chorus, and their feelings warmed:

O Home, we love you dearly,
O Home, beloved Home,
O Home, you become more dear, dear, dear
Every year.

The matron of the Home, Sister Anna, was dark and sombre. "But she loves the girls," Helene said, and Maria felt it was true, though she herself felt a reserve with her. One of Sister Anna's eyes was brown and the other blue, which unbalanced her gaze a little. Sister Anna asked Maria about her situation and was glad to hear it was satisfactory; if she needed assistance of any kind, she said, Maria was to call her at once, and Maria said she would.

Sister Anna or preachers she invited led the girls in devotionals that helped them get through another week. The girls were Marys to worship, Sister Anna might say, and Marthas to serve, just like the name of the home. The smallest room could become a cathedral of prayer, she told them, the longest drudgery transformed if done for their Lord. She recited poems.

> *Though I work as a servant*
> *For a meagre reward . . .*
> *My heritage, my honour is,*
> *"I'm a servant of the Lord."*

On Fridays Maria always felt a little depressed because it was another week until her next day off. She tried to recollect what she'd heard the day before. Sister Anna reminded the girls they were sent to the city for reasons. Purposes bigger than they could see. She wanted the girls to be strong and sweet. At the same time. She called them open letters, writing God's love to the citizens of Winnipeg, to those who had employed them.

□

Anni told Maria and Helene she was fifteen, said her last name was Enns but it made no difference, she had no family left, and her closest relative in Canada, a second cousin of her mother's, was a certain Nikolai Peters. "My parents are mounds in Russia," she said. "I can be a Peters as well as anything." She refused to say how she managed to get to Canada as an orphan.

"If you're the only one of your Enns family here, the name is important," Maria scolded. "You represent them. My parents taught me that. Surely yours as well." Anni turned to

Maria, but her eyes were skittish, not meeting her gaze. Her hair was parted down the middle of her head and she wore a white, tightly bound shawl, the line of white scalp flowing into it like a river meeting the ocean.

"My parents are mounds," she said.

Helene interjected, gently, "Oh Maria, but if we marry –"

"I'm proud to be a Klassen," Maria said.

Privately, when they discussed her, Maria asked, "What's the matter with her?"

"I guess she's young, and afraid." Helene tried to find the best reasons for everything.

Anni worked in a grand house of rosy-red brick, white stone trim, and large lawns on Wellington Crescent that she called a mansion. Sister Anna, the Mary-Martha matron, had asked Maria and Helene to call for her on Thursdays, to keep a bit of a watch.

The first Thursday, an April afternoon in 1928, Anni talked in her crepe paper voice without stopping, over the bridge, down Portage, through Eaton's. She claimed the house had twenty-three rooms. She was one of several servants, but the last of them, she said, and it was an awful position to be. "I'm at the bottom," she declared, though her voice squealed higher when she said so.

Helene wanted to know what the girl at the bottom did. "I'm below head cook and kitchen helper and butler and lady's maid," Anni replied. "I'm doing what's left. Each of them thinks they own me for their worst work. Whatever they don't want to do. Bothersome things. Not about the house sometimes."

Anni said the cook insulted her, told her the country was full of shifty, dirty foreigners. The cook was from England, poor as the next person and very fat, Anni said, nothing special, but she'd called Anni a foreigner. The cook said her master would agree; he hated Germans and Jews and Poles and Hungarians and Russians too. When Anni protested, saying she was Mennonite, the cook just laughed.

Anni said the butler drank. He was different when he drank; he tried to kiss the cook. She walloped him, so he tried to kiss the kitchen maid. She was frightened, but let him do what he wanted. His breath stank, Anni said.

"You're too young," murmured Helene.

One evening after they accompanied her home, Helene and Maria stepped inside Anni's mansion. She begged them to; her pleas pulled them in. Anni's people were gone, she said, to New York or someplace far away. The other servants seemed to be gone as well, at least for the evening. There was no sign of the nasty cook, the lady's maid, the drunk butler, the timid kitchen maid. Maria wondered if they really existed. They must exist – the house was too large for Anni to handle alone. She seemed incapable of anything but spinning her endless tales of complaint, taking up so much of the time on the way to the Home and back that Maria and Helene had no opportunity for conversation with one another. The way Anni had talked, the other servants inhabited rooms like putrid smells and now there was no sign of them anywhere and the house was immaculate and very elegant.

Anni showed them her cubicle in the basement, then led them upstairs for a tour. Her room was damp; even the bed where they sat for a few awkward minutes felt cool as water. Maria was nervous about wandering through the house, nervous because of Anni's boldness, acting as if the house was hers. But she was glad to leave the basement.

Maria and Helene followed Anni, and peered into rooms from their doorways. But Anni ran into them, turned on a low-burning lamp here or there, knew where all the switches were. She told them about the furniture and decorations in every room and as she pointed to them, Maria felt as if the features in question stretched towards her like carvings in relief, pleased and flattered by the mention, as if they'd been waiting for them in the shadows.

Anni's knowledge of the house was astounding, not just in what she said, but in her familiarity with the concrete parts of it. She hadn't been there more than a month. Maria imagined her scooting about the house at night like a mouse. Anni works here, she reminded herself, of course she'd been in and out of these rooms on errands, and when cleaning them. But still, it seemed remarkable. Grating too. Anni accepted the praises they offered the house as praises for herself. "Thank you very much," she kept saying, as if she'd put it all together. As if she'd matched the green and navy furnishings, the lovely Persian rugs, the velour draperies, as if she'd decided on the flawless arrangements and effects of the rooms. For all her frailty, Anni's attitude was hard and provocative.

When she started to lower a pulley chandelier so they could see the filet lace workings on the shades, Maria burst out, "Oh leave it Anni, we can see it from here! And what if someone comes?"

"You've got to see it. It was ordered especially for this room! Don't worry, don't worry!" Anni's voice sounded hoarse. "Bella's at her sister Martha's. Henry's at Captain Mercy's. He knows him from the war. Rose is out with her beau. And they've let Betty go."

So she and Helene had no choice, they had to gather round the fixture and notice every little part of it, the satin-ribbon-bound wires, the small pendant balls. It was intricate and beautiful, no doubt about that. But all the time, Maria kept thinking, this grand house isn't that much better than the Lowrys'.

It was larger, that was all. The tastes and instincts were the same; only the scale was different. Anni wanted them to be impressed, but Maria refused, out of loyalty to her own household; let Helene exclaim as much as she wanted.

The staircase, however, was wider than any Maria had ever seen. Set above the huge foyer, the stairs curved and ascended as if floating in air. They were covered in a long-tufted carpet of green and tan and the banister, though it followed the curve of the steps, seemed to pursue its own graceful line as a vine reaching for the sun. The three of them climbed up and down the stairs, silently. Even Anni stopped her squealing explanations.

But in the main drawing room their diminutive guide dropped onto the sofa, a soft mossy green sofa with flowers in peach. She crossed her legs and mimicked the mannerisms of a lady, turning her head, jutting out her chin, fluttering her hands, blinking her lashes, patting an imaginary string of pearls around her neck and then a cloche hat on her head, and most shockingly, miming the drawing of a cigarette to her mouth, breathing in, out, moving the hand with its imaginary trail of smoke away smoothly to rest on her knee.

It was a clever imitation; Maria and Helene couldn't help but laugh. Anni giggled too. All her teeth showed when she laughed. She bent over and laughed some more until it sounded hysterical and her narrow shoulders shook. She began to cough. She coughed off her pretence of the grand lady. Leaning over and coughing she seemed a child again, a crone-child, white and bony. Just bones, lacking flesh and brain. Anni didn't belong in that room. Perhaps none of them did, but Anni least of all. She sank back against the sofa after her fit of laughter and coughing, as insubstantial as a crumb.

Then the next week they heard that Anni had collapsed. *Zusammengebrochen*, it was said, "broken together." Someone thought she'd been taken to the hospital, or maybe it was onto a train bound for the Nikolai Peters farm.

This explained why Anni hadn't been waiting that afternoon when Maria and Helene called for her. The butler answered the door and insisted she wasn't there and neither did he know where she was. One girl at the Home said she heard from someone else that Anni raged and screamed until the police were called. Maria couldn't reconcile this with the image of breaking in Anni's case. It seemed to her that Anni would have collapsed into the middle of herself, losing whatever extended her being as she fell, soundlessly, as soft and weightless as meringue.

Everyone saw it coming of course. That's how they all talked about it. Everyone saw it coming. The troubled peep-like voice, the uncanny shafts of cleverness. Anni was drying all along, becoming brittle, getting ready to break. The white skin that seemed as delicate as porcelain, and pretty too, was actually bloodless, turning into dust.

Helene said, "Poor girl. Apparently she hasn't had a period since leaving Russia."

The two friends recalled how Anni had slumped against Maria's shoulder during a sentimental recitation about the beauty of a mother's hands at the Mother's Day program in the Mary-Martha Home. Maria had turned to see what was wrong but all she saw was the ghastly white parting of Anni's hair and her white paper carnation perched against her collar. Maria wore a red carnation because her mother was alive; Helene and Anni wore white ones because their mothers weren't. Maria assumed she was crying silently, sagging like that. But when she straightened, Anni's eyes were dry and vacant.

Still, *zusammengebrochen* was a shock.

Helene, ever sympathetic, said, "We're all the same in a way. So out of place."

Maria murmured "Yes," but she didn't agree. Back in her garret room, she opened her narrow window for fresh air, kneeling to the screen to feel it. The house hid the moon from her but its tender light played over the back yard and she heard the murmur of the streetcar far in the distance, a cricket's whirr closer, under the porch perhaps. She felt the gust of cool air that stroked over her face. She felt it. Of course! The fluids in her body ran as they should; she was vital, strong. Body and soul.

She'd had her period every month. She was regular in every way. The moon behind the house was the same moon shining in the Crimea. Like a continuous luminous line, Maria there, Maria here, she was the same person, under-laid with the steady surging of blood. She recalled the white

94

petals of the bird cherry blossoms powdering the ditches, the white stone fence (the low sturdy fence that marked and established), the acacia trees, chaste as angels in a row, under this same white moon. Alive and vigorous. She too. Her heart beating when Aron stopped her at that very spot, her knees trembling when they parted. She'd gotten out, she was here, increasingly fluent in English. She had a good home to serve in, friends like Helene. One of these months Aron would come and they would marry. They would be a good match.

Kneeling at her window, Maria took a kind of vow. It was a vow that she would never break. Never crumple as she believed that Anni had. She cried a little then, for homesickness, and waiting, and sorrow for the girl, resentment of her too, going brittle without their knowing it (none of them had really seen it coming), and as she cried, these lumps of sadness dissolved.

❑

Near the close of 1929, the stock markets crashed and Canada, like the world, spiralled into recession. Maria was vaguely aware of these events, which sounded serious, but the intimations of worry at the Lowry house were incidental: mostly Mr Lowry in a bad mood and his wife Edith explaining, "Oh, he frets about money, about the times, but when I do, he says there's nothing to worry about. Thankfully he's not risked our lives with foolish investments. He's still in, not out."

In, not out.

New clothes appeared that winter, and all the seasons following as usual, and there was no restraint in shopping orders. The Lowrys purchased a piano and added a day girl twice a week to do the heavier cleaning and the laundry, in a new washing machine installed in the basement. The day girl would take her instructions from Maria, Mrs

Lowry informed her, or ask her first if there was anything she needed to know. They bought a vacuum cleaner. Mrs Lowry's round of social obligations, meetings, and appointments increased. She belonged to the Women's Club, charities, musical events. The children were busy with school and lessons, and games at the Club. James Edward still studied in Ontario and Eleanor entered college in Winnipeg. They talked of a bigger cottage in a year or two, at a different location, more prestigious apparently than Victoria Beach, and that winter, for the first time, James and Edith Lowry drove south for a holiday, this in addition to Edith's annual trip east to see her mother and brother and to drop in on James Edward.

"It's good to know all will be well with you here, Maria," Mrs Lowry said before the trip south, bidding farewell beside a mound of suitcases. "You're as good as a mother."

Maria smiled. Little mothering was necessary now, besides making the food and keeping the house in order. Mr Lowry's sister Josie and her family took care of the children's social engagements, picking them up in their car. Bobby had discovered hockey, canoeing, tennis, and baseball; he was a virtual string of athletic games, each in its season and overlapping, "a terror in the water, on the court, on the ice," Mrs Lowry said proudly. He'd turned out to be a strong swimmer; the "nearly-unfortunate little episode" at Victoria Beach, as Mrs Lowry called it, was no permanent scar. He seldom kept Maria company in the kitchen now, as he had during her first year at the house, reading the funnies with her, correcting her English, speaking monologues about his life at school.

But he was still fond of her. "You don't need me, Maria," he said, to explain his growing absence. "You don't make mistakes anymore . . . Or maybe I'm just used to them."

It was her own family – the Klassens – whom the Depression affected. Many Winnipeg families were as solidly established as the limestone buildings that graced their city. On them, the economic downturn hardly made an impact. But the Klassens and the rest of Maria's immigrant people were still like fresh-made clay. There wasn't enough work to be had and crops were poor. The travel debt was far from paid. There was no end in sight for her family's need of Maria's monthly help.

"If I felt things were improving in Russia," her father wrote her, "I would seek an opportunity to return." Maria knew things weren't improving in Russia, she knew he wouldn't go, but the tone, the reversals of his hopes, angered her. Hadn't he urged her to learn the English language and Canadian ways? Now every letter remarked on the importance of Mennonites resisting integration and keeping up the German language.

Maria grew discouraged too. She hadn't heard from Aron again. She wrote him a second time, and a third, the words of the letters nearly identical. She sent them off like Noah sent out his raven and dove, trying to get some prospect for landing the ark. She'd been waiting a long time on the strength of a meeting on her former village street, a nervous exchange on the stoop the night before leaving, a solitary letter. It wasn't much and it seemed even less as time passed.

Maria kept her hopes up by praying. She prayed about Aron's obligations to his parents and the suggestion she'd read between the lines of his letter that his father didn't want to emigrate. By now the organized emigrations of Mennonites from the Soviet Union had been terminated anyway, so Maria had to find new words for what Aron needed: intervention, miracle, escape. She prayed for every solution she could think of, believing in them all. But she became discouraged. Her entreaties changed to wails. What could be the matter that he hadn't written again? Sometimes she stopped praying for weeks at a time, trying to absorb the *No* that seemed obvious enough, but this distressed her too. It made her feel guilty, as if she'd let Aron down on the

Canadian side of their last communication, abandoning what she'd promised.

Some hymn or Scripture at the Thursday devotional or the Sunday evening service at the Mennonite mission church would grip her then with its embrace of assurance and she could imagine again that the fault was simple: news of Aron's emigration hadn't reached her. He could be in Quebec City that very moment or even disembarking at the CPR station here. This would galvanize her to fresh prayers, to pleadings for a sign, and sometimes when she read the Bible on her own she thought she'd found one. *He will come forth*; any phrase like that might jump out at her like a promise specifically for her. Occasionally Maria dreamt of him, the images elusive on awakening but some narrative of arrival remaining with her into the morning. But even in dreams Aron escaped her; she never saw him face to face. She was beginning to forget what he'd been like.

Mail with Russia was unreliable. Perhaps he hadn't received her *Yes* and was growing discouraged as well. Sometimes she imagined him in prison, or dead. Or alive, but haggard with longing. It tormented her that her chastely eager words might not have come into his possession. Or that his reciprocal tenderness might be wasting away in some shoved-aside postal sack or delivered to the wrong address and simply thrown away. The options of fate were numerous; there were many scenarios to explore. But it was tiring; the trial of the severed connection was bad enough. And there was no one she could tell about her flimsy pact with him.

The fact that she'd brought her brother and Helene together tightened the bond between the three of them. Helene joined Gerhard in southern Manitoba. They teased her sometimes, on rare occasions when they met, teased her about young men they knew. They wanted to reciprocate the matchmaking favour she had done them. Even then, she couldn't bring herself to tell them of Aron. He wasn't solid enough to tell about, nothing like the objects such as new dishes or linens they showed her. She answered their teasing with careless disavowals, or changed the subject, but she knew they thought her exceedingly particular.

Late in the same year as the stock market crash, rumours, and then news! A miracle of the kind she'd prayed for. Mennonites fleeing to Moscow in the thousands, it was said, word ripping through their Russian settlements like a prophet's cry that some were given papers to exit; it was possible again. They had abandoned their homes and piled into the summerhouses of the capital. The men, organized to work with the documents, tramped from one office building to another, while the women waited in nervous flutters of intercession and fear, and all the while the Soviet police were plucking them away like feathers on a chicken, tossing them back to the places they'd come from or to exile north. But – for some – it was miracle. There were hundreds, it was said, who escaped.

It made no difference to Maria that the news was shapeless and full of uncertainty. This was the opportunity Aron would have seized. He would be there, on the lists marked with their priceless stamps and signatures. His name passing from one bureaucrat to the next – "This young man says he has a woman waiting." Ah . . . throats clearing, winks; old men remembering their old wives once slender and beautiful, pleased to assist – "This fellow must go." "Of course." "Of course." Passing every hurdle. Crossing the border beyond the grim Red Star. What did it matter that these immigrants were destined for Paraguay, or Brazil? He was out. They would find one another.

Maria received a letter from Russia before the hard facts of the miracle could be clarified. A letter from her cousin Lena. Her curling script ran over the paper in straight lines from the top of the page to the bottom. In an earlier letter, soon after Maria's arrival in Canada, Lena had written crosswise again over the sheet. Without it, this letter seemed half empty. But of course; there was little to say.

My dear Maria, Greetings from your old homeland. Now I must take up my pen when I would rather see your face. I come on paper to wish you God's presence this year, as I know you have a birthday coming, and a new year of life lies before you. We are facing many trials here but I have come to you in this letter to tell good news, news full of joy, and when you hear it, I know you will be glad with me too. I am engaged to Aron and by the time this arrives in your hands, we will be married. I wish you could join us for the festivities, although they will not be anything like years ago. If only it were possible for us to visit you and Uncle Johann and Tante Susanna and all your siblings as is the custom before the wedding day. We are filled with happiness in spite of many other sorrows. Aron sends his best wishes as well. Your loving cousin, Lena.

Lena had tried to shape her letters the way they were taught in school, yet they coiled and turned, deceptively warm, deceptively spaced, sparse and to the point, as if she meant to make it easier for Maria to read what they said. How could she miss them, these words of steel, sharper than the curving teeth of a plough? Aron and Lena were married!

So here was the reason. Aron wasn't desperate, or dead, or making his way westward to find her. No understandable, forgivable errors had turned her fate. The possibilities she'd constructed to explain the long silence had never included this. She'd been waiting all this time in her solitary station, willing to be desired and yearned for from a distance, only to discover that the tracks of his desire hadn't run very far in her direction. That was her fault of course; she should have realized that if her memory waned (though it flared up now), how much more would his, with conniving Lena near, twisting her advantage.

Maria held herself in check and read the letter again. She was in her room, alone, but she composed herself as if others were watching. She allowed no alteration of her face while she comprehended the facts, made the necessary adjustments, believed what was true. She kept herself on guard for the moment the true force of the disappointment would hit. As long as she could, she would keep her feelings at bay. There'd been a tiny woman in the Molotschna who held the door shut against a whole band of Makhno's men; of course it made no difference in the end, they broke through anyway, but she managed it long enough for her children to escape by the windows of the front room. With her husband already dead she refused to give the rest of the family over without a struggle. When they finally pushed in, the terrorists were astonished at the size of her. There must be someone else in the house, they said, creeping about the house poking weapons into every corner and bed, searching in twos and threes as if expecting a giant to overpower them.

Maria stared, inert, over the field of her hopes. Nothing grew there anymore, not a blade. She held back the shame of being supplanted, her humiliation before Aron and Lena. She didn't want to think of the letter she'd written Lena after Aron's letter to her, merrily, in a paroxysm of revelation. Yes, she'd actually written, "How fortunate you are, dear cousin, living in the same village as my Aron! Your eyes can see him and I envy you for that." They'd be laughing, repeating her lines with a delicious inversion, kissing at the end of it. *Aron sends his best wishes as well!* Ha. Lena had stolen him away.

She must think it through little by little. Not let herself be overwhelmed, or break. How fortunate that she'd kept the matter quiet with her family, Helene, the girls at the Home. It would be so much easier without the pity and knowledge of others.

Lena's letter arrived on a Monday. The week that followed was appropriately grey, sky hooded with cloud, as it should be for her future's collapse. The snow cover was mottled, also grey, the earth naked in spots, electric light required by day, all the rooms and her tasks tinged with yellow. Indecisive spatters of snow drove against the windows before a temperamental wind. It beat at whatever was loose; the atmosphere was chalky. It was too fantastic, a miracle more miraculous than anyone deserved, Aron surging over the sea, arriving to rescue her. She'd built a house of straw. All she had left to remember was his smile, and even that was blowing away. A fickle smile. Weightless.

On Friday Maria dropped the letters – Aron's letter and Lena's – into the pocket of her work dress, as if rubbing them together all day was necessary to substantiate her loss. When she went into the sitting room in the evening to gather the coffee cups she put the letters on the tray. They reminded her of crusts, or bones eaten clean, of no particular interest except disposal. Mrs Lowry was upstairs attending to Bobby's bedtime; Mr Lowry had retreated into his study and closed the door.

God meant it unto good. The story of Joseph flitted about her head, trying to gain her attention. *He meant to bring it to pass.* Maria let the words play but could neither grasp nor believe them. *Unto good?* The ginger jar on the mantelpiece and its Chinaman in his flowing blue robe and black hair looked smug and reassuring.

The fire was low. Maria set down the tray. She moved the fire screen aside and pushed the letters into the flames. They shot up white, temporarily excited while they devoured the paper, and then they dropped, sated, steady again to the wood. Maria gathered the pale green cups and saucers, dusted a few cake crumbs into her hand. She glanced at the fire. There was no evidence left of the letters, no charred corners or unburned incriminating words, only the consoling heat. By morning the fire would be dead, the ash cold.

Maria wrote Lena and Aron with her congratulations. It would be her last letter in their direction and if it failed on its journey, so be it. She crafted a lighthearted note of lovely times at the Lowrys' summer residence, at her family's farm, at the Mary-Martha Home. She rushed from one thing to another as if grabbing meadow flowers for an informal bouquet. It was more allusion than detail, and uniformly cheerful.

She was especially pleased with her final sentences: "You say you wish I could have shared your festive day, but even that joyous occasion would not have persuaded me to return. We do not look back as Lot's wife did. Every day we are thankful that we left when we did."

A cruel implication, perhaps, but with that, Maria considered the matter of Aron Ediger closed.

3

JAMES EDWARD STAYED in Ontario the summer of 1930, although he came for a short visit in spring. Maria was hanging the dishcloth at the end of one day when he strolled into the kitchen.

"I'm something of a collector," he announced. "Let me show you this."

He sat down at the kitchen table and swept his long arm over the oilcloth to indicate he wanted her across from him. He grinned as if they regularly met after dinner.

"Here," he said, "it's the most valuable thing I've got."

Maria sat down.

James Edward set a delicate silver case on the kitchen table. He opened it and lifted something wrapped in wax paper out of it. He parted the folds of the paper wrap carefully with his fingernails, then looked up at Maria with a pleased expression, as if what he'd expected to find was nevertheless a surprise to him. He pushed the packet towards her. It seemed small and vulnerable on the huge blue hibiscus blooms of the table covering.

The packet contained a set of playing cards.

Maria flinched. Cards were worldly; they were wrong. Her people didn't play.

But he was so proud of his cards, so preoccupied in lifting them out of the packet, her apprehension didn't even register with him. Well, she thought, let him be. But why had he come? Why this? Why show *her*?

Maria had never been this close to James Edward before. As she watched him, absorbed in some purpose of his own for being here, Maria suddenly found herself longing for his face, his length, his leanness. It swept over her like an ache. Suddenly she felt that she loved him and she wished he were hers.

The thought shocked her as much as the cards had. She wondered if they were the cause of it, if they had malevolent powers. She stiffened and drew away from the longing, just as she'd retreated when she looked down and recognized the contents of the packet.

Then James Edward handed her two of the cards. Maria hesitated but she felt she was in control of herself again, at an inward distance, so she took them. Surely James Edward, and the gesture itself, were guileless enough. He'd come into the kitchen like Bobby used to, after school, to eat something she'd made that day, telling her what happened since morning, expecting her to listen to everything but not mind about anything in particular. She was the maid, a kind of stand-in for any number of other companions or witnesses.

"Careful," James Edward was saying. He meant his precious cards; he wanted them held properly, the way he held them, by the edges.

One of the cards had a red king on it – a red king with dark eyes. On the other was a queen in black. Both were drawn with sharp, stylized lines and the colours were flat – red, black, yellow, white. She thought the figures grotesque. As soon as she could, without appearing rude, Maria put the cards down. She ran her hands along her work uniform as if they were dusty. She picked up the tarnished silver case.

"I could polish this for you."

James Edward frowned at the suggestion. Maria put the case back.

"Just think," he said after a moment. "These were used by my great-great-grandfather. Not much used, though. Thankfully. His wife was a rather strict Methodist. A bit of a fanatic. So they weren't used. Probably not at all. They're in excellent condition. They'll be worth something."

He ran his finger along the edge of a small stack of them. He said, "It's quite a story how I got them."

Maria didn't ask for the story because distance meant wariness, and he hadn't liked her offer to polish the case. One minute she imagined she loved him, the next she despised him.

But he seemed to be waiting for her to speak.

"What do you do with them?" Maria finally asked.

"I don't use these. I have others for playing."

"And with the others?"

"Games."

"Games?"

"Patience, casino, pinochle, red dog, bridge —"

"Red dog?" The names sounded like the hierarchies of fallen angels.

"Poker, hearts, and euchre. Gin rummy, blackjack, skat. Cribbage and five hundred . . . Card games," he said, into her silent incomprehension.

He gathered the cards he'd removed from the box. He patted them even. His fingers were long and the hair on his knuckles was fine and blond, curved towards his skin. His nails were short. He lowered the cards into the case and carefully closed the paper folds over them.

He snapped shut the tarnished silver case. "Edmund Hoyle," he said, leaning back in his chair and fixing his eyes on the wall. *"A Short Treatise on the Game of Whist: Containing The Laws of the Game and Also Some Rules.* 1743. Etc., etc. From which we have the expression 'according to Hoyle'. In the proper way, that is. Though rules have changed. Whist for four. Bridge for four. Cribbage for two or three or four. Invented by John Suckling. Sir John Suckling . . . Do you know what a suckling is, Maria? A suckling is an infant or an animal not yet weaned."

"So much you know about games?"

"Bridge for four," he went on, "grew out of whist." He smiled past Maria's head as if he had an audience in the pantry. "Games grow."

Then he looked at her directly. "Did you know that, Maria? Games grow – they grow from these seeds, from these fifty-two cards. Skill and chance in one combination or another. And then one plays, and plays some more, well enough perhaps to beat an opponent – and sometimes even chance." He winked and said, "A good partner is an asset too." As if they were old friends, as if they'd pulled off their share of card table victories in their day.

The cards weren't pretty; the figures had been strange, cold-looking, and the names for all their uses even stranger. "Do you play so many games?"

"All games are adaptable," he said. "You could play all your life and never run out. Good times for a lifetime. Shall I teach you a game?"

"No," she said firmly. "No thank you."

James Edward laughed cheerfully as if he didn't mind, and carried on. "Take poker for example. You make a bet – on what you hold, or what you hope to hold. And off you go. Royal flush, straight flush, four of a kind. Full house. Round and round and round and round. Highest rank wins." He banged the case on the table and the dishes on it chimed.

"Money?"

"Money, or other obligations." He swept his hand over the oilcloth as if gathering what he'd won.

She was fascinated by him. She couldn't help it. She didn't understand his talk of cards but he was fascinating just the same. But playing all those games, round and round! The hours it must take, the rules to remember, the idleness! The awful king and queen glaring at the players.

"And every game you know so well?" she asked.

Then she remembered she'd asked that question already. She blushed.

"Like I said, Maria," – he cradled the silver box in his hands – "I never play with these. This is my collector's set, the one I look at now and then. The one I'll sell if I ever need to. Though I expect I'll pass it on to my son and I'll hope he does the same to his. Can you imagine? They're from my great-great-grandfather. Though it's a bit of a story how I happen to have it."

The games made no sense to Maria, but connection with the past certainly did. "I think it's wonderful," she said earnestly, "to touch something your great-great-grandfather touched."

His expression was quizzical. He said, "I mean it's money in the bank."

"You're not selling the cards. Didn't you say you wouldn't sell them?"

He frowned again.

"But to answer your question, Maria," he continued after a pause, smiling with pleasure as if their conversation finally made sense to him. "About the games. I don't play them all, certainly not. Some are for the young and some are for the ladies. Some are for men, some for company that's mixed. Some are popular today, some may be tomorrow. What do I play? I play poker.

"But Maria," he warned, affecting a tone of severity, "I didn't say that to have you mention it to my father, Mr Lowry, or to Madame Lowry either. My father likes to win as much as anyone, but he does it absolutely safely, and the dear mother, well, she has an abhorrence of gambling that is . . . is rather pronounced."

"I guess I wouldn't like it either."

"No," he said. "I don't suppose you would." He chuckled, but his eyes upon Maria seemed thoughtful. She believed for that moment he realized to whom he was speaking, that he saw her as someone distinct. He got up then and left the room, but later she remembered that he'd waited a moment at the door, as if he'd wanted to stay but wasn't sure how to prolong the conversation. She remembered wishing he had thought of something, to make it possible.

□

Spring cleaning, Mrs Lowry liked to say, was nothing less than "chasing winter out of the house." The chasing involved a week of frenzy in every room. Every wall, ceiling, object, fixture had to be dusted or washed. All the curtains came down for soft beating or laundering. All the windows were opened as widely as they went. The sleeping porch too was unlocked and its dust and cobwebs attacked until even the air seemed cleansed, ready for summer breezes and the start-up scent of the lilacs along the driveway.

Mrs Lowry generally helped with this – "I love to touch the whole house this way occasionally, to feel it's mine," she'd said on one occasion – but in 1931 she spent most of the week at the side of her best friend Iona, whose daughter had been hospitalized. Maria and the day girl took care of the cleaning.

On Saturday, though, when they capped the orgy of scrubbing by cleaning and changing the outside windows, Mrs Lowry was there, and Mr Lowry too, climbing up and down the ladder to remove the dust-streaked storm windows and put in the screens for summer. The weather was wonderful that day, and everyone was cheerful. Mr Lowry teased Maria several times and Mrs Lowry made sandwiches and coffee, which they ate together on the front porch.

But in the evening the Lowrys were refined people again. Mr Lowry had hired a man to wash and shine the car and so they dressed in bright spring clothes and went off driving, the black fabric rooftop folded down to the rear seat. None of them looked at Maria on the back door steps when they pulled out of the driveway, except for Bobby, who was squished between his sisters and waved until he was out of her sight.

The car turned onto the street; Maria turned into the house. The house was perfectly clean but Maria's winter was loneliness and it hadn't been chased away. She'd not expected, of course, to be invited on the drive. Hoped, perhaps, but not expected. Sometimes she was included, sometimes a vital part of things, but this could never be assumed, that she belonged.

She wandered through the silent, pristine house. One room to the next, upstairs and down. Aimlessly, stopping and starting. She'd pause as if searching for something. Something missed in spring cleaning perhaps. The freshly washed and ironed curtains hung crisply from their polished rods; there was nothing out of place.

Maria's loneliness was of the most difficult kind, a separateness felt in a houseful of people. Compared to situations some domestics put up with, hers was a good place to work. If she stopped to count her blessings, they formed a considerable list. But she was only an accomplice to the Lowrys' homey delights as a family around a table, to the pleasures of guests and parties. It was no small task to run a household with ambitious parents and young people with wide circles of friends. It took intelligence and judgement to put out meals for their dinners and gatherings. But could she make an invitation of her own? Say, "Please come Saturday for an all-in-one-pot supper or Friday afternoon for a cup of tea?" She had social instincts too, but how could she express them? She could have friends over if they worked in the area, but they had to visit in her own small room.

She trudged there now, thinking to bring her embroidery down, sit outside with it for a while, in the freshened summer porch perhaps, but the sight of the meek, meticulous blooms disgusted her. She returned to the main floor, wandered through its rooms again, then climbed the stairs to the second. She stood in the doorway of the master bedroom.

The ruby-coloured cover on the Lowrys' bed stirred Maria with its inaccessible beauty. What was it like to have one's particular side of a bed? To open that side, the blankets like a letter, the other side opening as an answer, to awaken mornings and see another's form, hear breathing, or if waking late, be surrounded by evidence of him, by his quite peculiar habits, habits not one's own, but his, separate but overlapping. With the possibility of colliding and then the wonderful exclamations – "Oh, I'm sorry dear, excuse me," or "After you, darling." To open his drawers and smell a man's smell, to be comforted with that lingering scent of him while he was away.

Maria opened Mrs Lowry's closet door and stared at her dresses. She touched three or four of them on their sleeves. She counted the hatboxes overhead. She left the master bedroom and climbed the narrower stairs to the third floor room. She'd just washed this area too; Mrs Lowry said James Edward might return to Winnipeg this summer to work.

The room stretched the length of the attic level. Maria surveyed it by a narrow beam of light that searched in through a crack between the curtains. The room smelled faintly of tobacco, soap, and shaving splash, like the men's department at Eaton's.

Except for the centre of the room, and the bathroom and closet built into a dormer, the attic ceilings were low and sloped. Cupboards and bookshelves were set into the sides. The books were neatly arranged, their heights waving along the shelf. But they didn't tip in various directions as Mr Lowry's did, or sit half in, half out. These were the books of James Edward's boyhood, no longer used. A folded deck chair, its striped canvas gently rounded, leaned against one wall, evocative of the outdoors and oddly out of place.

A bureau of dark wood and the bed, covered with a red blanket, took up one end of the room. There was also a roll top desk of the old style. On the other end a sitting area had been created with a large chair and a footstool, both of them draped with a dust sheet. James Edward owned a museum table – a tall narrow table with glass set over a drawer in which various objects he'd collected were displayed. She'd seen them all before – postcards in a fan shape, marbles in a bowl, a pewter saltcellar, letter openers, a moustache cup, a line of paperweights, the silver case of cards – and they no longer interested her.

Maria was tempted to remove the dust cover, to sit on the brown velour chair that had been a gift for some achievement of his, but it seemed too much trouble to lift it. She dropped down on the cover instead. The slit of light, golden and loaded with shimmering dust particles, fell over her lap, over her left hand resting on the arm of the chair. She thought of her older now-married brother Gerhard, and of the Crimea, of wildly divergent things: paths lined with crushed snails, the pile of hay into which they jumped as children, the pretty gables of the train station at Spat, and her mother in a picture taken before Maria was born, wearing a hat with a rim like a bowl, full of flowers. And Aron, whom she'd believed she'd forgotten. He was married and it was probably a sin to dwell on him now, she thought. But if a sin, it was not of desire but bitterness. Bitterness that she was alone and he wasn't.

It had darkened considerably by the time some creaking of the house startled Maria and made her scramble out of the chair. Had she dozed off? Were the Lowrys home?

The house was as empty as before. Maria's steps echoed down the narrow stairs, down the wider ones, through the dining room and kitchen. It seemed to take a long time to get to her room, as if the house had expanded while she reclined in James Edward's large comfortable chair. Or, as if she'd grown heavier and slower with the weight of her desolation.

□

That same spring Maria turned ill, the first time in her working years she'd been seriously sick. One morning she was unable to lift herself from her bed and so indifferent too, had Mrs Lowry said "I'm letting you go unless you stand up and work," she would have answered, "Well, I'm finished here then." There was nothing to be done for it; she couldn't move.

When she didn't appear Mrs Lowry ran up the narrow stairway, knocked, called fearfully through the door, and then seeing Maria, shouted for Frances and Eleanor to give her a hand. They unlocked the door between the servant and family quarters and half-dragged Maria into the bed in the extra room. She stayed there for more than a week.

Later she recalled, with the vagueness of a dream, someone washing her with a sponge, then dressing her in a soft garment that smelled of lemon. Everything had been very white around her and she remembered falling into the whiteness with relief, with something akin to happiness. If this was death, she thought, there was nothing to fear. Once she opened her eyes, expecting her mother, and sure enough, there was a fond, worrying gaze upon her, but the face resembled Mrs Lowry's. The face gasped "Maria!" as if thrilled with her feat of waking and then a hand stroked her forehead with a cool cloth in commendation.

She thought that the homeopathic doctor Derksen had come, the tall, thin man with lank curly hair her parents consulted on occasion in Russia; she thought he stood beside her bed for quite some time, deeply engrossed in the analysis of her case. When Maria asked Mrs Lowry about this later her mistress smiled and said, "Our doctor is older and balding and I would have to say he's on the heavy side. He's the one who was here."

By week's end, Maria was able to sit up and eat some soup and bread. Several days later she was well enough to return to her room for the night and soon after that to resume her duties. By then it was the end of the month, the day she was paid. Mr Lowry gave Maria the same wages as always. She reminded him that she'd been ill, that she hadn't really worked much for nearly two weeks. "I think we can overlook that," he said. "My wife was very concerned. She'd want me to pay you, I think, for your excellent efforts to get better."

□

Maria was washing the dishes, and crying. Unstoppable, swimming tears, running over and down her cheeks. She rarely cried. But she'd just recovered from the flu and something inside her still seemed weak. She wasn't even sure what the tears were about. Was it fear that illness and recovery in this home had further fixed her destiny here, that she'd never escape this endless repetition of domestic work for others? Was it the photograph she'd wanted so badly but hated now?

When the Lowrys raised her wages at the beginning of the year she faced the temptation to keep more for herself. She overcame it but made one request of her parents, that she could have her picture taken. At a studio. Two girls from the Mary-Martha home, Liese Schellenberg and Gertrude Regehr, had asked if she'd join them for a photographer's portrait. It wouldn't cost as much if they did it together.

Father was the family correspondent, but this time Mother wrote. She said that Maria had probably earned an indulgence by now; if she felt it necessary, she ought to go ahead. Maria sensed her reluctance. Her mother's health had declined and bewilderment had invaded her assurances of God's care and her general optimism about the Klassens' prospects. The only thing that seemed to invigorate her gratitude now was what she heard and read about the suffering of their people in Russia who had not been able to leave, sad and desperate letters in the Mennonite papers that reminded her how much worse it could be. "We are in great need and ask for help. We feel compelled to beg for assistance because hunger hurts. The children go about hungry and eat weeds from the field." Or, "Widow ____ of Sagradowka pleads for assistance. The family consists of nine persons, one of them a cripple. All suffer greatly, with everyone hungry and on the way to starving. Please send help."

Liese, Gertrude, and Maria had their appointment posing in the photographer's studio, all wearing their serving uniforms. Mrs Lowry seemed amused and flattered to see Maria depart the house on her free Thursday afternoon, wearing her uniform.

The picture turned out well. Maria liked how she looked in it. The girls inscribed each other's copies and Maria sent one home, and kept one for herself. She considered giving one to the Lowrys, but what would they want with a picture of Liese and Gertrude?

After a few days, however, she was sorry she'd bothered with the photograph. She regretted the expense and the way the image had tricked her into permanence as a domestic. There they were, smiling serenely on her shabby dresser, three servant girls in their uniforms as if they'd reached some pinnacle of success.

And downstairs, she was crying at the sink like an idiot.

But no one was home so she didn't check her tears.

Then there was a noise and it wasn't just her snuffling. James Edward had come into the kitchen. He was searching for something in a drawer. Maria was so preoccupied she hadn't heard him enter and now as she turned in her fright, he saw her. Saw her bleary face.

He asked Maria if she was alright.

Maria focused on the dishes. "Yes."

"Are you sure?"

"Yes. Yes."

But would he think her tears were unhappiness over her position or his family or his mother, who'd just nursed her while she was ill? She had to say something.

"My mother's not well," she offered.

James Edward moved closer and seemed to be contemplating this. Maria felt fresh tears rising because of his attention. She bent further into the sink, scrubbed harder at the scrubbed-clean pot in her hands.

"I'm truly sorry," he said.

He said again that he was truly sorry. Maria didn't speak or look at him, and then she heard him leave, slowly and quietly.

□

The next evening James Edward arrived in the kitchen at the end of Maria's workday with a large wooden box-like tray. "Remember the cards?" he said.

When she nodded he ordered her to sit down; he had more things to show. Other collectibles.

A quick glance and Maria knew she'd already seen most of the things on the tray, and dusted them too, because the museum case wasn't completely airtight and had occasionally needed a careful flick of the duster over its contents. But he was explaining that a collectible was more than a pretty thing, more than a luxury, more than an interesting object, though it might be any one of these; the point was, it was something of value. Perhaps it was old or rare or unusual. It might also be current, not especially valuable yet perhaps, but its future potential guessed at: a chance taken.

He collected marbles, he said, and he showed her his favourites: a pink one of real marble, one of glazed pottery, marbles of glass and onyx and clay. He had a glass marble with a frosted white rabbit inside it. He put the marbles carefully, one by one, into Maria's palm. She smiled and tried to be friendly and cheerful, to show him that yesterday's tears had been an aberration. She ran her fingers around each one and murmured over it. She could see why he'd want to collect marbles, she said. The pink one felt cool and seemed to grow colder the longer she held it. She buried it inside one hand until it felt like a lump of ice and then she passed it back to him.

James Edward showed Maria his letter openers next: a miniature elephant of carved ivory and a brass eagle claw holding a ball. He took an old moustache cup with blue and pink flowers out of his box as well as an alligator nutcracker. Maria pretended she'd never seen them before, even though all of his collectibles had been rotated through his museum box. He showed her his collection of paperweights, heavy blobs of clear glass containing fruit – a pear and a peach – and some with patterns of coloured glass or green leaves. He handed her postcards, spoons, and stereo cards.

"Not all this stuff is old," he repeated, "but it will be some day. Every piece is unique for some reason." He recounted where he found various items and how much he paid.

He told Maria that he wasn't collecting any more. He'd been too busy with other things, and besides, a person's interests change. "Though you never lose your curiosity," he said, "and you'll take a look and sometimes buy, just in case." He showed her a bulldog toothpick holder of porcelain and a souvenir silk bookmark of the 1893 Chicago Fair with a view of the Women's Building. He explained that this was memorabilia. He also had a weather thermometer in the shape of a bird.

The last things James Edward pulled out of his box were his Lindbergh things: bookmarks, souvenir coins, a postcard picturing the "Spirit of St. Louis," a photograph print of the plane, and a round likeness of the pilot with a mirror on the other side.

He asked her if she knew about Lindbergh.

Of course she did but Maria wasn't sure what he considered adequate so she replied, "A little." Then he told her the story, everything about the flight across the Atlantic and the flyer's subsequent and ongoing fame.

When he'd taken everything out of the box, all the items spread out on the floral oilcloth, he asked, "Did you bring anything interesting along from Russia, Maria?"

She needed a few moments to think back to the small pile of straw bags and cases they'd had with them and what they'd packed inside. They'd brought as much as they could, but they'd already lost or sold most of their possessions by then. Her father had carried the personal papers, and her mother clung to a shawl that had been her late mother's. Maria had the choir book, but what was valuable about that? They brought a few photos and the family clock. But mostly they had bedding and clothing and food for the journey.

"Nothing," she said at last. The list of what they'd left behind was a long one, but that wasn't his question.

"I'll give you something," he said. "Get you started." He pointed at the Lindbergh souvenirs. "Pick something from here."

"Oh no!" Maria said, remembering his speech about the future value of collectibles and thinking he pitied her because he'd caught her crying the evening before. "My mother will soon be better."

"Sure," he said easily. "I know."

He picked up the mirror. "I've got plenty of Lindbergh stuff," he said. "You can have this."

She protested again but he put everything back in the box except the mirror.

"See," he said, lifting it up to her eye, "it's got your face on it. The very lovely Maria."

He left it behind on the table, so she had to take it with her to her room.

□

James Edward started coming into the kitchen after dinner for a second coffee and a second dessert, when he had nothing else pressing that evening, he said, to talk to Maria while she did the dishes. He'd begin with, "Hello there!" like greeting a neighbour over the fence. As if her presence in the kitchen was coincidental. He'd launch with a question or two but James Edward did most of the talking and then he left when his cup and dessert plate were empty. Maria found the topics intriguing.

Had she heard of Alfred Adler and his work on inferiority complex? Albert Schweitzer, his book on the mysticism of the apostle Paul? Was she interested in sports, especially baseball? What did she think of the news from Europe? Did she care for politics? Did she know the north face of the Matterhorn had finally been conquered by climbers?

The conversations didn't proceed, however, on his terms alone. In a brave moment's pause after his very first question, the first evening after the collectibles display, Maria decided to be honest about what she knew and what she didn't. She would feign nothing for his sake, nor allow herself to be mocked or humiliated in any way. Her haziness about his motivation for their strange new companionable relationship seemed to require her planning for all eventualities. She remembered the advice to housewives she'd read in the *Rundschau*: let him have the last word, remember he's a man but not a god, be reasonable, allow him to know more than you, honour his mother. But she wasn't exactly a housewife to this young man – this James Edward – perhaps not quite a friend either. While she figured out what this was about, she would defend her dignity, her intelligence. After all, Mrs Lowry had praised her once, in an especially congenial mood, as "a smart young woman."

Maria also had to get her work done. No use trying to hide the fact she was still the hired help. She was disadvantaged because her hands were busy and her face was flushed with toil, and her legs were aching. But he would simply have to talk around the clatter of pans and plates and sometimes her back to him. And so he did, though he'd raise his voice or pause if there was noise, and sometimes he'd get up from the table and stand down the wash counter from her so he could see her face as he spoke. But he never picked up a dishcloth to help. Nor did Maria expect that he should.

As it turned out, Maria had heard of most of the matters he mentioned, from bits of her reading here and there. It seemed to impress him. And when she admitted how little or how much she knew, linking it with an upturn of tone and a question to indicate she was interested in more of, say, Adler's work, the explanation James Edward then revealed to her was as pleasurable for her as it seemed to be for him. He wasn't condescending with his knowledge but had a good teacher's best gift: his own excitement and his confidence that the other would care and naturally grasp at what was expounded.

How curious he was, how far and indiscriminately his love of knowledge ranged! Maria feared this would make him arrogant; warnings about pride from her upbringing asserted themselves. But she and James Edward seemed compatible in their aptitudes, even though he was further ahead in actual education, and in English. Maria began to read the newspapers and magazines that came to the house (after the Lowrys were done with them) with even greater intensity and thoroughness. The things he mentioned could be found everywhere in their pages, as well as links and discovered facts of her own. She thought of the Scripture phrase, *light sown as seed*, though she couldn't remember where she'd read it. Maria kept her own pursuits of learning to herself unless they could be offered with integrity, but she believed she knew more than he did about European and Russian affairs; the German Mennonite papers often carried such news.

Maria's ideas about James Edward changed. She'd seen him at parties where she had to serve. There he was attractive, yes, but too loud, too boastful, his manner towards his female guests bold and suggestive. The enthusiasm he brought into the kitchen seemed different to Maria, as if it predated these social events. She knew his opinions were rather liberal, but the balance of light and dark she'd seen in him shifted among her stacked dirty plates and scraps, a table dusted with flour from baking, the stovetop spattered with gravy or soup, the air often hot and humid by evening. He seemed less brittle in these surroundings; there was a kind of innocence about him.

Mrs Lowry discovered her son's new after-dinner entertainment. She followed him into the kitchen one evening and demanded, "What are you doing in here? Bothering the maid!"

"I'm not bothering Maria. Am I, Maria? Say so, Maria, and I'm away." The repetitions of the name seemed designed to annoy his mother.

"It doesn't matter," Maria said quickly.

"Perhaps in these troubled times, high-born princesses will be found in low-born situations," James Edward said, dramatically.

"That's not amusing," Mrs Lowry said.

"Remember the story of Cinderella in the cinders? Perhaps it's here before our very eyes!"

Mrs Lowry grimaced and asked if he was the prince or the pumpkin.

"Mother!" he squealed. "You're quite a wit." He lifted his cup, slurped noisily at his coffee. "The prince, of course."

"I should think there's enough opportunity at our dinner table for your many ideas," she said.

He slurped again. Maria was disappointed by his lack of respect.

"Get out of here, James Edward," Edith Lowry said. "Stop bothering Maria!" Her rigid back as she swung out of the kitchen was a final word of disapproval.

Without any of the haughtiness he'd shown seconds earlier, James Edward asked Maria if his presence was a bother.

"I'm not used to it," she admitted. "But it's very . . . interesting."

"What's the harm in it?" he demanded hotly of the door behind which his mother had disappeared.

"She leans on you," he said. "Though she thinks you're all to her credit. Good mistresses make good maids, that sort of thing. Something to hold over her friends. When they're talking about the insolence and sloppiness and thievery of their girls. We've all heard the story how she gave up every-thing for a spell to train you. How it paid off for us all."

"I *am* good," Maria said. "Maybe the others should get Mennonite girls. We're honest and we work hard."

James Edward laughed. "You're quite without irony," he said. "It's refreshing."

"I don't know what you mean."

"No decadence. Consider it a compliment." He grinned and stood. "I guess I'd better obey my mother."

□

He did not heed his mother's command. May became June, the weeks wore on, and James Edward's evening visits to Maria increased in frequency and length. The things he talked about became more personal. He told Maria about his studies in law. He enjoyed law, he said. It's what his father wanted, but fortunately, he liked it. He had friends who felt the pressure of their fathers' careers but not the enjoyment. It wasn't easy, he said, to sort out one's relations with parents, to separate the self, though the work being done by the psychoanalysts was a help. He alluded to examples in their own home, in the homes of his friends. Maria was aston-ished how freely James Edward talked about things like that, about relationships. His examples disturbed and excited her in a way that discussion of theories and news did not.

Once she interrupted him, offered another view. "My parents decide, and we honour them," she said. "Honour your father and mother. That's what the Bible says." She felt the simplicity of this truth was superior to the analyzing he did, which only made her anxious.

"Sounds good," he said. "The Bible is our guide."

"You think so?"

"Oh, absolutely. It's foundational."

So they weren't disagreeing. She'd misunderstood what he meant.

One evening, James Edward offered Maria his family history. He said his English forebears who settled in Canada had a vision of what they would do in the country, the kind of society they would create. What they were leaving behind, what they were bringing along. They thought of themselves as custodians of the need to live decent and upright lives, to work hard, to transfer institutions. James Edward made the English – by which Maria understood the broad swath of people who grew up speaking that language – sound noble and very compelling. He made them sound like the rock under Canada's truest identity.

The tale of his genealogy rambled into a lesson about the constitutional monarchy, how it developed from Charles I onwards, and how it differed from the system of government the Americans had. Then he asked if perhaps she was bored.

Maria's "No" popped out like a supplication.

"Tell the truth, Maria."

"I did. If you get tired of law, you know, you could be a teacher. You're very good – as a teacher." It was the most direct and intimate thing she'd said to him so far.

James Edward pushed his empty cup towards her to be washed. "Well, thank you very much," he said. "That's awfully nice of you."

He stood up. "I like you," he said. Then he kissed her.

Maria's work in the kitchen was finished. She'd dried her hands. She was taking off her apron. He'd risen as if to go, but he stepped towards her and put one hand on the left side of her head. His fingers reached over her ear. Maria lowered her eyes from his eyes, but only as far as his mouth. She saw it coming and then she felt his lips touch hers. Just a touch, a slight pressure, then lifting.

He moved back and she could see his mouth again, forming words. She heard him say, "Your lips are truly inspirational." Then he was gone. As if it was a line of poetry. As if, at recitation's end, he had to exit the stage.

Maria clenched her apron. Her hands formed fists around the fabric. She began to shake. Her whole body shook and felt hot and unsafe, as if she were a bushel of leaves being tossed to a fire.

□

It seemed to Maria later that Peter – her uncle, her friend, her rival of sorts – was somehow involved in her troubles, though the role he had played wasn't clear to her at all. Had she presumed some warning, some rescue operation? According to her mother, Maria was supposed to rescue *him*, from his vague impiety and irregular attitudes, so why should she fault him for not being strong enough on her behalf?

Perhaps it was precisely that: his weakness, and hers. Their shared blood. Maria was supposed to follow the Klassen line, not the Konrad side with its implications of moral decline in the poverty of the hovel at the edge of the grandparents' village in Russia. Mother escaped it but Peter wasn't making enough of an effort.

He left Manitoba soon after attending to the Klassens' arrival in Canada. He lived in Saskatchewan, then Alberta, briefly in B.C., then Alberta again. He wrote Maria's parents only when his address changed. In 1931, he returned from his sojourning and he had a bride with him. Agathe, one of a row of Koop daughters from Coaldale, Alberta. She was barely twenty and shy at first. Peter brought her to Winnipeg and they rented the third floor of a North End house.

Maria began to spend her free Thursday evenings with Peter and Agathe instead of going to the Mary-Martha Home. "I'm so glad that Peter's back," Mother wrote. "You'll be a light to him. Our prodigal is still too restless."

"So glad you're going to Peter and Agathe's," Mother wrote in another one of the postscripts she contributed to Father's letters. "I trust you're strong enough. You know what I've told you."

Mother hadn't told her anything much, Maria thought, bleak from her useless waiting for Aron and more aware than ever that she wasn't married, and had no prospects either. She recalled from her brief breaks home how Mother's sighs punctuated conversations, as if to say *we're in Canada now*, a transitional sound, needing the heave of breath to leap over the miles. Maria's visits to Peter and Agathe seemed that kind of breath, not seeking the prodigal for Mother, but looking for a firm landing of her own. Chastened a little from the pride with which she'd wanted Peter out of the kitchen the day she was hired. Coming to see him and Agathe because all he could speak of was *here*, of Canada, and she had to fix that in her head again. Until she lost Aron, she'd believed she was no longer attached to her Russian past. After she lost him, she flew at the slightest provocation to old land-scapes and memories. These hurt, when she got there, but it was hard to tear herself away. She wanted to be firm with herself, forget the Crimea completely, and Peter, for all his flaws, seemed so fully, so freely, here. In Canada.

He just wasn't religious.

Peter returned to Winnipeg with stories about their people, people he met or heard of in all parts of the West. They were dramatic tales but confused, his sources often steps removed from the events he described. He said, for example, that Johann Wiebe who was the cousin to Johann Loeppky had said the two Sawatzky brothers from Tiegenhagen, who had also been briefly in the Crimea, in Schoental, were sharing a house somewhere near Dalmeny, Saskatchewan, they and their wives, one of whom was Johann Loeppky's stepsister. Or something like that. The wives drew a line down the middle of every room of the house. It was that hard for them to get along.

"*Ach*, Peter," said Agathe.

Well, if it wasn't so, he blustered, they'd certainly talked about lines. Maybe they were too poor to buy chalk or a pencil.

"*Ach*, Peter," Agathe said sadly, as if it was her own gossiping husband who'd been marking up floors with the stubborn females of the Sawatzky clan.

And Peter had met up with that Martin Loewen who seemed to know everyone, who'd told him many things. He'd told him that Abram Derksen had said the Peter Ennses from the same village had been royally cheated – by an Englishman with a rotten farm to sell. He thought it was near Boissevain, though that surprised him because someone else said the farms were excellent there. Enns sat and bawled until at last his son piped up and told him to be quiet. That boy was just a child and he had to set his father straight.

"*Ach*, Peter," Agathe said, her voice soft and chiding.

Maria listened, amused or distressed, whatever the stories seemed to demand. Her parents would have been more diligent in asking for the details. Father would have his reservations. Accuracy, to him, was everything. Mother would probe, to establish for a certainty the relations of the people involved and then make her judgement from that. She believed families possessed certain traits or characteristics. Once she knew the family connections it was easy enough to dismiss or to verify any story. For this reason, Maria supposed, her mother emphasized the Klassens' lineage rather than her own; its reputation seemed impeccable thus far.

Peter and Agathe's third floor was little more than an attic: just one room divided into two by a cupboard where Agathe cooked on a hot plate. She had no ice-box. In winter the rooms were cold and food could be preserved against the thin outer walls but in the summer the slant-roofed room was far too hot; they carried butter and milk and meat, when they had it, into the dug-out cellar three-and-a-half floors below.

They said it was temporary. Maria pushed through the shabbiness and pervasive disrepair of the rooming house, climbed the stairway lining the far walls of the house, where the window of each floor's landing gave a progressively higher view of the crowded street and the wash lines below, and the warmth of their welcome made her feel virtuous for surviving the passage from the street to their door. She had to keep coming. They liked her. They asked her questions and wanted to hear what she said. They were intensely curious about the Lowrys, but not in the scrutinizing, discerning way of her parents. They didn't seem to worry, or seem jealous of her either. They laughed at her scruples. With them, she relaxed.

Agathe's reticence had been a first and false impression. She proved to be as fearless about living in the city as Peter was. "I won't miss the sugar beet fields," she told Maria. "Not one bit." Neither saw the city's dangers as clearly as the preachers or the matron of the Mary-Martha Home. They mingled with the other tenants and joked in English with shopkeepers and neighbours. They poked fun at the foibles of the Poles, Hungarians, Jews, or Germans, as if they as Mennonites were superior, but with an air of affection that lowered the barriers, it seemed to Maria, instead of keeping them up.

Peter got a job in a watch repair shop – for pathetic wages, he said, and on some evenings he ran deliveries for the corner grocery store. Agathe took in laundry, using the washtubs of their landlady on the main floor. "She charges us dearly for the water, the power, the space," Peter complained. "But what can we do?" He shrugged. Agathe boiled potatoes for starch for the shirt collars and she and Peter ate the potatoes, cold, for supper.

After some months, talk of the third floor as temporary ended. Peter lost his job at the jeweller's and he and Agathe were reduced to living on what they earned between his deliveries in the basket of his secondhand bicycle and her washing orders. The house in which they rented their room seemed to decay visibly from visit to visit. Or was it coincidence that the weather was dull and overcast exactly on the Thursdays Maria came, that the dust balls in the corners seemed to grow every week?

That winter, the windows were heavily iced and the smell of grease – fried sausage and potatoes – seemed to solidify too. The room panted for air in spite of its humidity and chill. Agathe sometimes hung laundry inside instead of out. "I don't have to damp it to iron it," she said. "It never dries completely."

Their first anniversary arrived. Maria was barely in the door and Peter said, "I went on the dole today."

Agathe was struggling at the window to raise the inside pane. The wood around the glass was broken or warped, it seemed, and hindered her attempts. "No other Mennonite man would dare," she growled. She wrestled on with the window, her brown housedress rising and falling over her hips. Maria pitied the woman, won by her uncle's bravado, her ambition already reduced to the want of some air. Her feet were bare.

"How do you know that?" Peter barked.

The window finally yielded an inch. Agathe propped it up with a spool of thread and turned. "I've heard them say so. Or their wives." Her tone was mild now, almost sweet.

"All of a sudden she's going to church *Frauenverein*," he said to Maria. "Getting together with all the other Mennonite women."

He addressed his wife. "So they say they've got their pride. I say, what's it got to do with pride? The grocer takes the orders himself. Or his ten-year-old son. I don't know how he reaches the pedals."

"Peter sold the boy his bicycle," Agathe interrupted. "Half of what he paid for it, used. His last gift to the man. After he'd cut his wages."

"I'm as Canadian as the rest of them standing in line. And I chopped wood all afternoon. Do you think it's easy for me, Agathe?" The look Peter turned on his wife was beseeching. "I want something to eat on the table. Every day after washing, potatoes!"

"He sold the bike and we've already spent the money," Agathe went on.

"You enjoyed it too!" he roared.

"We went to the theatre. We can't think beyond today." Agathe sighed. They seemed children caught in a misdemeanor, confessing to Maria.

They all heard at that moment a loud sound of something breaking beneath them, a thump, a piece of furniture falling perhaps, then a woman's voice pierced with rage and a man's in answer, shouting. They heard scuffling, another thump, a scream.

A door slammed and there was silence.

"New tenants on the second floor," Peter said. The three of them seemed frozen then, no one looking at the other, as if the sounds of violence from the second floor were echoed by the tension on the third.

Peter broke the spell. "Oh come, Agathe," he coaxed, sitting down and patting his lap, "come here. Cheer up. We had a good time, didn't we? And we bought you the shoes."

"Lovely shoes," she conceded sadly. "For what?"

"Maria won't come again if our faces are hanging like this. Didn't we get the ham and cream for our supper tonight because of her?"

"Because of our wedding day."

"Yes, but she celebrates with us."

Agathe·prepared *vrenike* for supper. She and Peter ate heartily but Maria wished she'd gone to the Mary-Martha Home. The delicious dumpling pockets with their heavy cream gravy took an effort to swallow. She was choking on her uncle's only asset, the second-hand bicycle he'd sold to see a film, buy shoes, get groceries for a supper. She felt a rash hunger for a dish of mixed vegetables or a consomme.

But Peter enjoyed himself and he had music on his mind. "I was talking to a fellow the other day, an English fellow," he said, "and I suppose I implied that Winnipeg isn't that special. Compared to Europe, I said. He called me ungrateful, said I didn't know how lucky I am they let me in! So to make the matter clear, I had to explain I've been to Kiev and St. Petersburg, and also Berlin. St. Petersburg? he said. St. Petersburg? Again, St. Petersburg? Nothing else but St Petersburg. As if it had stuck in his throat. Maybe he thought Winnipeg was the world's biggest city. Let him think what he wishes, I said to myself, by then I knew exactly how little he knew. Just to add to his string of St. Petersburgs –"

"He probably knows it as Leningrad," Agathe said. "He was probably confused."

"I told him I'd been to the opera in St. Petersburg."

"You've been to the opera?" asked Maria.

"No, and not to St. Petersburg either," Agathe informed her.

"I was making a point," Peter said. "Some of our people have gone. Some of our people aren't unfamiliar with the opera, Maria. Among us they imagine themselves rather splendid because of it, but my point was in relation to this *Englischer*. I borrowed some experience because I needed to set him straight about who we are. Where exactly did he think we'd been living?"

"*Ach*, Peter," Agathe said. "Why don't you tease Maria, ask her if she has a boyfriend yet?" She laughed like a child.

While Agathe ran to the cellar to bring up a jar of pickles someone had given them, which she'd forgotten to put on the table, Peter said, "She's miserable because she wants a baby. We're doing everything and nothing happens."

Maria had no idea what to say to this so she said nothing.

When it was time for Maria to leave after supper, Agathe insisted on seeing her down the stairs and to the door. She had something to tattle too. "Peter smokes too much of the money away," she said.

"I thought I noticed the smell of cigarettes," Maria said. But she didn't know what to say to that either. Her mother hoped she'd be a good influence, but it was obvious she had no impact at all.

☐

The Mary-Martha girls had been warned of potential improprieties by the men of the house. But the warnings were oblique and since James Edward's subsequent behavior was polite and perfectly correct, Maria concluded that his kiss didn't fall under the admonitions of the matron and the preachers. He continued to stop by the kitchen several evenings a week. He didn't mention the incident or attempt to kiss her again. At first she'd feared he would, but as the days passed, she grew sorry that he hadn't.

Still, she appreciated his subsequent forbearance. Good that they were friends, she decided. It was a blessing, she told herself, for her to have this camaraderie, unusual as it was, something to shorten the days, something to anticipate. Yes, she decided, they were friends. She liked the word "friend." She often forgot while they talked that she was a servant – an immigrant, German-speaking servant, less educated than he. She mulled over things during the day to tell him in the evening; she organized and practiced her ideas so she would be ready.

Maria told herself their conversations were an education. In Canadian history, in ways of thinking in the English mind, and in many other points of knowledge. One evening James Edward explained the peculiarities of the Lowrys' church denomination, for example, and the events around the recent troubled Union. He'd been in favour, he said, of the Methodists and Presbyterians combining. He told her he was a Christian, of course, surprised she hadn't taken this for granted. Maria was grateful. She hoped she could share with him soon the history of her church and people, the history of her family.

"I don't care for James Edward hanging around and bothering you," Mrs Lowry told her the morning they drew up lists for the summer move to the cottage.

"It's not bothering me. I'm doing my work."

"It would bother me. It would slow me."

Maria was peeved and unusually blunt. "You'll have to forbid him then. I don't invite him and I don't mind."

"I'm not blaming you. I'm saying I don't like it."

"He talks. I listen." Like a friend, Maria thought. Like I'm a sister. She couldn't help remembering Aron's *my dear sister in Christ*. Perhaps Mrs Lowry didn't know her son as well as she, Maria, was coming to know him.

"No need to encourage him," Mrs Lowry persisted.

Maria was silent.

"He's on the rebound. His long-time Ruthie dropped him – for his best friend . . . I always suspected she'd hurt him someday. Funny how one anticipates these things . . . Not that I'm heartless to what he's feeling."

Her tone was less confiding than deliberate. The teacher's tone. "He won't admit it, but it's hard on him. He's unpredictable. Apt to set his affections . . . elsewhere. Anywhere. He's fond of women, Maria. He's good at it . . . If you understand what I'm saying."

What Maria didn't understand was the word "rebound." She repeated the word in her mind so she wouldn't forget it.

She looked it up in Mr Lowry's dictionary the next day when she dusted the library. *Rebound: spring back from force of impact; cast back; recoil*. She read further, and then she found what she was looking for. *Rebound: After being rejected by another.*

Mrs Lowry wished to accomplish another rejection with this information? Maria too knew a rejection of sorts. Her loyalty to James Edward simply increased. If Ruthie was that vain and faithless, it was good she was gone. But while he suffered, Maria thought, he was welcome to talk to her.

□

Indeed, the photograph of James Edward and his Ruthie had disappeared from the mantelpiece. It had perched against the ginger jar like a small bird and then, without notice, it flew away. Now the vacancy in front of the jar seemed important. Maria sensed it whenever she had duties in that room: a pouch of empty space like a nest, waiting for a new picture, an alternate pairing.

It was the story of Esther that Maria mulled over now – the story of a young woman set into a foreign place for divine and sovereign purposes. She seized the story's meaning for herself. Believed its application could be for her. *Who knows but that you have come to the kingdom for such a time as this?* She dared to imagine she'd been prepared for him. That a course of help had been opened, in this unlikely manner, for her loneliness and for the needs of her family. She thought something had changed between her and James Edward, that their individual purposes were pushing to the surface, begging to be acknowledged and joined. He'd asked her if she knew how pretty she was. He'd told her that her bit of an accent was pretty too.

She wasn't unaware of the hurdles, the resistance there would be to an interpretation of her life after Esther's example. But there it was, the unfilled spot where the photograph had been. Maria put herself there, in a new picture, reclining against James Edward, not audacious-looking as Ruthie, but serious and determined.

And she wanted to touch him. His shoulder or arm perhaps. She continued to serve at the table with her practiced invisibility, that fluid invisibility required of a servant, but she longed to be someone of flesh and meaning for him, to touch him while she lowered a platter of meat or a dish of vegetables, to anchor on him in the midst of the family. Maria's own parents were undemonstrative. She'd never seen a kiss or flirtation between them. But when her mother served the table, she placed the food before her father and sometimes if one hand was free she pressed her flat palm on his back as a kind of leverage while she leaned forward, and sometimes he looked up at her with a slight smile as if to say she was welcome to use him this way.

This was all Maria had wanted.

□

One spring day when Maria was a schoolgirl in the Crimea, her teacher took his students into the meadows outside the village. He taught them as they wandered – about the flowers, the butterflies, the larks, the history of the Mennonites. He flung his hands east and west, north and south, as if the sky behind him were a map. That winter had been colder than usual, and long, but now spring had come and they could see the mountains in the distance and all of them knew, over the mountains lay the sea. The sea and coast, where oranges, grapes, and lemons grew. Mr Dyck, their teacher, told them about people who lived in the mountains. About the Tartars, their mosques and their mullahs. When he taught inside the one-room schoolhouse, the Mennonites seemed powerful and righteous and their settlements filled Maria's world. But that day, outdoors, she felt jubilance like a flame inside her, as if she'd been ignited by the sun, because she'd grasped something which she'd known but never really known, that there were other people with lives as interesting and self-contained as her own. Mounted Tartars with scimitars glinting at their waists. Russian women in tiny sitting rooms drawing tea from samovars. And other places too: the salt plains, the long flat plains behind the mountains, the mountains, and the sea.

That day she felt as if she'd been hoisted – to soar in

her mind – over the place of her birth, away from the village and over the times of her people and their geographies, and for a moment she felt she saw everything that existed, so much more than she'd supposed: a godlike view. And she remembered thinking, *and God saw that it was good.*

When Maria finally had a chance to describe herself to James Edward, her friend, one evening when everyone had left the house but she (and apparently he, for he emerged from somewhere and finding her in the kitchen, invited her to the screened-in second level porch, where he pulled his chair close to hers like a secret and began to ask her questions), this was the memory she told him first. She couldn't duplicate its remembered intensity, but she tried her best and she felt he understood what she meant. Unexpectedly her voice broke at its conclusion and then he put his arm around her briefly and encouraged her to continue by asking more questions. She told him about their journey from the Crimea. The station at Spat, crossing the border, Southampton, the ocean voyage. She introduced her brothers and sisters: *Gerhard Susanna Katherine Hans Wilhelm Margarethe, and the baby Erna, born this spring.*

"Once you asked me what I brought from Russia," she said. "This is all I have." A museum table, she thought, of memories.

"Yes, yes," he said. "Very good."

It was an earnest conversation, too earnest probably, and dangerous, his physical proximity colouring everything. But she went on bravely, saying the best she could about each member of her family, creating a legacy for him to share.

James Edward listened well when he wanted to. She'd never had anyone outside her family listen to her with such concentration. He kept his hands around his knees while she handed him her stories, her verbal portraits, like eggs.

But even eggs are stronger than what she gave him! The house empty, everyone gone, and the voices of children somewhere on the street, the western sun playing into the room in one corner but the rest in shade, the grey mesh of the screens on three sides like a curtain that shut the two of them into each other. After some time he shifted, put his arm around her shoulder and left it there, turned his chair at an angle, leaned forward, his eyes on her face, his straight fair hair loping over his forehead like a tassel of gold. One by one her sentences hardened in that mellow and comforting light and by his willingness to hear them; they didn't disappear and even she could believe they were significant.

"How did your father get the papers?" he asked. "What is your older brother doing now?" "How old would your father be?" "How are they managing, your parents?" "Does your family like Canada?"

(She would never deny he knew how to listen. His powerful listening, his interest, led her on. Seduced her. She wanted him to know who she was. She told him about the choir, that in Russia she'd played guitar, that she loved to sing, that she was fond of children. She tested him with generalities and as his interest held, she gave him particulars. Much could be assumed in conversations with people of her own background and language, like the girls at the Mary-Martha Home. But here there were gaps, and James Edward had to work to span them. She believed that this effort, more than anything else, proved that he loved her. He'd endeavoured, she believed, to discover that she was complex too, that in the fundamental and human they were the same. Never mind background, class, and language. They were man and woman.)

On this evening they found out they were born in the same year, on the same day of the month, three months apart. While he was waving his infant hands at the world, so was she. "Think of it!" he exclaimed, as if it were portentous.

"Think of it," she repeated. Born on different continents and now they were sitting side by side.

☐

But he never used the word love, not even when kissing her for the second time, later, in the dusk, in the sleeping porch. (Or the third time, the fourth time, the fifth and last.) A longer, fervent kiss, as if a continuation of the first with more detail, more elaboration of its meaning.

Maria put aside the cautions that might have been – should have been – stopping her. She used the word love in her mind even though he didn't say it and later she remembered this and wondered why she'd ignored its absence in his speech.

It was the word she'd wanted for them and so she used and mis-used it. *Love bears, believes, hopes, endures. Love so unending . . .*

Love didn't end, but whatever she and James Edward had together had ended.

So, the word love wasn't allowed. But what word could one use instead? For what they had shared?

☐

Mid-August, the Lowrys left Maria at the Victoria Beach cottage with a week's worth of instructions, to thoroughly clean the place and do some painting. The porch and touch-ups. They wanted to offer it for sale. They returned to Winnipeg and arranged for her to take the train back to the city at the end of the week.

It was extremely hot and humid, had been that way for days. Even morning brought no relief. Instead of thinning through the night, the air grew steadily thicker with heat, more oppressive. Maria had her work to accomplish in spite of the weather. It made her tense.

Fearing it would rain, she painted the porch first, on Monday. If she worked hard, she would have hours to spare for herself, perhaps an entire day. She painted quickly, almost feverishly. A tremulous agitation had seized her, the sensation of suspense. Something would happen, she felt, something she was helpless about and unwilling to prevent. James Edward was in the vortex of her mind. He was planning to return to Toronto soon for his final term of studies and she needed to know his intentions. The next week she would visit her family and she needed to reach that haven safely. She felt that James Edward was near.

Late afternoon, Tuesday, he walked into the cottage. "It's my week off," he said. "I'm staying with McCormicks. I told them I was coming here to read."

"Is it too noisy to read there?" she accused. The McCormicks were elderly. "Are their grandchildren with them?"

"I knew you were here."

"What are you reading?"

He handed her a slender volume and she read the title. *All Quiet on the Western Front.* She turned it around in her hands and opened it to his marker, near the middle.

"All's quiet here," he said. "Are you happy to see me?"

"I don't know." Maria took a step back.

"Well, I'm glad to see you."

She waited.

"Sit down," he said. "I'll read to you."

"But you don't want to begin again!"

"I'll read from where I am. It's interesting anywhere."

She obeyed, choosing the small willow chair. He chose the sofa. He sat sideways, one leg lifted along the length of it, the other on the floor. He was completely at ease, his manner friendly and disarming. The way he was. Maria relaxed a little. He began to read.

Forgive me, comrade. We always see it too late. Why do they never tell us that you are poor devils like us, that your mothers are just as anxious as ours, and that we have the same fear of death, and the same dying and the same agony – Forgive me, comrade, how could you be my enemy?

James Edward had a pleasant reading voice: a flat, even tone. He didn't insult her by adding inflection or exaggerating things to make them clear. He trusted her to follow the story without beating it out. He read a long time, perhaps half an hour, and didn't look up in between.

Sometimes Maria heeded the words, sometimes she found herself slipping under them, lulled by his voice, hearing other thoughts of her own until she snapped back to the story. Or she might stay at a picture the author created too long, long after he'd moved on to something else. Sometimes she found herself watching James Edward. Studying him. Seeing not the details but him as a person who didn't mind her eyes on him, who sprawled before her with assurance she envied, as handsome as she'd ever seen him. Yes, she was happy he'd come.

His tunic is half open. The pocket-book is easy to find. But I hesitate to open it. In it is the book with his name. So long as I do not know his name perhaps I may still forget him, time will obliterate it, this picture. But his name, it is a nail that will be hammered into me and never come out again . . .

Through the verandah screen door Maria saw that the sky was changing. She saw it turning brown and muddy behind the trees while James Edward read. A storm was brewing, a fine storm, she thought, that would empty the heat out of the air. She was glad; it's what they needed. It would make things easier. Once the storm cleansed the air, her forebodings would disappear.

James Edward paused and then Maria asked him if she should make tea.

He said, "Oh no," strongly, as if the suggestion were

inappropriate. But he stopped reading when the noise of the storm began.

Lightning and thunder squabbled over them while they listened. "Come here," he said, patting the spot beside him.

She went. She'd never been afraid of storms but it couldn't hurt to sit beside him. He put his arm around her, drew her close. It couldn't hurt to lean a little. She closed her eyes, perceiving through the lids the lightning flashes and hearing the thunder that followed, like a stone wall thrown up around them. She was safe against him. Happy. Soon it began to rain, a gushing, extravagant rain that poured onto the cottage roof like a bath running over their heads. They listened to it in silence. It would have been impossible to hear each other properly in any case. She felt his body as if it were drawn for her, a thick inked line from his fingers against her elbow to his arm along her upper back, the curve of him under his arm into which she was curled, and his chest – the essential stroke of the piece, bearing the full significance of their mutual arrangement.

The rain stopped as abruptly as it started and Maria jumped up. James Edward rose more slowly and stretched his limbs.

"Have you ever danced?" he asked.

Maria shook her head.

"Would you like to try?"

She said she didn't know.

"Take off that uniform. That cleaning dress. You've worked enough for today."

He opened the door to the verandah. A ribbon of cool damp air flew in and wrapped itself around her. "I won't touch you, I promise!" he laughed.

He meant to reassure her; he meant it. He was dependable. Not the languid sophisticate he tried to be with his friends. This was James Edward as he really was, as he wanted to be.

Maria went to her narrow bedroom to change. She had

only one good dress along, the one she intended to wear on the train trip back to Winnipeg. It was a pale blue summer dress passed along to her from Mrs Lowry. Maria noticed in her small mirror that her face was flushed. She hadn't worked quite enough for the day. She would have to double her efforts tomorrow.

When she returned to the main room James Edward asked, "Don't you have anything besides my mother's old dresses?"

"It's my dress now."

"You'd look terrific in the new things. Your colour would be red, I think. I can just –"

"I send most of my money home."

"I know, I know. You look marvellous, really. But you could loosen your hair."

"So many ideas you have today." Maria smiled but she didn't touch her hair.

"Twenty-three and quite lovely," he said. "With no opportunity to meet a good Mennonite farmer."

"No opportunity," she said.

"Come on, I'm going to teach you to dance."

"There's no music."

"I'll sing."

He took up "Better Days are Coming" but lost the words after a line or two and began a "ta-dum-ta-dum-ta-dum" in a tune he seemed to be improvising as he went. He danced about alone, comically alone, out to the verandah and back in again, hearing an orchestra in his head perhaps. Maria began to laugh and he laughed too and finally she lifted her hands to imitate his hands and then she took a step like one of his and then another, and in this fashion they danced. She followed him and their feet clipped along the painted wood floor and outside the birds sang and the sunshine sparkled on the wet trees and grass. Water dropped from eaves and branches and the porch roof, plinking rhythm along with them. Maria's restlessness had vanished.

He said, "I promised I wouldn't touch you while we dance, but may I take your hands to show you this particular step?"

She gave him one hand, then the other. His hands were large; they were warm and dry.

"Your voice is good," she said.

"Thank you." He swung her after him, still muttering a beat that was easy to follow. He led her around until both of them were breathless. They stopped and he dropped her hands and bowed. "Well, Maria," he said, "that was terrific. You have the makings of a dancer. Maybe I'll pop by tomorrow and teach you something else."

He kissed her for the third time and this time she felt that she was kissing him too. Then he picked up his book and left, letting the screen door slam and whistling down the path.

Maria slept poorly that night, the agitation returning to possess her again. She felt she should pray but her thoughts wouldn't conform to the relinquishment of prayer. But she remembered some words of a psalm and wondered if they were intended for her. *When the Lord turned again the captivity of Zion, we were like them that dream . . . our mouth filled with laughter, our tongue with songs.* Surely the purpose of her life was different than she'd supposed, different than her family supposed. "God has put you where you are," the preachers often reminded the lonely, homesick girls of the Mary-Martha Home when they gathered on Thursday and Sunday nights. Surely it was providentially planned. James Edward was intended for her, and she wouldn't be lonely again.

☐

He brought her a flower, a wild rose with its five pink petals and furry yellow middle. "It wasn't easy finding one that wasn't washed apart by the rain," he said.

The wild rose was a simple flower, very basic. "Thank you," she said. "I like it."

She was in her working dress. She'd stayed at the cottage to work. She'd washed the cupboards, inside and out, and dragged the mattresses onto the porch to air. Thinking of James Edward coming by, she'd made a fire and baked scones.

"I made scones," she said. "I didn't have currants though."

"They look good."

"I'm used to a wood stove from Russia," she said. James Edward glowered at the stove as if it was vulgar, something one wouldn't want to get used to.

She took the flower to her room, slipped it under a pile of cottage novels to press it.

"Did you read your book?" she said when she returned.

"Finished."

"It's very frank, don't you think? The parts you read to me yesterday?" Maria had hoped he would read again.

"Everyone's talking about it. It blows out our notions of war."

"Perhaps I could read it too."

"I'll bring it over for you."

They didn't read, they didn't dance. She changed, into the same dress as the day before. She asked him if he wanted to take a walk, it was past supper, but he said he was tired of people and didn't want to see anyone.

So what did he want?

She made tea, and they drank it and ate the scones. He told her she made tea like an English woman. But he was quieter than usual. Maria decided if she waited, he would tell her whatever he'd come to say.

He wanted to be close to her, he said. Maria sat down on the sofa and James Edward sat down beside her.

"You're shivering," he said. He put his arm around her and pulled her towards him tightly until she stopped. Then he was touching her neck and shoulders and she felt her skin dissolving, turning to water. But his arm seemed a high firm bank, holding her in. He knew everything. He was very fond of her, he said. He loosened her hair.

He opened her dress and carried her into his parents' room. Maria was tall but he was strong. He flung the dress on the chair, and his own clothes over it. He threw an old blanket the Lowrys left behind over the naked mattress. This room was the nicest in the cottage, with its high window and the trees pressed against it. It was on the cool northerly side and a bird chattered in the branches against the wall. Just that day Maria had rubbed the glass clean until it was as clear as no glass, and the screen too, all the grit washed away. She heard him latch the door, felt her skin like water, her body powerless, pliable, as loose as loam. Yearning not to be alone. There was a shocking whiteness about him that she sensed rather than saw and his smell reminded her of cinnamon. He said her name. He repeated her name, as if giving it to her in the English manner of pronouncing it, urgently christening her to be his very own, and she clung to him, receiving it that way.

Later he went away to swim and Maria got up, pulling the blanket after her. She needed to wash it, or the centre at least, with its incriminating dots of blood. They would marry, she thought to herself, and this matter would belong only to them.

□

By Friday the list of tasks was finished, the cottage clean. James Edward didn't want to return to the city with Maria. "My parents think I'm at Lake Manitoba with friends," he said. "They're expecting me Sunday. They have no idea I'm here."

"Let's go to the island," she said. "There might be late berries to pick."

He said it would be better if people didn't see them together.

"That wouldn't matter," she said. "Not now."

He took her face between his hands and laughed and kissed her. It was not a laugh to concern her. She thought they would surmount what had happened; she thought they would soon be married.

"I would love to wade over the channel!" she begged.

"Your zest is remarkable, Maria, but I insist on staying right here. Besides, you won't want to miss the train."

He had a book with him. *The Maltese Falcon*. He began it while she packed her bag, but he didn't read it aloud. She sat down in the rocking chair, her case at her feet.

"Don't you want to start your book?" he asked. He meant the book about the war.

"On the train."

"Don't mind me then." He lay on the sofa on his stomach, his book open on the floor. Maria leaned back in the rocking chair and closed her eyes.

"I'll see my baby sister Erna when I go home next week," she said. "I've never seen her."

James Edward murmured but he didn't seem in the mood for conversation.

She drifted into sleep, then jerked awake. It was time to walk to the train. She rose, picked up her case.

"I have to go," she said.

He twisted and grinned up at her. "It's been terrific," he said. But he didn't move.

Well, they would see each other in the city.

"So, goodbye," she said.

"You're really terrific, Maria. Really. Beautiful. Smart. The best of luck to you!"

He was like a boy sprawling there, so free, so unencumbered, the hair a tousled flail of white and gold, the mouth nearly unbearable in its beauty. She remembered how she'd wanted to touch him at the table, put her palm on his back.

Now she'd touched him. It made her itch inside, this knowledge of his skin – and hers. It seemed like hunger; she wanted to feel him against her again.

"Thank you," she said.

She'd hoped he would see her off at the train.

But they'd meet again in Winnipeg. He was probably afraid to be seen here together; it was as strange for him as for her. They would need to tell their families, make their plans, announce them. Everything in its order.

"Goodbye then." At the threshold Maria turned and waved. James Edward waved back. It seemed silly – and disappointing – to be waving. Maria closed the cottage door. She knew if the Lowrys sold the cottage this would be her last sight of it. She'd planned to take a last look at the point where the path angled sharply away, but when she got there she forced herself to go on without a backward glance, in case James Edward had gone to the window or the verandah. She didn't want to wave again.

□

Maria spent the next week with her own family on the poor failing farm. Her mother was in bed much of the time, though she insisted it was nothing serious, this touch of tuberculosis; she was getting better. The Health Nurse had come round to give them instructions. Maria worked the entire week with a kind of fury, the hidden current of guilt and desire impelling her to reform conditions around her, to spare for a few days her younger sisters and brothers, sending them off to play while she cooked and cleaned and mended and ironed, all the while listening to her mother and watching her as a servant would, for any indications of need or command. Maria was eager to return to the city.

The farewell from her family would have been painful except for her longing for James Edward, nearly strangling her, it seemed, with the strength of its pull. He was heading back to school in the East, but not for a week. They had only one week to make plans, decide the future. Everyone would be surprised, of course, but they'd manage it together. Convince his family, and hers.

She was barely back at the Lowrys, barely inside, barely into her day uniform, and Mrs Lowry was rattling off instructions for the coming week. Among them, "Clean the attic room. James Edward's left for Toronto."

Maria heard the words, felt them turn her over inside as an hourglass is turned, anticipation dropping away. Disbelief in its place.

"Gone back?"

"Well yes, of course. To school."

"He's gone back." Maria was forgetting herself, speaking the fact aloud.

"What does it have to do with you?"

Maria shrugged as if merely confused instead of draining away. "He went early," Mrs Lowry said. "There was a message from Ruthie – the girl who broke with him in spring. I gather she wanted him back." She spoke impatiently but distinctly. It seemed important that Maria comprehend the details. "He was thrilled and took the first train out." Mrs Lowry sighed. "Let's hope he won't regret giving her a second chance."

James Edward's room was a clutter of half-measures: the bed coverings half pulled over, drawers half open, a few summer clothes in a neat pile, others discarded haphazardly on the floor. The books had been riffled through, some had fallen over. It seemed as if he'd packed in a hurry.

Maria worked from one end of the room to the other. She worked mechanically, not believing he was gone. It seemed a stupid wish, but she fixed on the notion that he'd left her a message. He'd know she would be cleaning his room. He'd leave her an explanation. She stripped the bed and ran her hand over the mattress as if stroking his back. She shook the used sheets and clothes before dropping them onto a pile of laundry. She picked up a light blue pullover and gave it a shake. The sleeves jerked downward apologetically and she spotted something in the pocket. But it was a newspaper clipping, not personal: the obituary of an English author. It had nothing to do with her.

She was too numb to think. Far too numb and too fearful – sure now that everything had gone awry – to be sentimental about the mess he'd left behind. She finished the room, then peered at the collectibles in their museum table, each in its place, looking quaint and rather puny without his eager explanations or his hands caressing them. The key was in the lock but she didn't lift the cover. She hurried down the stairs and around to her room to get the book he'd loaned her. She ran back and set it with the books on his shelf. *All Quiet on the Western Front*. She'd had no time on her holiday at home to read and she couldn't finish it now.

When Maria passed the sitting room she saw that the photograph of James Edward and Ruthie had returned to roost in front of the ginger jar. Presumably they were still standing close, both of them wearing their widest smiles. Mrs Lowry said he was thrilled. How could it be?

4

MRS LOWRY SETTLED into the worn seat of the train coach and sighed with pleasure. She slid her arms out of her coat sleeves and tented the garment around her shoulders. She spread a brown flannel blanket over her skirt and legs, and set a book, a packet of sweet biscuits, and an apple on her lap.

She leaned over to root about in the bag at her feet. "Would you like to read, Maria?" She pulled up a handful of women's magazines, sliding them apart a little like a fan. "The scenery will be exceedingly dull, I'm afraid, and it will take us the day."

Generally Maria liked magazines, with their interesting stories and their crisp advice, but she said "No thank you," rather vehemently, surprised that Mrs Lowry didn't realized a magazine might be painful, even impossible under the circumstances. Maria knew the sentences of women's magazines, their fantasies and scoldings. *If a woman wants to get married, she can. The trouble with today's old maids is that they set their sights too high when they were young.* Or, *"She flushed with rapture, and couldn't look at him, she was so confused and grateful."*

Maria had no wish to encounter sentiments like that today, or to read of current colours and fashions, forecasts about hemlines and waistlines, Christmas decorations and recipes, ideas for entertaining and parties. These issues would be full of the approaching holiday and she hadn't had a Christmas off in all her years of working. The Christmas coming up would make five of them away from home.

Plus, she was pregnant.

Mrs Lowry pushed the magazines back into her bag. She opened her book and again sighed cheerfully at the long happy prospect before her, this excuse for a day of uninterrupted reading that always carried with it, she'd told Maria once, the very nicest memories of her childhood, those years when she'd been allowed to pass one vacation day after another with books, with no responsibilities whatsoever except those of a reader to character and narrative. Her mother had been a restless and active woman, Mrs Lowry said, never able to keep at reading for more than a few minutes, but she was in awe of her daughter Edith's ability to concentrate on stories; she'd protected and encouraged the child's hours of solitary amusement as if they brought some necessary consolation into her own life.

The train departed the station and Maria turned to the window. She turned her head with her shoulders so she was quite separate from the other passengers in the car, but most deliberately separate from Mrs Lowry. She turned so not even the corner of her eye would take in the other woman, engrossed in her novel. Maria knew, as servants do, the tics and gestures of her mistress and felt she couldn't bear to see the twitch of her head while she read, the flickers of absorption that marked off lines while the pages accumulated. Mrs Lowry was disappearing into another world. Her ability to read under the circumstances seemed an act of desertion.

Under the circumstances. Maria had been nauseous. Mrs Lowry had come upon her vomiting bile into the kitchen sink. Maria had seen Mrs Lowry's look of revulsion.

"What's the matter with you, Maria?"

Maria said she didn't know.

"Maria!" Mrs Lowry grabbed her shoulders.

"Something's wrong."

"You know what's wrong! He admitted where he'd been!" She'd run angrily out of the room, up the stairs, and come back with a small brown bottle. "It brings your period on," she'd said.

"I've never had trouble with that."

Mrs Lowry asked Maria how she could be so dense. She told Maria to read the label. She was shouting. Maria blinked back the tears rising behind her eyelids. She took the bottle upstairs and set it on the dresser, as if adding an ornament to the small collection she'd gathered over the years: a china candy bowl covered in roses, a plaque that said *Mein Herz ist bereit . . . – my heart is willing, God, to sing and to praise,* a glass swan with a long neck, the Lindberg mirror.

That evening she lay on her cot for hours, not moving, not sleeping, her eyes fixed on the ceiling. James Edward was gone, she was pregnant, and *it brings your period on.*

She'd finally roused herself to get ready for bed. She took the bottle with her to the bathroom. It stood on the lip of the sink while she washed. Then she poured the potion into her chamber pot. She didn't know what she'd do but in the murk of her brain she knew she couldn't take it, whatever it was, whatever she did. Perhaps James Edward would come back to her.

But he hadn't come back; Maria's failure only grew worse.

Now she stared listlessly at the landscape as the train pulled through it, barren, winter-pressed fields with their small dips and falls and their meagre clumps of leafless wood, the land frozen into stupor and oblivious of their coming, their going, their passing. So this was the great western prairie. Elevators rose on the horizon here and there like arrows lifted clumsily to impale the sky, and here and there Maria glimpsed a cluster of houses, roads, fences, a small town, spattered it seemed on the vast plain, under a vast grey sky, nothing more than flecks on the face of an unsympathetic and gloomy geography. This was a wilderness and she was a Hagar, driven away. *Into that great and terrible wilderness.*

When the rail line curved, she saw the spuming smoke of the steam engine torn askew by the wild wind over its neck. Everything else seemed still. The snow undulated in pale shades of blue and grey that looked like stone to her, as if etched in another era, before the trains perhaps and not touched since. She saw a herd of cows close to the tracks, unperturbed as the clattering giant roared by. Their heads were uniformly turned to the train at the same angle, as if encased in frost. *And I was a beast,* the psalmist had said. *So foolish was I and ignorant: I was a beast.* Impressions, snatches of texts, memories came and went in her mind.

Eventually, Mrs Lowry had taken her to the Lowry family doctor, the one who attended Maria at the house when she was ill with flu. She'd waited in the doctor's office after the examination while he and Mrs Lowry conferred in another room. There was no doubt by then: she was pregnant. But Mrs Lowry never asked whether she'd taken the contents of the bottle. She'd sown the wind, as the Scriptures warned, and she was reaping a whirlwind. It was that simple. She'd sat there waiting for Mrs Lowry as if for salvation, her own mind bereft of response, of strategy. But sullen too, left in a corner as a naughty child. The office was sparse and uninteresting, far too parsimonious for the physician's genial air.

After Mrs Lowry retrieved her, she had taken Maria to a small café for lunch. There were no customers in the place besides themselves. Mrs Lowry placed their order and then she told Maria she was letting her go; she told Maria to think about what she would do.

"Do?" (How dull she'd been that day!)

"Surely you've realized you have to go home."

"I can't go home."

They'd argued back and forth. That she had to. That she couldn't.

"You have to help me," Maria begged. "I don't want them to know."

She'd found herself saying, "I helped you. I saved Bobby, remember?" She said that if Mrs Lowry helped her, she'd leave immediately afterwards.

"And the baby?"

"You can have it."

Mrs Lowry had looked at Maria with astonishment, as if she'd over-estimated her intelligence. "That's ridiculous, Maria."

"It has to be a secret."

They nibbled on sandwiches and on it went, one intense sentence after the other.

"Maria, you're such a total, incredible fool. I warned you!"

"You left me there alone."

"Were you forced? Were you forced?"

Maria was miserable and confused. "No," she finally said, twisting her napkin around her left hand.

They ate in silence for a time, until Mrs Lowry said wearily, "He's gone back to his Ruthie, Maria." This sentence seemed to dislodge her essential kindness and her tone grew gentler. "Nothing will change that, you know. And you're in trouble."

Both were true. Ruthie had summoned him back and he'd gone. *Thrilled*. And Maria was pregnant.

"You've got to help me then."

Mrs Lowry said she was sorry to lose her; she'd miss her competence. Her cooking. Said she dreaded the thought of training another girl to the point Maria was now.

Maria pushed her desperation at Mrs Lowry. Talked about her mother's tuberculosis and the shame it would be for them, her coming home in this state.

The owner of the café, a thin bald man in a large stained apron, had hurried over at one point to see if they needed anything else and waited even when they said no, looking from one to the other as if to offer his services as a mediator. Mrs Lowry shook her head at him impatiently.

Maria said, "I saved Bobby, remember?"

"You said that already."

"And he's – James Edward, I mean – he's your son."

"Not technically, if you really must know. My husband was married to my sister first. She died and then he married me. Only Bobby is mine by birth."

This information was new and startling; it explained Edith Lowry's relative youthfulness, but Maria refused to be distracted. "But you love him as your own," she insisted. "You're his mother."

"Of course I do. I promised my sister –"

"They can't know . . . You said you'd be grateful forever – about me saving Bobby."

After this battle, which they'd taken unsettled back to the house with them, Mrs Lowry conceded. She said she would figure something out. She agreed that no one would know. Shortly she'd decided to send Maria to her sister in Saskatchewan, to work for her, as if to do her a favour. She instructed Maria to write her parents that this was Mrs Lowry's temporary wish and that she, Maria, had been happy to do it. "Tell them there may be extra money in it," she said. Maria should also prepare them for her service ending in spring. ("I'm helping you now, but I'm not taking you back. Not after this.") Mrs Lowry informed her there was someone in her sister's vicinity who wanted a child.

These solutions seemed to animate Mrs Lowry. She said she'd take care of the documents and come along to her sister's place; it was a good excuse for a visit.

Now she turned pages, lost in her book, and Maria watched their progress over the prairie. Stops at stations along the way hinted at purpose, at significance – buildings painted red, the sheltering angles of wood roofs over platforms, the shouts of men loading and unloading luggage and boxes, the puffs of visible air when doors were opened and heat met cold. In one town a child was blowing and scraping at a peep-hole in the iced-over pane of the station's private quarters. Maria observed the child in parts, a mouth, a hand, an eye. She thought it was a girl, five or six years old perhaps. She remembered the advertisement: "Smiling faces, tender skins, Allenbury's Nursery Powder." She noticed these gestures of vitality but was unable to rouse herself from her apathy. Why get involved? The train pulled away and the things she had seen in the station ceased to matter as it gained speed.

Maria was careful about only one thing. She averted her eyes from names on signs or buildings that might reveal where they were. She knew, from the Mennonite newspapers, the places in Saskatchewan where her people had gone – *Rosthern Watrous Glenbush Herbert Hepburn Greenfarm Elim*. She had no idea where these settlements were situated, whether north or south, on this rail line or another, but if she landed near one of them, she didn't want to know it.

They were going to the farm of Mrs Lowry's sister; the farm was in Saskatchewan. That was all Maria knew, all she needed. She'd told Mrs Lowry not to mention the name of the place. "Don't give me the address. No information. As long as I can work there and stay inside the house." When the conductor came by with announcements of stops, she slid her hands up to cover her ears. Mrs Lowry attended to the tickets.

They travelled on, eating sandwiches in the middle of the day, but not speaking, not until Mrs Lowry finished her book. She clapped the cover closed. "Well," she said cheerfully, "that carried me quite away! Oh, but isn't the landscape dull in comparison." She was ready for conversation.

Maria shifted in her seat. "You told me everything is planned?"

"It's all arranged."

"My father knows many people . . . Our people, I mean, here in Canada. My mother is ill. It would kill her if she knew."

"I suspect she's hardier than that, Maria," Mrs Lowry said. "But I can assure you, my sister Gladys and her Martin won't be talking. That should be the least of your worries.

"They're good people," she continued. "They've suffered like everyone else in Saskatchewan, these years. Not that they'll admit it, mind you.

"*These* years," Mrs Lowry repeated, meaning the combination of unemployment, financial failure, crop failure and economic recession plaguing the entire country. She touched her fingers to her hair. "It gives me an awful feeling to think that hoboes may be clinging to the rods above our heads at this very moment."

"Do they ride passenger cars? Do they ride in the winter?"

"The thought of it," Mrs Lowry said impatiently. After a pause, "Oh, they're managing. He's decently established, his father came early. But it affects them, sure it does. The drought, the prices, the wind. You'll hear the complaints. He was working along in the Wheat Pool and I think it's collapsing. And I should warn you. Gladys may exhibit – oh, what shall I call it – a touch of oddness now and then. What's annoyed me, to be frank with you, Maria, there's a depression on and they buy a new radio. They buy a new chesterfield suite. I'll be called upon to admire it all and what am I going to say?" She took a biscuit out of the packet.

"Well, people are different I guess," Mrs Lowry said. "I've been lucky, to be sure, James can turn a single dollar into two but if it wasn't there, we wouldn't spend it, I can tell you that. We keep an eye on what we can afford. I've always considered what's possible."

Maria murmured in agreement but she jerked fitfully towards the window. Her reflection in the glass disappeared into the endless vista of patched snow and earth, into the stalks of dead grasses protruding like ragged upended brooms in the hollows.

Maria said, facing the glass, "I appreciate all you're doing for me in this situation."

In the silence that followed Maria supposed Mrs Lowry was thinking of something equally generous to say, something warm about the past nearly five years. She listened to the movement of the train, noticed how it separated into parts, one a faint monotonous clicking over the seams where the rails were joined, measuring their progress, and the other, a steady rolling hum of the iron wheels along the horizontal line, pulling forward. That sound strained ahead; the other resisted, marked time.

"Of course, I never expected it of you, Maria," Mrs Lowry said at last. "You presented us with another impression altogether. Perhaps I should have stuck to my resolve that very first day."

Saying this, Maria thought, was harsher than nothing at all. To respond to its errors and implications, to explain, however, was simply beyond her. That would need far more confidence and vocabulary than she'd gathered so far.

□

Mrs Lowry's brother-in-law, Martin Anderson, met them at the station. He drove them to the farm down a series of straight narrow roadways, mostly bare of snow though flanked here and there by grey and rutted drifts. The farm seemed a good distance from town.

She's gone visiting a Model T. Maria had come across the expression somewhere and James Edward explained it. It meant a girl, not married, off staying with relatives for a stretch of months – relatives she might not even have, but gone away under one pretence or another – to have a baby. The reason for it may have happened in the back seat of a Model T.

Martin's Model T sputtered, hobbled along, was

dreadfully cold inside. Just as Maria was beginning to despair of reaching their destination, the vehicle summoned the energy to turn and pull up a long lane, lined by a tall wide hedge that looked spectral and bereft without its leaves.

The house that came into Maria's view was a large, two-storey building with a verandah on one side. Its scale was grand but it seemed worn, as if it had tired of keeping up appearances. Its white exterior had not been renewed, it seemed, for a very long time. The barn, the storage sheds, the animal pens scattered behind it, were in similar condition. The entire collection was set on a slight rise of earth at the end of the lane. Maria spotted a patch of bush in the distance but there were no trees in the yard. The impression of the farm upon her, in spite of its solitary tiredness, however, was one of sympathetic compatibility with her own condition. It seemed a place that would demand very little of her.

Mrs Lowry's sister Gladys was a flurry of greetings and gaiety. She was a short woman, and fair-haired, in contrast to her older sibling. She pressed her hands around Maria's in welcome and said she'd been looking forward to meeting her very much. She searched Maria's face, as if trying to place her. She and Martin had visited the Lowrys in Winnipeg several years earlier, she laughed, but who noticed the Help?

Then she took Maria to a room upstairs, a square corner room with windows in two directions, which contained a single bed and a sewing machine cabinet as a table. "I hope you'll be comfortable here," Gladys said. "Please, make yourself comfortable." Her tone was imploring. She gestured towards a narrow cupboard in the corner, the doors open and shelves empty for Maria's things.

"My husband Martin was born in this room," she continued. "He grew up on this farm. He was an only child. We moved in with his parents when we married. There were never any problems with it, all of us living together. His parents were wonderful people. They're both gone now of course. Mother about a year ago now." She darted a hand over her mouth as if someone had just reminded her she was talking too much. "Oh, but I'll let you unpack," she said. She scurried out of the room.

The bed cover in Maria's room was a patchwork of squares: greens and yellows and browns. The only decoration was an embroidered motto on the wall at the foot of the bed: "Love makes the Home." The colours of the lines had faded to pale shades of themselves, except for the points where the thread punctured the cloth, still bright, a hint of how the motto looked when it was new.

Maria opened her case and realized there were no children in the house. She remembered the Andersons' visit to Winnipeg: Gladys' high spirits, their furious pace of shopping and amusements. That the two of them came alone. They had seemed to be in their thirties, certainly beyond the flush of young marriage. Maria had asked Bobby if his uncle and aunt left their children – his cousins – behind.

"They don't have children," he stated, chin thrust up proudly. "Not even one!"

Their childlessness. Two people alone on a farm. A large house. Suspicion immediately shaped itself into fact: Gladys and Martin must be the couple that was taking her baby.

This conjecture lifted, at least a little, the terrible sense of numbness Maria had been feeling for days. It gave her mind a small mystery to fasten upon. But she couldn't ask Mrs Lowry to confirm it. Mrs Lowry wouldn't tell her anything now, not after Maria had begged her to withhold every piece of information. Or, she would go on and on for paragraphs and not reveal a thing. She might haul out the sentence she employed when her children's excuses were flimsy: "You seem to have a weakness, my dear, for reaching conclusions that are wholly unwarranted!" She would remind Maria that she'd been adamant about her disinterest.

It was true, she didn't want to know. This knowledge had come to her in spite of herself.

☐

Maria liked Gladys and Martin, though she sensed that her own unhappiness prevented her from comprehending them plainly. They were shapes and sounds, impressions as if through leaded glass. They seemed kind. They seemed friendly. Solicitous. She was supposed to be working for them; they were her master and mistress these months but they seemed to possess no zeal for the roles. Rather, it seemed they were helping her. They all ate together, used first names. Mrs Lowry had warned Maria to be grateful and she wondered if she was showing it enough, but the intention was all she could manage; she wasn't sure if anything practical showed itself above the helpless prostration of her spirit.

She fulfilled her duties reflexively, bringing forward from long practice the servant's attentiveness. She learned where things belonged – plates here, cups there, pots over there. She learned Gladys' preferences. The farm routines. She'd always been quick at picking things up, at imitation.

The first major task was cleaning the house, Gladys said, and then they would tackle the Christmas baking. "Are you up to it?" she probed. "If we give the place a thorough cleaning for Christmas? I'm afraid I didn't get to a fall cleaning. Or a spring one. I must confess, I hate to clean. Getting your room emptied for you is the biggest cleaning I've accomplished for years."

"I'm up to it," Maria said. "I'm feeling fine."

They worked together. Gladys was almost jovial over dirt, cobwebs, and stains they encountered. She expressed no indignation, no good-riddance. She was more concerned that Maria not tire herself. "Don't work too hard now. Not too hard," she would insist. She made Maria rest from washing walls, ceilings, floors, and cupboards up to two hours every afternoon.

"You don't want to strain yourself," she said, "and lose the baby."

Lose the baby? I wouldn't mind losing the baby, thought Maria. She'd defied Mrs Lowry over the medicine in the bottle, not wanting an end to the affair, needing its evidence. (Of what? Her love, their love, her fault, his?) But now, without fantasies or hopes, she wouldn't mind. Hearing Gladys' constant worries, she wondered, could it happen that easily? Could one lose a child by cleaning?

So she gave herself completely to her work; she strained, stretched, and hurried, daring her body to punish her. Nothing untoward happened. She grew weary, slept soundly. That was all.

Perhaps cleaning's effect was cumulative. She waited.

They all seemed to be waiting. After his chores Martin worked at the kitchen table, bent over a sheaf of papers he pulled out of a drawer, shuffling them, making notations. Maria supposed they were his farm records, but the way his back curved over them, she sensed it was more ritual than work.

Once he lifted his head and asked, "Can you figure it out? Drought and heat, and that's when it rains without stopping in China. They have those terrible floods. It's like something's gone crazy in the world . . . Do you know what it's like to see the crops green, and filling out?"

Maria and Gladys were washing up the dishes and both of them had glanced at him, but it wasn't them, it seemed, as much as the room he was asking. "Mid-June, we're halfway there, you're holding your breath. The heat and dust storms come, dust so thick you can't see the barn from the house. It's too hot to sleep, but that's not the reason, you're worrying over the crops, and you just know every time you turn in bed, they're shrinking in the heat of it too. Course the sunset's been beautiful every night. The dust makes them glorious. If you could make a living from beauty. You're thinking, well the rainbow's a lovely sight too, how about a rainbow. How about some rain."

"Oh Martin, I know what you mean," Gladys soothed from the sink.

"The skies heavy with clouds twenty-four hours at a stretch. Night or day, you'd check, and there they were, low, like they were touching the roof. But not a drop. Not a drop of rain. The clouds moved on."

Maria also knew what he meant, she understood that helplessness. These laments weren't new. She was thinking of her father. She could have said, "Well there's always next year," but she knew Martin would eventually say it himself. Every disappointed farmer said it at the end of his worrying, like Amen at the end of a prayer.

Gladys changed the subject. "Maria, you'll have noticed, I'm sure, we haven't had our children yet. Perhaps it's just as well, with the crops these years." Her tone was blithe and hearty. "Lots of time for children, my mother-in-law always said. She had to wait for her Martin too. She'd always say, 'and certainly worth the wait, wouldn't you say?'"

She pivoted and spoke in his direction. "Remember Martin, how your mother would say, 'Worth the wait, wouldn't you say?'"

Martin didn't look up. Perhaps he hadn't heard her; perhaps he felt he'd responded to this observation often enough. The fears and assurances of waiting waved about them, like streamers in the wind. The strange wavering fears and assurances of waiting.

□

Maria was afraid through all of December. Her position seemed relatively safe, her alibis sure, but she was still afraid she'd be discovered.

What if her parents, through some bizarre intervention, found themselves suddenly rich – rich and healthy and confident enough to journey from Manitoba to find her, to carry her home in triumph? What if there was some emergency, some unstoppable longing that sent them searching for her, checking? What if her mother had a premonition of Maria's state, confronted Mrs Lowry, forced everything out of her?

Maria's sense of danger increased when December's temperatures turned unusually warm and Martin said the mild weather conditions were true throughout the western provinces. Maria had counted on deep cold, on heaps of snow, to impede mobility, postpone activity. It even rained one day, a fine, intermittent drizzle, and Gladys told her that someone had spotted a butterfly; her friends had mentioned this novelty at the social on Saturday. "Butterflies in December!" Gladys said, delighted. "Can you imagine?"

If her parents came, Maria's secret could not be hidden. She hadn't thought ahead – at least not clearly enough – to the signs. No one told her what to expect, that the landscape of her body would alter this drastically. Her mother, she thought, hadn't changed that much when she was pregnant, but of course Maria never knew her as a young woman, slender, pregnant for the first time. Maria's breasts had grown larger, softer, weaker, the nipples darkened. A network of delicate blue veins like streams had risen to the skin. The lump under her pelvic bone grew upwards towards her navel, stretched the tiny pit into level ground. On her abdomen, pinkish streaks had appeared, like tracings of granite. She felt herself visible in a new way and couldn't fit into her clothes. She had two second-hand maternity outfits Mrs Lowry had produced for her from somewhere, which she wore, alternating. Neither of them, she thought, suited her.

Hanging the laundry one afternoon, Maria heard the dog erupt in a flurry of barking and realized they'd come. She dropped the clothespin in her hand and dashed inside, collapsing against the porch door, breathing noisily.

Gladys heard the commotion and came running. "Are you sick?" She seized Maria's arm. "Tell me, are you in pain?"

"No." But her heart pounded. "No."

"What's the matter then? What happened?"

"I heard the dog and it frightened me. It's nothing."

Gladys stepped to the porch window, surveyed the lane. "There's nothing Maria. There's no one coming. No one will find you. You're safe here. Really." She looked at Maria and her forehead wrinkled with concern. "Come, sit down."

Maria protested, ashamed that Gladys had guessed the reason for her reaction, but she allowed herself to be guided to a chair. "Don't get up," Gladys commanded. "I'm going to make you a cup of tea!"

She filled the kettle. "We've got to take care of you," she said. "Pregnancy brings changes and frights of all sorts. Stay sitting.

"Stay!" Gladys repeated, though Maria hadn't moved.

Gladys placed the tea before Maria in a sky-blue china cup. The tea was sweet and milky, prepared the way Gladys drank it. She'd forgotten that Maria didn't take milk in her tea. But the sweet creamy liquid tasted good and her breathing and heartbeat calmed. How foolish she'd been, jumping like a gunshot because that harmless old hound had barked. Dogs will bark at anything. Perhaps he was worrying a butterfly. (In December!)

"Look," Gladys coaxed, pulling a chair beside Maria, opening the farm paper, pointing to an advertisement. She pointed and read, "A real organ grinder's monkey with a smart red collar and a gay red cap. Very brown and warm and furry, and quite ready to dance, when he's held by the string. 75 cents.

"Isn't that sweet?" Gladys giggled. She meant to distract Maria. She'd tried it other times, when the afternoons waned and she ran out of chores for Maria to do. "Look," she'd say, reaching for the catalogue, opening to the toys and showing her a train set, a truck, little wooden figures, dolls named Patsy Ann. "Look," she'd say, "they have such lovely things for babies. For children." Was this a family trait, the search for diversion in the miniscule? It reminded her of James Edward and his collectibles, his marbles, his "Look, Look!" Beguiling her with objects.

Gladys left Maria to contemplate the organ grinder's monkey and went outside to finish hanging the clothes. "Stay!" she'd said. Maria watched her through the window, the sturdy body bending to the basket of wet things, straightening and reaching to pin, bending again. Like a mechanical doll, up and down. Short determined jerks.

"Look!" Maria muttered aloud to herself, watching Gladys finish the job she'd been doing and drinking tea as Gladys liked it, their positions reversed. "Look. The tiny woman goes up and down." She felt unaccountably vicious.

She watched Gladys finish the clothes, saw her walk across the yard to the barn. She saw Martin saunter from the barn to meet her, the two of them standing and talking. She had no sounds to identify what they talked about, just their little steps backwards and forwards and sideways, and their movements, Gladys' arm lifting, the slight shift of her head to indicate laughter, his hand pointing at something in the field. Their gestures and words weaving in and out. She was telling him of Maria's foolish fright, no doubt. Or perhaps it was something as mundane, as ordinary, as the weather, or the antics of one of the animals. But to have this daily conversation, the comfort of belonging, each other!

But how sudden the shock she'd just experienced, how sudden and unexpected, how momentous the effects. Would the palpitations have been enough? Probably not: they'd been too short. The changes pregnancy brought to her body might be soft and curved but they also seemed tenacious. But I wouldn't mind, Maria thought, if I was frightened so much that it loosened. If I were jolted, if the child disappeared, if I lost it. Spontaneously. God willing, of course.

Maria closed her eyes. She'd mocked Gladys. Unfairly. Gladys, so anxious to help, to protect her from harm, and Maria? She craved an accident, the sight of blood. She always peered at her undergarments when she urinated, yearning for a sign, a smudge. More than that, a clot. Now she held her teacup in both hands, pressed it against her lips and imagined the journey of the tiny fetus, imprecise and shaggy (the size of a peach or a potato perhaps?) loosening and swimming down in a rivulet of blood. Declaring, ah, here I am, and you're finished with me now. Maria wished it would tug away, set out, come and die. The sensation of that lump slipping through the tunnel from her womb would be ecstasy, she thought. She could go home, delivered.

But Gladys – Maria was even more sure of it now! – would be bitterly disappointed.

□

On Christmas Day, Maria rose early, with Gladys. She helped Gladys get the turkey into the oven. She made soup of the turkey neck and feet and giblets. She peeled the potatoes and set the table. When everything was ready and Gladys caught sight of the first vehicle at lane's end, Maria climbed up to her room as they'd arranged and turned the key to lock it.

Martin's three cousins and their families were coming from some other place in Saskatchewan. "Have some dinner," Gladys told Maria. But she was elated and flustered with the prospect of her guests and needed Maria's help to the last moment. Maria wasn't hungry anyway; she was exhausted.

It was barely noon but she undressed for bed. Beneath her she heard the merry calls, the excitement. More families arrived, with further excitement, and soon the house sounded full. Children ran up and down the stairs, even tried her locked door, but Maria slept and woke, slept and woke.

She dreamed strange dreams. She'd taken possession of a house, a small house set on a vast tract of what seemed to be flatland, though it was shadowed, as if mountains lurked nearby, and behind them, other hostilities. The inadequacy of the dwelling dismayed her; she'd been promised something better and she was angry at someone – the seller perhaps? – who had misled her. Once installed in the house, however, she found there were many more rooms than the exterior revealed. They led from one to the other and branched off corridors as far as she could see. She wandered through them with growing frustration. Every room needed repair.

The rooms were full of people. They were playing cards around tables, singing around pianos. A choir practiced in one of the rooms, a man plucked at a guitar in another. No one seemed to notice how decrepit the surroundings were. She shouted at them to get to work, to fix and clean, and they glanced up briefly but paid no further attention.

Maria woke from these explorations, disturbed by them, and slipped back eagerly to her uneasy sleep, to the house of her dreams, as if something could be salvaged. She reached a modern kitchen. The table was set. She counted the settings: twelve of them. The room moved as if on a train, passing beautiful scenes – trees, lakes, huge patches of flowers lit with the most brilliant sunshine imaginable. The scenery distracted her from her obligations to prepare for her company. It gripped her as a spell. The guests were arriving any moment and she wasn't dressed. She couldn't find her way back through the maze of rooms to her closet. She knew there was a red dress hanging there that she'd not yet worn.

Maria woke again, sorry that she'd woken and wouldn't know who was coming to dinner. It seemed to her that James Edward had been expected as a guest. She tried to drift asleep once more over the noise of the Andersons and their relatives. They seemed to be having a wonderful time. Laughter rolled up through the floorboards like water beating against the floating dream box of her room. She didn't mind that she was alone at Christmas this year. Any impulse by her family to see her, any unusual curiosity would pass with the season. She'd reached a major crossing safely.

□

The next morning Maria rose early again, long before Gladys and Martin got up. She was thoroughly sated with sleep. She tiptoed downstairs with her German Bible and made herself porridge and coffee. The house was askew with the previous day's excess. Cold cigarette butts filled the ashtrays and the house smelled stale. Maria ate, then read the Christmas story in German. She also read it in English, from the large family Bible in the sitting room. Then she wrote her family a letter.

> *My dear family,* she wrote, *greetings. This is the season of Christ's birth. Even though I am far from you, I can reflect on the truths of these days and be with you all in my heart. Don't be anxious, or pity me. Today I read, "To give light to them that sit in darkness and in the shadow of death, to guide our feet into the way of peace." These days I have been busy baking. The house here was full of guests for Christmas. We made English recipes and also some of mine. The pffeffernuesse I made (and taught Gladys to make) were much appreciated. Don't you think it is generous of the Lowrys to help their loved ones through me in this way? It has not been unpleasant to be in the country instead of the city for a while. As you know, I was not unwilling for a change in location. But my thoughts are to the future. I was very hopeful, Father, at your last letter's reference to North Kildonan. You may recall that when I heard of the new settlement several years ago I mentioned it to you. I urge you to explore the possibilities. I have also been thinking along these lines: that spring would be a good time for me to end my service for the Lowrys and*

return to the family. If you were in North Kildonan this
would be easier. I could find a day job, either in service
or at a factory, which I believe would pay a little more.
I know that Mother has been waiting patiently to draw
the family around her again. Mrs Lowry has intro-
duced another girl to her household while I am here,
so I think spring will be a suitable time for me to leave
my service for them without upsetting their routine. Let
us look forward to spring, and consider this seriously.
Continue to address your letters to Mrs Lowry, as I do,
for forwarding. Packets go back and forth on a regular
basis and she suggested this was the easiest way for us
to communicate. She told me she had written you about
my work here. Your loving daughter and sister, Maria.

It was awkward to write letters from Saskatchewan.
Letters left tracks. This one sounded more pious than she
had a right to sound, perhaps, but the Scripture quotation
filled some space. And surely it was rich and full of meaning.

Maria was relaxed this morning. Contented. Christmas
was over and they hadn't found her.

She began to clean up the clutter of the Christmas Day
celebration. She wanted Gladys and Martin to sleep as long
as possible. She would surprise them, like an elf on the sly,
everything tidied by the time they woke. She wondered
about the animals but decided the barn chores were none
of her business. Perhaps once in the year the animals could
wait. She padded silently about the house, straightening and
putting away and washing the dishes left unwashed, amazed
how quickly everything could be accomplished, how rested
and full of joy she was.

When she finished, she decided to return to her bed.
Gladys and Martin had still not stirred. Crawling under her
covers, Maria felt a tremor – slight, but distinct – below her
belly. She'd felt this before but now she understood what it
was. It was the child. It reminded her of bubbles bursting,

or ripples that follow the plunk of a pebble in water, or the flutter of wings. Of all these things.

Maria was astonished. Someone within her had moved and spoken. Not she, but someone else. So this is how the child speaks, she thought, this is how it says "I'm alive." She lifted her nightgown and put her hands, both of them, over the fluttering place. The little bird, she was thinking. The little turtledove. These expressions were gurgles and coos of her own but they were only names, endearments. She wasn't thinking of a bird at all, but of someone human, like herself.

Maria sat amazed, unmoving, her hands on her belly, allowing the unexpected miracle to ring through her being as long as it would take. She felt her fingers merge with her skin, as if they were burrowing lines into the womb. Her awe might cloud over in a moment, the problems of her situation re-assert themselves, but she waited, savouring as long as possible. Like the time at Victoria Beach, the *aurora borealis*, Mr Lowry urging the children out, explaining, and she listening for a while, then slipping away and finding her own spot alone on the cliff, nearly running along the path to get to the little nook she knew in the trees, private and with a view of water and sky, to watch without any explanation the mysterious green dance of the lights across the sky. It was wonderful beyond words and when she became aware of herself she discovered her hands were clasped. *Oh God . . . oh, oh God*, their posture had seemed to be saying.

And now she was bound again with wide-eyed awe: the little one is a butterfly, twisted out of his chrysalis. He's stretching and hardening and lifts into the air. He alights. He or she alights on me. I'm a flower and I've opened just in time. *When Elizabeth heard the salutation of Mary, the babe leaped in her womb.* But it's I who leap, Maria thought: the child greets me, and perfectly still, I'm leaping.

□

"I know this place is nothing like my sister's," Gladys said.

"It has a good situation," Maria assured her. "On a bit of a hill."

"A bit!" Gladys chuckled. "That's right!"

"The upstairs windows. As if you could see the world," Maria explained. She meant, as if this was how the world ought to be seen, in broad sweeps where nothing was hidden on the way to the distant horizon, from any window one might choose. And in the summer, sashes lifted, the possibility of placing one's elbows on the sills and daydreaming again. She would be gone by summer and wouldn't have a chance to do it.

"Very nice thought," Gladys said gratefully. "What I'm thinking of though, is that I'd hoped to keep the chesterfield nice, and the chair. I covered them at the beginning but it wasn't practical and we're using them every day. Now they're showing the wear, wouldn't you say?"

"They're very comfortable."

Gladys sighed. "Well, we're not in the city. I tell myself that. But it bothers me sometimes, you know, thinking it's not like Edith's at all. I'm sure you've noticed."

"I like it just as well," Maria said.

"Do you mean that?"

"I do."

Of course Maria had noticed the contrasts. And all of them favoured the Lowrys. Favoured the city, which in truth she missed as well. "A dear house," Mrs Lowry would say, a compliment meaning it was well below her standards. It needed papering, modernization, an overhaul in every room. The plumbing was rudimentary.

Maria shared Mrs Lowry's standards, but she'd surrendered them for now. She liked the shabbiness, creaks, and worn experience of this grand old house. Its air of humility. The fact it was wood, not brick. It better suited remorse, she thought. Expiation.

Its unevenness, its mixture of the old and new, filled in around her, around the waiting and her womb, a house of smells, odours that gathered and faded, that met and left her again as she passed from room to room, coming down the stairs or going up them: cheap varnish and dusting oils, tools and rope, the foliage of geraniums, beans on the stove, sour milk, and perspiration. Piled yellowing newspapers. Dust. The dust crept into the house even in winter; on very windy days it was rubbed loose from the frozen bare patches on the fields around the house. It layered on everything and embedded itself in the new chesterfield and chair, where it released whiffs of fine, dry earth when they sat down too quickly.

There was a sharp smell of liniment, medicinal remedies, wine. Smells from the barn, of hay and animals and manure. Damp wool socks and mittens and scarves, wet wool drying. Maria loved the smell of their clothes in from the line, fresh and clean. Even when they came in stiff from the cold and collapsed in the warm kitchen, they smelled of the sun, seemed to belong to other times beyond her pregnancy, far beyond the coming birth.

Catalogue orders had entered the rooms with a haphazard flourish. In the sitting room, the chesterfield suite, moss green, plump and round. The handsome walnut console radio receiver with its bevelled panels, standing on its short legs like a short stout gentleman, swelling with a dignity hard to contain, as if it knew it was the most elegant thing in the house, in a class by itself.

The radio receiver was the reason Gladys' wish to keep the sofa unused and the ottoman in its place could never be fulfilled. The radio drew Gladys and Martin into the room and relaxed all the formal inclinations they wished to possess. They drifted there evenings like children after the piper, for the comedy and music hours, the preachers and the politicians. They turned on the radio and twisted their bodies and limbs into the furniture in order to be comfortable as they were taken away into other worlds from their ordinary ones. They were enchanted and Martin would start to tip and fall asleep.

"Your house is comfortable," Maria said.

"I hope you don't mind that I gave you the smallest room."

"It's not that small. It's plenty."

"You're in the room where Martin was born. It's going to be the birth room. The other room, the bigger spare one, well, you've seen it. It's such a clutter. So many of his parents' things. They moved out of the big room when we married, insisted we take it. Said it was the master's room. Insisted. We haven't bought much ourselves, you know, just the radio and the chesterfield suite. I'm bumping into something of theirs at every turn . . . There's not a day goes by I don't think of those two one way or another."

"I guess you miss them."

"Well, you live with them, you miss them when they're gone." Gladys was knitting and stopped to count stitches. "My own family, we were four of us. A boy, and then three girls. I'm the youngest of them all. We grew up in Ontario. But I imagine Edith's told you all about us."

"She hasn't said that much."

"Charles is still there. Doing well, though I couldn't tell you exactly what. A rather lot of everything. Business, I suspect. No unemployment in his life. No drought, no grasshoppers . . . Just between us, Maria, they might be feeling a little sorry for Martin and me occasionally, but it's nothing of his fault, the prices and all. And he does love farming. Martin goes a long way back, you know, same as everyone, to good family I mean, up through the States. Solid people. In that way we're all alike. It makes it easier if your backgrounds are the same, wouldn't you say?"

Maria grunted her assent and Gladys carried on. "Adela was the oldest. A beauty. That was her ticket, I guess.

It filtered down a little, you know, through Edith and me. Mostly used up by the time it got to me." Gladys gave a hearty laugh, as if nature's tricks were hilarious.

"Adela's death was dreadful, you know, a young wife and mother. It certainly made it easier that Edith was there to fill her place. It kept the children and James in the family. We were so proud of Edith. The way she took over. She took on James Edward and the girls as if she'd borne them herself. We used to say, she loves them fiercely! Fiercely. You know what I mean? Really, it was as if Adela had never left them motherless, except of course, Edith wasn't Adela. They were really quite different, Edith and Adela . . .

"But I knew she was longing for one of her own. The others were Adela's and Adela was such a star. Edith never said so exactly, but I could tell. I saw her often then. I wondered if James wasn't against it at first. He'd watched Adela suffer, after all. Sometimes it closes you up a little. Edith understood that, she was very good. She's determined though. I'm sure you've noticed. Well, she got her Bobby. He made her life complete. I saw her when she was carrying him and she absolutely glowed. At least to me it was all very clear. A little sister grows up watching . . . I could tell. I was there when that baby was born, did you know? I've never seen anything like it. You'd think she woke up and found herself in heaven. I don't mean to frighten you Maria, but that birth was something else, the pain and all. But she was gritting her teeth and never made a complaint, no noise, nothing, and when it was over, she couldn't move but she laughed as if ready to dance!"

So Mrs Lowry didn't make a sound, Maria thought. And neither will I.

"Oh yes, her dear and desperately longed-for Bobby," Gladys went on. "Her Bobby. And then she nearly lost him in the water. Except that you saved him for her. The whole family heard the story! I imagine it's why she's been so willing to help you and everything."

Gladys concluded with a contented cluck. "So it's working out for everyone."

□

Martin left for the North. Gladys said, rather vaguely, that he got an employment contract and would be gone several weeks and that it was fortunate she had Maria for company. "Times being what they are, he jumped at the opportunity," she said.

Until now the evenings had belonged to the Andersons. They occupied the sitting room, listened to the radio. When Maria joined them she felt herself a stranger, as if the setting sun had thrown up a wall between them that wasn't there during the day. In spite of their polite invitations to stay, Maria usually excused herself to read or embroider alone in her room, or to sleep, while the pleasant murmur of their fond though intermittent conversation and the sounds of the radio drifted up to her.

Gladys' invitations were more pressing now and Maria sensed she was afraid to be alone. She stayed downstairs with her until they both retired to bed. They spent the evenings knitting. From a commode in the spare room Gladys had produced a pile of sweaters to unravel and re-wind into balls for new garments or blankets or rugs. Each of the old sweaters had a history connected in some way to her husband's parents – histories that Gladys explained. The brown one, for example, was never worn: her mother-in-law made it to celebrate the return of an older cousin of Martin's, name of Albert, serving in the War; he'd survived until then, and not without valour either, and just a month before armistice, he was killed. What to do with the sweater? Her mother-in-law cradled it in her arms and cried over it, then put it away, as if she hoped Albert would come by later to claim it.

"I think we can say it's not going to be used by him," said Gladys, "and it's a little old-fashioned looking, wouldn't you agree? It's not Martin's fit either, though I know he'd never wear it, even if it was, out of consideration for his cousin and his mother. He watched it coming together. It took her a time to finish anything, and every time she'd pick it up again, she'd repeat his entire biography. Albert was her sister's boy. They hailed from Manitoba I believe, though I've forgotten that for sure. They were all so proud of him, going off to serve. So by the time it was finished, a month before he died, she'd knitted his life into it, over and over. Not a long life, of course. She was a talker, Martin's mother was. As much as I am I guess. Both of us talkers with our quiet men. The two of us, we got along fine."

When the unravelling was completed, Gladys said, "What if we used the lighter wool for some children's or baby's things? As gifts and such. We could . . . we could send a few things along with the baby."

This was fine with Maria, so every evening Gladys closed the outside doors, drew the curtains tightly together, and they sat down to knit, interrupting their labours only for a mid-evening cup of tea. Gladys seemed to feel the radio was Martin's prerogative; she seldom turned it on with Maria in the room. They sat on either end of the chesterfield, both sets of feet stretched to the single ottoman. Maria's fear of detection had eased considerably since Christmas, but Gladys checked all the doors again while Maria made the tea.

"I know of girls," Gladys said on one of their January evenings, "heard of them anyway, girls in your position, rushing into marriages because they're in the family way and once the excitement is over, people settle down over it. Once everyone has told everyone else. Those without sin casting stones as it were, but most often letting them fall. Most of them do eventually."

"I'm not getting married."

"I've heard of girls not married and it's the same thing," Gladys said. She repeated the drift of the argument, that people settled down over scandals and life went on.

Maria considered this and wondered what Gladys wished to convey, or wished to know. She said, "My father, he's a preacher. He's a farmer, but he preaches too. On occasion. My mother –"

"They'd turn you out?"

"Not turn me out . . . But everyone would say, look at the Klassens' Maria . . . They'd have to account for themselves. I'd have to account for myself – in the church.

"My mother was poor," Maria continued. "She offered her life to God and that's when things changed in a way that amazed everyone but her . . . my father's proposal, I mean, and –"

Maria stopped. She'd said too much. It wasn't relevant either. "So," she said. "So." A feeble ending but she hoped Gladys was satisfied.

The needles of both women clicked for several minutes before Gladys said, "Well, I suppose it's more complicated if you're really religious. In an obvious way, I mean . . .

"Not that we're not religious," Gladys went on. "Don't get me wrong on that. I understand what you're saying."

Perhaps she understood, perhaps she didn't. For it to really make sense, Mother would have to be here. If Gladys knew Mother, the need for secrecy would be clear. Mother often said, "I always knew I was destined for something better." Mother loved her children and never scrupled to say so. Children, she would quote, *a heritage of the Lord, the fruit of the womb, a reward.* How wonderful they were, these children – her children.

But would she have pride to spare for an illegitimate child?

"My mother suffers from tuberculosis, and she had a baby in spring. She's not well," Maria said. "Not well at all."

"I'm not saying it wouldn't be a shock among us too," Gladys said. "I know what you mean . . . I guess you couldn't have married the lad?"

So had Edith Lowry protected herself and James Edward as well?

Maria answered that it hadn't been possible.

"Well, there's something for others out of it," Gladys said. "That's worth considering. Those who are getting the baby will be happy." She spoke slowly now, as if examining her words before letting them go. "Hard for you, but something good . . . for others."

"Do you know them then?"

Gladys hesitated. "Yes," she said. "Yes, I'd say so. They'll be good to the child."

Maria gave her a searching glance. She heard anxiety in Gladys' voice and now she saw it on her face. Gladys was barren. How obvious it was! Dry and useless, plump at the middle, but not from child. Her expression announced her defeat.

Maria set down the sleeve of the toddler's jacket she was constructing and yawned. She stroked her swelling womb as if examining the ripeness of a fruit. She was tall and well-proportioned, young and unlined, bulging beautifully in the way a woman should. How fertile she was! She saw Gladys turn slightly, knew she'd seen the hand move over the child in his cocoon and despised what she'd tried, and succeeded at, provoking: the other woman's envy.

Maria picked up her knitting again. Her thoughts tightened like a fist. What good was English family, a cheerful disposition, language and possessions, everything Gladys and Martin Anderson and James and Edith Lowry had, set beside barrenness? Even Hagar found a well in the desert, cold water in dark cold depths. Even she was useful, while the barren Sarah watched, weak with longing. *Sarai said of her maidservant, Perhaps I shall be built from her.* It robbed Sarah's judgement, diminished her, turned matters upside down: the maid into mistress.

Maria thought that Gladys might have answered the question – "You and Martin are taking the child, isn't that so?" – if Maria had asked it. But she didn't need to ask. Gladys was dependent on her, deeply in her debt, because of the baby. She was trying to repay her with her various remarks and attempts to understand. The bright "Oh, we'll have our children yet" a thin veneer, webbed with cracks. Maria recalled the unnatural, high pitch of these utterances.

"You're probably right," Maria said carefully. "People would get used to it, after the shock. Maybe I should keep the child. Go home with it. You may be right . . ." She let it hang in the air, then, "I wonder if it's possible to withdraw from the papers I signed. Do you know if that's possible?"

She sensed that Gladys' body tensed; she heard the halt of the needles.

"Well," Gladys began, releasing excess air on the word, "the people would be disappointed. I . . . Naturally they're in great anticipation. I mean . . .

"Well, it's your decision," Gladys said after a while, her floundering replaced by a calm tone and overlaid with a smile. "I mean, they would give the child a very good home. That's what I meant, that they'd be disappointed."

But the fear hadn't been expunged. Abruptly, Gladys wound her work around the needles and thrust it and her ball of yarn into the satchel beside her. "I think I'll get to bed now," she said. She nearly stumbled as she left the room. Maria pretended not to notice.

□

Maria couldn't sleep. Over and over the accusation: You're the one!

She fought it. Which one? What are you talking about? *That cruelty. That horrible cruelty. You think she'll be his mother in your stead. Not knowing for sure is secrecy's price and you wanted to pay it. Then you want knowledge as well. Power. You have it and beat her with it. You think you know she'll be his mother. She'll be as good as you would be. Better perhaps. You uncovered her envy because you're also envious' of her. You know what you did, how stricken she blundered upstairs. She was stricken.*

You despised her. Thought her afflicted by God – because she's barren. Thought yourself blessed – better – because you're not!

This conviction was stronger than any Maria had ever felt before, the pierce of angry words within her almost physical in thrust, as if another voice, even more angry than her conscience. She acknowledged the charges as true but the picture of what she'd done to Gladys still wouldn't disappear. Then she crept out of her bed and knelt on the floor. She pushed the rug aside, stretched her arms along the chilled wooden surface, felt them protest the cold. She waited until they were as cold as she could bear. She prayed for mercy.

But then she had to creep along the hall and knock at Gladys' door. It was a timid knock; if Gladys didn't answer, she would wait until the morning.

"Yes?" The voice was clear and wide awake.

Maria pushed the door slightly ajar. "Oh Gladys," she said in a rushed tone, "I'm terribly sorry to bother you, but I just wanted to say, I really don't know what I was thinking earlier. Last evening, I mean. You know about taking the child home with me. It's impossible. I've really not changed my mind."

"I understand, Maria." The sentence sprang out of the darkness with surprising authority. As if Gladys was used to people offering nighttime confessions at her door.

"I don't know what I was thinking," Maria said. "I certainly won't be changing my mind."

"You go to sleep now," Gladys said. "Sleep well now, you hear?" Her "Goodnight" was muffled behind a blanket, but it seemed a benediction and a pardon.

□

The sewing machine was biding its time in Maria's room. But in the middle of February it was fitted with a spool and bobbin of thread and Maria began to sew. Her facility with knitting and embroidery had given Gladys the idea and once she was possessed of it, her zeal on Maria's behalf was boundless. "I think you might have a gift for dressmaking, for costuming, clothes, you know! An aptitude for – for, textiles!"

The evidence seemed scanty. Several knitted child's things by now, a pair of pillowcases and three tea towels, all of bleached flour sacks, hemmed on Mrs Lowry's old machine before she came, "fancied up" as Gladys would say, with flowers, butterflies, puppies, scroll-like lines. Maria was making them as gifts for Mother or her sisters. She was consistent and particular, but didn't think her skills unusual. Gladys pressed her assessment. "Look at your hands," she said, "your long fingers compared to mine. No wonder."

"I learned some sewing from a woman in Russia," Maria owned. "Everything by hand, though. She made little bonnets that the elderly women wore."

"I hate sewing, I really do. It goes so slowly and never turns out as I'd imagined. I don't mind knitting, but really, my talent is the garden. I don't want you thinking I can't do anything," Gladys laughed. "I do have *that* talent at least."

Maria's first pieces by machine – a smock for herself and pants for Martin – aroused Gladys to further excitement. She would find fabric, she said, and use Maria to bring their wardrobes into order. Maria could make things for the future as well. They were running out of housework; the walls had been washed and there were weeks to go before the Easter baking.

Gladys returned from a trip to town with a pile of second-hand goods. "We're not living in clover, I've got to admit, but I didn't come to these used things by walking up and saying we needed them, that's for sure. I had to make some excuses.

Good thing I have friends where I need them." She sniffed at the clothes derisively. "Some do-gooder town in Ontario filled up a boxcar. All their mothballed things for parched Saskatchewan."

She pulled out a long pale green dress, ruffled, gilded, lined with petticoats. "What do you think the cows would do if they saw me coming on with this?"

"But we could take it apart. We could –" The pieces were coming open and back together in another arrangement in Maria's mind.

"That's what I was hoping you'd say, Maria! We could make me a frock, Maria! I haven't had anything new in I don't know how long!"

Maria had an eye for it all right, how fabric could be draped and turned, fashioned to advantage. The dress came out beautifully, and then Maria was called upon to comment on everything in Gladys' closet, to offer suggestions for alterations, trims, and accessories. Gladys agreed with everything Maria proposed.

Gladys returned from an afternoon away to visit friends with another sack of used things. Her voice was affectedly casual. "You know, Maria, you could make babies' and children's things. Little coats and so on. You know what I mean?"

"But there's no one to fit them against."

"I've got patterns, pictures. A doll or two. You've got ideas. You're here anyway, Maria. Edith told me to keep you busy."

◻

The sewing machine stood in front of the south-facing window. The low winter sun warmed Maria's arms and her bent head and the pretty black body of the Singer. There was nothing anywhere, not in the empty snow-patched fields or the clear pale sky to impede or distract her. How different the landscape seemed than the day she'd travelled across it from Winnipeg. The open spread of plain and sky felt strangely sheltering now. It was a contradiction. The place with nowhere to hide had become a refuge. Sewing, and so much time to think.

When had she lost her way?

There was no answer in tearing seams open, or in stitching them together. Was it the city's fault? Sister Anna said the city was a maelstrom. She said Winnipeg was the Indian name for "muddy waters."

Or was it simpler than that? Maria had imagined herself living as the Lowrys did. Not a servant. She'd tacked a picture onto her wall of the Prince of Wales riding a horse on his ranch in Alberta. And a pretty scene of Naples. She could name the pride, the covetousness in herself. But her involvement with James Edward was harder to define. She couldn't find the vice that contained him. Or the two of them. She tried not to be angry with him, to forget that he'd left without a word, that he'd not meant what he said. But what had he said that he could be blamed for? She missed him and he'd humiliated her by not missing her in return.

She'd fallen short of how marriage was supposed to be, how it was supposed to begin, but weren't there parts of it, still, worth receiving? In the sleeping porch, surrounded by green, the way he listened? The way he said her name? Maria in English. But she'd been robbed.

She needed a Solomon to send a sword through it all, to divide the parts that were wrong, the parts that were pure, the parts she could rightfully look at and those she should bury without another glimpse, ever! She needed a Solomon badly. When the two women came arguing with a living baby that each of them claimed and a dead one neither one wanted, he said, well, cut the living child in half, and each of you can have a piece. And the woman who spoke the truth was broken with love for her infant son and cried, oh my lord, give her the child! Don't kill him! But the woman who lied said, fine, divide him then. So they knew who the real mother was.

Maria needed someone to say, you can dwell on this but not that, it simply increases your need of forgiveness, going over it again and again. Sometimes, it seemed, she was assessing it all in front of everyone she knew. People from Minlertschik, Tschongraw, Winkler, wherever her people lived. Her father and mother, Gerhard and Helene, Sister Anna, all the Mary-Martha girls. Even Uncle Peter. Voices like blackbirds. Curious and sceptical. Picking at her sin like chickens at corn. Reminding her that the sinner shouldn't weigh the evidence, or assume forgiveness too quickly. When a woman opened her mouth on a point of theology, they cawed at her, it should be heard with suspicion. *For she was deceived.* If Maria picked up her own sword to discern, wouldn't it slice at the wrong place?

She would be tempted to justify herself. To claim greater mercy than allowed in cases such as these. She'd already been tempted to too much joy on account of the child, because he was alive. She imagined the child a boy. Well, it might just as well be a girl. *Talitha kum*, she would say then, *little girl, arise.* Soon-living, risen from the sleep of her womb, the dark grave, released from her. How could she condemn the child? Male or female?

But who would speak for her, who find wisdom for her now? Getting closer and closer, and backed into her corner, grieving and pleading her guilt. Let me speak to this, she was pleading. To this and to that. James Edward: *Speaking with his feet, teaching with his fingers.* Sowing calamity. Maria: *Clinging like a fool to the bosom of a stranger.*

She remembered cutting lilacs for a spring bouquet. Mrs Lowry wanted a large bouquet. Lilacs, Mrs Lowry said, were a lavish sort of flower. They didn't last long on the tree or cut in water either, but the bunch had to be lavish. Mrs Lowry had been shopping and the stores were full of their fragrance. "More, more," she'd called down from the sleeping porch. Maria's hand was full but she cut and cut until she couldn't hold another branch. At the doorway she looked down at her mound of mauve and green and then she looked at the row of bushes and couldn't tell from where she'd taken the flowers.

On the evening she and James Edward talked in the screened porch room wrapped in summer air, their foreheads touching before they kissed, she'd remembered that day of the lilacs, Mrs Lowry calling down to her. Ordering her to cut the blooms while they were splendid. Because they wouldn't last.

The aftermath was the maelstrom. At the place she'd fallen, the waters seemed calm.

□

Dear boy, she imagined whispering to him while they gawked and pointed, in the worst, most unexpected of places, there are moments of joy. Many things, dear boy (yes, she imagined the child a boy), happen at the same time. These are matters too difficult to judge.

Do I need to be sad when I'm feeling fine and the sun shines? When I've discovered the pleasure of sewing? When I puzzle over remnants, worn-down garments, and discover another use in them? When I come up against collars, wonder how they're sewn and then open them backwards and understand the way it was done? When I can turn around and build another collar like it without anyone telling me how? I'm going home and I'll make my living at sewing. I'll persuade Father to buy me a machine; it will pay for itself. I've always given him my wages.

You can't come along, though, because of the way they're looking at us and the questions they would ask. I'll tell you the problem, my boy, and you tell me if there's any answer. People know for themselves that they can be forgiven after they've sinned. And everyone learns eventually that even mourning doesn't follow an unbroken line without moments of forgetting or merriness. But they don't believe it for others. They don't approve of it being possible for anyone else.

Would they believe that even my fear is gone? That you called it away, you little butterfly? I would always be large with child in their eyes, never a virgin again. No matter how often the blood flowed down to prove I was clean. Empty and innocent. You could be in my arms, growing up and then a man, taller than I am, and still they'd see my big fat shame. They would follow us like mirrors. They would taunt you: Who is your papa and where did he go?

Maria knew she would soon have to turn away from him, sever her connection as a scissors through cloth. But for now she spoke to him tenderly in her thoughts and explained these matters as best she could. He'd persisted, so she was protective.

When he moved, she quieted him with monologues. He seemed to sleep then, for hours, as if she'd wooed him into submission with her lullaby of thoughts. Sometimes she would disappear into forgetfulness too, until she brushed an arm against her protruding belly and experienced a small shock, remembering who was there, and why.

◻

March opened with a blizzard. "The roads will be impassable," Martin, home safely from his work in the North, declared at breakfast the day it began.

Maria was having trouble with her ankles and feet; every day by noon they were swollen and sore. She spent much of the day with her legs up, doing whatever hand sewing was necessary on the pieces she'd put together in the morning by machine, or knitting – more socks, children's sweaters, caps. "And make some small mittens!" Gladys urged, "Various sizes! Perhaps I can pass them on, sell them! You know!"

The day the blizzard climaxed, Maria climbed onto her bed with her handwork. The wind howled around the house, hurling snow and pellets of frozen earth against the windows. But the storm's fury felt benign. Tucked under a blanket, inside her room, it was just another layer around her. Nearing the end, it added further cover to her secret. Gladys said they had everything for the birth. She claimed she would know what to do if the child outraced the doctor's arrival, though this was unlikely, she said, it being a first delivery and all. Maria straightened her spine, shifted her position to relieve the discomfort in her lower back.

"You know the Lindberghs, don't you?" Gladys called, running up the stairs and bursting into the room.

Who didn't know the Lindberghs? America's handsome hero, that brave man crossing the ocean alone, just him and the "Spirit of St. Louis," all the way to Paris?

Just like a child he simply smiled,
while we were wild with fear.

She had him on her mirror from James Edward. Who didn't know Lindbergh, his elfin wife Anne, their curly-haired Charles Augustus?

"Their little boy's been kidnapped!"

Maria didn't know if someone had passed this along the telephone line or if Gladys had gleaned it from the radio receiver through the cackle and tumult of the storm. It seemed remarkable, frightening, that they suddenly knew of this terrible news. Gladys clutched her hands, and then they flung open as if against her will and she ran downstairs again. Maria heard the door slam and supposed Gladys pushing through the whirling snow to find Martin in the barn, to tell him too. The Lindbergh baby kidnapped! How strange to sit on the bed, to hear this, to feel the shock of the news but not need to move, not need to do anything but absorb it. She shivered.

They learned more from the radio in the days that followed. Excited voices from far away provided regular bulletins. They learned as much as could be known at least, about the kidnapping and the search for the criminals. The storm abated and Martin went off to town. Gladys hadn't left the house for weeks, insisting Maria not be alone "in case something happened."

He brought newspapers back with him. "I cried last night," Gladys told Martin and Maria, "just thinking of that poor mother. Muttering prayers for her every time I turned." Gladys repeated everything she got from the radio and papers, as if they couldn't hear or read for themselves. She sleuthed with the press and police, weighed the evidence, spun the line of guilt from the black-haired child's nurse Betty Gow through her boyfriend Henry Johnson to whomever it was he had tipped off about the family's movements, a gang from Denver most likely. Heartless, they were: just after money. Gladys was angry that the authorities didn't realize what was obvious to her and settle the matter.

The loneliness of the Hopewell house without its round-cheeked little Charlie merged with the isolation of Gladys and Martin's farmhouse and the recently postponed spring. Maria slept poorly, unable to find a position in which she could rest for long, the baby stretching, kicking, turning. "You're having a big one," Gladys said. Maria dreamt that a blond blue-eyed boy was caught in the drifts along the lanes of the farm. She opened the white front door and she saw him, but feared to move from the warmth of the house into the cold night wind. She evaluated his cries against the cries of the darkness, the wind, the strange howling animal noises, and she didn't move. She locked the door.

In the morning Maria remembered the dream and was distressed over her failure to act. Wasn't she as concerned over the Lindberghs as Gladys? It was only a dream, she reminded herself, peeling potatoes for dinner, last year's crop, hauled from the cellar, getting soft, tubes growing out of them. Martin had been sorting through them, setting aside what they needed for planting. He informed Maria that Saskatchewan was having the coldest March in more than a decade and then he left the house. He returned just as Gladys began to wonder where he was. A rabbit dangled from his hand; he grinned broadly over his miracle.

The rabbit tasted delicious but Gladys couldn't enjoy it. "I'm glad your father isn't here to see this," she scolded her husband. "How hard things have gotten."

"Who do you think taught me how to snare it?"

"Still."

They learned that hopes for a speedy recovery of the Lindbergh child had weakened. The next day the hopes were propped up again because rumours had it the boy had been returned, though secretly, to give the kidnappers time to escape. The police were convinced he was alive; they continued to say so in the papers. Maria dreamt of the blond dimpled boy again, wailing in a snow bank within sight of the house. This time she peered at him from the upstairs window. She wasn't surprised to see him; the border authorities had been warned to watch for the thieves entering Canada. The border was long and unprotected. Maria knew that much about the country.

She saw him clearly, heard him cry, yipping like a small dog, but she was still afraid to rescue him. If she did, she would be famous. She would be discovered too. The dream was so vivid and logical to her that she wondered when she woke whether she had peculiar, extraordinary powers. Unable to shake the question, she went for a walk down the lane after breakfast, much to Gladys' surprise, for the day was grey and the wind brisk. Maria walked near the place she recalled from her dream, looking for a sign of him, listening. There was nothing. Of course.

Good Friday passed, and Easter too; March yielded to April, the $50,000 ransom paid to the kidnappers in a careful exchange. But the Lindbergh baby was never returned.

The story no longer got headlines. Gladys still mentioned it now and then, a wistful wondering where poor dear Charlie could be, and what was the matter with the American police anyway? Martin watched the weather. It had turned warmer and he waited for rain. He wanted to plough and to seed.

□

Maria was summoning Scripture urgently now, desperately. *If we confess our sins, he is faithful and just to forgive us our sins.* It said so; it must be true, but Maria didn't feel forgiven enough. Gladys had come down with a cold. Her fits of coughing were awful to witness, that struggle to get rid of the tickle in her throat and the struggle for air, her face growing florid, her body bending in two, her eyes full of tears when the urge to cough was finally over. These fits, which Maria observed with embarrassment for Gladys' sake, because of the contortions they required to get through them, made her ashamed, as if something once purchased within her was up for barter again.

She remembered Mary Magdalene, *out of whom he had cast seven devils*. Jesus met her on the resurrection morning. After the tomb was empty. Would Maria have to wait for the birth before it was real? To the woman caught in adultery he said, *Go and sin no more*. She read through the Gospels, using as a bookmarker the rose James Edward had given her, now pressed between a folded square of onion paper. One of the petals was missing and the remaining four were drained of their gentle pink hue. The yellow centre had faded to white. It was a relic meant to reform her of her past. She placed it unhappily back in the Bible whenever she ended her reading. Had she entered into her pardon, beyond all doubt?

Gladys produced yards of a soft gauzy white fabric and a large piece of white cotton flannel. "The layette," she explained. "Make it all up into diapers. Receiving blankets and nightgowns. Just sew it all up until it's gone."

Maria stared at her, puzzled.

"A present, a present," Gladys said quickly. "We'll send it along with the baby."

This was simple sewing and required no thought. Maria's mind wandered over the white material under her fingers, thinking of blankets folded on the shelves at the Lowry cottage, of sheets and burial shrouds. As she finished the four seams of a blanket, she folded it and thought, this isn't a receiving blanket – as Gladys called it – but a giving one.

She knew women sometimes died in childbirth and she begged God to keep her alive. Her foot rocked the rhythm of her plea on the treadle.

Gladys and Martin set up a bassinet in the room where Martin's parents had spent their last years. "Martin slept in the same little bed," Gladys said.

Maria asked, "But when will the baby be taken to the people adopting it?"

Gladys seemed impatient. "Well, we can't know when the birth comes. We can't make these arrangements in advance. It will be best to pack you and the child up at the same time, after your confinement, I mean, and you're better. We won't be pushing you out. Ten days perhaps. We'll take you to the train, and the baby along, to the parents."

"If they're waiting, will they wait that long?"

"It's a complicated thing, Maria."

Maria had opened the large walnut cupboard in the room where the bassinet stood. It was usually locked, but she spotted the key, forgotten in the keyhole, and tiptoed to the old commode and opened it. It was full of baby things, children's things, all the new diapers and blankets and night-gowns and shirts she'd made, and more. All the children's coats and mittens and dresses. Not a single thing sold. No layette wrapped to present as a gift with the baby. There were pads and bunting and sweaters and caps, and blankets of wool and lace and flannel. Enough for a prince or a princess. Half a shelf was taken up with bottles and pacifiers, baby oils, tins of talcum powder and china bowls with diaper pins and packets of soap and smelling salts. The entire cupboard was crammed with supplies for a baby of their own. Maria closed the commode and tiptoed away.

Sadness returned to her at the end of her term and she wearied of sewing. One day she glimpsed Martin walking on the land beyond her window, his head and shoulders bent as if pulling the field behind him on a yoke, sorrow walking to meet travail, it seemed, helpless against the inexorable heartbeat of time. The child wasn't moving much now, also dispirited perhaps by the cataclysm approaching. If only she could help, hold the sun from rising or setting, lengthen the night!

She slept several hours every afternoon. All pretence of serving Gladys and Martin was gone. She helped them with the diffidence of a guest, felt herself an intruder, imagined they were as eager to be rid of her as she was to be rid of them. She passed hours alone in her room.

She read large chunks of the Bible at a time, looking for final words that may have escaped her. She wanted to seal off this part of her life. But the question danced beside her as she searched: could she take what she found as meant for her? Really meant for her? *Every male that opens the womb shall be called holy to the Lord?*

Or, *Behold, a woman in the city . . . a sinner, when she knew that Jesus sat at meat, brought . . . stood . . . weeping. Kissed him.* Jesus said her display of love had proved she was forgiven.

The rose marked the place, the Bible was closed, Maria's condemnation remained. *If He would have known who and what manner of woman this is that touches him: for she is a sinner.* Her dreams were filled with odd but fleeting images. James Edward returned and she repeated her folly, scattering her repentance out the window like feathers to the wind. She sank against him with gladness – he had loved her after all! – and woke relieved and then frightened at what she'd done. Her hair, all her dark shining hair, cut in the refugee halls of Southampton, wrapped in a receiving blanket. Desire thick as honey between her thighs as she rushed into a room full of people she knew, carrying the bundle like a tray, heading for him across the room. He was explaining something to someone in his animated way. Everyone staring at her, as if they'd formed rows like a choir, singing *"Bubikopf! Bubikopf!* – Bobbed hair, Bobbed hair, Just like a boy!"* She heard an argument, someone crying, Women get headaches from their long, long hair, and another retorting, Has anyone ever died of it? She was going to open the blanket but then she stopped just in time. The baby was in there, though now it seemed to be Anni, her eyes scrubbed clean of their unfocused and milky stupidity. Her mother followed her into the kitchen, admiring the range, the refrigerator, the dishes and pots. She was touching everything with faint mutterings of envy and then Maria's bundle slipped and something broke on the floor.

The pains began. They crescendoed and fell back. Rose again. Her legs were damp; she felt an involuntary gush of liquid. She didn't cry. She bit her lips, she closed her eyes. Gladys pressed wet cloths against her face. Far away from her, Maria heard voices, Gladys' voice and then another's. She was sure she hadn't cried out. But perhaps she groaned; it seemed she was losing something at her throat and it may have been sound. It disappeared in spite of her. Whatever she released seemed imperative now, a stream, a blur of swift-flowing expiation – pain and confusion and breathlessness seized from her, hours-long it seemed, until she gave up and let the end of the tale come true.

5

AFTER THE BIRTH, Gladys praised Maria, for being brave, for the good colour in her face, for the baby. "It's a boy," she said, "just like you predicted. A big, solid boy."

"The Klassens are tall."

"Want a look?"

"No." Maria didn't want a look, or an earful about him either. Gladys was bursting with information, but Maria wouldn't ask about weight, or length, or his features. She wouldn't ask if he was normal or flawed in some way either, though she surmised from Gladys' high spirits that all with the boy was as it ought to be. He wasn't hers. When Maria heard his cries in other parts of the house, she heard Gladys next, rushing to respond, soothing and cooing. It was the sequence of sounds she had chosen, she told herself. She wouldn't give him the breast either. She willed him to be satisfied without her, willed herself into unconcern for him, into satisfaction about what she had done.

On the fourth day after the birth, Maria slid out of bed to walk about her room. She felt well and wondered why she shouldn't get up. Gladys had been waiting on her as if she were invalid. She wrapped a thin counterpane around her nightgown and shuffled barefoot down the stairs. Gladys was asleep on the chesterfield. The room was a mess. It looked as if it hadn't been tidied for days. But the blanket over her body was straight and smooth. It seemed to float on her. Perhaps Martin had just covered her. Maria padded into the kitchen and found him sitting, his back to the doorway, his feet on a chair, and a bundle on his lap – the baby, tightly wrapped, placed along Martin's legs, head towards his knees. Martin didn't move as Maria entered and then she noticed he was sleeping too, his posture stiff and upright though his head lolled. The child was also asleep. Maria felt she'd stumbled upon a fairy tale whose inhabitants were under a spell.

She hadn't intended to look at the child but she did, for a moment. She saw that his hair was long and dark. That a tiny fisted hand curled against his cheek. That he was beautiful. Beguiling.

Perhaps she drank in the sight of him longer than she realized, for a groggy voice startled her. "You should be in bed, Maria." It was Gladys.

Maria reddened. "I'm feeling fine!" she said. "I want to go home now, to Manitoba."

Gladys brushed by her to lift the baby from her husband's lap. "Don't rush," she said distractedly. "Next week."

Martin stirred, dropped his feet to the floor, rubbed his face.

"You ought to be resting in bed," Gladys told Maria. "Another week at least. I'm going to be firm." She pressed the child close, tipped her head towards him.

"I'm feeling fine," Maria said. The soreness of her breasts was of no consequence.

Martin stretched, then stood and ambled to the window. "I wonder if you two see what I see?" he said. "I believe it's rained. I'm sitting here waiting and it starts without me." He laughed ruefully and headed outside.

"Any little rain, he thinks the Depression is over," Gladys said, also sounding pleased. But she was speaking to the baby. Maria fled back to her room.

◻

Putting in her final days at the Anderson farm, Maria received a letter from her father, forwarded along with a letter from Edith Lowry.

They hadn't tried to reach her, Father wrote, she couldn't have come on sudden notice to get there in time. Mother was dead. And buried.

In the end, she died of pneumonia. "She wanted to see you once more, but we submit ourselves to God's will," he'd written. "We conducted the funeral the way we are used to it from Russia."

Maria read the letter twice, lying flat on her back. Then she folded it and set it aside. She stared at the yellow moisture stain in the corner of the ceiling, its butterfly-like shape. Her mother's death wasn't a shock; she knew Mother's condition had been worsening instead of improving. Father had said as much for some time. Still, to miss it!

She was tempted to be hurt that they hadn't tried to contact her by telephone or telegraph, but it was so like her father, ponderous and indecisive in the face of trials, though briskly energetic in projects of other kinds. But surely it was a mercy. The burial was the day of the birth.

Maria considered, tentatively, then more boldly, the matter of mercy. If Mother was dying anyway, the timing of her death seemed providential for sure, designed specifically for Maria perhaps. If she'd had lingering worries about returning home, they were slipping away, the intuition of her mother now silenced. It was a mercy; yes, it must be a mercy.

And her duty was obvious. She would take her mother's place. Her father and siblings needed her. (Wouldn't Mother have wanted it?) Any disarray of her body because of the birth could be accounted for as grief. Maria's path was clearer than it had been in months.

When she remembered to read Mrs Lowry's note,

Maria also learned that final papers to sign would be waiting for her at their house when she returned to Winnipeg, though she would only be expected to stay around for a day or two. As previously agreed, Mrs Lowry said, Maria's employment with them was finished. In other news, Mrs Lowry was busy with clubs and committees, the children were fine, and James Edward had married his Ruthie. It had been a hurried private affair in Toronto, she wrote. They would celebrate with a party when he brought his bride for a visit in summer.

□

The weather was hot when Maria reached Winnipeg. She disembarked from the train and entered a city pitched by the heat into a state of irritability. Everyone felt obliged to talk about how hot it was so early in the season, it seemed. Mr Lowry, who picked her up, was unusually talkative, Maria thought, but his words were mostly about the weather. The buildings of the business district through which the car passed on its way from the station to the Lowrys' startled Maria with their size but they struck her as over-anxious too, and the streets and walks more crowded with automobiles and pedestrians than she remembered, people looking rushed and strained. Only children appeared happy, jumping hopscotch, pulling wagons, running merrily in the heat.

The maid's room at the Lowrys' house was occupied by Dorothy, the new servant girl, and the guest room by a cousin who had come to the city for business, but Eleanor and Frances were gone for the weekend. Maria was given their room for the night. She didn't sleep well. One moment she was hot, pushing her blankets away, and not long afterwards, she was chilly and in the stupor of sleep pulling them high about her neck. Shortly she would be over-heated and rid herself of the blankets again, her skin gulping for the touch of air.

In the same way she'd found herself indulging and

resisting in turn the memories that enveloped her in the familiar house. As soon as she stepped over the threshold, she felt the subtle wrap of flower scent and tobacco, the spirit of elegant imperturbability radiating out of wood and pictures and draperies and the cool, darkened sitting and dining rooms. They were arms reaching to welcome, the sensation firm but exquisite. Then as she undressed, laid down on Frances' bed and scrutinized that room in the waning light, she found the decorations – the sense of the entire house in fact – overbearing, overwrought. She recalled how she'd cleaned here, in this very room, bracing herself not to feel the smart of its snobbish plaids and charming floral prints behind the girls' careless assumptions that she would always be picking up after them. She missed her plain enclosure at the farm, the colourful patchwork on her bed.

Compared to the farm, the city was noisy at night. A train whistled, then another. Traffic squealed and honked from all directions as if crazed by the heat. Voices and music lasted late; she thought she heard the streetcar, the gong of a clock, bells. Or was she dreaming? It occurred to her, after some time, that she must be dreaming, because everything was quiet. Desperately and strangely quiet. A bit of a wind came up and she listened for the faint whinny of the clothes-line pulley in the breeze. She didn't hear it; Martin must have oiled the hinge in the post at last.

Though she slept poorly, Maria felt refreshed in the morning by the fact that Gerhard would soon be picking her up. Indeed, she felt quite thoroughly rested by the thought. She came downstairs and Dorothy informed Maria she would serve her breakfast in the dining room. The newspaper lay on the table, unrolled, and there it was, the large black headline. News that the stolen Lindbergh boy had been found, dead in the hills near Hopewell. While they were thinking of him alive, needing their rescue, he was already dead, thinly covered with leaves and debris not far from his home. On the night he went missing, he was dead, and everything that followed was a massive exercise in futility.

Maria read the stories carefully and folded the paper. She wondered if the new girl followed the news, if she had any curiosity for that sort of thing. She wasn't Mennonite; she was an English girl. She seemed pleasant, what one might call hearty. She'd served Maria well.

Edith Lowry came down the stairs in a new short coat. It was teal blue, a stunning colour, completely current. "It's nice to have you back," she said, "even if only for a night."

Mrs Lowry was on her way out and Maria hadn't planned what to say in farewell. She wished she could have gone directly to her father's house but she'd come to pick up the box of possessions she hadn't taken with her to Saskatchewan. (She'd dispatched the paperwork without looking at the details the previous evening.) And Gerhard was coming into Winnipeg anyway; he'd purchased a used car and was driving in to finalize negotiations for their move to North Kildonan – he and Helen and baby John, and Father and the children.

"I won't be here when your brother comes," Mrs Lowry said, "so I'll say Goodbye. I put a bag with some clothes beside your case. Things I'm not using anymore. The new girl isn't my size, as you are." She smiled wryly. "You have your figure back already." Maria tried to return the smile but her mouth seemed frozen.

"Your wages are in there too, as I'd arranged with Gladys, and some extra. A little extra for five years."

Now Maria managed a slight sound in her throat, a stammer of thanks, but she was inhibited by the other woman's efficient generosity and the dazzling coat. Mrs Lowry sounded as she always had, like a teacher in September, lively and competent and distant, so far beyond Maria again. The coat's brilliance set off her eyes; they sparkled with energy, with affection too, but professional affection, for her poor stammering pupil.

"In spite of everything, I trust you'll carry good memories away with you," Mrs Lowry said. "All's ending well. And I've written your parents a little note, in thanks for your service. If you ever need a reference, I'll give you a good one."

Maria considered mentioning that her mother had died, but Mrs Lowry seemed in a hurry.

"Goodbye then, Maria."

Maria straightened her shoulders, attempted to straighten her face. She floundered a little; her lips and chin trembled.

"Goodbye." Maria's voice found its way safely through the quivering and the word emerged with a full, proud tone, even more assured than she'd hoped. Mrs Lowry stepped towards her and lifted a hand. It wasn't clear if she intended to shake Maria's hand or embrace her but Maria didn't move quickly enough and the lifted hand fell awkwardly back to its place.

A car tooted at the street; Mrs Lowry's friend and her driver had arrived. The door closed behind her. Through a slit of lace in the curtain Maria watched Mrs Lowry bend into the vehicle, one hand holding her hat. She was a teal blot, and then it disappeared.

Maria went to the broom closet, found a dust cloth and an apron to wear. She slipped the kitchen scissors into the apron pocket. She told Dorothy she would help with the cleaning. "I'll dust," she said. "I have nothing else to do while I'm waiting for my brother." The girl looked perplexed but she nodded.

Maria climbed the stairs to the third floor, the cloth swinging at her side. She opened the door and slipped into the unoccupied attic room. The room was hot, the air close. Moisture rose on her forehead. The room hadn't been spring cleaned yet, it seemed, nor had James Edward been back to gather his books, furniture, collectibles.

The key to the lid of the museum table was still in the

keyhole; James Edward wasn't afraid of his valuables being stolen or disturbed. Perhaps his interest had diminished further, now that he was married.

But he would still be attached to the cards. Maria wrote her name with her finger in the dust of the glass. She wiped it away, turned the key, raised the lid. The cards were what he prized most, he'd told her, because they were the oldest and in excellent condition, and both cards and box had come down from his grandfather's grandfather or some long-ago forebear. They'd be worth a great deal, or would go on to his son. (Did he know he had one?) Maria recalled how she'd approved of the second scenario. The imperative of family.

She opened the silver box, unfolded the paper wrapping, turned the top card over. There again, the haughty medieval king in red. James Edward said his name was King of Diamonds. Maria stared at him. There was certainly something sinister about this king. She had the urge to tear the inhuman creature in half, to let her anger show in jagged edges. But no, she would stick to what she'd planned during the train ride back to Manitoba.

Maria took the scissors out of her pocket and cut the card in two, straight through the middle. She placed the pieces back as if they were still one card and then she closed the box. At first glance James Edward might think the cut was a piece of thread or maybe a hair lying over the king's shoulder, some foreign fibre caught there, touching the precious ancient monarch by mistake. He wouldn't realize, at first glance, that the card was ruined.

This was her gesture for the end. She felt it was a good one, not too large, neither too small. It wasn't large enough for revenge – as if that was hers to exact! – but it had its consequences, it made a mark, like punctuation closing a sentence. She glanced at the bookshelf and saw that *All Quiet on the Western Front* stood where she'd left it more than nine months earlier. She decided she wanted to read it after all and would take it along.

Maria put the cloth and apron and scissors away. She slipped the book into her bag, gathered her coat, her case and box, and set everything she owned neatly in the entrance. She sat down on the chintz sofa to wait for her brother. She contemplated beginning again. She thought of Genesis, how everything began the first time. *In the beginning,* she remembered, *God created the heavens and earth. And the earth was without form, and void; and darkness was upon the face of the deep. And the Spirit of God moved upon the face of the waters.*

PART II

Five Decades

1932 – 1983

6

Now, how to appear but still remain hidden? How to stay alert to the cracks of her secret? How to fill them in, rub the edges smooth so nothing would be visible?

She was home. It was not far from her former place of service – the city accessible for the price of a streetcar fare – but the two places seemed a long and momentous journey apart. When she migrated from the Lowrys of Crescentwood to the Klassens of North Kildonan, Maria told herself she'd crossed the sea at last to reach the place she'd been meant to reach when she first came to Canada. She'd arrived greatly altered, she knew, and chastened, but she was – finally – ashore.

And then, the anxiety, in her bed, one night after the other, as if she were still underway. She would wake, at midnight, or early in the morning, her stomach aching or her heart racing as if it would leap from her chest. She wouldn't know immediately what the matter was – was there an intruder or fire in the house, or some other danger? Fully awake, she knew it was fear. Fear of discovery, of not being what she had wanted to be, of not being what others supposed her to be.

She calmed herself in various ways. She pushed back with words. She said the names of what mattered. Of course, her father and the household and all of her siblings mattered, but there were only three names of utmost importance: the baby Erna, her small sister Margarethe, her young brother Wilhelm. Counting them, naming them. One, two, three. Erna, Margarethe, and Wilhelm.

She thought about the three of them, so dependent on her still, thought of each one of them, bringing his or her face and body into her recall, and since she slept near the girls, at one end of the room from them, she listened for their breathing, or for some sound from the boys' room one door down. She listened until she heard some noise to prove they were much more real to her than her own clattering heart and anxious intestines. She thought through a list of what they would need from her the next morning. She reviewed the previous day and saw she had succeeded well enough in what they needed from her then. She chose again her new and ordinary life. Her unexpected, and limited, life. She hid what she had been deeper inside who she had to become.

Maria told herself that she would be what others needed. What they could admire. Surely it was possible to shrink in parts and emerge more strongly on the surface. She reviewed the cautions she had placed upon her speech and mind. They were firmly in place. She reminded herself to watch how others related, responded, to her. To see if any mistrust had been aroused.

Careful, careful, careful, she told herself, in answer to her fear. A girl in her position couldn't be too careful.

□

Eventually she landed at a day where effort that strenuous seemed in the past, or even forgotten. A day like this.

The young woman forked the cooked potatoes from a pot on the stove into a half-empty serving bowl, filling it for a second round at Sunday dinner. Her fingers were long and faintly marked with the signs of her daily duties in the garden and kitchen: a slight discolouration of the forefingers, a little roughness on the tips, the pale ivory line of a nearly-healed cut. She wore no rings. But her hands, gripping the fork and bowl, were beautiful.

The woman herself was beautiful. She was thirty-two, at the time of life in which women have both youth and maturity at their disposal. Her face was unlined and her dark hair gleamed. As she carried the steaming dish the few steps from the stove to the table, her gored skirt with its twelve seams and perfect two-inch hem undulated prettily around her legs. The dark green fabric of the skirt had been worked into a narrow trim on the collar of her white blouse and she wore a starched white apron tied with a wide bow. Had she been photographed at that instant, caught in the noonday light in the act of serving food, she could have been the model housewife for some advertisement in a women's magazine. The kitchen was too crowded, of course, the home much too small, the accessories of the scene too sparse, but the woman herself looked the image of domestic contentment.

This woman, of course, was Maria, who had returned to her family eight years earlier, in 1932, to take on the mother's role in the family. She set the bowl of potatoes near her youngest sister Erna. The baby she'd taken in charge as a toddler was nine now, a slight and delicate-looking, tenderhearted child. Maria touched her on the shoulder. "Pass Papa the potatoes, please. His plate is empty."

Maria's return had coincided with the Klassens' move to North Kildonan, a community northeast of the city of Winnipeg where Mennonites had begun to settle in the late 1920s. They moved onto one- or five-acre lots east of Henderson Highway. They cut new beginnings into the scrub woods of poplar, willows, and oak. They uncovered the dark, rich soil. They planted large gardens and raised chickens and cows.

The "Chicken and Garden Village" grew, and a decade after its founding contained more than a hundred families. The Mennonites liked the rural and closely-knit feel of their community, with the city just close enough to serve as a market for their vegetables, chickens, and eggs. The street-car ran north and south and connected them to day jobs or periodic meetings with their co-religionists in the city's Mennonite churches. Locally, they gathered for weekly religious observance, meeting first in homes and then putting up church buildings. Several of them opened stores. They were close enough to walk to these stores or to each other's homes to borrow a cup of sugar or to gossip a while. They were near enough to help one another and numerous enough to keep their German language intact and most of their children within "the fold."

Maria's father, Johann Klassen, moved to North Kildonan in the midst of grief over his wife Susanna's death, getting barely anything for the farm near Winkler beyond the debt still owed on it. Gerhard and Helene came too, with the enthusiasm of a young married couple. Maria joined them with her secret and resolve. All of them, except second daughter Susanna, who had married Henry Rempel of Gnadenthal and lived on his parents' farm in southern Manitoba, put their resources together for the down payment on two adjoining lots. Maria offered her final wages.

Like the other Mennonite settlers, they built primitive houses, scarcely bigger than their chicken barns. These dwellings would eventually be enlarged and improved. Hans bicycled into town to peddle produce and eggs. They invested in a sewing machine and Maria took in sewing and alterations, securing regular customers in the better-off area of North End Winnipeg, off Scotia Street, through a chance remark by one of the domestics from their church who worked in a home in that area. Once a week she delivered what she'd finished and measured and took new orders. She set a good price from the start, and got it.

To the raising of chickens and vegetables, Johann Klassen and his sons added a repair shop in a shed in the back yard. They accepted anything that was broken –

machines, tools, motors – and could nearly always fix it. They did good work; there was always something waiting for repair.

The Klassens were poor, but so were the people around them. It was hard times everywhere in the Thirties. But they felt they were making a go of things, slow as it might be, and that their efforts would someday be rewarded. They felt they might even pull ahead of others within their community.

Katherine married Peter Penner of Steinbach; they hoped to move to North Kildonan too. Hans had recently married Ida Fehr. Maria believed she'd fulfilled her mother's wishes of keeping the family close to one another – except for Susanna, who was, however, in the province and thus not so very far away.

"This is a lovely meal, Maria," Ida was saying now. "Everything tastes delicious."

"It's a simple meal." Maria sat down and ate a bite of chicken.

"But in each part, as simple as it may be, the flavours are drawn out perfectly," the pretty blonde girl pronounced. "And the chicken is moist and tender." Father glanced up from his eating to give Ida an interested look, as if she'd said something unusual, and then directed a kindly look towards his eldest daughter who for eight years now had been setting meals like this on the table.

"Thank you," Maria said. She couldn't help thinking Ida was trying too hard.

"It was my chicken," Erna whispered shyly.

Ida didn't hear her. "I know," Maria whispered. "Thank you."

"This is what I've grown up with," Hans grinned at his new bride. "Such meals. Haven't I told you what I'm used to?"

Ida flushed as if he'd rebuked her, but said, "It's all very fine."

Maria stood to replenish the serving bowl of carrots. Ida asked if Maria was getting time to eat.

"Oh yes," she said. Again the smooth, authoritative movements at the stove, the gracious serving movements at the table, all meant to assure there was food enough, plenty of everything.

"Maria was a maid in a big house," Erna inserted, her voice stronger this time, "and she says she can't eat without jumping up between every bite. Isn't that so, Maria?"

"I always get enough," Maria said.

At the head of the table, Father Klassen, his shoulders slightly stooped when sitting, had removed his suit jacket. His stiffly starched white shirt was still closed up to his neck and the wide dark tie was tight around it. He would loosen it soon, perhaps after his coffee, perhaps just before. They were all still in their Sunday best. Church dress, with its particular primness and discomfort, was taken off in stages. Sunday meant the contrast of white and dark colours around the table (white and black, white and navy, white and dark green), bits of lace on the girls' collars, the strong noon sun falling on Saturday-cleaned floors, a gleaming stove, and golden gravy; it meant this particular clink of the best dishes and the sound of stiff Sunday shoes, and these mingled smells of chicken and coffee and soap and starch and perspiration when the men removed their jackets. And it meant these voices, unhurried and polite.

Father Klassen rarely said much at meals, as if his hunger had to be stilled before he could think or speak, but on Sundays he seemed more aware of his family than on week-days. He might lift his head from his plate occasionally and look about him, as if to check who was here and who was not. It was a look of appraisal, the well-practiced eye of the householder over his crops or flocks, but it wasn't critical on Sundays.

Maria observed his manner, his once-a-week gestures of attachment; she was particularly alert herself on Sundays when she prepared the most important meals of the week, the ones at which one or more of the married children might be home. She glanced frequently over the table, made surveillance of the needs of each person and of the diminishing mounds of chicken, potatoes, bread, and vegetables. She listened for the nuances of conversation, listened if any kind of guidance or diversion might be required. She watched the youngest three – Erna, Margarethe, Wilhelm – over whom she still had maternal oversight, watched how they behaved. Today there was also the factor of getting used to Ida.

Ida was too eager, but she was a prize for Hans and the family. Her clear paraffin-coloured skin seemed the sign of how valuable she was. She came from a good Mennonite family in Elmwood that had been in the Winnipeg area longer than they had, her father a businessman and prospering. He'd been mentioned in the newspaper not so long ago because of a hefty donation to the Red Cross.

Maria passed the pickled beets, a perfect deep red, to her new sister-in-law. Wilhelm said to Ida, in English, as if wanting to offer her something as well, "Maria learned her good English when she was a maid." Wilhelm was nineteen, as tall as his father and with the same slightly stooped shoulders. "She reads English books late at night."

"Not that many in English," Maria said anxiously in German. "Very few English books actually."

Language was an issue in the community, and something of an issue in their home as well. Maria tried to catch her brother's eye but he refused to meet hers. Wilhelm was a stubborn boy.

"Of course I learned English well," she said. "I had to. Even as Father told me I should. But now I'm home."

"English is useful to establish ourselves," Hans said. "And to prove we're loyal Canadians. But our real world is German."

"I would think with Canada in the war and everything, with the war against Germany, we should make the effort to speak English," Wilhelm said. He used German this time, as they always did in the family, but even in his familiar tongue he spoke in a rush. It often seemed that Wilhelm decided what he would say in advance and then recited it with the school-boy's terror of forgetting what he'd memorized.

"That matter we've settled well enough, Wilhelm," Hans said pleasantly, though with the condescension of the older and now married brother. Hans was the best looking of all the boys, Maria thought, and so sure of himself. He put his cutlery correctly on his plate as she'd taught him and wiped his mouth with his napkin and smoothed the dark narrow moustache under his nose. He pushed his chair back a little and rested one white-sleeved arm on the back of Ida's chair, lightly touching her shoulder with his fingers, as if to remind his family and Wilhelm in particular about his success in winning Ida, perhaps the loveliest young woman in the entire fledgling Mennonite community.

"We've settled these things, Wilhelm," Hans reiterated. "You weren't at the church meeting, but it came up again, and the agreement is very strong, that we must keep the German language. It's fundamental, especially with the children attending English schools."

Maria asked her father if he was ready for coffee. He nodded and she prompted Margarethe and Erna, who rose as one to help her gather and stack the dishes, cut the pie, bring out fresh plates and forks and coffee cups. Ida stood to join them but Maria waved her down.

"But I'm part of the family now." Ida handed her flat black purse to Hans and squeezed past him to join the females.

Now there were too many of them at the worktable.

"You speak English just as well as anyone I've heard, Wilhelm," Ida told her younger brother-in-law as she brought him dessert.

She's missed the point, Maria thought, catching the grati-tude in the boy's eyes. "Thank you for your help, Ida," she said. "Really, I think we can manage the rest."

"I love to help," Ida said. "What else would I do, just sit there and talk business with the men?"

It wasn't exactly business talk, but something more restrained, something in keeping with the Sunday admonition to rest, to cease from work. They were speaking of a certain Mr Loewen from Morden, the brother to the Loewen here, for whom they were intending – hoping, that is – to build a new house when he moved into the settlement. They were adding the business of building to their machine and tool repair. Katherine's Peter was a skilled carpenter and when he joined them, it would be possible. Since it was Sunday, the terms of the proposed contract for the Loewen house weren't discussed directly, but Father observed that the Morden man's brother was especially cordial this morning after church. It seemed to him the matter would soon be concluded in their favour.

"Don't encourage Wilhelm too much about English," Hans told Ida when the women joined them at the table again. "I don't agree with any notions of half and half. We'll speak German."

"Your sympathies for the Brown Shirts will get you into trouble yet," Ida returned peevishly.

"Brown shirts, nothing of that. I'm talking about our church meeting last week. We're setting lines against more than a bit of politics." Father nodded and Hans went on. "Papa gave a wonderful defense of the language at the meeting. You weren't there, Wilhelm."

"Wilhelm was working late on Mr Falk's car," Maria said. "Hadn't you and Papa asked him to finish?"

"I was finished," Wilhelm said. "I didn't want to go."

Maria stood to refill coffee cups and offer seconds of pie. "The pie is delicious," said Ida.

"I'd say something at the meeting if I felt it was important," Wilhelm said. "I'd say it in English too."

"I'm sure you wouldn't," Father said. "Even Chamberlain said it's impossible to think deeply and clearly in English."

His tone indicated the topic had been concluded.

They finished their dessert in silence. Maria reminded her father then that everyone was done. He cleared his throat. *"Gesegnete Mahlzeit,"* he said, announcing the "Blessed meal" that signalled they were free to leave the table.

□

Maria had embraced the pioneering life with the uncomplaining energy produced by remorse. She tended and fussed over her private rehabilitation like a sapling nourished from seed until tall and established and the seed forgotten, absorbed somewhere in the depths of its beginning. Hard years, they'd been, physically wearing, but in the sum – looking back, at least – she thought them surprisingly happy. She'd begun to awake each day with anticipation and once her sister Margarethe had said, as if she'd made a happy discovery too, "Maria, you're always singing or humming!" It was true, though Maria was mostly unaware of it.

She was aware, however, that others marvelled at her. She felt it a measure of success. Although she was friendly, Maria confided very little and socialized mainly with her family. Still, things were said and they got back to her. She works so hard, *Tante* Friesen, Lena Rempel, Frede Martens, Greta Braun and others said to each other; she's young but manages everything as if she's far, far older; she strides with such pace, such determination. And *always* singing! It seemed remarkable for a young woman, a single woman, though they suspected it had something to do with freedom from pregnancy and conjugal duty, not to mention the worries over children – children of her own, that is. Still, the work demanded of her was enormous and her competence remarkable. So good at everything, and quite a seamstress too. She picked up a lot in those years of working out, they said to each other, some very good ideas. Even picked up some airs, they muttered on occasion, and one of them couldn't help noticing that Maria hadn't concealed her look of pride when the items she made fetched the highest prices of their category at the last auction for missions. She brought the city along with her, another woman grumbled.

But, speaking of pregnancy and duty to a husband, didn't she want it? They wondered and murmured, the other women did, about Maria, who had moved from girl to woman in their midst, and still unmarried, and wondering whether she would or she could, so bound to her sisterly duties. These things came back to Maria too. And things concerning her father.

Her father, people noted, seemed in no hurry to find another wife – but who needed one with Maria in the kitchen? It might have been better, they mused, for a man in his position as lay minister to seek another partner, but why should he rush into it when his children were tended so well? He was mourning a very long time, they noted with approval and disapproval, but conceded that his late wife Susanna was a wonderful woman, at least according to their Winkler contacts who knew her: always so respectful of him! And Maria, a true mother to those children, the only mother they've got, *Tante* Friesen, Lena Rempel, Frede Martens, Greta Braun and the others remarked sympathetically, though they felt a little sorry for her too, not having her own, her own flesh and blood.

The women of the community couldn't ask Maria, for while she was willing to discuss the weather or gardens or handwork, she responded to anything personal with silence or remarks so cheerful and vague it discouraged them from further enquiry. She couldn't be engaged in gossip either, which only enhanced her air of aloofness. They saw that she was talkative enough with her sisters, and her friend and sister-in-law Helene, but those women provided no useful information either. The younger girls didn't know whether Maria would marry or not, they would say, and Helene's disposition was so optimistic, she managed to turn every question into a further compliment of Maria's various efficiencies. The women definitely tired of asking Helene.

There were men whose expressions of interest, whether in her figure and features or her proficiency in running a household, had also gotten round to Maria. As far as anyone knew, however, she wasn't open to suitors. There was no encouraging coquettishness in her and she seemed so attached to her duties it chased ideas of love out of their minds. Men she might have married eventually married others.

No one knew the source of Maria's confidence or the source of her disinclinations. Maria felt she wasn't like other single women, forced into a long extension of girlishness in their parents' house, forced by common custom to defer to married women – women who had penetrated those mysteries of sex and birth around which they drew a circular line of inclusion. Those who were mothers ascribed Maria's assumption of equality to her sacrificial identification with the maternal role and gave her space beside them, if grudgingly, because of that sacrifice. Maria took it because she felt herself their equal. Whether they knew it or not, she thought, she'd crossed over their line and belonged where they were. But she would never explain or defend it, and if it was required, she could pretend a humble or old-maidish naivety as well.

She didn't talk about her five years of service; she never mentioned James Edward's name aloud. She never spoke of Saskatchewan either, nor were questions ever raised about why she had worked there. In the Klassens' history, that particular year was marked by Mother's death. "The year Mother died," they would say in reference to 1932, as if their own histories that year were completely subsumed by that event, as if nothing else of significance had occurred.

Maria rarely uttered James Edward in her thoughts either. The features of her lover faded; she couldn't remember him whole but only in parts – the colour of his hair, his lips curved downwards towards her like an overripe tulip, his large bony shoulders. Occasionally something evoked his memory, some fragment of sensation, a smell, or the movement of a stranger, and then for the briefest of moments she remembered him or felt him against her, but she dealt harshly with these memories when they came and he grew ever more indistinct. She weaned herself of the humiliation of his swift flight back to Ruthie; she concluded the matter had been jinxed somehow, or foreordained. Her own part was an error – yes, a sin – and terrible enough, but it was finished.

As for the baby, he was unknown and meant nothing to her. In time, he seemed a phantom. The wound of pregnancy healed; the loss of virginity and the stretched and opened womb grew small and tight; it was closed. She no longer felt, eight years past the birth, that her body had suffered discontinuity. As the Low German proverb said, it was all so very long ago, it was hardly even true anymore.

□

The immigrant Mennonites needed to survive, spiritually, culturally. Maria did too. She read the German newspapers. She read the local English paper they shared with Gerhard and Helene. She listened to what the men reported from church meetings, to the Sunday sermons, to the gossip and opinions of those around her. Assimilation had its dangers; she knew that well enough.

But she had Wilhelm and the two youngest girls to raise, her nieces and nephews to influence, her own inescapable love of beauty to satisfy. She made their surroundings pretty, insisted on extras that appealed to her, pushed the children to excel, plied them relentlessly with compliments and reminders of their Klassen family worthiness. Sometimes, she realized, she sounded exactly like her mother.

She made the girls go to German Saturday school, and to go without complaining. She made them speak German when Father was near, let them chatter in English when he wasn't.

She read them German stories and books, and *Anne of Green Gables* and the *Just So Stories* and other books in English. She never hindered the fantasies inspired by catalogues. She started them on scrapbooks of the royal family after the shock of Edward's abdication: pictures of the young sisters Elizabeth and Margaret, posed with their mother in identical plaid jackets and skirts, knitting needles in hand while their mother held the wool, or the two of them in riding uniform, or sitting on grass in light checked blouses with ruffles, their pet Corgi between them.

She was completely inconsistent – protecting with all her energies their German Mennonite enclave, yet striving English-ward. It was that old weakness of hers and she knew it, but surely they had to fit in here, improve, develop, expand, become more secure on their own terms. Be something again.

Maria arranged that the whole family attend the annual Mennonite music festivals, even as far away as in Winkler. She turned attendance into a tradition. She persuaded her father that while she played guitar, the younger girls should study violin. She insisted he start saving for a piano. "They're such good girls," Maria told her father when she wanted him to buy the things she thought they needed. "Such very diligent girls."

☐

But Wilhelm. For Wilhelm the two worlds – the Mennonite world and the larger world with its dangerous "worldliness" attached – couldn't be brought together or satisfied by English stories, scrapbooks, or new choir oratorios. Maria was sewing and he sat down beside her, rubbing his right hand over the left as if twisting a screw. Then he unfurled his announcement with a self-conscious flourish: "I smoked a cigarette today."

His way of confessing, with defiance and fear co-mingled, unburdening himself before she found evidence of what he'd done and accuse him herself, was familiar to Maria. She'd been listening to Wilhelm's sins since he was eleven.

He confessed candy stolen from the neighbourhood store and she trudged with him to the shop and held his trembling hand while he blurted his theft to the owner. On the way home she told him she might find a way for him to earn back the penny he'd given up to pay for the sweet.

He told her he spent the day at the riverbank instead of in school and she marched him to the teacher's house to report it and ask for mercy – and to ask as well that the matter be kept confidential between them. When Wilhelm killed one of their chickens out of season because of some fury against his brother Hans he wouldn't or couldn't explain, Maria set him grimly near her to pluck the skinny bird so she could prepare it for supper, but when her father asked why they'd taken one so young, Maria mumbled "It happened" as if it had been an honest mistake.

She knew what she wanted to avoid. She'd seen Wilhelm and her father entering the shed, both faces rigid, and she'd heard the whistle and catch of leather striking inside it. She'd seen them emerge as they went in, silent, their faces as dark and unyielding as before, nothing resolved in either one of them. So she was glad when the boy came to her with his misdeeds; it was better than that kind of affair, and if she sometimes felt that some right of the father was being circumvented (the unspoken rule being that she was responsible for the girls, he for the boys) she told herself that the bit of remorse and fear in Wilhelm's twisting hand and the concrete steps she took with him to right the wrong were enough.

It was hard being the mother in circumstances such as these, she comforted herself. She couldn't discuss the training of the children with her father in specific terms, not as his equal. She was his daughter too and there was distance in that.

Father told her that Wilhelm had the best fingers for

machine work in the shop. Maria said, "But he thinks he's just your fetch-boy, Papa."

"Gerhard and Hans are married men. Shall I be sending *them* on errands?" Then he added, with a bitterness she hated to hear, "He's baptized, he's a minister's son. I wish he'd behave that way."

What could she say? She wouldn't ask what incidents he meant. She had her own examples and didn't want his. There was a belligerence about the boy that seemed to infect whatever he did, and though her father's love hadn't failed any of them, Maria began to fear that it might fail Wilhelm, his youngest son.

And now he'd smoked a cigarette. Maria sighed, turned the dress she was working on inside out and shook it to check it over. She'd finished the machine work and only the hem and over-casting were left.

"It was awful," he said. "Really. I was coughing. I guess I don't like it."

"It's a horrible habit, so don't get started. And don't forget you're a church member."

"It was at Uncle Peter's."

Maria dropped the dress onto her lap and glared at him. "And look how poor *he* is!"

Peter and Agathe lived nearby, in a two-room house Maria's father built them in the east front corner of the Warkentins' place (the two women were second cousins) and Peter found work as a gardener on a Winnipeg estate. It didn't pay much but it suited him and Agathe kept a cow. They agreed to pay off their house through milk, butter, and cream.

"A bit of tobacco, my dear. One cigarette," Peter answered Maria when she took it up with him later, rubbing a ruddy cheek as he spoke as if to measure exactly the size of the object they were dealing with before he continued. "In my opinion, one cigarette is no problem at all. Neither are two, I would think, though he ended at one. Not even finishing that one, if you want to know."

He paused. "That's what the Reformation was all about, Maria. Or maybe it was the apostle Paul who grasped it first. No one condemned to death because of human commandments."

This was Peter's charm and his danger. A rebellion, not against the ideas they accepted but of how they might be interpreted instead, leaping from a single cigarette onto the theological rock of the church. She wondered if she should argue church history and theology, of which she also knew something, or if it would go as it always did, she sputtering a kind of acquiescence because he'd come round to talking about weakness, forgiveness, and grace. Which she also relied on and knew more of, she believed, than he would ever know.

They were sitting at Peter's tiny kitchen table.

"One cigarette, dear Maria. He told you, didn't he, how awful it was? I said to him, now you don't need to try it again. Do you think I encouraged him? Don't you realize I'd like to be rid of it myself because of what it costs and my wife always nagging at me? And not joining your church because it's considered a sin? But Wilhelm? One cigarette. I like that boy, Maria."

"What's that got to do with it? You want to stop, then stop."

Maria remembered Martin Anderson bringing out his pipe. "I'm going to nurse my pipe awhile," he would say, as if it was a habit of compassion. It involved more lighting and futile puffing than anything else, the whole exercise a series of starts and stops, a silly waste of time, stinking up the house. The only time she'd appreciated it was shortly before her departure from Saskatchewan when the smell of disinfectant hung in the house because someone, Gladys she assumed, had gone crazy with its application.

"I like Wilhelm," Peter said stubbornly.

Maria wasn't that afraid of Wilhelm's cigarette either. She was more afraid that Wilhelm liked his Uncle Peter as she had liked (and yet despised) him, and that in fact the three of them – she and her brother and their uncle – were all too alike, tainted by something adventuring and flaccid in the bloodline, something her mother had broken away from. But had, after all, passed along to two of her children. Did attractions for pleasure and beauty, a lack of will and over-much dreaming, certain tendencies, inhabit some people more than others? Perhaps Wilhelm couldn't be stiffened into a Klassen at the core.

Agathe was seated at the table with them and said to Maria, "If you could talk Peter out of his smoking you'd accomplish everything I've been unable to do and I would thank you. I think of the cost."

Peter shrugged. "Maria thinks of Wilhelm. My dear wife nags over the cost. Suppose I stop smoking. They'll let me into the church. But maybe they should keep me out because of our bickering."

Agathe clucked with disgust but Peter reached his arm towards her and chuckled. "Which we don't take so badly ourselves, do we?" Agathe's expression softened.

She was still childless and Maria knew she was deeply unhappy over that. She saw that the rims of Agathe's eyes were puffy. "I'm just asking you help me with my work of raising the children, Peter," she said. "Especially with Wilhelm. Help, not hinder me."

She absently rubbed circles on the table top with her forefinger. "I'm trying to be a good mother," she went on. "I'm trying to do what my mother would have done."

Peter laughed. "Your mother would have been far, far harder on me, Maria. I'm glad it's only you."

☐

Maria's love for her brother Wilhelm was like a funnel, opening from a wide source but focussed, intensely singular. She came to believe that if the hidden thing in her life had any redeeming feature at all, it would pour here, as a balm, into this brother of hers. Whatever good could be brought out of it must be directed to him.

He went to the theatre, to *Gone with the Wind*, thoroughly enchanted and thoroughly miserable over his transgression. He challenged his father with theological questions at the supper table. Who did Cain marry? Why had God commanded all that killing in the Old Testament if they were supposed to be conscientious objectors? If God knew everything, what was the point? Where had the devil come from? Father Klassen always answered briefly, with a fork held midway to his mouth, and then he continued eating. To Maria's mind, he rarely answered the questions well. A tense stillness would settle over the table, as if they had to pretend they'd had a pleasant conversation, though permitted only one a day. Maria felt the unfinished business of the two men like a burning sun that wouldn't set, the boy's mad stirring and stupidity, hungry, it seemed, to be punished. Wishing, it seemed, to actually outgrow or find the end of his father's patience. And from the older man, the growing disdain that merged with his fundamental dislike of doubt and the satisfaction he found in his own answers as he gave them, the assumptions of his authority and what was obvious to him making him blind to the boy's need.

Love bears and believes and hopes and endures; it never fails. But of course it could. It would fail here, unless, Maria felt, she could keep it from failing, bolster it, deflect what they intended for one another, until the day that Wilhelm was mature enough to understand his father. Until he allowed himself to be understood.

□

One early October afternoon while Maria was lifting the earth around a tight cluster of carrots, carefully so none of them would be damaged by the fork's tines, she spotted

Wilhelm heading her way and knew there was trouble again.

She straightened, her arm levering her aching back, and watched him coming. It was the end of the season of cabbages, cauliflowers, tomatoes, potatoes, and beans, the precious harvest meaning some money for the winter and preserves for themselves, and she was thinking how brief the garden's span ultimately was, from spring to fall, and hoping the girls were doing their chores indoors, finishing the ironing and getting supper ready. There was still so much to do before winter.

And thinking too that she loved this place. This prairie place. This nest against the city wall. And wondering too, not for the first time, who'd been here before her, dreaming in this very spot. Indians had been glimpsed in the lush woods of Fraser's Grove on the other side of the streetcar line. Camping there. This question was a kind of melancholy that sometimes came over her. It was not generally her way, or the way of her people, to waste worry over what had come before them in the places they lived. It was their own history, with its wanderings and sorrows and triumphs, that they remembered and celebrated, not the land's. The earth they settled upon was assumed to be new and empty. As if prepared, readied and waiting for them. Their memories concerned lines of migration over maps, or lines strung through genealogies of the same names used over and over. Lateral lines, blood lines, not layers of dirt or bone.

"I've enlisted," Wilhelm said, kicking at the side of a cauliflower stem with his boot, dislodging the root. He nearly stumbled and it took some of the force out of his declaration.

So he repeated it, legs steady now and arms akimbo before her. "I've enlisted. I'm off to the war."

It was surprisingly warm this day, for October, but there was something false and unreliable about the heartiness of autumn heat. Maria lowered herself to sit on the ground. The soil beneath her was cool in spite of the air. She hadn't heard him correctly perhaps. At the same time, she felt herself give way as one gives in to sleep, to the knowledge she'd lost him, that he would go the prodigal's path, that she couldn't prevent him.

A gust of wind fretted against the strands of her hair that had escaped their pins. The stalks on the orange and green heap of carrots she'd been building softened in the heat, sagged away from their roots, despondently it seemed, betrayed by what had sustained them. She remembered the book about the awfulness of war. It took no effort at all to see its troughs and ridges, its trenches, the black and white contours of its shadows and flares. She heard the unnatural sound of her voice, like a high-pitched explosion. "You've enlisted?"

"I'm going to war." Wilhelm pulled back his shoulders.

"I wish you wouldn't make fun of such a thing."

"I'm not joking."

Of course he wasn't. Of course not.

Perhaps the facts would help. Surely he'd have answers to questions of fact. "Why? When?"

The world's second war was in its second year. They were all aware of it. Father's interest was extensive: he followed the battles through the papers and radio, and he and the older sons discussed the campaigns. The conversations came from a certain perspective. They were conscientious objectors; non-resistance was a tenet of their faith. The discussions she overheard concerned how to articulate this position, how to help the Mennonite boys of soldiering age explain it, gain alternate assignments. Still, there was a certain enthusiasm about the progress of the battles and Father examined his map of the European continent often. Wilhelm had never been interested in the discussions, or the map.

Otherwise, however, the war had had little to do with them so far. Hans might have to go to the CO camp, but even that was not to be feared. They and Ida's parents would look after her while he was gone and his position in the business covered until he returned. Indirectly, the war had actually helped them. Canada's economy had rallied in the face of it, there was demand for many products again, and better prices. There was no denying the war had been good for the country. And for them. They had their piano and Father said one of the houses they were building might be for themselves. He put in his name for another lot, on speculation.

"Today," Wilhelm said. "I've been thinking of it for a long time."

"You should have said something."

"So you could talk me out of it?"

"I would have told you how wrong it is. I still will."

"I've enlisted, Maria." His voice was colder than she'd ever heard it.

She ignored it. "Wilhelm," she pleaded, pushing herself up from the ground to face him, "you belong to the church."

He pitched his foot against the pile of carrots. "I've asked you to call me Bill," he stormed at her, "and I'm telling you now, if I hear you say Wilhelm again I won't speak to you! That was the Kaiser's name and I'm not on that side. I want you to call me Bill."

The earth seemed to rush towards Maria's feet and clot there. She wished she could kneel in it, break it apart as it congealed in front of her. She wanted to concentrate on the carrots, get them free and into the root cellar. He'd never spoken to her this way. There was a man's anger in it, anger against her and no one else, and the words not as rushing and tumbling as before.

"I've enlisted as Bill," he said. "That's the name they'll put on —"

Have it then, she thought, and she leapt in with "Bill, Bill, Bill." If he would be prodigal, she would play the extravagant father, giving whatever he asked for – his inheritance. She'd call him Bill already, as long as he wouldn't finish the sentence, though she felt she'd already heard and could see it, his name on a tag, to identify his body. He was probably thinking a crisp pack and outfit neatly printed, or some notice of valour, but all she saw was the name on the notice of his death. Bill Klassen. In the paper. Half an inch at the most.

Well, let him have his tiny name. "Bill," she repeated, spitting the word at him with a venom that astonished her.

He laughed – his victory obviously unexpected – but there was hurt in his eyes, all his irritation gone. Maria was making his name a joke.

"Thank you," he said.

Weariness overwhelmed her. She laughed too, briefly. She said "Bill" again but softly this time, though she sighed at the end of it.

He misunderstood; he thought they'd been reconciled. It emboldened him. "My name is Bill Klassen," he declared to a pile of rotting tomato stalks. "I'm here to fly a fighter plane!"

His voice turned younger and wistful. "I want to fly," he confided. "Remember, Maria, when you made us run outside – to look at the geese – coming or going, spring or fall, and you said, isn't it wonderful, and I – I was desperate because they could fly and leave and go other places? I envied their wings. Remember how they flew so low over us? It was dark, remember? And once we heard the wings because they weren't honking for some reason – and then I imagined that sound growing louder, and a motor, and the wings stable –" Wilhelm stretched his arms.

"It's your fault, Maria," Wilhelm said.

He was looking this way and that, not at her, dreamy and thinking everything was just fine because she'd called him Bill in a gentle way, had agreed to one thing. As if that would undo his foolish decision. "It's you who got me interested, Maria," he said, "because of the birds, the stories of Lindbergh –"

"Lindbergh!" Maria interrupted furiously. "Lindbergh?"

"Yes, because you said how magnificent – you used

the English word m-m-magnificent, Maria —" but he was stammering now, as if afraid of her, as if sure and already ashamed that he'd misused or mispronounced the big word. "That flight over the ocean – you said, that's the spirit of not giving up we Klassens have too, and —"

He'd gotten it wrong, she thought, what she'd been trying to say. Now she wanted to say "Wilhelm" to hurt him, to make a fist with his old name against him, but she swallowed it. She'd said Bill and Bill it would be, as long as she could remember to use it when she spoke to him.

"Stay here," Maria said. "Work on the carrots while you wait." She thrust the garden fork into his hand. She marched over the rows of the garden, her feet sinking into the loose spent earth. At the porch she dropped her shoes, rushed into the house and up to her room.

In a moment she was back, holding the round Lindbergh mirror. She waved it in front of him, inches from his face. He backed away. "This Bill is a fool," she said. Her vehemence had only increased. "You think enlisting is like smoking a cigarette or going to the theatre? It's far bigger, but for you, it will turn out the same. You choke on the tobacco. You tell me you're miserable in the theatre because you shouldn't be there. Do you think you'll fit? That they want you?"

"They wanted me."

"They want men, they want bodies, but they don't care about you. You want to belong but they don't want *you*. Not in particular." Her perception of the first war and this one too was only of its rottenness, like that repulsive feeling in spring when one reached for potatoes or carrots in the dark root cellar and encountered something soft and decaying.

"They were glad I'd come in," he said.

"Of course. Of course." What was the use?

"Lindbergh, the hero," she said, turning the mirror, mimicking his euphoria about flight.

She flipped it and held the mirror to his face again. "The boy who wants to be Bill."

She twisted the mirror, said "Lindbergh the flyer," turned it back. "Not Bill the flyer. Still only Wilhelm. Who's never been in an airplane. Who knows nothing about sitting in the cockpit of a fighter plane!"

Wilhelm flushed. He jerked and seized the mirror from her hand. "You said you'd call me Bill! And you're not my mother either!" He heaved the mirror against the house. It bounced hard off the wall, dropped into the hollyhocks. The dry stalks shuddered.

The back door opened and Erna appeared. "What was that noise?" she called.

Neither Maria nor Wilhelm answered. "Did something fly against the house?" Erna called.

"Yes, Erna," Maria shouted. "Something flew against the house. Go back inside and do your chores."

"Just Lindbergh flying again," she grumbled to herself.

Erna retreated and Wilhelm said, chastened, "I'll find it."

"You can't imagine the trouble you'll have with Father or your brothers," Maria said.

"I'll always be in trouble. There's no end of trouble if I stay. It will be easier for all of us."

"That's not true," she said. He tramped off to the flower bed and her sentence wailed after him.

He found the memento immediately and brought it to her. The mirror was broken and dusty.

"I don't want it," she said. "You can throw it away."

He held it out to her, waiting.

"Throw it away," she said. "I don't want it."

"May I have the picture then?"

His inexhaustible eagerness exasperated her anew. "Have it! Have it! But you ought to know that Lindbergh is opposed to this war. He's doing everything he can to keep America out. He's no one to look up to if you've enlisted."

"I'm going."

"Have it, have it! And put the carrots in the tub. Clean

up the hoe and fork. Tidy up here. I'm going to see about supper."

Bill, she thought. What a short, unpleasant name. A fragment of what his parents had intended when they named him.

□

Wilhelm's enlistment, as Maria predicted, unleashed trouble and complication in the family. The brothers Gerhard and Hans were contemptuous, the sisters worried and pitying. Father's emotions were more difficult to gauge. He was surprisingly restrained. After his initial "Our church's position is, we don't bear arms," he said nothing further.

The news zigzagged through the community, of course, and there were questions and bids for information about what had possessed the young man. Maria felt she was going about with a fever just under her skin, wearing Wilhelm's shame like a flaw obvious to all. She assumed he would be excommunicated from the church.

Once, coming to the door of her father's room and leaning on the door frame while he scrutinized his Europe map, Maria blurted, "I'm afraid he'll die over there."

"You don't know," he said. "God knows." There was little conviction in his voice. "But yes, it's certainly possible." A tone of forced magnanimity, as if granting her a wish. But he seemed to be speaking of some unrelated young man, some other Mennonite son, not his own.

"I know your heart is motherly towards him," her father said. He'd seen the tears she couldn't hold back when Wilhelm left, how spontaneously she hugged him, how they clung to each other for a moment, Father waiting for his handshake and formal embrace. "He made the decision. He chooses the consequences."

It wasn't a mother's heart, she longed to protest. Somewhere she had a child who meant nothing to her, about whom she desired not to think except as the reason for a path in one direction and not another. But the child existed because of her; he was a consequence impossible to alter. Though he meant nothing to her, he existed. She'd changed the world in that way.

But life proceeded after consequences. Surely Wilhelm could realize what he'd done, return to them, to his faith. Many Christians went to war, he'd told her in his defense, but in the context of their church, he knew his act was a spiritual rebellion. And there, she felt, the future in terms of Wilhelm was being ignored. Surely the meaning of consequences was greater than that and, past fear, Wilhelm could be back.

Back to sing in the choir, carrying the tenor section or the basses, whichever section needed help, so large was the range with which he was gifted. Jacob the patriarch ran away after cheating his brother, and then he dreamed and heard a blessing, saw angels strolling a ladder. After his treachery!

And Leah, the patriarch's wretched first wife, feeble-eyed. She was so unloved, God made her fruitful. All her sons, one after the other, named for the stages of the unending contest with her sister, competing for the love and seed of one man. But divine help was then pushed Rachel's way when she angered her husband by blaming him for her barrenness. Her maid gave sons to her: Dan, the vindication, and Napthali, the poet, appreciated by his father for his delicate words. And she too, at last, given sons – from her body.

Blessings were irrational, out of turn – that's what those stories told her. People chosen and kept in the oddest ways, rivals blessed, both of them. God somehow managed to be on everyone's side. And in spite of her fears, wasn't there enormous hope in that? But she hadn't been muttering of this to Father, had she? Muttering her unconventional observations?

"Mother was so worried about you being alone in the city," Father was saying. "She always felt she'd done a terrible thing to allow it."

There was a pause. Maria longed for the sound of a bicycle on the wooden walkway, Wilhelm whistling, "When you wish upon a star" or "You are my sunshine," songs her father didn't know.

"I guess she worried for nothing," he said. He smiled at her kindly. "You've done a good job for us, Maria. I want you to know that."

□

The top of the Heintzman piano was a place of honour. Here, on a crocheted runner, stood the wedding photographs of her siblings: Gerhard and Helene, Susanna and Henry, Hans and Ida, Katherine and Peter. And the family groupings: Gerhard and Helene with their children John, Helen, and Louise; Susanna and Henry with their sons Henry and George. The photographer had posed Gerhard and Helene's children leaning against their seated mother as if she were a tree and they small ladders against the trunk. There was a photograph, made informally at Hans' wedding, of Father Klassen; another of the three single sisters Maria, Margarethe, and Erna.

There was no picture of Wilhelm on the piano. Before he left, Wilhelm gave Maria and his father each a photograph of himself taken by Uncle Peter. He was standing in uniform, smiling brashly in front of Peter and Agathe's small house. No denying it, Maria thought, he was handsome in that uniform.

But neither Maria nor her father had offered their picture of Wilhelm to the displays on the piano. She set hers against a white vase on the table beside her bed. After several months she put it away, into a drawer, wincing again at the cheery "Your brother Bill, remember me always" on the back.

She prayed for him routinely, once a day, calling him Wilhelm in her requests that God keep and protect him. Beyond that, she didn't think of him often. His infrequent letters were brief and there was little to be learned from them. He wrote in English and sounded immature and awkward. He hinted at boredom, at wanting to use his training. He was loading planes on a British base, he wrote eventually, but still hoped to get into the air. He hadn't earned his pilot's wings yet, he said, but there were other positions to get him up and over.

Then he astonished them by sending a photo of himself and a woman to whom, he said, he'd become engaged. Her name was Grace Berton.

"An *Englischer*," Father said sadly.

The comment irritated Maria. What else did Father expect from England? The two young people were standing in front of a gate in some kind of garden, their faces unclear at a distance. Grace was much shorter than Wilhelm; she was pressed into the crook of his waist, with her head turned slightly and laughing up towards him, as if it was a great joke that they would be married.

"She seems nice enough," Maria said. "Though not much can be gained from a picture."

"A picture tells us nothing," Father agreed.

This photo didn't make it onto the Heintzman either. It travelled with Maria for a while, in her pocket or bag until all the married sisters and brothers had seen it. Then it stood with the letters from Wilhelm behind the good dishes in a high kitchen cupboard. When they got the news two months later that Wilhelm's plane was downed on his first mission as a gunner, the photo and the correspondence relating to his military life were tied with a string and removed into Father's room, into his box of papers and keepsakes.

Father had opened the official missive that said

Wilhelm was presumed dead, read it and pushed it across the supper table to Maria. "As you feared," he said.

That evening their devotional reading fell upon a terrible passage.

> *He lurks in a hiding place as a lion in his lair;*
> *He lurks to catch the afflicted;*
> *He catches the afflicted when he draws him into his net.*
> *He crouches . . . and the unfortunate fall . . .*
> *He says to himself, God has forgotten;*
> *He has hidden his face, He will never see it.*

"So," Father said, adding a gloss to the text. "There it is. Be sure of yourself." He clapped the Bible together with unusual force. When he continued, his voice was quiet, confessional. "I've been anxious over his soul this whole time, and now I'll never know how things stood. No one should put their parent through such uncertainty."

Maria and Erna and Margarethe stared at him, then bowed their heads as he did. Maria squeezed her lids tightly against tears while he prayed.

She did not hear what he was saying. Her secret suddenly surged within her. It was consolation; it filled her with certainty. God had been with Wilhelm too.

☐

The Flood had done its damage, was finally over. There was no damage to his house, Peter mused, or any house of his Klassen relatives, though his brother-in-law Johann had insisted that Maria and the women folk of his clan leave the city, even if they weren't under evacuation orders. He wanted them safe and dry and out of the way, so they'd all crowded into the Winkler farm house of Susanna and Henry and their four children, where they had been – to hear Maria speak of it – packed as tightly and neatly as cordwood. His

Agathe wasn't with them though, as if it made no difference if more dikes burst and he and she were forced to clamber up their chimney and sit on it, clinging to one another as their home lifted off its foundation and floated away.

Well, it hadn't come to that, and the foundation wasn't that fragile either, as bad as it had been, the Flood of 1950, capitalized and dated now for the history books. Not as bad as carrying them away; they weren't in the low areas of St. Vital and Kingston Row and all those other places talked about over and over again in the papers. Just weeks of panic and sogginess, and then Maria and her sisters gone and Agathe left behind at home with him. Though now they knew it hadn't been a party, all of them pressed together at Susanna's, and Maria ill and miserable the whole time on the Winkler farm, her body reeling like a piece of cork in turbulent waters, she said, hearing rain against the window and constantly worried. She had said all this this afternoon, visiting, and then he'd hurt his Agathe and so he'd fled her hurt and tears and anger, fled now to his chair beside the shed in the back yard, watching the sky. He was a sky watcher. What room was there for bitterness in the changing panorama of sky?

"I'd volunteered to take care of the laundry," Maria had said, coming round for her visit with a piece-for-two of her fresh platz, as if to apologize for the fact she'd been away, "and was hanging out the diapers. I guess I collapsed."

When she opened her eyes, she said, she'd thought for an instant the diapers flapping over her head were clouds.

"Clouds of diapers," his Agathe had sighed. "So many children in that house all at once," and then she and Maria were naming them all, but he thought Maria looked sad and uneasy, describing how many days she'd been in bed, and no one taking it as seriously as she, her younger sisters and nieces laughing through the weeks they were there, and then those silly exercises they'd been doing out of a women's magazine, bumping their hips against the walls for ten minutes a day. Exercise for Hippy Hannahs, or something like that, and when Maria said none of them had hips enough to speak of, Susanna had pushed it away with, "It's a silliness that does no harm."

Peter heard the indignation in Maria's voice, so he'd mentioned, nothing hurtful intended, that Agathe had been as happy as she'd ever been while they were gone, as happy as he'd ever seen her in fact, thinking herself with child at last, though he hadn't believed it himself, not for a moment, not without more evidence than a week or two. How many false hopes could one chase before one gave up on a futile habit, he'd said. But she – Agathe – she'd been happy the entire time they'd been away, as if she needed them gone so the child-wish could set, but just because it was a week longer than usual, what did that mean?

He'd sensed Agathe stiffening, but thought nothing further – honestly – until Maria was gone, for it was Maria who seemed unusually critical today, complaining of Susanna so proud – and bossy! – to be in charge for a change and poor Henry hiding in the barn the entire time (as if he had an option, Peter had thought while she talked of it, those silly girls knocking their hips against his walls). She would never speak ill of her family, but rather defended it, and now she was giving him these kernels, not to please him and his penchant for gossip, but out of some disappointment of her own.

Then Maria was gone, her empty *platz* plate too, and Agathe had flown at him, her fist against his chest, wailing that it wasn't the kind of thing he needed to broadcast and why in the world had he talked of her like that, to Maria yet, when it wasn't true, there was no baby, then saying she was happier than he'd ever seen her?

It was a muddle of accusations that only confused him and so he'd escaped here, to the shed, grabbing the chair he kept there for sitting outside, for sky watching, glancing as he took the chair at the last year's calendar still hanging on the rough shed wall, a picture of a chalet nestled in the mountains with its announcement beneath, "Care Saves Wear! See your Esso dealer," and he'd been briefly saddened by the thought of a year over and never retrievable again, though he'd hung the calendar there for the picture and the sky behind the mountains, rose-coloured from the unseen setting sun.

The sky. How he loved the sky. He'd imagined, as a child, that everyone was the same as he was in this way, until some of the boys had laughed at him for always talking about what he saw, and he'd stopped speaking of it then, but not stopped looking, and after so many years he felt he must be nearly alone in the world in his secret obsession about what the sky was like at the moment. It seemed his private burden, and his private joy. Every time he stepped outside he looked first at the sky.

Many days there was nothing there in particular but the palest shades of blue and an immense sense of unassuming patience, a kind of mercy he was no less fond of than the extravagant displays that clouds could mount. He didn't watch as a farmer, for he was a gardener, not a farmer. Of course the weather affected his work, but it didn't affect his living. He was a gardener of decorative plants and grass and if it didn't rain it meant he'd be taking stored-up rainwater in pails around the gardens in a wheelbarrow to keep the plants going for maximum effect. A little sweat work, that was all.

He watched the sky for some other reason, not for God exactly, whom he assumed much further away than even the sky. For movement, perhaps, though often almost impercep-tible. For movement of clouds. And colour. When Agathe imagined him just sitting there, bored or smoking or lazy perhaps, he was watching. He remembered certain pictures, small sequences. That one last summer, spectacular mounds of white sliding by in front of the steely blue behind it, as blue-grey as slate, not threatening as much as stern. Like the law, and love surging past in that glorious triumph of white, he'd suddenly thought. Crazy, what it made him think of.

But now, here was Agathe, her eyes red, dropping to the ground before he could offer her the chair, her head on his lap. She said nothing and had closed her eyes, so he said, "I liked it that you were so happy."

She didn't answer or protest, so Peter went on. "Maria seemed rather cross because of Susanna."

Agathe raised her head, her face turning prim. To Peter, her look announced that once again, she would have to clarify the world of women.

"Maria was sick, Peter, and Susanna took care of everything and everyone. Instead of Maria doing it. And Susanna is married, which irritates Maria too."

"Susanna's not the only one married. Why would that bother her?"

"But Gerhard and Hans take their women for granted. It's bearable being with them. Those women have their bits of misery too."

"Susanna's Henry never says a thing."

"Have you seen how their eyes meet?"

Peter couldn't say that he had, and he lifted his own skyward now, surreptitiously though, thinking this conversation nearly as mysterious as his wife's rage not that many minutes before.

"Susanna talks enough for both of them," Agathe said, "but she always says she's completely dependent, she calls him her Gibraltar, and if you happen to see that look, you believe it. She's completely happy, and I imagine he is too. Maria's probably seen it too and it would make her envious I suppose."

"She said he lived in the barn while they were there."

"Just those weeks, Peter! And it's an expression. It's an expression!"

"Well, I hope I'm not so bad as all that to you," he said.

"There's nothing to envy in us, Peter!" Agathe's voice rose with the bitterness he often felt but could not hang onto for long, and now he saw something in the sky that he was sure had just arrived for him. He couldn't help himself. "Look," he said.

The sky had deepened, ever so slightly, and a solitary wisp of cloud, like a bit of cow hair caught in a fence barb, had formed to float on its surface.

"What, what?" she cried.

"That clump of cloud," he said.

"*Ach*, Peter," Agathe sighed. Once again, she leaned into his lap.

□

One day in 1951, Edith Lowry telephoned to ask Maria for tea. It took a moment, until Mrs Lowry identified herself, and then Maria thought, Yes, of course, I knew her at once. Her hand holding the black receiver weakened as she recognized the long-ago voice. It was nearly twenty years since she'd heard it.

"We're at the same address," Mrs Lowry said. "Not even the furniture has changed."

"We've been pilgrims," Maria said. She meant they'd been moving around in North Kildonan, from one house to the next slightly bigger one. She'd just settled into the latest of these, in fact, built since the flood. But she regretted the phrase immediately. The purpose of the movement was strictly material, not spiritual at all, as the expression implied: *I'm a pilgrim, I'm a stranger, I can tarry but a night.* She'd been proud of their mobility because it showed their growing affluence. But suddenly, in the face of Mrs Lowry's two sentences, it seemed unstable and capricious.

But, not even the furniture? The Lowrys' house must be looking very dated by now.

She didn't really want to go, but what could she do?

She had no excuses. Maria accepted the invitation and they agreed on a time for her to come by.

The Lowrys' red brick house appeared smaller than Maria remembered it. Perhaps the growth of trees had revised the proportions. But, the house and yard seemed well tended, though one of the lions at the porch was disfigured: half its mouth was chipped off. Why hadn't they repaired it?

Maria and Mrs Lowry were formal with one another. "Come in, please, come in, let me take your coat." "It's so nice to see you again." "Please be seated." They glanced furtively at one another but neither mentioned that the other had changed. Neither mentioned the span of years since Maria had last been here.

Mrs Lowry was dressed simply in a black wool dress, a strand of pearls about her neck. Her hair was dark auburn as before and piled about her head in much the same fashion as earlier but it had a different sheen to it now. Maria suspected it was dyed. Her lipstick was a bold thick red, the rouge visible on her cheeks. She looked slightly garish, or careless.

They hurried to small talk, about the weather, the current news, about Maria driving herself over. Maria was privately pleased to discover that learning to drive was a feat Mrs Lowry hadn't attempted herself but heartily approved of. "I think it's wonderful," she said. "Why shouldn't women get about on their own?"

When Mrs Lowry said, "Well, let's have tea," Maria nearly sprang up to make it, but it was Mrs Lowry who rose. "I don't keep a regular girl anymore," she said. "Things are different nowadays."

Maria had no idea what Mrs Lowry wanted or why she would revive their relationship. Could she anticipate friendship? Such a friendship would have the one ingredient none of Maria's other relationships had, the knowledge of the child she'd borne. Sharing this truth made her cautious, but it attracted her too.

Waiting for Mrs Lowry to reappear from the kitchen, the

visit barely underway, Maria felt herself disappointed. The feeling of being a young immigrant servant was creeping upon her. Oh, how many things there were to learn! So many fine points in proper service, in proper behaviour, in running a household Canadian (or English) style. They had to be acquired, one by one. Would one ever be finished?

> *Don't pass someone on the stairs, but wait at the top or bottom.*
> *Offer food on the left of the person being served.*
> *Remove the dishes on the right.*
> *To plan a successful menu, first taste it in your mind.*
> *Don't ask, "Would you like some more . . . ?" thus drawing attention to the fact that a portion has already been eaten, but ask, "Would you like some . . . ?"*
> *Every meal should have at least one interesting dish.*
> *Crescendo to the main dish, diminuendo to dessert.*
> *Keep the water glasses filled.*

All the maxims, great and small, had been sung into Maria's repertoire of rules for living. The Lowrys had seemed to know them all of course, but it occurred to Maria now, they'd been honing themselves for upward advancement by passing them on; her progressive refinement kept their own goals in view. They weren't finished with their ideals when Maria lived with them any more than she was with hers. They yearned and planned and arranged and pursued. "Better days are coming," one of the songs of the day had promised, "wait and see."

Remembering, Maria felt that a friendship of equals between her and Mrs Lowry wouldn't be possible, tea together in the sitting room notwithstanding. Maria consoled herself against this assessment by reminding herself that the exclusive knowledge they shared – her given-away baby – was really nothing more, nothing better, than sharing many other things. Mrs Lowry knew only that and Maria's five years of service, but what did she really know of her, of her history and life before, or after? The one thing Mrs Lowry knew wasn't important any more. Even though Maria's own family might be missing that one piece, they knew vastly more. And they loved her.

A fire, begun but untended, burned on both sides of the fireplace. The heavy curtains in the room were half drawn. The room felt grey and dim, as if bulbs in the lamp fixtures were missing or dusty. As Mrs Lowry had warned over the phone, the furniture in the room was the same, the same tables and lamps and sofa and chairs, though the chairs had been recovered with different fabric – in a light walnutty brown colour – and there were different draperies to match. The overall effect was still well composed and elegant, though faded and somewhat old-fashioned by now.

She wouldn't mind a peek at the kitchen. Had the back rooms been re-arranged or were they also preserved as they were in the past? She tried not to think of the house, however, not to notice it. But she remembered the third level room and suddenly worried that Mrs Lowry had called to interrogate her about the ruined King of Diamonds.

Then Mrs Lowry was back, attentive and brisk, and the ritual of tea and cake was underway. Maria remarked on the teacups – a white leaf motif on a deep pink band – and Mrs Lowry explained they were Minton-made; she got them in 1940, she said, for their anniversary. Mrs Lowry told Maria that she and James lived in the large house alone. She had a day woman two days a week, someone who cleaned and did the laundry, but as to the meals, she managed herself. Maria took a piece of fancy cake from the tray and saw it came from a bakery; the pieces were exactly the same size, the cuts obviously made by a machine with a long blade, and the swirl of chocolate over the glaze almost too perfect. That's why there was no aroma of baking in the house, just the smell of furniture polish, wax, tobacco smoke, and Mrs Lowry's perfume. Why shouldn't Maria also buy from a bakery sometime when she couldn't get the Saturday baking done? Her guests would be shocked, have the same haughty reaction she'd just had, then do the same thing the following week.

"I'm planning to re-do the sofa as well," Mrs Lowry said. "Or maybe I'll finally order new. I've just gotten attached to this stuff, I suppose."

Then she paused and said, "Robert Russell was killed in the war."

The war had been over for six years.

"Bobby?"

"Yes, yes."

Maria said she was terribly sorry; she hadn't known.

The bleakness of her voice must have touched Mrs Lowry, for the older woman's lips began to quiver. This in its turn drew tears from Maria. Commiseration swam between them.

"That's why I called you," Mrs Lowry said.

She got up, went to the mantel, returned with a framed picture of her son in uniform.

"Oh, he looks very good," Maria said. She touched the glass as if to touch his face. Why hadn't she been told?

Mrs Lowry took the picture and held it upright on her black lap. She leaned forward and talked about Bobby, who at some point after Maria left their service seemed to have grown up into his distinguished double name of Robert Russell. Edith Lowry told Maria how he graduated, how he joined the Air Force, how he earned his wings, how he was killed in heroic action. Over and over the name Robert Russell sounded in Maria's ears. Mrs Lowry said he was married before he went overseas but they hadn't had children. "She's re-married. It's only fair for someone so young. I wished they'd had a child though."

"Don't you have grandchildren?"

"Oh yes. Five. James has three, Eleanor two. Frances hasn't married. She's a missionary in Burma."

Snobbish Frances a missionary? It was almost more surprising than Bobby dead.

"But —" Mrs Lowry lowered her voice as if she feared an eavesdropper, "you'll remember that Robert Russell was my only son. You know what I mean. There's something different about that."

In spite of the length at which she spoke about Bobby, Mrs Lowry seemed finished with grieving. The black dress was for taste, Maria felt, not for mourning. The visit must have been an opportunity to tell the story to someone completely new to it, however, to someone keen to hear it, someone who would gasp involuntarily, hear it as the bad news it was, for the very first time. Maria wondered if the other woman had missed the sense of loss, the sweet melancholy of sorrow, and needed someone completely new to invigorate it. Then remembered Maria. A chance to talk about her son and pretend it still pained her unbearably. To reassure herself perhaps that she couldn't live happily without him.

"You rescued him for me once and I still lost him in the end," Edith Lowry sighed. "He was a wild boy, though, I have to say that. I had my hands full with him."

"He taught me a lot of my English," Maria said.

Mrs Lowry said she could tell Maria hadn't been using it enough.

The fire had crackled down. The steam pipes gurgled and clanged at a distance. Maria heard the slight warning hiss of them, the heat coming on. Obviously Mrs Lowry hadn't noticed how cool the room had become. As soon as the room was warmed, Maria thought, she would leave.

"I had a brother . . . Bill," she offered. "He was also killed in the war."

"I had the impression you people didn't participate."

"He went anyway."

Mrs Lowry seemed to be contemplating this. "He gave his life for our freedom, Maria," she said after a while. "No

244

matter how much we miss our brothers and sons, I comfort myself knowing they gave their futures for ours today. It was worth dying for . . . I'm relieved actually – glad, I mean, that someone in your family went. You came to this country for what it offered and your brother must have realized it takes sacrifice to keep the freedoms you came for."

Mrs Lowry believed it. Maria only half believed these sentiments, with their cadences of rippling flags and marching – she'd tried to believe them, at least, to justify Wilhelm's premature death – but they shamed her. She was unable to talk about Wilhelm in the way Mrs Lowry talked about Bobby. Her brother's death seemed less necessary than Bobby's, less noble. If only she could bring him into her hand the way Mrs Lowry set her son in the room, his eyes so clear and merry, in a framed photograph taken in a studio. But it wasn't just that. Her brother never earned his wings. She couldn't imagine Bobby and Wilhelm as comrades. Her brother would have fallen inwards – she was sure of this – around the Robert Russells of the barracks.

The dead Robert Russell might be gone but he remained still whole on Mrs Lowry's lap. His name was on a church plaque, she had said; Maria imagined the sunlight touching it through the stained glass windows. Maria attended church with them one Easter many years ago and remembered the mellow light, red and blue and yellow and green, and the names of local fallen soldiers of the Great War. But she couldn't hold Wilhelm in one piece, not as a decent picture, not as raised letters speaking his name, not even as a wounded body. He had scattered. That's what explosions did. She assumed his body had flown apart into soft fleshy lumps that dropped to the earth as rain, there to be tumbled about and further broken, clods of dirt on the bleak wintry earth.

Of course she wanted to tell Mrs Lowry more about Wilhelm, but she'd been reminded her English had suffered. How could one describe this wayward brother of hers anyway?

She'd tried hard over Wilhelm, and thought for many years she'd done well. He always came to her for confession. *She who is forgiven much, loves much.* That's what Jesus said. Maria had poured so much love into Wilhelm.

How to describe the two of them?

Maria told Mrs Lowry that her mother died the year she left service and that she'd been taking care of the household and younger siblings since then. "My brother who died in the war was a wild boy too," she said. This caught in her throat a little. "I had my hands full too."

"They died for us, Maria. You have to remember that."

Mrs Lowry asked how she'd been keeping otherwise and Maria gave a short report. She told of her brothers and sisters who were all grown and married now. She told of her sewing. She mentioned that some in her family were musical. They were heavily involved in the Festival; perhaps Mrs Lowry had seen their names in the paper? She mentioned by name the businesses her father and brothers had founded. She said a little about each one. She thought Mrs Lowry was impressed.

Then Maria said she ought to be going, and she stood up to do so. The telephone rang in the hall. Mrs Lowry excused herself and left to answer it. After a moment she stepped back and said it was long distance, from her brother's wife; would Maria wait a few minutes, please?

Maria couldn't help herself. She stole to the mantel to look at the photographs. They'd been talking about Wilhelm and now she caught a glimpse of him. No, not Wilhelm. What was she thinking? But someone similar for sure. The dark and wavy hair, the wide smile, askew at the same angle, the body tall and gangly. Looking both stubborn and vulnerable. A Klassen if ever there'd been one, shades of her father. It was her son. Who else could it be? He was posed with Martin and Gladys and they were all smiling broadly, looking extremely pleased with themselves, looking straight at her. He was looking at her and she couldn't turn away. All she'd planned was a glance at James Edward and his Ruthie and children – Mrs Lowry said they had three.

"You and I each lost our only son," Mrs Lowry said cheerfully when she returned and saw Maria by the mounted photos. "That's Raymond there. With Gladys and Martin."

Maria said she really should be going now, it was late, and she'd had such a lovely time. The awkwardness returned and she and Mrs Lowry resorted to formal phrases until she could get her coat on and get out of the house.

"A lovely reunion," Mrs Lowry called after her, just before she closed the door.

Maria patted the blighted lion cub on the head. "Raymond," she said aloud. So that was his name.

When she turned her car at the street corner she glanced sideways and back. The Lowry house was hidden behind its neighbour except for the winking windows of the attic room on the third floor, just under the roof.

7

ANOTHER TWO DECADES passed before Maria had to pick up the thread of her Lowry connection again.

(And what colour was the thread? To such a question she would have said, not scarlet, that's for certain. Scarlet was a notion that forgiveness overrode. The colour of something long buried underground, pale perhaps or very dark; and anyways, she would have said, how can you know the colour if it's deeply hidden, away from the light of the day? What difference does it make, she would have said, exasperated.)

Just days before she and Edith Lowry met again, in 1971 (as if the incidents were also connected, underground, or overground perhaps, *as far as the heavens are over the earth*), Maria found herself weeping in the tiny bath of a shabby though surprisingly expensive London hotel. She was weeping like she'd never, to her recollection, wept before, in great gushing sobs and gasps for breath, unable to stop herself but conscious at the same time of the extravagance of it all, letting the water run to muffle the noise, pressing a towel against her eyes, swabbing at her mouth.

(But still letting out some of the sound. It seemed important to let some of it go. To howl a little. As if the sobs were plugs of pain that wouldn't disappear unless they deliberately popped and dissolved into the steam.)

Maria knew she was weeping over Wilhelm that day,

but images of her long deceased mother, her father – more recently deceased – and then the baby boy in Martin's arms, and a great variety of other scenes appeared in her mind, appeared and vanished again, as if they were the visual track of the shuddering sound that possessed her. Her mother turning, only her profile visible, but the expression on her face one of her own separate self, a look perfectly contained and – at that moment at least – not of someone attached to her husband or children. Her father's stubbled cheek and his body sinking into his chair (it was the house in Russia) and some hue of fear or horror on his face. She was five or six then, or maybe seven. Then the image of his old body in the coffin. The white of a diaper billowing into her face at Susanna's as she crumpled to the ground. A dresser set she hated. A chubby woman shrieking questions through a hole in the hedge. Flower-like shapes opened larger and larger behind her eyes while she wept until they exploded and fell into the ocean of memories that was her life.

□

And what had opened, closed, exploded, changed in twenty years?

Ah, the Flood, yes, with the illness seizing her while away. Pushing her into a corner of Susanna's house. Voices and laughter around her like lamps blinking in the faraway dark. A sense of being small and compact, as if bundled into a sack. Trying to claw her way upwards, then feeling relieved to fall backwards, to nestle in the warmth of a hole that was private and utterly safe. In the foggy haze on the morning they had packed and departed the city, the dikes they passed seemed like stone walls out of antiquity. Something that would last forever.

Then, lying in her cot, fed her sister's chicken noodle soup, not as tasty as her own, feeling for the first time anger and waves of envy, strange grief over what keeping her secret had actually done. How it had turned her into something partial, and false.

She'd fought the grief, the foreign notion, immediately. She would work at it harder then, she told herself, she would make herself real, make her decision true. But the regret she'd felt had caught her unawares and ached in her along with her illness, like a prediction of uselessness.

Then in 1957, she reached the age her mother had been at her death. Forty-nine. The Christmas before, her father and Margarethe and Erna (who'd married in summer) put money together and bought Maria a dresser set. It was a heavy silver-toned Priscilla set she later saw advertised for $34. They wrapped it up with a store-bought card in English that said, "For all you mean to us," which each of them had signed.

When Maria opened the box, the dresser set glimmered at her with an oddly jaunty air in spite of its weight and ponderous ornamentation. She exclaimed over it, but wondered whose idea it was. She'd never expressed an interest in a dresser set. Dresser sets were given to girlfriends or wives. Later she spread the mirror, brush, and comb on the crocheted runner on her dresser but no matter which way she arranged the pieces, in three parallel lines leaning left, then right, or in a fan shape, she didn't like it. The set looked formally romantic but also sinister, she thought. She supposed it was a reminder she had finished raising the children and could reclaim youthful accessories if she wished, after all this time. Middle-aged women had dresser sets too, of course, but she had nothing to match the set's assumption of the boudoir. Her father and sisters should have given her some kitchen utensil or appliance.

□

She had found herself, sometimes, staring at her father. He might be sitting in his comfortable brown chair, engrossed in the newspaper, his legs crossed and a worn slipper dangling loosely over the toes of his raised foot, and she on the sofa opposite, crocheting the tablecloth she was making for Erna and Peter's belated wedding gift. She might hear his lips part as if he was going to speak; she would look up. But he was absorbed in his reading, seemingly unaware of her gaze. And she would think, "That's my father," and be startled by this as if it were a newspaper headline. Who was he, this familiar stranger?

Or the question caught her when she walked by his bedroom door and noticed him busy at the desk beside his bed, studying charts and Scripture texts and articles and books of prophecy. By day he was businessman and builder; evenings he worked at mastering the End Times. He sometimes preached on the prophetic texts, when it was his turn to preach, or wrote about them for the denominational paper. He'd also been writing about television, warning about the deterioration of morals and its effects on children and the church's growing accommodation to the fashion of the world. He sometimes wrote of the continuing need for the preservation of German, urging the Mennonites to establish classes for the cultivation of the language. To keep them going once they were established. People would tell Maria how much they appreciated her father's articles.

Sometimes she passed the compliments on; other times she kept them to herself. Yes, his words flowed in a logical way from one point to another, but in her opinion – though she never voiced it – her father was becoming unreasonable. He refused, for example, to speak to his grandchildren in any language but German. He actually pretended not to understand their English, though he was fluent enough with his non-German customers. It was for the children's sakes, he told Maria. But he scared them away with his false insistent ignorance. Maria spoke German in his presence to keep the peace, but when he wasn't around she switched to English with the children and young people, as they preferred.

Nor was she interested in the details of the Second Coming or the events before and after it. She couldn't fathom the quest to decode the unknown future. If it took so much work to unravel the sequence of things, she sometimes thought – aware of her irreverence – perhaps the order wasn't meant to be obvious. Surely the end of the world would unfold as God willed it in spite of preachers' charts and their elaborate schemata. But she felt vaguely ashamed in thinking this. Surely any kind of specialized knowledge, such as doctors and scientists engaged in, for example, required diligent study, endless detail, leaps and connections. Why not this? Perhaps her resistance was laziness, or a faith too small. Perhaps she was simply hoping the Second Coming wouldn't happen too soon.

Maria's father was still handsome then, though his hair was grey, his brows white and coarse, and his shoulders even more rounded. He needed glasses. He found a pair that helped him by trying various ones in a store. They didn't suit him, Maria thought, though perhaps it was merely the fit that was wrong. He refused to consult a doctor or specialist in eyeglasses.

But where was the likeness between them she'd always been informed of, always been proud of? Maria would fix her eyes on her father, narrow them, will this gaze to jog her memory about their common lineage. He'd told the children about his boyhood and youth, about the Crimea in the early years. She recalled him in scenes of the past. She could recollect things he'd said and done. She knew his tastes in clothing, his preferences in food, his opinions, and his stories. But, as much as she searched, she couldn't truly remember him. But why did she need to remember him anyway, with him present, mere feet away?

Bringing him a tray with a mug of coffee and a piece of buttered bread and jam one evening, all as he liked it, the coffee nearly white with milk, the bread sliced thickly, the butter scant, the jam piled full to the edge, she was gripped by an irrational, shocking wish to shout at him. The two of them lived harmoniously. And what would she shout about? She had no idea.

Did this happen to everyone? This anger that ties of blood, a common history, even hundreds of small details of day-to-day living held in common, could never bridge the distance between parent and child? Nothing could resolve the fact that he'd existed before she did. The fact that he'd caused her to be. That her essential self owed something to him, but his owed nothing to her. His stories of his younger self were simply that, souvenirs of himself, units of memory he owned but she didn't. When she stared at him, she realized he hadn't needed her protection for who he was, yet she'd kept her pregnancy and baby a secret in order to preserve the lives and reputations of her parents. She'd acted the way she did because of them, because of her brothers and sisters. Because of her strong belief in the connection, in the family unity, as if it were a cord as thick as her arm. In their breath as one breath, in her obligation to the blood she'd inherited. But it hadn't been necessary!

Or had it? A cleft of sadness distanced her now, because she'd forgotten what *father* had meant to her then.

□

And then there was Anni.

"Remember? Remember?"

It was Anni, gripping her arm in the foyer after church, her face inches away from Maria's. Anni Enns, the girl she and Helene briefly befriended in their days as domestics. The girl who'd broken down and disappeared.

Her breath puffing out "Remember?" was warm and surprisingly sweet. Maria moved backwards. Anni had grown fat and creamy in the face, but her gaze was still steady and unblinking. Maria had recognized her immediately.

The couple who'd taken Anni in after her collapse had

died, Maria discovered, and now Anni was staying with those relatives' daughter and her husband and children, the Sawatzkys, who lived in North Kildonan. But it wasn't clear how long they could manage.

Hurrying home from the women's meeting at the church several weeks after this first reunion, walking alone because she'd stayed to clean up afterwards, Maria spotted something yellow in the branches of the hedge at the Sawatzky house.

She stopped. Anni's round face with its pale round eyes peered back at her through a hole in the green caragana. She was wearing a snagged yellow sweater.

"Maria!" Anni said. She whispered hoarsely and opened her eyes even wider as if Maria were a rare bird she'd discovered between the branches. "Mar-i-a!" She drew out the syllables.

Maria greeted Anni, asked how she was doing. She spoke as if it were possible to have a normal conversation with her.

"Maria!" Anni tried to wedge her head further into the gap in the hedge.

"Don't, Anni, don't do that. You'll hurt yourself!"

But Anni got part of her head in and twisted slightly and gazed up. "What happened to your baby?" she squeaked.

Anni was sick and everyone knew it but hearing that question, Maria stepped back. The heel of her shoe landed on a stone. She teetered a little, moved off the stone, kicked it away from her. She swallowed.

"Get your head out of the hedge, Anni," she said, bending closer. "And what did you say?"

"Oh, oh, Maria, where's your baby?" Anni pulled out of the hedge and rocked on her haunches. "Your little baby boy, where did he go?"

"You and your bad, bad ideas, Anni! Stop it now!"

Maria's scolding only encouraged the other woman to moan, "Oh, oh, oh, where did you leave the baby?"

It was absurd, Maria thought, standing there talking to a crazy woman through a hole in the hedge, a hole Maria knew Anni made for herself by persistently plucking the fresh growth away from that spot. But the question worried her.

Did Anni know something or was it just coincidence, something formulated this minute from the shards of impulse and idea that collided in her head? What exactly was inside that head and how did it work? Maria wasn't unpitying of the woman and she admired the family that had taken her in. But this weaker woman aroused her fear, her uncertainty.

She noticed Frede Martens advancing along the sidewalk. Maria put on a merry, indulgent manner. "I'm making borscht for supper," she bent to tell Anni loudly, giving Frede a knowing look as she passed. Frede nodded and smiled.

"You had a baby," Anni told her. "The butler said."

Maria tensed; she could feel her heart pounding. But Frede was out of earshot. "What butler?"

"My butler." Anni stuck her head into the opening again. "You went away. You had a baby." She twisted her features into a pathetic expression. "But where did it go?" Her straw-coloured hair was loose and caught the stub of a branch. She shrieked and yanked herself back onto the ground inside the yard.

One of the Sawatzky children, a girl of about six or seven, ran across the yard to Anni as if to console a younger playmate. But first she peeked through the hole at Maria. "Is Anni bothering you, Miss Klassen?"

"No, no. I just stopped to say Hello."

"She had a baby, Rosie, a baby boy," Anni muttered. "But we don't know where he went. Did the flood wash him away?"

"Rosie," Maria said, relieved at the nonsense of Anni's assertion, "I hope you aren't paying attention to the things Anni says."

"Oh no, Miss Klassen," the child answered solemnly. "We pay no attention to what she says. Mama says she's grown up but something happened. Now she's got the brains of cottage cheese."

"Well, that's good," Maria said. "Run along and play now." The girl skipped away. Anni had cupped her head with one hand and was swaying, though quiet.

"Anni," Maria hissed through the hedge. "Don't you know God doesn't want you telling those lies?"

Anni stopped and squinted through the hole as if she were going to attempt to climb into it once more. Then, as if she'd peered through a tunnel and finally seen to the end of it, she started again. "Maria!" she cried. "What happened to your baby? Did he float away in the flood? Did he disappear in the river?"

"The river!" Maria filled the words with her indignation, as if the ridiculousness of it all was a scolding enough, but saying them, she felt afraid. The accuracy of Anni's incoherence disturbed her; on this lovely autumn afternoon, speaking to Anni, it seemed to her that God, whom she knew cared for the lowly and weak and even the dim-witted, had sat down beside Anni, sat inside the hedge and that she, Maria, was alone. Oddly forsaken, as if in fact something long forgiven needed forgiving again.

Maria trembled but she strode away in a show of confidence.

Anni did not stay in the Mennonite community of North Kildonan much longer. The Sawatzkys wanted to honour their parents' commitment, but it was hard for them, looking after Anni, having small children of their own. And she was constantly making up stories, others (like Maria) gently reminded them. Yes, they realized that. Stories could be damaging. She'd been saying, for example, that Catherine Rogalsky was alone with Benjamin Wiebe at her house on an afternoon when Abram Rogalsky was gone to tend to a situation with his parents in Morden; surely children shouldn't be hearing that. She wandered and picked up things, that was the trouble. Not necessarily true, of course.

Maria had mentioned her concerns to her father, since he belonged to the council of ministers; she had added her voice to those who encouraged the church to take action. The Canadian churches of their denomination were opening a hospital in Ontario for their "weak in spirit." Wouldn't that be a good place for Anni?

When Anni told everyone she met that Preacher Schmidt had stolen a hairnet from the store, they laughed. It was preposterous, of course. What would he want with a hairnet? The council finally met with the Sawatzkys, however, to discuss the situation. They said they'd assist them in getting Anni placed. Nikolai and Elisabeth admitted it was getting harder to care for her, though they'd grown fond of her and now that it came down to it, the thought of sending her elsewhere was difficult. She was capable of simple tasks and not violent. But yes, she was another mouth to feed and they were struggling to make ends meet. And if she could be helped, well, for her sake, yes, perhaps it was best. And there were the children to think of. All those stories!

Anni was sent to the institution called Bethesda and Maria was relieved. Something strange about Preacher Schmidt and that hairnet, though, Gerhard confided to her and Helene one afternoon at coffee. He knew of it from another minister in the case. The preacher had definitely stolen from the store, small items only, including a hairnet. He'd confessed to it, though. He'd been forgiven.

□

As more years passed Maria had become involved in the businesses of the family. She felt her life had renewed its purpose. Gerhard, with his son and sons-in-law, was head of Klassen Homes. Hans and Katherine's husband Peter looked after the automotive interests: the new car sales division and the repair division respectively. Their children were drawn into the work in various ways, though some of them studied music, teaching, and medicine. Erna's husband Peter was head accountant of both companies. Everything was "a going concern," they all liked to say. A family concern.

They had become, amazingly, rich. It was wonderful, and Maria couldn't deny feeling the importance of that. They kept her a vital part of things. She'd long given up her sewing in its repairing, adjusting, and tailoring-for-others variety. Now she sewed only for special family situations and became advisor to the customers of new homes about their window coverings. Sometimes she sewed the custom draperies herself. She made good money at this; she enjoyed it. No need to flatter or fuss over bodies. The house construction industry introduced the idea of model homes and Maria assisted in the decoration of those the Klassens showed.

She also helped at the automotive centre, with filing or writing orders. She came and went as she pleased; she wasn't required to be there, they told her, but was always welcome when she was. She took the summers off to garden and visit Susanna in Winkler. Her brothers established regular family business meetings and she made herself useful by listening carefully, memorizing details, occasionally offering advice. At one of these meetings her brothers told Maria they'd decided to pay her a lifetime salary for services rendered, whether she worked or not. She could stop when she was ready, or continue, as she wished. "You've been like a mother to us all," they said. "It's the least we can do."

After her father's removal to the nursing home, Maria often had someone from the family's next generation living with her for months at a time. It helped them; it helped her. First Susanna's Henry and then George came into the city, attending the Mennonite college. Anna and Betty came too, for shorter periods, taking summer jobs at the car dealership. Maria promised her nieces and nephews jobs, then told her brothers to find them positions and pay them a decent wage. "They're studying," she reminded them. She provided room and board in exchange for their mowing the lawn and keeping the drive and sidewalks cleared of snow.

She began to buy her clothes off the rack, at good shops. She travelled. As surrogate mother and grandmother she hosted large family gatherings at Christmas, Easter, and Thanksgiving, insisting on full family attendance. She kept track of birthdays and anniversaries, and bought gifts to celebrate. Men landed on the moon and Canada commemorated its centennial with an outburst of pride and exuberance, hosting the World Exposition in Montreal. Maria went too, with Gerhard and Helene. Expo was so wonderful she urged her nieces and nephews to go, offering to pay their fares. Many other people of Maria's age, even her siblings, complained about contemporary trends and the younger generation, their hair and their music, the upheavals of the civil rights movement, hippies, and Jesus people. But Maria honed a reputation for acceptance of, for confidence in, youth. She was clearly getting older but she'd made herself essential again.

□

Perhaps she shouldn't have resisted the prospect of Father's remarriage. Not that it was ever certain, not that she had done anything more than raise her objections to Gerhard, more than beg him to do something. Their father might have an eye on Widow Hiebert, Gerhard had said.

"But she never stops talking!" she'd protested.

Gerhard said, "Our mother was talkative too. It might be cheerful, more talk around here."

He'd said, "Not to keep house, of course. You do that well enough."

As if she'd asked the reason, he continued, "For the same reason as the first time. To have a wife."

One couldn't fault Widow Hiebert for lack of cheer. But

they were different, these refugee Mennonites who came after the war.

"It's all about the daughters," Maria said. "How hard they work, how they've suffered, how sweet and gentle – "

Gerhard laughed, as if he found the trials of women amusing.

"Endlessly," Maria said. "The lives of saints."

Widow Hiebert, two daughters, one daughter-in-law, walked out of Russia. They'd walked beside a roughhewn cart in a winding, miles-long procession of women and children and ancient men. A soldier harmed one of them, that much was openly stated, although the manner of the harm never delineated, and then the daughter-in-law died along the way, several days after her baby was born dead and had to be abandoned in a ditch. The dear husband and father gone before that, when the losses first began, although even earlier there was the dear village and the dear house and then the dear things they'd packed, all taken by others or simply left behind. And her dear dear sons, snatched for the army and never heard of again. And after all that, the separation of mother and daughters and their finding one another – it was nothing short of a miracle. The widow and her daughters suffered every imaginable loss, every deprivation. They were happy, grateful, then, for being alive, for what they still had.

But their gratitude seemed a rootless, restless thing. Their homelessness was with them still, like anxiety, their lack of attachment except to one another. Happy for their little house; saying so, over and over. As if it were a refugee shelter they could not fully trust to be permanent.

If Father married Widow Hiebert, Maria would have to listen, and listen some more, until the Klassens' own memories of Russia and their immigrant hardships had yielded to the babbling woman's tragedies. To the Trek and its multitude of sorrows. Smoke and steam rising from fires and soup pots in a line of dots over the countries of war-torn Europe,

Stalin on the one hand and Hitler on the other, and mud and more mud and enamel dishes and the smell of manure. Animals in tow. The stench of decay and ethical compromise. Who knew what had really gone on in those camps?

"And besides," she'd asked her brother, "is she really a widow? She told me they don't know if her husband is living or dead. What if he's still alive?"

"I think we can assume that he's dead."

"If you've been encouraging Father in this matter," Maria said, "please discourage him again. Remember Mr. Reimer? An old man in love is a ridiculous sight."

Let Father focus on business. After those hours of business, let him fill his mind with his books. With his studies of the newspapers and Bible.

Gerhard was eating a second piece of her pudding torte, washing it down with coffee. Maria rarely drank coffee in the afternoons, but in the midst of this conversation she'd poured herself a cup.

"I don't want it," she said. "You have to stop him."

And perhaps he had, because nothing further came of Father and Widow Hiebert. Her brother never explained, but Maria felt guilty, and grateful. She had the early photograph of her mother as a young wife, the one with the flower-filled hat, enlarged and framed at her own expense. She hung it on her father's bedroom wall, as a gift.

□

Johann Klassen was active in work and church until his early eighties, then rapidly lost his memory and health. Hardening of the arteries, the doctors said. He spent his last years unaware of his accomplishments and as his condition worsened, his children put him in a nursing home.

Maria visited her father three times a week. She made herself stay an hour. She never entered his small room without hoping the haze in his head would clear for a moment, that he would recognize her. This didn't happen, not during his last eighteen months. She usually brought him something to eat, perhaps a pudding or his favourite peppermint cookies. He resisted the staff in the seniors' home over food but whatever Maria fed him he received submissively and she supposed that he knew her voice at least and was calmed by it. She talked to him about everything, beginning with the world news and the weather and then the happenings of the children and the businesses. She talked to him in long linked paragraphs, unlike any conversations they'd ever had when he was well and at home. It was like writing regular diary pages, she sometimes thought, though not records that lasted, merely an exercise of organization and recitation that made the time pass and gave the visits a routine. He seemed content enough to hear her go on.

One day, impulsively, Maria put his hand in hers and stroking it, said, "Oh Papa, I have to confess. I had a baby, you know." Tears welled in her eyes at his unchanging gaze, as if she had recited a list of stock market numbers, but then it made her laugh. She laughed aloud at herself for saying such a thing. It had no impact whatsoever and yet it had been spoken and entered the vast repository of the earth's delivered sounds. Father sat listlessly in his brown recliner, an afghan she'd once made him over his lap, one hand limply in hers, the other as limp upon the afghan. One of the nurses had put a record on the player in his room: the Handel's *Messiah* recording he'd loved ever since he'd first heard it sung in church. But the needle had stuck and was slipping back over in the same groove. "Speak ye – comfortably – to Jerusalem," the tenor soloist sang during Maria's one-sentence confession, then "and cry unto her, that her warfare – her warfare – is accomplished – plished – plished – plished."

"Think of it, Father," Maria whispered, laughing, lowering his hand with its parchment-like skin and standing up to give the record needle a push forward. Father didn't know her, nor had she ever really known him. Not really. But she loved him. Love was worth more than knowledge could ever be.

As the solo gave way to another – "Ev'ry valley shall be exalted" – Maria recalled how the *Messiah* had worked its way into the fibre of their souls. That and the other oratorios her people had been taught and grown accustomed to. The magnificent chorales and cantatas. Her father was one of the first to purchase a tape recorder – large machines then, with one reel slowly emptying itself onto the other, the music they heard in the concert halls and churches now pouring into their own rooms, the slow swelling invitation of the violins, and then the comfort. The comfort for the people. *Speak ye comfortably to Jerusalem . . .* The promises of valleys raised, hills lowered, terrain made straight, the vista of continuity and peaceful ends. Progress in every direction, yes even that. The upheavals of time already gone, now made smooth as promised.

□

Her brothers Gerhard and Hans had acquired cottages at Victoria Beach. They were among the first Mennonites to break into the English enclave there, among the first to get summer homes away from the city. Maria enjoyed mentioning this casually to women at church, to the girls at the tills of Redekop's Grocery; any comment about summer, especially the heat, might bring it on.

"Helene," she could say, "and Ida, they've asked me to join them at Victoria Beach." Mrs Lowry had always talked simply about going "up to the Beach," but Maria preferred to use the full name. She had conquered the V sound early in learning English, and to say the word with its five hard prim syllables reminded her of her competence; it had the clean, fussy sound of assimilation and success.

But, in fact, she seldom joined her relatives at their

summer homes. "I spent too many summers at Victoria Beach when I worked," she said to the regular invitations.

"But you won't be working. Come and rest."

"What would an old woman like me want on the beach?"

"You're not old!"

And so the conversation went, back and forth, and every summer she was asked, and every summer she found reasons enough to stay home with her flowers, her own back yard, her own car and the freedom it gave her.

Once she gave in, for two days, drawn in a sudden fit of nostalgia for the closeness of the trees, that thick green. If she expected to be overwhelmed with memories, however, she wasn't. Her family's presence there overlaid the past and its vague familiarity. Black and white photos of the earlier years that hung on the walls of the café at the Moonlight Inn seemed lifted out of a world otherwise hidden in fog. Nothing pained, nothing swarmed over her, no reason not to come again. Yet she found herself impatient with the sandy grit beneath her feet. Descending the steps to the beach seemed an effort that immediately overheated her. She sat near the water beside her nieces and nephews one hot afternoon, making an effort to be enthusiastic, and it worked: she drummed herself up into feeling wonderful, enjoying the sun searing against her. Wonderful, that is, until she wound her way up the stairs and into the shade again and discovered she'd burned badly. It was the worst case of sunburn in her life.

"Does it all come back?" Ida asked brightly, meaning Maria's reminiscences of being a maid at Victoria Beach. It was a dry year, the beaches were wide, the mosquitoes few, the sunsets splendid, the very best of all summers for such a holiday, but nothing came back. Maria saw the lawns where the train tracks had been, the climbing aspen. She regretted that she couldn't spread her body along the fat lower branch of the tree, but nothing came back.

When Maria declined urgings to stay longer, Ida

lowered her voice. "It's the memories, isn't it? There's so many memories." Ida regarded Maria's years as a domestic with great admiration, the source of her skill as a house-keeper and hostess, and referred to them often as if they'd elevated her sister-in-law to her own standards and tastes.

"It's not the memories!" Maria snapped. She simply had no interest in lolling about the place. Her skin itched, and the water, which she enjoyed even more than the trees, wasn't visible from Ida's cottage in any case. If she wanted water, she would rent a little cabin in the Whiteshell, she thought to herself. Her family owned at Victoria Beach now by money and merit. That fact was the only solace the place could give.

□

The rise and fall of generations, the ponderous yet all too swift movement forward, the losses. Father dead. Her dearest sister-in-law and friend Helene, lost to cancer. Erna widowed – her Peter dead of a massive heart attack, a relatively young man. One grieved and mourned, but there was no point in anger. Sadness intertwined with a rising sense of her own diminishing store of years, of the spiteful injustices of aging.

Less was likely to happen to or to change for her now. This was also a loss. She realized that she'd always hoped, without specifically thinking so, for the unfinished parts of her life to be resolved. She wondered if other people also went through their lives yearning to pick up and weld together the discrete pieces of their past. Expecting that someday, tomorrow or next week, or any time ahead in the mystery of the future there would be answers waiting, satisfactory answers to various hurts and puzzles, or even repetitions of the best events already transpired.

Did she expect life to resemble stories? She'd once

read that no important character introduced into the plot of a novel, in a professionally written novel at least, could be allowed to appear or disappear without justification, without being assigned a compelling reason to exist in the text. Without some satisfaction for the reader, or protagonist.

Her own narrative, it seemed, had not been well composed. She'd sometimes daydreamed, for example, that she and Aron Ediger would meet again. She imagined him showing up in Winnipeg after finding his way out of Russia via Germany, during the new slim openings of the Khrushchev era in Soviet Russia perhaps. They would sit on her garden swing in the late afternoon, and he would speak to her in the way he'd once written, *My dear sister in Christ*, explaining absolutely everything. After that pious beginning, the fantasy usually degenerated into a wishing that felt intense and physical. She imagined he'd been in prison, in the Gulag, that he'd suffered enormously. Of course Lena had been a good wife, they could grant her that, but she was gone now and he had his first and deepest love, Maria, beside him in the garden, the colourful comox on their long stalks waving at them, sparrows splashing in the white bird bath. She figured he might have a dozen dreadful secrets for her one and for that reason hers wouldn't matter to him at all. She imagined, vaguely, a wedding, but most of all she saw them intertwined. She was amazed, even dismayed, at the sexual yearning that could still suffuse her on occasion. This yearning couldn't give Aron a recognizable face, only the imagined nearness of his body, hard and lean, as if neither of them would notice they weren't young any more. Not at all what they'd been.

She sometimes daydreamed of James Edward too, a surprise meeting somewhere. Perhaps at the symphony, while visiting his mother and taking in a concert. Nothing lengthy. Even words stolen in the crush of a crowd would be wonderful. They ought to be possible. "Oh, Maria, you're as beautiful as ever! I've often wondered how you were doing."

More pointedly, "I had to marry Ruthie. Oh, it's gone well enough, but . . . and you've been happy too? Good. That was such a brave thing you did. Our son resembles you. He's a fine boy; I've kept up with him a little . . . All the best to you, then. All the best." Suave, irresistible, selfish James Edward grown wise and beneficent in the interim.

And the lesser questions answered too. About Wilhelm's last hours. Where her father's mind resided during his decline. Whether her mother, had she lived, would have guessed her secret.

Word eventually came through Lena's relatives in Ontario, from her mother's side, not the Klassens, that both her cousin Lena and Aron had perished, Lena in a lumber camp in the north, and Aron in 1937 in one of the purges. He was arrested by the Soviet interior police and shot ten days later, not more than twenty miles away from the village. So much for conversations on a garden swing, for lying close between her starched white sheets. What an unseemly imagination she had, making love with a man already dead!

She blamed the stories she'd read and heard and hung on to, happy-ending fiction. She grew suspicious of these, even as her nieces and nephews introduced her to other less predictable books. She began to read more widely, more indiscriminately but then, she tired of novels. She turned to non-fiction: travel books, biographies, histories. Sometimes she devoured a devotional book, perhaps by one of the popular Christian writers recommended to her. Often she found herself inspired at first, only to feel uneasy with its ideals long before she reached the last page, as if she'd eaten too much dessert. Even the happy endings of devotional books, she realized, couldn't be entirely trusted. She didn't doubt that all would be well, someday, past death for sure, but life itself, she thought, had its share of disappointment and nothing, she kept reminding herself, could tie up all the stray ends of that.

□

The weeping in London came about because Maria and her widowed sister Erna had a free day on their England tour. Maria was restless. This trip hadn't been as enjoyable as others she'd taken. The weather was miserable and there was no end of small confusions and problems. The tour leaders were apologetic, but apologies weren't enough to rescue the holiday.

Maria peered through the high window of their hotel room. Grey rain washed dismally over the chimneys and roofs and courtyards and streets, grey over grey over grey. She and Erna had already been out to shops in the vicinity. Their black umbrellas dried by the door.

"There's something I've been thinking about I haven't mentioned yet. Perhaps it's foolish," Maria said.

Erna asked "What?" without raising her head; she was paging through a souvenir album of the Tower of London.

"Do you remember that Wilhelm got engaged? To a Grace Berton?"

Erna looked up.

"I have her address," Maria said. "She sent a card. After we got the news about Wilhelm. She'd married someone else and I kept the card and address . . . I'd be curious if she's still there. If we could talk to her, for a few minutes, because of him."

"Do you think she'd remember him?"

"I don't think you'd forget someone you once planned to marry."

Erna, who always acquiesced to Maria, agreed it might be worth a try.

The clerk at the hotel desk helped them find the number, and sure enough, Grace lived at the same place from which she'd written some thirty years earlier. It took some effort to explain who they were, but she sounded reassuringly ordinary and said they could come.

It was a long ride by taxi into a suburb of drab rowhouses.

"I scarcely remember Wilhelm," Erna said. "I just remember how sad you were after he left."

Maria didn't respond and Erna continued. "I was actually glad when he was gone. Then the house was calm and you were calm. You were sad but there was peace and quiet."

"Is that how it was?" Maria thought she'd been controlled and serene. She lacked the energy now to assert her own version of the past, however; she was wondering what she wanted from a meeting with Grace. Perhaps she and Erna should have explored an old church or gone to an art gallery instead.

They lapsed into silence.

The taxi stopped in front of a porch awash with buckets of flowers, bright purples and blues but bedraggled in the rain. Maria told the driver they wouldn't be long and asked him to wait.

Grace was a friendly round-faced woman. She invited them in, gestured at two straight-backed chairs near the table. "Now I see Billy again," she said, scrutinizing them. "He's coming clear. You can imagine I've been trying to recall him since you rang.

"My man won't mind your stopping," she went on cheerfully, "he knows what the war was like. Still, a good wife don't keep photos of earlier men. I'd quite forgotten how Billy looked."

She nodded at Maria. "I suppose he'd be looking most like you if he was living, if he was old. Not that you're showing your age, ma'am, not at all . . . "

Maria smiled. The room was crowded with mismatched furniture, a television set, newspapers and knickknacks, the untidy detritus of a lifetime, it seemed. The sofa was covered with a broad pile of unfolded laundry. Grace pushed the pile aside and lowered herself onto a cushion in the corner.

"Thank you for having us in," Maria said.

"We're here in London, and it made us think of our

brother," Erna explained, "and we thought, well . . . it couldn't hurt to try. To see someone who saw him before . . . Of course we won't take much of your time. We don't mean to bring up sad – "

Grace laughed, a pretty rolling laugh. Her face was lined but her teeth were even and attractive. "Oh no, you needn't worry 'bout that. I've got me a very good man and we've been married long. When I tell him who was here today he'll be right interested and he won't mind either. He knows what it was like. He knows how many men some of us went through before we found a love that lasted. A love that lived, if you know what I mean. I tease him, saying it's awful so many of the lads had to die, but he wouldn't have me today if at least two of them hadn't been removed before he got the chance of looking my way." She laughed again.

"Oh, they all thought they was gallant, handsome, cocky boys," she said, "you could see how they come over, the Canadians and all, with their notions, and then you'd watch, it wasn't ever what they thought, and the homesickness would sit down so heavy on them. Especially with the waiting. I pitied Billy, I did. He never fit in so well with the others, you know, there was something of the stranger in him. He was good-looking, of course, and I was young. He was plenty appealing for all that. He told me about being . . . what was it he was again . . . ?"

"Mennonite?"

"That's it, Mennonite. I'd never heard of such a thing. I've forgotten so much! But you sitting here, it's coming back in bits, just now . . . Ah, he said he spoke German. But he'd come to fight them. But he wouldn't say a word to prove it so I supposed he was teasing me. He was a little different, you know, I felt that. And then he was drunk and he said something and it wasn't English, and I thought, oh my land's sakes, it's German! I knew it was. I pitied him, I did. I felt afraid for him. It wasn't that he didn't interest me, you know, us with our very young blood! We were all of us falling in love so fast, my friends and I, catching it as it came, because they didn't know – and we didn't know – we didn't even have tomorrow perhaps, and to love and be loved was worth something we thought. It was wonderful, that love, like a strong drink to take away the fear. Ah, Billy was afraid, he was. But he never said so. I never did either. He wasn't used to drink and then he drank too much. I was nearly carrying him back and it could have been trouble, but it worked out, I guess. I've lost the details. And he was grateful though. That's how it started and then he asked me to marry him and I said, well, sure, why not?"

Grace stopped. She seemed to be at the end of her memories of Wilhelm. She began talking about her three daughters and their husbands and their children and their vacations at the sea. She picked up loose photos from the table beside the sofa and passed them along.

Maria found an opportunity to break in. "We have a cab waiting," she said. "We really have to go." She rose from the hard chair. "Is there anything else," she asked, "that you remember? Bill hardly . . . he hardly ever wrote." She hated to admit it. "Did he mention us?"

"Billy and me, well, we hardly knew each other," Grace said. "My parents were strict, you know. Even though I've made it sound like we was wild young women. We was only really alone a time or two. I worked at the base. You mustn't think anything happened, I wasn't that sort. Not beyond a kiss or two, you know. Billy always said he loved my voice, my English. He was good looking, so tall. I remember that. I was a slip of a thing. I guess I fell in love with that, and kind of looking out for him, you know, he being so shy and quite out of place. I did a lot of chatting. It seemed to cheer him up. You're lonely, I said. I'll wait and marry you. I made the proposal, yes, that's it! It's my nature, spoiling a man. Making him a cozy little place. I'd even go to Canada, I said."

The woman was no help. Maria stepped to the door.

"I see him now," Grace said, "the face comes back." She peered at Maria's face again as if to get behind it. "Yes, indeed, those were the days. Some of us having two, three loves before we might have one that lasted, and if you were even a little bit pretty, you found a soldier who would give his heart away. Canada seemed an adventure all right. I don't think I'd have minded either. Everything's possible when you're young. Not to say I'm not happy how things turned out. None of us know how it could have been otherwise, do you ever think about that?"

Maria realized they should have brought her a small gift, some token of their appreciation for the intrusion. She hadn't thought of it: an uncharacteristic lapse.

"If you ever come to Canada," she had to say instead, "you'd be welcome to visit us."

"Oh," Grace laughed. "No, no, no. I'll not be starting any visits like that! I'd have to make one to the United States of America as well! Up to the sea, that's a holiday for me."

"She pitied him," Maria told Erna, getting into the cab. Then she turned sharply to look out the window for the ride back to their hotel. She felt she was going to cry. More than cry. Weep. She sensed a rare and staggering force of emotion rising and a need to let it spill; it was dangerously close to the surface. She kept her head to the outside. She forced herself to watch for the sightings of what she'd seen on the way. It was a long habit of hers; she'd been a passenger so much of her life. Even though she drove, on important and interesting trips she'd gone along with others, a third party, usually in the back seat. Heading to their destination she would take a seat on the right side and returning, she sat on the left, so she was facing the same view either way and could look for repetitions of what she'd seen going, an odd or beautiful farmyard, a building, a natural feature, anything odd or beautiful that provoked her interest. It was like following Hansel and Gretel's strewn pebbles or crumbs back home. She'd convinced herself she preferred to deepen rather than unduly diffuse her knowledge of new places. Now she spotted the ram figure perched on a pole above a storefront that she'd noticed earlier. She thought of the stolid endurance of the inanimate object, letting the rain divide over its back as it must, whenever the weather dictated. Maria's urge to cry was overwhelming.

It would burst; it wouldn't take much (and it was coming) to dislodge the lump of suffering in her throat. It was a dangerous position to be in, her younger sister right there. I can't, she told herself, do it here.

What was the matter with her lately? The very idea of visiting Wilhelm's old fiancée! The rain blurred the shape of the day; it could have been morning or evening or afternoon. She felt disoriented. Her need to howl was crowding higher and higher.

Water slid down the cab window in a thin shifting stream. Maria guessed it wasn't disappointment but grief that swelled within her: the grief of returning to Wilhelm's past, as if the fighting were still underway, during the Blitz perhaps, as if he'd dropped out of the sky just moments ago, a bloody heap onto a soggy sidewalk. *He was quite out of place.*

She and Erna weren't stopping to search for him either, weren't giving him commemoration bigger than hearing the woman and her list of loves. Wilhelm was of no consequence to her or Grace or Erna, of no consequence to anyone. This was the horror of it, the horror of death. For a while the departed one was alive, and real, and important to someone or other, and in such a short passage of time, the same person was of no consequence at all. Death posed a fatal reduction in every case except for the very few extremely famous, and even these individuals didn't make a personal difference to anyone later. Their names and contributions were simply used by the living for their contemporary ends. The horror of her own death, its undeniable victory over all she'd supposed otherwise as a young woman, this knowledge that she had scarcely affected more than a handful of people already – oh, and even *that* mattering was far too peripheral for comfort! Out of place. She too had been. Still was, in a way.

What was the point of carefulness then? For whom to guard one's life, watch one's words? She'd kept Wilhelm as a pale unclear figure poised with his face towards her, pale but lit by the soft light of her mercy, but now she knew he'd long departed even that. He was like a piece of clothing hung in a museum, empty; the bloody heap was a costume to which he would never return.

The cab reached their hotel. Maria pushed a wad of bills from her purse into Erna's hands and found her voice to say, "Here, I'll pay but you look after it, and get us something to eat please, I'm chilled and have to run a bath – "

Maria rushed away, the rain of her sorrow beginning to fall before she reached their door, making it difficult for her to place the key in the keyhole. Erna would take a long time with everything, perplexed perhaps that Maria had deserted her, but not likely surprised either. But she wouldn't complain and in the meanwhile she would search well for exactly the right thing for them to eat.

Later, Maria's emotion purged, Erna returned, apologizing, with nothing better than a package of biscuits and two battered apples.

"You spent a lot of money on our fare," Erna said. "Shall we split it?"

"No. It was my idea."

"I hope it wasn't too disappointing."

Maria said that Grace seemed nice enough.

"But can you imagine her in North Kildonan?"

Maria got up and faced the window. There was a crack between the bleak roofs of their vista where she could see the traffic move and people under umbrellas like mobile mushrooms. Her brother had been homesick. Awkward and pitied.

"We can keep some things to ourselves," she advised,

her voice hard. "That he got good and drunk, for instance. What difference would that old news make to anyone now?"

□

Erna feared Maria's anger. Her sister didn't show it often, but Erna knew Maria turned away from her in the taxi. It was raining much too hard to be curious about the sights. She'd put a scarf on her head and pulled it very tight. That was the telling gesture.

A gesture of her relentless self-control. Of her control, period. A scarf pulled tight. Like her need to manage the curtains and everything else. Maria opened the curtains, Maria closed the curtains; she was the guardian of the light.

"I'll do the curtains," she'd said when Erna closed them at her house once.

"I'll do the curtains," she'd said firmly this morning when Erna opened them in their hotel room.

"Sorry," she'd said lightly moments later as if to erase the previous tone, "just being motherly. I keep on forgetting." *Motherly.* Her prerogative, then.

"I don't know how people can keep their curtains open all evening," she'd said that day at her house. "I don't know how they can stand everything closed in the middle of the day." But Maria's practice was random, its patterns perplexing. Some evenings she left the drapes alone, and some days she pulled them shut. She might open them and then close them an hour later, and every time she moved them, she shook them slightly; the pleats had to be arranged just so. What measure of light, too much or too little, motivated her judgements? Erna couldn't remember this fussiness from earlier but now, it seemed, those who were with her had to bear the brightness and absorb the dimness, as she alone decided.

The interlude of living with Maria, after Erna was widowed and in her transition to a smaller house, hadn't been an easy one for the younger sister. Maria believed it was good for both of them, however, that it took the sting of death out of Erna's bitter shock.

Well, perhaps it had. How could she know if that terrible time would have been worse on her own? As it was, it had been so difficult she still refused to think of it much. It was simply something she'd survived. She was certainly glad to be in a home of her own again, mistress of her own surroundings. She seemed to know when, and how, to open and close the curtains. Or was there some knack to it she still had not learned? She thought of Ida, her sister-in-law, even richer than the rest of them, because of money on her side as well as the Klassens. Ida hadn't mastered the art of windows any more than she had; she flooded the house with yellow summer sun and then begged for air conditioning until she got it. "I can't endure the heat," she said, "except in Palm Springs in the winter. Desert heat in the winter is fine by me."

Erna was inclined to agree; she'd always liked Ida. She'd gone along to Palm Springs with her and Hans six months after Peter died and felt her first hours of happiness, of forgetfulness, there. But Erna knew that Maria, who as a matter of principle had never said a negative word about any of her siblings or their spouses, disliked Ida, and disliked most of her opinions too.

When Maria wrapped herself in silence, Erna left her alone. None of them, in fact, ever tried to penetrate that rigid silence, nobody besides Wilhelm, but she couldn't recall how he'd done it, or why, except that she remembered her stomach hurting when he tried it. It had made Maria tense.

Best to let her mood pass, the not-speaking run its course. Best to let the brightness swing back on its own. As it always did.

Erna was the youngest, the baby, and no one in the

family trusted her insights, she felt. "It's difficult having a sister as mother – I mean, a sister who's like a mother," she'd ventured to one or another of her siblings on occasion, but no one asked her what she meant, or even agreed. The category of "sister who's mother" seemed to exist for no one besides herself, and she felt perhaps she hadn't been capable of assessing it properly, that she'd marred her powers of judgement by all the idle hours she spent dreaming of her real dead mother, giving her qualities not quite opposite but still very different from Maria's. It was her foolish, futile imagination.

As everyone always said, Maria had been a wonderful substitute. She wasn't mean. She wasn't neglectful. She'd been fair. She'd worked from morning to night. Sewing, cooking, gardening. Helping them with their reading, their music. Doing their hair. Erna knew, from being a mother herself, that Maria had done an excellent job.

But she'd longed, oh how Erna had longed, for her mother. The one she couldn't remember. And so she'd been discontented, inventing someone else – covertly – who held her on her lap and stroked her head and told her how ecstatic she'd been at her birth, when she first received her to her breast from the womb.

It was an ungrateful habit, Erna thought now, and one paid for these things. Maria turning her head in the cab, then leaving her to negotiate with the driver, to find a shop and purchase food, to look after everything while she hurried upstairs to indulge her chill and discontent.

The fate of being a widow, of being old, perhaps. Thrown back once more into original family relationships, companions for one another on travel tours and not able to escape. She paged through the Tower of London souvenir again, nibbling at the crackers. But she'd liked Grace, and even though she could barely remember Wilhelm, she was very happy now that he'd been loved by the high-spirited blonde woman before he died. That she'd got him safely back to his quarters when he was drunk, and later suggested he marry her.

□

So, Maria was home from the London trip, but barely in the door when the telephone rang. It was Edith Lowry on the line, insistent that Maria meet her for lunch. Yes, it had to be today.

An hour and a half later, Maria was following Mrs Lowry through the narrow spaces between the tables in Eaton's dining room. It was just past noon and the restaurant was crowded. They passed several tables that would have been suitable. When Mrs Lowry reached the end of the room she stopped to survey it and then began to weave her way back. With every step Maria felt her purse, coat, and lunch tray growing heavier in her arms. Jet lag fatigue drained at her strength.

Mrs Lowry chose at last, a table along the wall near the restaurant exit. Even then she stared thoughtfully around the room before claiming it. Maria had never seen Mrs Lowry so unsure of herself. And what a strange meal she'd assembled on her tray. Two desserts (a small white cheesecake with blueberry sauce sliding over the edges and a vanilla pudding in a parfait glass), a plate of crisply fried potatoes with gravy, a warm dinner roll with three pats of butter, and tea. Maria selected a vegetable soup, tomato-red and thick, still steaming, and a whole wheat bun. According to Maria's skewed sense of time this wasn't the hour for lunch. But the attractive, nutritious moderation of her selections compared to Mrs Lowry's hodgepodge rallied her appetite.

If resolutions didn't appear as life wore down to its end, she thought, there were certainly ironies. She couldn't help thinking of the many Thursdays she'd stopped in Eaton's on her afternoons off. It was that moment of entering the store that was clearest in her memory, that single step from one sphere into another, like getting into a rowboat and pushing off, feeling briefly the exchange of land for water: a tiny shift and then engaged with another element altogether. She and Helene and the other domestics had rushed from the sidewalk and the bustle of the street, and in one swift turn of the revolving doors they were in a world loaded with merchandise, smelling of flowers for the seasons, perfumes, pine and candle wax, a world of things new, unworn, and sealed, and the exquisite rustling sounds of wrapping tissue and salesladies' murmurings.

Now she was "dining" here, as she had before, but never with her former employer, an ancient-looking woman now. Once more decades had passed since they'd last met, discussing the deaths of Bobby and Wilhelm over tea. Edith Lowry's face was crisscrossed with lines.

What she wanted this time, Mrs Lowry said, popping the decorative cherry from the pudding into her mouth, was to pass on that Maria's son wished to meet his mother.

"His mother?"

Mrs Lowry jumped on this evidence of sloppy listening, like the teacher she'd been. "You, Maria! You had a son!"

Maria concentrated on her soup. I'm sixty-four, she thought, and she's able to humiliate me still. She heard the clatter of dishes, the ring of the cash register at the end of the cafeteria line, the din of dozens of conversations.

"Surely you haven't forgotten you gave birth to a child."

"Of course not. I've been travelling and I'm tired."

Mrs Lowry squeezed her tea bag with a spoon, muttering that one couldn't get a proper pot of tea nowadays. She flipped the bag onto her saucer with disgust, as if she were beaching a fish. "It's a bit of a new thing, I suppose," she said.

"What is?

"The search for the mother . . . the birth mother. As you'll remember, his parents know my sister Gladys, and through them . . . well, it's come to me."

"His parents know your sister Gladys!" Maria mimicked. "His parents *are* your sister Gladys and –"

"Alright. So you know."

"I figured that out when I was there."

"So there's no long chain," Mrs Lowry said calmly.

"No chain. And I saw his picture at your house. You said he was Raymond."

"Yes. Raymond. And Raymond wants to meet his mother."

"His mother is Gladys."

"Yes, yes," Edith Lowry scowled. "Birth mother, Maria. He'd like to meet the woman who gave him birth."

Maria reacted instinctively. "I'm not going backwards to all that. Nothing about me, not my name. Tell him that."

It was Mrs Lowry's turn to mimic. "No information. Tell him that. Very simple."

"We wanted to do it that way."

"That's what you decided."

"You wanted it too. We agreed."

Who knew anymore what either of them had wanted? She didn't want this now, even if it was the newest and latest thing. Nowadays an out-of-wedlock birth wasn't cause for a secret, but it had happened then, not now. And that's where Raymond belonged. Meeting Mrs Lowry for lunch for this reason was a letdown.

Mrs Lowry looked up and around the room as if Maria wasn't there. Her lipstick had crept into the openings of the tiny lines emanating from her mouth. Her eyes brightened; she'd spotted someone she knew. She stood up clumsily and waved. "Mrs Tees! Eileen!" A tiny woman with wavy white hair fluttered to their table, tray in hand.

"Edith," she cried. "Lovely to see you. Don't tell me you're Christmas shopping already, you organized dear, you!"

"No, no, not this time," Mrs Lowry said, "I'm just here lunching with an old friend." The two women began to exchange all the news they could think of.

Mrs Lowry hadn't introduced them, Maria thought, but she'd said "an old friend." A phrase as pretty as a blue-green egg in a nest, come upon by chance in a thicket of grasses.

When the other woman moved on, Mrs Lowry returned to her subject. "Raymond's having some difficulties," she said, "and Gladys suggested it. You shouldn't think it's something I'm doing behind her back. She was fond of you."

Maria didn't answer. The conversation struck her as fanciful, something she might wake up to discover she was dreaming.

"He's in difficulty," Mrs Lowry repeated.

Maria sighed. "What kind of difficulty?"

"Well, of a general sort, really. He's a kind man, really very conscientious. His wife had polio. She's here in the King George. It depresses him. Naturally. He gets discouraged . . . How could it harm, Maria? It might be something touching for you."

"Does he need money?"

"Money!" Mrs Lowry laughed. "He doesn't need money. He took over the farm. It's much bigger now, like a business really. And he's the only child Gladys and Martin have. He'll inherit everything."

Maria felt proud that Raymond didn't need money. It was the Klassen coming out in him. Their entrepreneurial bent, the ability to turn up the right stone in the field, the one under which the treasure was buried.

"Something touching," Edith Lowry said again.

Did Mrs Lowry think Maria needed something touching? That she was that starved for emotion?

"Apparently – I'm told – there's this ache they feel. A sixties child, too old for his time . . . In our day, yes, we believed the fate of an illegitimate child would not be improved by living with his mother. But . . . He's depressed. Have you never thought of meeting him?"

"I can't say that I have," Maria said. "Not really." It was true. She'd yearned for various kinds of resolution but not, she was sure, for the resurrection of her son.

"Nobody in my family knows," she said.

"You're a church-going, Christian woman, Maria. I'd imagined it might make a difference. For Raymond . . . in his difficulty."

This was surely intended to provoke her. "Why doesn't he meet his father then?" Maria asked.

"The father's unknown."

Maria glared at the other woman. "You know who the father is!"

"The papers say, Father unknown . . . Raymond isn't looking for his unknown father."

"You lied then."

"Even the father doesn't know he's unknown." Mrs Lowry flashed a tiny inscrutable smile. In that moment, she didn't look old and wrinkled and changed at all. She was Mrs Lowry of more than forty years ago.

Maria forced herself to be calm.

"James Edward doesn't know?"

"Not unless you told him and I doubt you're exchanging letters. Why would he know?"

So he'd never been plagued with regret or thoughts of responsibility? He'd gained an adopted relative and never realized the boy originated with him?

"Ruthie's been good for him," Mrs Lowry said. "They've gotten nicely old together." She chuckled.

Maria was tired to the bone; she had to get home to sleep off her travel exhaustion. She was much too tired for the veneer of good manners. She told Mrs Lowry – crossly – that she could inform her son, James Edward, let him deal with Raymond in his difficulty, as she called it.

The other woman reminded her of the earlier wish for "hush hush." They argued another round about that.

Then Mrs Lowry provoked her again. "I've never been

able to put my finger on you, Maria. Haven't you got the natural sentiments of a mother?"

"I'm not his mother!" Maria wanted to say that she'd mothered her siblings, but this protest, just this one, was all she could manage.

"But you are."

"I gave him up."

"Raymond is a decent man. A little discouraged, but decent."

"Secrets grow small and no longer exist," Maria said. She'd composed this sentence years earlier and liked how it sounded. Now she finally had the opportunity to say it aloud.

"Well, I don't believe that for a moment, but never mind. Raymond married Lillian and Lillian got polio. They were only married a year before she got it. She's in the King George. Here in Winnipeg. It's hard to visit her. Understandable, I guess. They had a baby girl. He hardly knows her, as Lillian's sister raised her. He sees her sometimes when he comes to Manitoba. She's up and married too, just a year ago or so, married awfully young, mind you. He's depressed, that's what I think. Martin's passed on and Gladys worries and pushes me for ideas. As if I'm supposed to know everything about children . . . Sometimes Gladys wishes he'd simply divorced her. It's much too hard on him."

The wife's name was Lillian. "What's the daughter's name?"

"Eileen."

Raymond, Lillian, Eileen.

"The answer is no," Maria said. "I don't think it's wise. And I've got to go. I've just come back from London and I can't keep awake." The soup wasn't as tasty as it looked. Mrs Lowry could clean up her tray.

"I've got a wedding coming up," Maria said, as if this would finally explain everything. "My niece Marilyn's getting married. She's lived with me for some years. She's from Alberta but she's getting married here. So I'm doing the mother's part of the planning."

Maria put on her coat. She intended to stride away.

But she was so very weary. Her legs felt rubbery and it seemed to take a long time to pull herself through the doors, to find the elevators.

On her way through the main floor and to the exit she passed a display of masks. "Halloween!" a notice blared. "The possibilities are frightening." Ghoulish faces, their eyes dark holes, their mouths jagged. They jeered as she neared and probably laughed behind her back as passed. *Haven't you got the natural sentiments of a mother?*

□

Edith Lowry picked at her fries. She shook the salt shaker over them angrily. They were cold and tasteless.

She wasn't hungry and Maria had walked away.

That didn't turn out so well, did it, Edith my dear? she thought to herself.

The dining room was still crowded. So many flushed and excited women, wraps and parcels piled around them like booty brought back from a war. She saw Mrs Tees at a distance, chattering non-stop to a friend. There were a few men in the restaurant too. From Eaton's or nearby offices, she supposed. Men in grey suits leaning forward, towards each other, eating without looking at their plates, as if their discussion was a game in which they mustn't lose sight of the ball. At the table next to hers, a young couple ate with their heads down, not speaking. They chewed their food with deliberation. They'd come from the country, she guessed, for a full and exhausting day of shopping, and a meal out was unusual and no pleasure either.

Had she told Maria that James had passed on, five years ago, of a heart attack?

284

Had she told her she was thinking to sell the house, move into an apartment? Her children kept pushing.

Had she told Maria she was getting too old to arrange things like this – getting her and Raymond together? To run interference, as her football-playing grandson would say.

She didn't mind Raymond staying with her when he came into town. She'd always liked the boy. He'd made her sister Gladys happy, that was reason enough.

Well, he was a man by now and she'd pronounced him stalwart, to Gladys' satisfaction. "Oh, he's stalwart, he's stalwart alright," she'd said. "Steady and quiet and stalwart." A stalwart boy, a stalwart man.

In the last years, though, quiet had crystallized into dullness. Taciturnity.

Until last night, sharing an evening snack. He'd begun to probe his origins, insisted he had to meet his mother. Asking questions and asking for her help with a drill-like efficiency that amazed her.

"Well," she'd said, excited by the chance to effect some change in him, "I helped her with it then, and I could give it a try. Helping you now, I mean."

She'd assumed Maria would be thrilled.

That stubborn girl.

She could never find fault with her work. Maria even higher expectations of herself than Edith had had of her, it had seemed to her then. But there was no doubt she was stubborn. In her servant-like subservience she'd still managed to express a confounding immovability.

She'd remembered it today. But she still couldn't understand it.

What would she tell Raymond now? How would she phrase Maria's refusal so it wouldn't deepen his gloom?

The sounds of voices and the thin white messages of cigarette smoke swarmed and mingled in the air. Edith Lowry stared at her food. She pushed it away. She looked around. She saw a room full of tables. How many would there be? Napkin holders, sugar containers, salt and pepper shakers in standard issue chrome and glass anchoring every one of them.

She rubbed her eyes. Lines from the *Book of Common Prayer* ran into her thoughts. She seemed to see, to hear, to be speaking them. "O God, merciful Father, that despisest not the sighing of a contrite heart, nor the desire of such as be sorrowful; mercifully assist our prayers that we make before thee in all our troubles and adversities, whensoever they oppress us; and graciously hear us, that those evils . . . "

The lines had faded; she'd lost them. She reached for her cup, drank the last of the cold sweet tea.

She couldn't remember the rest of the prayer.

Oh well, she thought, Amen to all of it.

8

THE WINTER DEEPENED and passed, one white day after the other. "Raymond in his difficulty," as Maria thought of it, often presented itself to her mind, but just as often she pushed it away. Mrs Lowry had said, "One visit to Saskatchewan, you meet somewhere for lunch, tell him you love him but of course you had to give him up, you had no choice about it really. Tell him and it will settle his sadness. Exaggerate the circumstances if you must. Or meet here, when he comes in to see Lillian. One small thing, and a world of difference."

At the cottage, Mrs Lowry used to close her books – those light romances she read in summer – with a dreamy smile, stretch her limbs, and head for one of the girls or Bobby or her husband James, whoever was nearest, exclaiming "You're such a sweetheart" or something like that. Usually, the affection was incongruous with the moment. Its recipient hadn't been caught up with her in the emotional tangles of her book and, more often than not, responded with irritation. Mrs Lowry seemed just that naive about an encounter between Raymond and Maria. She imagined it from the outside, Maria thought; for all she knew, Mrs Lowry might even scheme to follow, hide behind a fern in that restaurant in Saskatchewan and dab at her eyes, hoping to behold a grown man's depression disappear after looking on the face of an old woman he'd met for the first time.

One small thing, and a world of difference. Maria

resisted the arguments Mrs Lowry had raised, kept resisting. No matter how cautiously a meeting might be arranged, it would undo the life she had chosen and constructed. Break into the secret, shatter the person she'd become. Did Mrs Lowry think she was one of those Russian nesting dolls, or an onion that could be peeled back, one layer the same as the next, just smaller versions of herself all the way inside? She was more like a box, something essential locked away.

But she liked the box by now; it was familiar and not unattractive. She kept busy. She had the wedding sewing to do – the bridesmaids' dresses and Marilyn's going away out-fit. She and her sister Erna went to visit Jake and Margarethe in Alberta for ten days, and after that she had to organize the church bake sale and missions bazaar; she'd agreed to head it up this year. She was knitting afghans for two nieces and she had a spring bus tour to the southern United States to think about and read for: travel books and histories, photos and maps. She liked to study the places she toured before she got there.

Change: it was too much to ask of her, at her age.

Maria was bending to remove a roast chicken from the oven one evening, for the meal she was about to enjoy with her niece Marilyn and fiancé Alan who whispered and gig-gled in the living room while she did the last things in the kitchen. The chicken skin was crisp, the meat of it tender. She was bending and she realized whom she had to protect.

Herself.

Where this insight – or accusation – had come from, Maria didn't know. It struck the retina of her soul like a spark, and it hurt.

So she wasn't hiding it for the sake of her family, be-cause of their prominence or professions or positions on boards and committees. One nephew a minister, another teaching at the Bible college, another a physician, and one a singer of some renown.

Whatever deception she'd practiced had been for herself.

She'd re-created herself after her failure and liked what she'd made.

Maria said "Nonsense" to herself and decided to have a good evening with the young couple. She was currently living alone but would soon have someone with her again. Marilyn would be back for the month before the wedding, and next fall Maria's nephew Frank – Marilyn's brother – would be attending the college in Winnipeg and would live in her basement. Then there would be the evidence and solace of someone near: the run of the bath or shower, a toilet flushing, footsteps on the stairs, music at a distance, crumbs on the counter, the driveway cleared of snow while she was away. Days might go by without them seeing one another, for Frank said he wanted to eat his main meals at the dormitory dining room and Maria had the wisdom to give her young relatives generous belonging and trust without interference. But she would provide his weekend meals. "Bring a friend," she liked to say. She enjoyed listening to young people talk. If their views perturbed her she would simply concentrate on their plates and make sure they got plenty to eat.

□

But the truth that confronted Maria as she opened the oven to her perfect roast chicken must have damaged her resolve more than she realized. It seemed the only explanation later for what she did the day after her niece Marilyn's wedding.

Maria hosted the post-wedding reception gift opening and get-away ceremony at her house. There were more gifts than expected and the eating took longer too, but just at the moment Maria feared the length of the proceedings would strain and possibly even injure the mood of the celebration, the young pair emerged from the guest bedroom in matching outfits, hers a white skirt and frilly red gingham blouse, his a pair of white pants and a red and white checked shirt. Marilyn couldn't stop smiling. Her shining long hair, parted in the middle, framed her face. Alan's face, which had been tensing through the interminable loosening of paper and ribbons and exclaiming over cutlery, towels, and kitchen gadgets, looked relaxed again.

The bridal party scurried to get the confetti they'd concealed for this moment. Maria shooed them outside, where the girls lined the sidewalk like a bed of flowers. Squealing, they showered the couple, then everyone, all the bridesmaids and groomsmen and aunts and uncles and both sets of parents, closed in and surged after the couple to the car where Alan's friend Ron sat ready in the driver's seat. There were hints of a transfer of cars, of mysterious strategies for foiling the expected pranks of Alan's friends, all to get the couple safely to their honeymoon hotel.

Maria squeezed forward to give Marilyn a hug.

"Thank you, thank you, _Tante_ Maria," the girl was crying into her ear, "for everything, the use of your house and all you've done, for everything all these years I've lived with you."

"I love you as a daughter," Maria murmured. She knew Marilyn's mother Margarethe wouldn't mind her saying so, not her affable and accommodating sister Margarethe, just as grateful as Marilyn for all she'd done. Marilyn had lived with her nearly five years in all; what else could they expect but that she'd want the wedding in Winnipeg, that Maria's home would be, as it were, the bride's own, from which she would leave as a single woman into her new married life? They released each other with sighs of satisfaction and Marilyn slid after Alan into the car's back seat and the Buick roared to life, pulling away in a bound and a trail of honks, out of view down the street.

Maria made it clear that no one should stay to help tidy. She was going to leave everything and go straight to bed herself, she insisted, since it was already dusk; the house would be set to order in the morning. Margarethe was full of thanks and apologies; Jake, she said ruefully, now had a son-in-law as restless as he was. Their bags were packed; all they had to do was change from their finery and they'd be off. They would drive through the night, taking turns; the call of the ripening Alberta crops would keep them awake.

Jake was also grateful to Maria, but seemed unconcerned what she'd think of their immediate departure. Jake wasn't in awe of the Klassen clan. "You should be thankful I rescued you from that smothering bunch!" he'd told Margarethe once.

Margarethe, who'd passed this on to Maria with a giggle, said she'd answered him, quite seriously, "I'm not sorry I married you, Jake, but it's not been easy to be so far away from my family. Always getting together without me."

The last guest gone, Maria locked and secured the doors with their double bolts. Then she realized she wasn't as tired as she'd thought she was. The dining room table was covered with half-empty serving platters of food – *bodentorte, blaettertorte*, several varieties of *platz, perischke*, fancy cookies. On two silver plates, leftover slices of wedding cake sagged in piles onto white paper doilies. Pink rose petals had dropped onto them from the centrepiece. A single pink mint sat in the candy dish. Plates and cups covered the long kitchen counter. Other plates were scattered over the tables in the living room; napkins and wrapping paper littered the floor. The gifts were piled haphazardly, box lids open, in a wide swath by the basement stairway.

Maria looked over the mess, contentedly, for it represented a wonderful day, and then, putting on an apron, she tackled it. She worked systematically. She began with the living room. When everything was cleared and in its place, she turned out the lamps, drew back the curtains, opened a lower window. Cool air flowed into the room. It was close to midnight and the neighbourhood was quiet.

She restored the dining room next, then moved to the kitchen. I'm not tired anymore, she thought to herself, running a sink of soapy water and a second sink of a steaming hot rinse. The cool air from the living room window was flowing to her as in a stream, as if it had come searching and found her. She was tempted to turn off the kitchen lights and work in the dark, by the pale light cast by the streetlamps and homes of the neighbourhood and the rising half moon. I'm sixty-five, she thought. My health is good. The wedding was wonderful. We did it. Life is good. These were obvious acclamations. Simple thoughts. The right kind for this evening.

When she'd dried her best dishes, Maria set them on the dining room table. This much could wait, she decided; she would put them into the china cabinet tomorrow. She'd already made a huge, good start on things.

Passing Marilyn's room, Maria saw the wedding gown and veil in two heaps on the bed. The bridal slip was a white puddle on the floor. White stockings and white high-heeled sandals floated on top of it.

Maria opened the closet and saw that Alan's suit and his shirt hung in the closet, neatly and on separate hangers. His shoes stood together beneath them. This is how it will be, Maria sighed, bending to pick up the girl's clothes. Marilyn was careless and Alan was fussy. He wouldn't have noticed the dress on the bed today, or the pile on the floor, but by next month these habits of his wife would begin to irritate him. Maria wondered, as she'd wondered before, if they would be happy together. She feared there'd be stresses. Well, they'd have to work them out; she'd told herself that before too. Marilyn had so many compelling qualities; she was generous, affectionate, full of fun. And Alan was a fine person, precise and ambitious. "He'll reach his goals, there's no doubt about that," she often told Marilyn, whose radiant smile had always replied, "I know." He could also be tense and critical.

Maria lifted the dress to its full length. Marilyn was a big Klassen girl, as tall as Maria, and the dress was in the princess style. It would fit Maria. Of course it would.

The temptation was too strong. Maria slipped out of her rose dress. As she climbed into the gown she caught a glimpse of the pale loose skin under her elbow and nearly stopped. It was too late. The dress was on; it dropped and enveloped her. She thought it would be complicated – Marilyn and her bridesmaids had taken ages, it seemed, to dress – but there it was, she was wearing the bridal gown and the only difficulty was getting the zipper closed. With stretching she accomplished that too.

The skirt of the dress was A-line and fell away from Maria's bosom as weightlessly as mist. The pert stand-up collar hid the wrinkles on her neck. And then she saw her arms through the sheer fabric of the long puffed sleeves and they seemed to be the arms of someone else, smooth and sculpted, creamy white, as if fashioned of pearl.

Maria allowed her hands, softened by dishwater and smelling faintly of lotion, to play over the dress. Against her pressing hands she felt the tender filmy outer layer of the skirt. Against her legs she felt the stiff inner layer of taffeta. She had never worn so much white. She felt exotic, like someone other than herself.

Bending slowly as if the dress were glass and could break, Maria lifted the veil from the bed. She knew it was nearly ten feet long. She twisted herself under the headpiece and fastened the combs to her head. She walked out of the bedroom to let the train of the veil lengthen behind her. On a path of light from the hallway she entered her darkened bedroom.

She stared at her reflection in her full-length mirror. She was breathing heavily, and was startled to see her hair permed and softly grey in front of the white headpiece. Had she been expecting a girl, dark-haired and unlined? She was sixty-five. Dressing up, playing bride. Her face disappointed her, so much older than Marilyn's. And inside too. It was nearly fifteen years since she last bled as a woman, since there was any reminder of fecundity in the regular menses. She was grey and dry, as grass in autumn, hollow and dead. The softness of her curls was subterfuge.

But the veil and the dress made her lovely in spite of herself. Her futile maternity was covered; she was quite safe. There was nothing in this about bearing children; the dress spoke of love and uniqueness, an authoritative "you are beautiful" spoken through a once-in-a-lifetime gown. Maria stepped closer to the mirror. The white softened her facial lines. Even flattered her, she thought. She ought to be dressed in white when she died; it became her.

Encouraged, Maria stepped out of her bedroom into the bright single light of the hallway. The mantel clock struck two. Just one turn through the house, she thought. Just one walk through the kitchen and dining and living rooms, the fabric caressing her legs. She began to hum one of the songs the organist had played at the wedding, one of her favourites:

> O pow'r of Love, all else transcending,
> In Jesus present evermore;
> I worship Thee, in homage bending,
> Thy name to honour and adore . . .

What did brides think about as they walked down the aisle? Were they conscious only of the groom? Or did they feel, as she did now, that their skin pulsed, that they were nearly transparent, their entire body as sweet as the fragrance of lilies because of the admiration turned upon them, their entire being urgent and yearning, turning as pure and white as their dresses and veils?

She walked slowly through the rooms of the house, singing.

Yea, let my soul, in deep devotion,
Bathe in love's mighty boundless ocean –

Did they feel this strange blend of spiritual worship and body awareness, this intensity, like alabaster, from the toes to the fingertips, enough to make one weep, as if life were simply too precious to endure for long? Were they relieved to reach the end of that passage, at last? Maria went through the kitchen and rounded back into the hallway, the last turn before the short stretch back to her room to take off the dress and get ready for bed.

Something made her glance at the front door. A man's face was pressed against the glass of the square window in the door. Maria saw his eyes, the slightly parted lips. His astonishment.

Her hands flew upward to her mouth, but not before a sound like a moan burst out of her throat to end the warbling hymn. The face disappeared at the same time, as if snatched away from the window by a giant hand. She heard the sound of footsteps descending the porch. She leaned forward, the dress rustling around her, and managed to find the switch to darken the hall. She forced herself to the living room window; she parted the sheers enough to peer through. He was hurrying away, already to the middle of the street. Maria knew it was Raymond.

His gait was uneven, and halting, as if he lacked sufficient power to flee. His shoulders were stooped.

Raymond. Maria was too shocked and exhausted to think clearly. She'd recognized him. Of course. She knew now that she'd memorized the picture on Mrs Lowry's mantelpiece, that she'd been adding the years as they passed. She knew without stopping to count that he was forty-one. She'd known him immediately, as grotesque as he was, pressed against the glass, his look, in that split second she'd had of it, a child's who is the oddball of the playground, that child so hungry for notice he attracts only teasing or bullying. The kind of child none of the Klassens, not even Wilhelm, had been. She'd caught that beaten, desperate look just before their eyes met and he was gone. Peeping in like an idiot and then surprised, as if she'd scared *him*!

Well, yes: the dress. Whatever he'd been looking for, he wouldn't have been expecting a wedding dress and veil. Maria sank to the couch. She felt too dry for tears. What good was forgiveness, she thought, what good forgetting, if Raymond crept after her half a lifetime later, wanting something else from her? What was the point of forgetting, if he still existed?

The telephone rang shrilly.

And now, harassment by phone.

But how had he reached a telephone so quickly?

If she didn't answer and it was someone from the family, one of them would show up at the door, checking on her. And she in a wedding gown! Maria hurried to the ringing phone, tried to calm her panic. She picked up the receiver on the fifth ring.

"Maria, are you still up?" It was Ida. "I saw a light across the way."

"Yes, Ida, I'm still up."

"Not washing dishes, are you? I know you don't have lights on at night unless you're up. I wouldn't have called if I hadn't seen the light."

"Well, I wasn't tired after all. I hadn't planned to and then I wasn't tired," Maria said. It was only Ida, no emergency at all. She recalled Ida in her dress at the wedding – a very expensive dress, robin's egg blue and its pleats so narrow and numerous they shimmered from her hips as she walked. Like beams from her artificial white-blond hair. "And why are *you* still up?"

Ida paused. "Oh Maria, had you forgotten we're leaving on our holiday to Ottawa later this morning? I don't hold it against you, Maria, you've had so much to think of with the wedding. It went wonderfully, don't you agree?"

They'd already agreed on this many hours ago. "Yes, it did.

"I was busy," Maria went on, apologetically, "but I shouldn't have forgotten. I wish you both a safe trip and a good time and health."

"Oh thank you, Maria. But I'm worried about something, that's why I called. Did I leave my coat at your place? I'm packing, putting things away, and I can't find my coat. I don't know whether I left it at church or at your house. I don't need it for Ottawa, but I want to know where it is. Could you check the front closet?"

"Wait then," Maria said. She leaned over and grabbed a tea towel to wrap around the receiver. She thought the swishing of the dress might be audible. What a tiresome, inhibiting costume a wedding gown could be. Requiring stealth.

Ida's summer coat hung in the closet where she'd left it.

"Ida," Maria said, "it's here." Her voice seemed breathless to her. "It's here, so don't worry about it any further."

"Oh that's good to know . . . Is everything all right, Maria?"

"Yes. Why?"

"You sound a little different."

"It's after two o'clock."

"Of course. Well, I wouldn't have disturbed you if I hadn't seen the light across the way. I get a glimmer of it through your kitchen window from our window upstairs. I'll pick up the coat when we get back."

"Have a good holiday."

"Thank you. Goodnight now, Maria."

Maria hung up the phone. She was thirsty. She found a bottle of grape juice, half full, in the fridge. She gulped at it. But she swallowed too quickly and coughed. Grape juice spurted out of her mouth onto the bodice of the dress.

She stumbled to her room. Yes, everything had its just reward. A grape stain on Marilyn's dress. A peeper at her door. A flattened, despairing, unnatural face, grubbing for her.

Undressing, she glimpsed her naked body in the mirror. It seemed solid enough but she might as well have been a skeleton, her long-time secret pushing hard on the cage of her bones.

□

In the morning Maria telephoned Mrs Lowry for the information she needed and directed her to give Raymond a message. She placed Marilyn's dress in a plastic wrapper and drove to a dry cleaning establishment on the other side of Winnipeg. She couldn't risk meeting someone she knew.

She was the only customer in the shop. "A wedding dress to clean," she said. "There's a grape juice stain on the front."

The attendant, a chubby teenager wearing glossy pink lipstick, examined it and said, "Who got happy? The bride or the groom?" She laughed at her own cleverness and looked up, anticipating the details.

"Will it come out?"

"Well – "

"I'll pay extra if you give it immediate and very careful attention. It must come out. It has to be completely removed."

"It's amazing what can be done," the girl said.

"Mark it please so it won't be missed."

"It's hard to miss."

"Could that be rush, please? I'll pay extra." Alan and Marilyn's honeymoon was going to be short.

"Rush is extra."

"I said I'd pay extra."

"Tomorrow afternoon," the girl said. She tore the claim stub from the order invoice and pushed it across the counter. "Your daughter's dress?"

Maria took the stub. "Yes," she said. "Sort of." Her

hand was shaking. Parts of her had been shaking intermittently all night. She'd hardly slept.

She drove to the King George Hospital and parked her car. Raymond was sitting on a bench on the grounds between the buildings.

She walked towards him. "Raymond," she said.

He stood. "Mother."

Now her entire body was shaking and she could think only about landing safely on the park bench. She fixed her eyes on the worn grass and gravel at her feet so she wouldn't stumble.

Then they sat beside each other and for some time neither of them spoke. It was a warm day, the air heavy with the full, ripe disposition of late summer. Maria saw orange and yellow in a distant flower bed and thought of the profusion of orange and yellow marigolds in her garden. Her flowers needed attention, she'd been so busy with the wedding. She wanted to re-arrange the living room too. Take all the plants and decorations out, look at it in a brand new way. Perhaps she should get the walls re-done. How many years had it been since the last coat of paint? In a few weeks her nephew Frank would be moving in.

"Just tell him you love him but you had to give him up," Mrs Lowry had urged her, excited at Maria's call. Yes, she'd said, Raymond was staying with her. No, she hadn't given him her address. He was fully capable of reading a phone book, she said. And it was Gladys who told him her name; she couldn't be blamed for that. "Just tell him that," Edith Lowry said. "It'll settle him."

Well, he'd begged to see her; he'd ferreted her out. Let him speak first, apologize perhaps.

But if she confronted him with spying in her window, she'd have to explain the dress.

"A lovely day," she ventured.

"Yes it is."

Maria didn't see Raymond beside her as much as

sense him, and the sense of him seemed steady, without any nervousness at all. Her agitation settled and she glanced sideways. He seemed to have sunk into himself, into a sadness that fit him easily like an old shirt. His hands were loosely joined and his eyes half-closed.

This is my son, Maria thought. She was making an effort to learn this so she could move on to another idea. She recalled him saying "Mother." It was the first time she'd heard his voice. It sounded ordinary. Medium pitch. No particular strength or charisma, but nothing of the tortured unhappy child she'd supposed from last night's viewing either. He seemed depressed all right, weighted, at a distance – "Raymond in his difficulty" – but at the same time too contained, too aware of himself, to be patronized. Or scolded. Or blithely consoled. She couldn't think what to do with him next.

Finally she asked, "Your wife is in this hospital?" Maria gestured at the red brick building in front of them. Nurses were escorting several patients outside into the sunshine.

"In a lung. Then a respirator. Sometimes in a rocking bed. They do everything for her. Since 1953. Just after our daughter Eileen was born. She was always very lively. She was pretty . . . I was the happiest of men. She cried so much afterwards and I promised I'd never end the marriage. I didn't want to either. I meant my vows. Now she's used to it. She sees how I'm feeling. She tells me I'm free to be divorced. But she doesn't mean it. I promised. You can't break a promise you've made in front of God. Can you? She belongs to me." Each clump of words was gulped out on a single breath.

Maria didn't know how to respond. Not when he'd said so much, said "in front of God." Should she congratulate him on his faithfulness?

Should she say she wished her life had turned out differently too, that she knew what he meant?

A muddle of texts filled her mind – *all things work*

together for good . . . and now for a while, you are under
manifold temptations, the trial of your faith . . . nothing
but such as is common to man . . . and I can do all things
through him . . . and she nearly pulled one of them out, as
she often did for the encouragement of her siblings or nieces
and nephews, but she was stopped and vexed when she
remembered, this is my son. She clamped her mouth shut on
the thought. Such reminders would only sound hypocritical,
coming from her.

She finally came up with, "You've been very perse-
vering."

"Thank you."

"And . . . Ei-Eileen?"

"Lillian's sister Betty raised Eileen. She used to come
to the farm in the summer, sometimes at Christmas. But
we've been apart so much. I wish I knew her better."

"Your mother . . . Gladys. Is she well?"

"The usual."

"I've been afraid," Maria said. "Nobody knows." She
rushed out some sentences about the shock it would be to her
family if they knew of him.

She remembered Mrs Lowry's instructions. "I had to
give you up," she told him. She spoke a little louder. "I *had*
to. Nobody knows."

"That's fine," he said.

This was unsatisfactory, unclear. Frustrating. *Mother.*
It was all she'd ever been. Servant, surrogate, support. All
her life she'd been watching and responsible, to her parents,
then her mistress Mrs Lowry, and then her father and her
brothers and sisters and their children. The whole family.
Guarding. Nurturing them back to the prominence they'd
known in Russia. Keeping her mother's trust. Taking care
of everything.

Mother – it was nothing new. Mrs Lowry had practically
taunted her, wondering if she had the sentiments of a mother.
Blind to the fact that she'd filled a lifetime as full of mother

work as the handsome large building in front of her, the King George, such a solid and comforting place it appeared to be. She didn't want the responsibility of this stranger's sorrow, his despair, his circumstances beyond his control. Beyond hers. No mother could change his life, the polio virus that paralyzed his young marriage, the loneliness of a husband and father without his wife and child. No mother could take on the terrible decision he'd made to honour his vows.

But here she was. She'd given in; she'd met him.

"I never look in people's windows," she heard him saying. "I'm not that sort of person. I just wanted to see the house, and the light was on and I . . . I'm not that sort of –"

"Of course you're not."

She sensed him shifting on the bench.

"I don't wear wedding dresses at home either," she said. "It's the first time I've ever worn one. My niece was married yesterday and . . . I'm not –"

"Of course you're not."

They looked at one another. He smiled, almost imperceptibly, but it was the way Wilhelm had always smiled, lifting only one side of his mouth, a little coax in it. And a little tease. Raymond's eyes were pale and clouded with sadness but she thought perhaps they weren't asking her to bear it, as a mother might be expected to. A hint of amusement swam between them now because of their first strange encounter as the bride and the peeper.

"That's fine," he said. "I understand."

Maria lifted her hand towards him. The motion was tentative, but she chose to keep it going. She lowered her fingers and her palm to his arm. His arms were tanned and hairy. She felt the hair, the skin, and sensed beneath it, his sinew and bone. She thought of the blind patriarch Isaac, feeling the hands of his son to be sure it was his firstborn, the one for whom he'd intended his blessing. Maria touched Raymond's arm and felt she was giving him what she could.

□

One day several years later, Maria slipped two warm breads into paper bags and carried them tenderly into the car. She set them side by side on the front seat and drove out of the garage into the bright afternoon. She drove the short stretch to the house of Peter Konrad, her uncle, whom she'd never called Uncle. The grey pocked snow was shrinking back on boulevards and lawns, water trickled into street drains. There was grit under the car tires. The local school had just been dismissed and children scampered home with their jackets flung wide open or even removed altogether. Spring was "in the air," as the saying went; it was impossible not to be affected by the day's keen spirits.

"You're wearing your hat inside, Peter!" Maria greeted him, extending the breads to him. "Careful, they're very fresh."

"You think I'll squeeze them like a woman?"

"Peter!"

"Makes no difference to me if they're a bit out of shape."

Peter lived alone since Agathe's death, still in the house Maria's father had built them when they moved into North Kildonan. It had been slightly enlarged and upgraded, re-done on the outside, re-painted inside, but it was the same house, small and box-like, with only one bedroom.

"I said to myself, Maria's coming with her fancy car, better get the driveway swept. Guess I forgot about my hat.

"I don't know why you're still baking," Peter went on. "It's too much work."

"Have you ever had bread as good as mine?"

"Maybe not quite as good."

"I have the machine that kneads it. It's no work."

"As long as you don't think I couldn't go to the bakery. Buy it on my own."

"You'd forget."

The untidiness and slightly musty odour of Peter's

303

house always offended Maria a little when she entered; she wished she could give the place a thorough cleaning. But even the suggestion, she felt, would hurt him, so she'd never offered. And he'd stopped smoking, she was glad about that. As soon as she leaned back once against the worn blankets and afghans draping the sofa and they were visiting, she could ignore the disorder easily enough. She liked the fact that he kept the house warm. Her younger relatives talked about limited resources, turned their thermostats low, wore sweaters indoors, felt virtuous if they were chilly.

Maria and Peter conversed in Low German. He was the only one to whom she spoke the dialect. She'd slipped back to it after her father's death. She and her brother Gerhard had learned the dialect as their first language. When they were ready for school her parents decided the Klassen children would speak High German at home, speak the language of school and church and books. They'd been strict about the matter.

"Let's turn the television off at least," she said. "That's a children's show. Is the television always on?"

"I turn it off before I go to bed."

She smiled at him affectionately. They used their old, first tongue, and they repeated things like this from visit to visit, as if their relationship had reached its highest plateau and no longer needed innovation to sustain it.

"When I was the only one who had a television, I'd get company," he said. "Remember? Gerhard, Hans, their boys. All pretending they'd come to see their uncle. Every eye on the moving pictures, every eye on the pretty girls. But I always let them imagine they'd come to visit me."

"Things have changed."

"Me the old sinner, buying a television. Letting the devil into his house. Better go over and keep an eye on him, they said."

"I never came over for that."

"Not you."

"It's a noise-box, if you ask me."

"I need the noise."

He got up, turned off the television, plugged in the kettle. They would have a cup of instant coffee together and then she would leave. That was their custom, once a week. She came to his house. If he came to hers, he was fidgety and caustic.

"Well, you were always my favourite, you know." The teasing was part of the ritual too, his way of thanking for the bread. Maria rested her head on the back of Peter's old, spongy sofa, waiting for him to make the coffee. Her eyes were hurting and her hands ached; her arthritis was bothering her again. She liked to bring Peter his bread but resented using the dough hooks instead of kneading the bread dough by hand.

But bread was bread. They'd had communion at church on Sunday. She always looked forward to it now. The tiny square of bread, the tiny cup, the gestures of the hand required to "take and eat," to "take and drink," the quick tipping up and down of that clear plastic goblet, and the humility that filled the sanctuary, everyone quietly accepting their share, one for each, no more or less, as if they were all far too unworthy to receive even these miniscule symbols of salvation, never mind desire anything more.

The portions were entirely too small for the spiritual hunger and thirst of her old age, she sometimes thought, tastes so brief they were scarcely comprehended, but once inside her mouth they seemed to swell in their indefinable way; then they were enough. Once she'd thought, well, no wonder, it was his body and blood after all. She'd pushed the heretical notion away, remembering that for Mennonites there was nothing literal in those words; symbols didn't abandon their ordinary substance on account of a presiding minister's words; that was one of the things the Reformation had squabbled over, wasn't it, and weren't the Catholics damned, to a soul?

Well, I don't know.

Maria loved the convenience of "I don't know," the prerogative the church had given women: silence, no theological finesse or bold statements required. It made them lazy perhaps, but maybe not. She, at least, felt she could rest in the truth and squalor she'd cobbled together from what she'd heard and read and imagined. She could always say, as Mary must have, sitting at Jesus' feet, I don't know my Lord, what do you mean? Free to listen. The exact meaning of communion didn't seem important. She'd found room for fervour, for happiness, inside the small, formal movements, inside the expectation of sorrow coaxed along by solemn organ music and staring at the wood grain of the pew in front of her. But here it was again. Pasty bread: flesh. The onslaught of juice in her mouth: a taste of blood. Hadn't he said, *Eat me, drink me*. There it was, in the Gospels, his audience surely confused by the words. It horrified her too, but she liked the subversion of believing it, exactly that way, straight on.

Women, Maria thought, waiting for Peter to make the coffee (there was no point trying to talk, with him growing deaf and in the kitchen) – women, contemplating the hymn-book or the pew, ruminating, praying, saying "I don't know" to the legalisms and knowledge far beyond their designated role, privately asking, receiving the unconventional. Asking against the grain, against the common lines of churchly teaching. They could do that, and no one would know. She did, at least. Praying for Wilhelm a good resurrection. Praying for Raymond.

They'd met seven times already, every time he came into the city. She asked if they could keep it quiet between them. But why not lunch, some conversation? It was, "How have you been?" and that kind of thing.

"Are you tired, Maria?" Peter startled her. He had the mugs of coffee ready, weak and milky.

"Oh no. No. Not really."

"It's quiet in here without the television," he said. He was trying to set up the ongoing duel.

Remarkable too how much she'd come to love this uncle and friend of hers. She'd always loved him, but now her judgements had eased. The ways they were alike seemed all right to her now. Also their differences. Getting older had its compensations.

And what was happening now, pushing up through her windpipe, sitting in her mouth? Words forming, like water flooding past a barrier, and nothing preventing it. She asked him whether he remembered her working at the Lowrys. That first day outside the door. How she'd insisted he get her in.

"You liked it there, didn't you?"

"There would have been other opportunities. I'm sure Mrs Lowry wasn't the only fine woman in Winnipeg who needed a maid."

"Of course."

"Don't you ever think how life could have been different?"

"You liked it. I remember how you talked. Lowrys this and the Lowrys that. You seemed to like it."

"Remember when I was in Saskatchewan? The last year?"

"*Mensch* Maria, that's a long time ago."

"I was there half a year."

"I remember the skull bones of your mother – my sister – showing under her skin. I was angry they wouldn't call you home . . . Where were you exactly?"

"On a farm. And I didn't know she'd died until after the funeral."

"And that might have been different?"

"I was there because I had a baby."

She paused and, as if intending to erase the sentences

and re-write them, selected a lighter tone. "So what would you say if I told you I had a baby? Adopted by others."

Peter grinned uncertainly and rubbed his forehead. "So that's why you were there."

He lifted his cup of coffee, looked into it. "I guess I'd say you were luckier than we were. You had a baby. We didn't. You could have given it to Agathe."

Her truth had suddenly been easy to say. His seemed to have popped out easily too.

Then Maria felt they'd been silly, but both of them too old for it.

Peter laughed, as if he'd realized their mutual silliness at the very same time. "No, I think I'd probably say Maria is the model of perfection and it's simply impossible."

Her mouth felt as if it was bubbling with soda pop. "Impossible," she echoed.

"But it becomes you," he said.

She wondered if he'd comprehended what she said. She felt weak. "It's a secret," she said.

"I won't go announcing it."

"Impossible," she said. "We're getting old, aren't we Peter?"

Maria changed the subject then, told him her car was acting up but the problem was fixed. She said she'd had a letter from Alan and Marilyn in Vienna. She asked if he'd gone to his doctor's appointment; she asked him what the doctor had said. Then she finished her coffee.

"Well, you can turn your noise-box on again," she said, rising. Peter put on his hat and the red windbreaker with the name of his former employer, the furniture-manufacturing company where he'd done grounds work and maintenance for twenty-five years after his other job as a gardener ended, twenty-five years until he retired. He accompanied her to her car, opened the door for her.

A plane passed overhead and they both looked up and

watched for a moment the line of white exhaust sketched against the blue."I hope you haven't been missing the baby all these years," Peter said. "I hope you haven't been suffering."

"Really Peter, it's a secret so I don't want you to think about it. I haven't suffered that much." Maria got into the car, closed the door, and didn't acknowledge him further, though he offered a wave as she drove away, in case she looked back.

□

Peter Konrad stood on the driveway, watching Maria leave. She always had a new car to drive; her brothers saw to that. They looked after each other in that family. He benefited too, of course; he got the crumbs of their lavish success, bits of money and provision, given him by Gerhard or Hans, though he believed Maria was probably behind their occasional generosities. Recalling the freshly-baked breads, he turned and went inside.

There was confusion in Peter's mind over what Maria had said; over her joking, her wistfulness. He wasn't used to her saying things like that. Being that vulnerable. Although the house was too quiet, he left the television off. Maria's confession seemed to hover in the room and required additional time, he thought: some additional respect.

But Peter was uncomfortable, for he was a gregarious man, unable to live in silence. With Agathe gone, he had an even greater need for sound, for the human voice. He had ample opportunity, of course, to converse with his friends. There was a group of them who spent hours over coffee at the Norvilla or the Gordon. Sometimes he stayed later than they did, not yet ready to return to his solitary life. More than once he'd stayed into the evening, watching the girlie shows, to review his knowledge of the female form, he told himself, but perhaps, he was thinking now, it was simply the sounds he wanted, sounds connected to people, the flickering of intonation and syllable in the dancers' movements and music, the overheard exclamations and conversations of the patrons, the pulsating shadows and light of language, one word or many at a time, whatever was available.

He hadn't removed his jacket and hat. Something was bothering him; he felt uncertain. He went outside again. He scanned the sky – a cheerful, optimistic blue for this warm day in spring. But the driveway was far from finished. He got the broom, swept vigorously with short strokes to gather the sand, the gravel, the dust that winter accumulated, then abandoned. Could it be true? What had she said? She'd gone to Saskatchewan. Yes. He recalled it, some assistance for relatives of the Lowrys. Some urgent need for her help. She'd been changed when she returned, he was sure of it now, and some puzzle about her seemed to resolve because of what she'd said this afternoon, though he couldn't articulate either the puzzle or its solution. Still, the explanation rang true.

Impossible. It was a joke. She had no secret as enormous as that. Later, they'd laughed. He was the one with secrets, though not even secrets in the real sense of the word, but accusations that could be made against him, a black thread of them – if he was honest – as long as a highway. And unlike hers, his failures were public. Failures both general and specific: his sloth, his resentments, his envies, his blaming. His overall laxness. The family ne'er-do-well who might be tolerated as an amusing, charming, friendly fellow but never emulated. He'd always loved what came to him naturally.

Peter swept the grit into piles and then he headed to the shed for the shovel and a pail. The shed was a mess: his life in a sum, nothing hung, nothing orderly. The shovel blade, he saw, was resting on the damp earthen floor. It was rusting.

He seized the shovel and carried it to the driveway. He loaded the piles onto its flat pan and dumped them into the pail. As he bent, his stomach rumbled. He was angry – and hungry. The recollection of his childlessness stabbed at his intestines. The child, he thought. He and Agathe could have taken a child. It had been such a grief to Agathe; he could never comfort her enough. All their arguments eventually ended in tears, and when he asked why she cried, she always said it was over that. Only that. So if Maria had a baby, what had she done with it? Adopted, she said. She might have considered him and Agathe. At the very least, his Agathe.

Had Maria said baby, or boy? Peter thought of a small boy. But no, the child would be a man by now. How many years ago was it? Gerhard's son John, heir to the Klassen throne as it were, with his bold, gifted children strutting along beside him, was coming up fifty, wasn't he? Peter imagined someone smaller than John, someone lesser, someone lesser as he, Peter, was lesser, someone ordinary and of smaller ambition. He could have explained to a boy like that about his childhood in Russia, about village life, about those happy times that still came back to him, the hours out of school and with the herdsman, and the river he swam in. He'd come to Canada assuming he'd have a son for his stories and his river.

Peter straightened. He shuffled back to the shed with the tools and the pail, the sand heavier than expected. On the street a car honked but he didn't turn to see if it was a greeting for him. Maria would not have dreamed of giving the child to them. Of course not. She'd pushed at him to get into her fancy house, to serve that fancy lady, and some-where inside that house she must have met her match. But she would have considered Peter unfit for her baby. Worse than giving her child to a stranger.

The bitterness, the futility, the loneliness of his life in spite of his friends: Peter couldn't summon jollity for himself as he did for his friends and relatives. He had no real defences of his own. But if only – for Agathe's sake! They'd tried so hard, and Agathe ran out her years, one month to the next, careening between depression and submission, between prayers and hopes and resignation. She never won serenity. All she had for her trials was the abiding ache of her spirit and tears at the ends of their arguments. Peter slammed the shovel onto the cracked ground of the small shed.

Then he reconsidered. He searched for a nail to hang the tool. There were plenty of nails in the walls, put there in some burst of enthusiasm he and Agathe had on a Saturday to reorganize and clean up their lives, to cover the confusion they felt at their emptiness.

He hung the shovel, returned to the house. He loved Maria, his niece, like a sister, and it made no difference now. He wasn't even sure of what she'd said. He'd forget it. You're forgiven, Maria, Peter thought, if it's true, if I understood what you meant.

He laughed. "Peter," he muttered to himself, "don't go thinking of yourself too highly now, handing out forgiveness as if you're a preacher." He climbed the dilapidated steps and let himself into the house. He cut a thick slice of bread and saw how finely textured and white it was, just as he liked it. He reached for the jam jar. The jam came from Maria too. She made it herself. Thick red rhubarb and strawberry jam. She kept him stocked with jam and bread. Then he tried to imagine, as he sometimes did when he'd been thinking of Agathe, what the nature of his late wife's existence might be now and it occurred to him that whatever she did in the afterlife, she probably wasn't sad anymore. Surely the reasons she hadn't conceived a child had been explained to her by now; and surely, by now, she would be satisfied with that explanation.

Realizing this, Peter's eyes filled with tears and he stumbled to the table, tipping his hat off, dropping his head into his hands. He pressed his fists against his eyes, as if to hold steady until he could adjust to what he knew. After some time he noticed again the terrible quietness of the house but then he heard some boys outside, yelling, and also a barking dog. Ordinary, comforting noises.

He ate the bread and jam, and then he turned on the television.

□

A young woman connected with the Mennonite Archives telephoned Maria. She asked for an interview. She was researching the Mennonite girls who'd worked as maids, she said, the immigrant domestics of the twenties and thirties. Later she would write that these domestics "functioned as the first wave of the process towards Canadian Mennonite urbanization" but she didn't put it quite that authoritatively to Maria when she called. Her thesis, she said, was academic conjecture at this point. Maria wasn't sure what she meant, but she gathered the young woman simply wanted to ask some questions about what it was like to work in those rich people's houses.

Maria felt instinctively anxious about the unknown scholar, how interrogating she might be. But the fact that she'd become historically interesting – her category of women at least – intrigued her. And the young woman on the telephone sounded nice. A little timid, with a soft voice, not likely to push too hard.

Besides, Maria knew she would give nothing away. In spite of her meetings with Raymond, in spite of what she'd told Peter, that intention was solid. She could give what she usually gave if the topic came up. She could spread out her little store of first impressions and witty observations, the curiosities of another culture, just like the missionaries laid wooden spears and necklaces and gourds from Africa on church tables for their furlough reports so people got a better idea of how things were with the heathen. Though here it was from the other side of the city, from the elegant avenues near the river bank, an idea of how it was with the *Englisch*.

When the young woman came with her tape recorder and questions, Maria was ready. She had humour for her, and details of the house. It was amazing what she could recollect: menus, prices of things, smells, and the sometimes hilarious progress of learning the language. She agreed that domestic employment had been important in her life; yes, she said, she could probably agree that the girls influenced their community because of their experience, that in some ways, yes, they had eased their families into the city. She was aware of the budgies singing – she'd moved the cage to the back bedroom – and of the clock ticking as they spoke. Tick, tick, tick. Steady, she told herself. She hoped the young woman would feel at home in the living room, which she had cleaned thoroughly the day before, with its ferns and doilies and floral sofa, that she wouldn't think the soft beige fussiness of it too old-fashioned.

She enjoyed the young researcher's insistence on women's importance in the narratives of the past. She thought of Marilyn and other nieces and their friends, how they discussed and argued the women's liberation movement. Some hunkered down to defend the traditional approaches and others flamed with indignation, fighting for more room beside men – at work, in the church. She remembered Marilyn's excitement in one conversation, how she'd used words like equality and voice, hidden lives and possibilities. "Speaking out secrets," she'd said.

Maria had been listening to Marilyn and her friends, eating Sunday dinner around her table, and then she inserted a question. What did Marilyn mean, speaking out secrets? How would that sound?

"Just how we are as women," Marilyn said, "just being human across the board, if you know what I mean. More alike than different. Nuance and complication. Just saying what's inside, honestly, I suppose. Sometimes it might sound like unhappiness . . . but more often, I think, it would sound like joy."

What a delightful prospect altogether, Maria remembered thinking. "Sometimes I wish I'd been born for your times," she'd replied to the girls at her table.

But, she'd thought to herself later, when they were gone, even *not* speaking, one could hear unhappiness, and one could hear some joy.

□

In her seventy-fourth year, Maria revised her will, with her grandnephew, the lawyer John, assisting her. She asked him to come to her house so she wouldn't have to search for his office downtown.

He said he hoped he wouldn't be accused of conflict-of-interest, since he was her relative. "I know what I want," she said, "and don't worry about conflict-of-interest. I'm not leaving money to everyone in the family. I think you've all got enough of it."

John smiled at her meekly and Maria showed him her list. There were five items: beginning now, a monthly anonymous allowance for Peter until his death, and the same for Marilyn. "She lived with me five years. She's like a daughter," she said. "She always writes."

It wasn't just that. Alan's ambition, and a ridiculous one in Maria's estimation, was to see and know the world, one region at a time, coming back to Canada just long enough to work at roofing and earn enough to go again. He could live on a dime, but Marilyn couldn't. She would overspend and irritate him, strain the marriage. She deserved some room to breathe.

And then for the will, three beneficiaries, in three equal parts: the church, the Red Cross, the King George hospital.

"The King George here in town?"

"Down by the river there," Maria said impatiently.

"Where they have the polio patients."

"What's your connection there?" he asked. "Just out of curiosity."

"Do you have any idea how horrible polio was? Of course you wouldn't; they discovered a cure before you were born."

"You're such a caring person, *Tante* Maria. Even your will sets an example."

"My mother had tuberculosis. She wasn't at the King George, but I know people who were . . . Who are. The Red Cross, because my brother Wilhelm died in the war. And the church – that one should be obvious."

John looked through her papers, went over her assets, her accounts. He promised to get everything typed and shown for her approval, and then all could be signed and witnessed. He'd be in touch. "It's a rather unusual will," he said, leaving, "but a wonderful example. Most of my clients have such predictable wills. It's usually the children."

"I don't have children," she reminded him. "Just money."

"I know. That's what I meant."

These young people, Maria thought, so devoid of wisdom sometimes. Like the young tendrils of a very old vine, they seemed far beyond her reach, climbing up places she could barely see, never mind prune. She was no longer that interested either. They were busy and never thought of her. What did they know?

But on her seventy-fifth birthday, Maria's family – so large by now – gave her a party. Then Maria thought her family was the best in the world. Even the out-of-town siblings were represented. The party was held at Gerhard and Helen's sprawling house in the country, the house her brother had built for his second wife, also a Helene, though this one, rather younger, had dropped the "e". Helen called Maria "the birthday girl" through the entire afternoon.

The party had food, of course, and a program. The

Klassens liked programs. They liked to formalize their relationships and speak so that everyone could hear what ought to be said. An aimless open house or gathering with only small talk and food wasn't sufficient. A program solidified their identity as a family. It was also an opportunity for the children to show off their talents and practice performing in front of an appreciative audience.

This day they praised Maria in tributes, repeating how much she'd done for them – filling in as mother and grandmother – and then three of the grandnieces sang a trio around the piano, and another played her violin. Melvin, the preacher of the family, gave a short meditation. The program closed with a trumpet solo by a nephew and a poem by his small precocious son. After Gerhard's prayer for the food, Helen and Ida escorted Maria to the table heaped with hors d'oeuvres and tiny sandwiches and cakes. "Look at it, tell us what you want," they said. "We'll serve you."

"Oh, I can help myself," Maria said. "It all looks wonderful."

"This time, *we* will serve you," Helen said, so Maria said she'd like a taste of everything and then Helen and Ida turned her gently but widely, as one might turn a boat, back to her chair. The birthday girl was soon delivered a plate rich with the colours and tastes of the splendidly decked table: crackers and antipasto, a chunk from the cheese ball with its nuts and parsley, a chicken and mushroom turnover, sweet green pickles and a watermelon pickle perfectly square and pink and luminous, a miniature spinach quiche, three rolled sandwich slices with various fillings, and a glass of raspberry punch. Everything was bite-sized, uniformly made.

Coffee and slivers of cheese cakes and bundt cakes and dainty peppermint cookies followed. "Many of them your recipes," Ida reminded her. They kept bringing her food and Maria tried everything. The members of the family stopped by her chair, one by one, sitting beside her or standing above her as she ate. They gave her bite-sized reports of their lives.

They thanked and commended her. They gave her a hug or a kiss, a card or a gift. Once more they wished her a happy birthday and then they moved on.

☐

Peter stayed close to Maria during the party for her birthday. He was always invited to the Klassen gatherings and sometimes he went and sometimes he didn't but this time he was sure he needed to be there. He felt protective of her again, now that she'd reached seventy-five as he'd already reached it, though he couldn't explain why he felt responsible or what she might need from him now. She'd never needed him, but for that first time, arranging her employment with the Lowrys, taking her there, and even then, she'd taken over and pushed her way through the door herself.

Or was he clinging to her?

"Woman's food," he complained, sitting next to her, half a dozen tiny sandwiches on his plate. But Maria didn't hear him. She was busy receiving well wishes, one after the other.

He'd begun to eat the sandwiches. Now and then he looked up, to watch her for a while. An old man watching an old woman, he thought. He watched her well but as needlessly as the guard on the wall in the psalm Melvin had used for his meditation – *unless the Lord guards the city, the watchman keeps awake in vain.* How Melvin had gone on and on, all that sacrifice they were so in awe of, her working out, her taking over from her mother.

"And you, *Tante* Maria, for five years you worked out, away from the family you loved so much and away from the mother you loved. Except for about a week or so a year – isn't that right? – you were away from her. And you never really had a chance to be with her again, all this time in the city, which was a big worry for the parents apparently, the cause of daily prayers. The city" (he had needed to explain, he said, for those who didn't know) "was a place often feared by the Mennonites back then. And you sent money faithfully home to pay for debts and not only that but to put food on the table. Not once was there a complaint, not once a cry in the letters, saying, please let me stop. These are the facts, and though my cousins and I have been told them, I repeat them for the youth and the children here because they need to know . . ."

On and on and on he had gone, and other tributes in that same tone too, as if Maria was an idea or an emotion they couldn't get enough of, some honey-coated notion of her they wanted to claim as the virtues of their family. And Maria, attentive and serious in her growing blindness, head cocked as pretty as a dove, reserved as always, but taking it in.

Peter watched, unnecessarily now, as Maria lifted her head to each one who came to converse with her. She lifted her head as a sunflower lifts to the sun. As always, the admiration made her beautiful.

☐

It was hard to fall asleep after a party like that. So much food, so much coffee. And, they'd all said so much. Such wonderful things. There was so much to think about. So much. So very much.

She'd used her secret in various ways, Maria thought, this hidden thing – bending it to her will, making it serve as repentance does, to motivate, as receiving mercy does, to the giving of mercy. Especially for her brother Wilhelm's sake.

Then she was middle-aged, and fell into regret. She'd worried back over her servant years with a kind of fury, seeing every incident as a crossroads that might have led her the other way, if only she'd known! Nothing escaped her scrutiny then, not the first day, when she'd been so emphatic about her wishes, or any day after that. Endlessly she analyzed: why did I do what I did? Her loss seemed an injustice she'd inflicted on herself, the secret a snake-like creature that intended to choke her.

If I'd known. The phrase tore at her; she was like a garment on the line in a storm, being shredded by the wind. She might fix on one memory or another, draw it close as if with powerful binoculars, then watch herself with remonstrance, suggestions, fantasies, until she felt nearly dizzy with it all. Then she'd forget the knitting project in her lap, let the hot soothing tea in her mug get cold. The record on the turntable played to an end without her hearing it. She would feel her mind collapse from the sheer impossibility of her effort, only to find herself simply inside the crevice, at nineteen again, or twenty or twenty-three, doing everything she'd done.

Eventually she'd folded and unfolded these pictures so often, they seemed tattered and grey, and so, beyond her middle years, she hardened herself, expecting nothing, growing lonely on the inside, and on the outside more disciplined: demanding perfection. Meeting Raymond was a crack in her self-containment, a small break that both pained and relieved her. It wasn't a seismic shift, as she'd feared, and she'd become reconciled to their rituals of occasional and formal exchanges of cards or notes, of periodic visits in restaurants. For his sake. But perhaps, by now, also for hers.

By the time she was old – now she thought herself old – Maria knew that the phrase *if I'd known* was spoken easily outside the gates of any Eden that's closed, on the edges of the thick green mists of a receding innocence. By the time she was old, she knew it couldn't be proved one way or the other whether knowing changed anything. Re-living, re-imagining, regretting, even acquitting the past was complicated, and the narrative still unrolled more or less the same way. It was pointless speculation, this, because nobody was given another go at their lives, were they? And in the meanwhile, times had changed, and all the decisions she'd made and the reasons she'd made them, because of the culture, because of the church, were a currency lost to her.

Perhaps the long-kept secret had been unnecessary, but she'd climbed into the cocoon of her family and stayed there the rest of her life. She'd chosen it instead of shame. Her inner life grew rich and compassionate, her memories like a wall of chiselled hieroglyphics to press her hands upon, to feel for their comforting mystery, to mull upon. The very thing one determined to conceal might flourish beneath the efforts of restriction, she discovered, and so it became, in its own strange way, a precious possession. She alone owned its power and its sorrow. Even Raymond – the real Raymond she exchanged cards with or met for a meal – had not become a part of it. Not really. It was as if they were strangers who'd chanced upon each other on the King George park bench. Strangers, yes, except for the fact that he had said "Mother" and she had said "Raymond." (Even now, though, she still recalled the slight scrape of annoyance she'd felt, her resistance at speaking his name aloud, the one he'd been given by the Andersons. She would have called him John.) Her outer life was a wall smooth and elegant, different altogether. Eventually, on that side she grew lonelier too and on the inside, weary. Deeper than her silence was an ache for understanding, for the intimate disclosure of the self that made one truly human, and to which, she knew, her soul remained a foreigner.

But now the memories of her years as a servant, as surrogate mother to her siblings, had the pallor of acceptance, like a pale brown wash over every page of them. The hue of the piece still seemed a tragedy of sorts, still required her secrecy. But she was plagued with bodily aches that seemed much worse. She knew there was something very wrong with her health, something more compelling than secrets or arthritis.

Maria believed that she knew the meaning of the new pain deep in her bones; she believed she was dying. She was also going blind. The doctor had told her so. Slowly, unstoppably blind, he said. There was nothing he could do for it. Nothing that made any sense at her age.

He'd pulled his chair close to hers and leaned forward and his voice was kind and hesitant as it carried the diagnosis. She'd answered him, just as kindly, "Oh, that's okay. I really don't mind at all." She wanted to put her ancient, liver-spotted hand upon his young knee to console him.

He probably thought her odd. It *was* odd, but she'd felt a kind of alleviation. To be given at the end of her life a reprieve from the gaze of others. Did she think, like children do, that if her eyes were covered, she could not be seen? Of course not. But still, it was a rest from appearances. A disappearance of sorts.

That evening, after the visit to the doctor, she'd written Marilyn to ask if she might want to come and help her for a month or two. Then she'd made herself supper. She felt the layer of grey in her eyes, as soft as dust. She felt it thickening. But it wasn't bad yet. She could still see the butter bubbling, browning in the pan as she fried her egg. She saw the egg slipping down with a plop. How willingly it dropped to the heat! She saw her blue-veined hands tucking the halves of the broken shell together, a gesture of regret perhaps or comfort, and the egg clear and almost transparent and then, in the frying pan, its immediate transformation, that solid yellow, that solid white, like plastic. The Amur maple in the corner of her eye through the patio door, starting its own inexorable turn, to shades of autumn. Late strawberries in a white bowl on the counter, poised like red buds swelling. Her Gold Lace china. Ordinary things.

Moments like this were epiphanies of consolation. In the final revision of her memories, she would be tender and tolerant towards all that she'd been.

□

The last time Maria got the entire Klassen clan together in one place was at her funeral. If she'd ever wished to impress, she certainly did it now. It was a splendid day, the vast sky clear and cheerfully blue. Many of the trees were bare, and the others yellow and brown, the plain colours of the Manitoba autumn, except for the single Ontario maple at the corner of Gerhard's front yard flaming red and orange, but temperature-wise, far too pleasant for a funeral because the people stepping out of their cars at the church couldn't help but feel the exhilaration in the air and had to remind themselves the occasion was a sad one. But it was hard to be sad on an autumn day this glorious.

They had to make the best of the irony then and use the weather in a positive way for their mourning. After all, they remarked to each other, Maria had lived a long, full life, and she'd been suffering, and she was ready to go. She'd had that effect on them, people agreed; she'd made them happy, made them feel good about themselves. They could almost imagine she'd arranged the day this way just for their enjoyment. Everything fit her to a tee.

Some people said she looked like herself in the casket. Others said, not so much. For everyone who saw her, her body was a facsimile that blurred between what they saw today and the last time they had seen her alive. Each one considered: what was the final living thing I saw her do? How did she look then? She may have been hastily and freshly constructed for just this reason, it seemed, built out of paper and powder and wax, framed in cream-coloured fluted fabric in a box of gleaming oak, just for the last comparisons, for the last glimpse, to close the image of her in their minds. What happened to her when the lid came down need not be thought of. "Our sister," said the pastor of the church in his opening remarks, "is departed."

Like herself or not, she'd made sure in advance that she

had a new dress for the funeral and burial, and wasn't that just typical of Maria too, some of her sisters remarked, to plan ahead. The black crepe fabric had an expensive sheen in the muted light of the foyer.

The large church with its pale peach and white interior was full. The music was performed by the family and was tastefully sombre. Melvin had an excellent sermon. Later, people said it was a wonderful service. Even inspiring, in a funeral-like way. She was elderly, after all, and it wasn't as if death had robbed her best years. The cancer came suddenly, yes, but its course had been mercifully short.

And oh what a day! That vast radiant sky, so extraordinarily blue, the warmth, everyone blinking under the brightness during the burial. (Everyone but Peter, it seemed, scarcely able to lift his head.) Then into the cool basement for the funeral lunch of raisin buns, cheese, pickles, and sweets, and more memories at an "open mic."

Marilyn also shared anecdotes about her aunt, highlighting her gracious spirit, her trustful resignation, the last few months, while she'd been there to assist her.

"Good speech, Marilyn," her cousin Erica told her later.

"Thanks."

"You're lucky. You got close to her. I always found her a little intimidating myself. She seemed so pious. Or perfect, I mean. In manners and things."

"She thought she had to be an example, I suppose," Marilyn said. "But she wasn't much of a talker."

"Shy, perhaps." Erica had taken a personality test and knew she was shy as well.

"Maybe. She held herself back, I think."

"Her generation, I suppose."

"Probably . . . But she liked to look presentable. She didn't mind going blind, but – 'am I presentable?' She was always asking me that."

Both Erica and Marilyn laughed, amiably, at the vanities of an old woman, now deceased.

□

There was a slight young woman in her late twenties among the friends and relatives at the funeral who had no comments about the service or the skills of the mortician. She wore a casual grey skirt and short-sleeved black blouse and had pulled her blond hair into a ponytail with a black band; she looked as if she'd dressed in a hurry.

She *had* hurried, running behind as she always did; she'd grabbed the darkest things in her closet, and then she had trouble finding the church. She slipped into the back of the sanctuary moments before the service began. She got there just before the coffin was closed. She recoiled for a moment, seeing the body on display, not expecting that. But she stopped for a look. She'd never seen Maria. She had no reference for the body except the face of her father, Raymond Anderson. There was something, perhaps, to be glimpsed of him here, but it was too distressing, and surely ill-mannered, to explore what it was. Mother, son, enough. She took a quick glance and hurried on.

Her father had asked her to come, because she was living in Winnipeg now. "Please, for my sake," he'd said. He ought to be there in some way, he'd said, even if it had to be, as it were, through her. He'd asked her to keep an eye on the obituaries in the paper because he knew the woman was very ill. She wouldn't need to explain, he said, just go, slip in and out. She hardly knew her father, but she liked him well enough, with a little regret and longing because his circumstances had distressed him, and she was a pitying woman, unable to hurt a soul. She had a girlish frame, and outwardly, had hung onto the tentativeness it seemed to require. She also thought her father's commitment to her mother and his long sorrow over the polio attack had made him rather sentimental, but she assured him she would go. She signed the guest book in the church foyer with her first name only: Eileen.

She didn't follow the cars to the graveyard, nor did she stay for the coffee time in the basement hall of the church. She was glad for her father that he'd found his birth mother but she wasn't interested herself; she told him she had enough layers of family to keep her busy. After the service, she telephoned him to say she'd attended. She would mail him the funeral bulletin and obituary from the newspaper, she said. The music was very professional, and the dead woman seemed a paragon.

"What do you mean?" Raymond asked.

"Like a model in everything."

"Oh," he said, pausing as if to consider whether it could possibly be true. "Well, yes, that's good. Thank you, Eileen. I'm very glad to hear of it."

The following spring, Raymond drove to Winnipeg for one of his periodic visits to his polio-stricken wife. "I've got to close it off," he told himself. He re-read the short letters he'd received from Maria over the past years, the birthday and Christmas cards since their meeting at the King George. She always signed them Maria Klassen. He put these and the obituary and the bulletin in chronological order and slid everything into a large manila envelope and then into an archives box that he was slowly beginning to fill for his daughter Eileen. He wanted everything organized. Just in case things got worse and he couldn't cope anymore.

He spent half a day in and out of a downtown florist shop, unable to decide on an arrangement of flowers he liked. He finally bought roses, loose, wine-red roses on long stems, as many as they had in the store that day, more than fifty of them. He drove to the cemetery. He carried the roses in boxes to the graveside. He heaped them below the marble plate bearing Maria's name and the years of her life. The roses were a gorgeous pile of scent and hue, lavish against the fresh green grass, and tears came to his eyes as he realized there was nobody else there to enjoy them. Raymond had a poetic side to him, but it was the poetry of feelings, not of words. He relied upon common expressions for the sensations that came from deep within and often overwhelmed him. "Rest in peace," he whispered.

He knelt beside the flowers for a time. Then, hoping it wouldn't cause any trouble for her or her family, he drew a small card saying "MOTHER" out of his pocket and slipped it inside the mass of elegant blooms.

The card caused no trouble at all. No one from the Klassen clan saw the roses. Several weeks later, when a groundskeeper lifted the pile of dead flowers to dispose of them, the card slipped from its tangled prison of dry stems and leaves and fluttered to the ground.

The groundskeeper was an irreverent man, even though he spent his working days at a graveyard, and he was bored with his job. "Mothers, mothers, mothers," he answered the card in a singsong voice. He shoved the dead roses into an oversized garbage bag. "One mother after another." He picked up the card and tossed it into the bag with the dead floral memorial.

He was also a careless man. Something at a distance caught his attention and the bag went slack in his hand. The card fell out. It landed on the edge of Maria's memorial stone and slid down upright beside it. It nestled there the rest of the summer, until a storm wind in August blew it away.

Acknowledgements

This book has been underway a long time. Early in its writing, I was encouraged and helped by financial assistance from the DeFehr Foundation to research the 1920s Russian Mennonite immigrant experience in Winnipeg, the historical setting within which this novel rests. This research included interviews with Esther Horch, C. C. DeFehr, John and Mary Suderman, Katharine Klassen, and Anne Martens. Anne was particularly generous with her insights and information.

Frieda Esau Klippenstein's oral history project with Mennonite women who had worked as domestics, as well as other scholars' work on the "girls' homes," further oriented me to the thinking and dynamics of the period. Staff at every library and archive where I searched for materials proved both expert and wonderfully kind to me in their assistance. When I conducted an interview about her quilting with Alvina Pankratz in her old and beautiful Winnipeg home, for an article for *Mennonite Mirror*, I got a bonus: ideas for the layout and look of the Lowrys' house. *Secrets*, a small book by the Swiss physician and writer, Paul Tournier, provided psychological insights on the title subject.

The years that I returned to university to do an MA in history may have interrupted this work but they stimulated my thinking on the past in many ways and thus made their own contribution to this novel. Here I want to especially acknowledge Prof. Gerald Friesen and his Canadian history course at the University of Manitoba, which included the history of communication.

Writer and friend Sarah Klassen's response to an early draft of this novel was greatly appreciated, as was Sara Jane

Schmidt's review of the Victoria Beach sections. Many other friends, colleagues, and extended family members have helped me with their advice, reassurances, and cheer. Thank you to my sister-in-law, Agatha Doerksen, for her contribution to the cover via her painting, *Seasoned Offerings*. It's a piece that means a lot to me. At CMU Press, Prof. Sue Sorensen has been exactly what I'd hoped for in an editor; I felt blessed by her enthusiasm and her perceptive attention to the text.

The novel's protagonist, Maria, is fictional, yes, but to me she seemed a living character whose long habit of reserve often made her resistant to my stubborn poking about in her life. We eventually reached something of a mutual understanding, I think, and I'm also thankful for that.

My last, but deepest, thanks go to my children, who were still living at home with us when I started this book but are now grown and on their own, to my since-gained children-in-law, and to my husband, Helmut. All of them "leave me alone" in my writing, but never leave me without their warm interest, support, and affection. I love you too.

Dora Dueck
March, 2010